CU00921766

# AWAKENING

## THE DARK RITUALS BOOK 1

CATRINA BURGESS

*She'll do anything for vengeance, even confront death itself.*

Born a healer, nineteen-year-old Colina has been taught to fear dark magic. But now vengeance and survival are her only goals, and she seeks the help of the Death Dealers—dark mages who wield the death arts, drawing their power from the spirits of the unsettled dead.

Colina asks a death dealer named Luke for help. Little does she know convincing him to train her will be the easiest part of her journey.

Three dark rituals, each more terrifying than the last.

If she survives her trials, what will she become?

*For Nerd Boy.*
*You are my knight in shining armor.*
*Because of you, my world is filled with magic, every single day.*

# TRIGGER WARNING

**Trigger Warnings May Contain Spoilers:** Demons, Possession, Hauntings, Occult, Blood and Gore, Loss, Depression, PTSD, Fire, Hallucinations, Kidnapping, Cults, Gun violence. Also includes violent and nonviolent death, including the passing of a terminally ill young girl.

CHAPTER

# ONE

"Y ou want to learn the Death Arts?"

The look on his face was hard to read. It couldn't be every day that someone wandered into the shop and made such a request.

I tried to look more confident than I felt. He couldn't tell my hands were trembling slightly inside my jacket pockets, could he? I forced myself to keep my gaze steady and resisted the urge to run out the door.

My mama always said, you can always ask. The worst they can do is say no. But I don't think Mama was thinking about revenge and murder when she dealt out that piece of homespun advice.

He stood behind the counter with a questioning look in his eyes. He looked a few years older than I was—maybe twenty-two—and had shoulder-length blond hair. His black tank top sported a picture of a large red phoenix surrounded by fire.

My words seemed to catch in my throat, so I decided to look around the shop to buy myself some time. Every wall in the place housed a set of shelves, and scattered around the room were waist-high, freestanding glass cases. Statues with menacing faces stared back at me from between leather-bound books on shelves. Every flat surface was crammed full of exquisite bottles filled with colorful liquids, dried herbs, exotic feathers, and cloth pouches tied with ribbon.

Mixed in with these harmless-looking objects were other things. Misshapen bottles filled with red liquid—probably blood—from a human, goat, or pig... Who could tell? In a dark corner, I could make out the shapes of animal skulls. And something else. I leaned forward to get a closer look. What were those small objects hanging from a wooden pole over in the corner?

A chill ran down my back when I realized they were shrunken heads.

This was a magic shop, dimly lit, with items peering from the shadows where they hid. Some of them I'd only seen in pictures. At another time, I would have been tempted to spend a lazy afternoon exploring every nook and cranny. But not today. I was here with a single-minded purpose.

"I was told the owner of this shop could teach me the Death Arts," I finally said.

"I'm sorry, someone's playing a joke on you. No one here can help you, not with something like that."

I'd anticipated that my request would be met with anger or disbelief, but he seemed almost indifferent. Almost. Those dark gray eyes had a hint of wariness about them. He might act as though everything was okay, but I had the impression that, at any moment, I was going to get tossed out.

"Luke, you know who she means." A pretty girl with the longest hair I'd ever seen spoke from a doorway behind the counter. Her hair was the color of sweet yellow corn and fell just short of the ground.

"Darla, shut up."

Darla looked a few years younger than me. She had on a

long, flowing blue skirt covered in yellow flowers and a white bohemian shirt, the sleeves trimmed in blue lace.

"You're looking for our Uncle Franklin. He's out of town." She glared at Luke as she made her way to his side. "Ignore him. He's worried you're a Redeemer."

Goddess, do I look like a Redeemer? Everyone knew about the cult by now. They started up two years ago—a group of non-mage born who hated all magic. Most members were innocent enough, but there were fringe sects that not only reviled magic, but also sought out anyone who practiced magic for the sole purpose of "cleansing" the offenders.

In the last month, five people had been found drowned in local lakes, their hands and feet bound by thick rope. Obviously, this fringe sect of Redeemers—aka psychopaths—were watching too much of the History Channel when they came up with that idea. They believed anyone who was a witch would float, and the innocent would drown. These crazies proclaimed the poor souls who drowned were cleared of all charges. Little help it did them, being dead and all.

A group of Redeemers did take credit for the deaths, but not in any way law enforcement agencies could track. The news reported that flyers proclaiming THE CLEANSING HAS BEGUN and REDEEMERS WILL TAKE BACK OUR WORLD had appeared on various city streets.

How does someone prove they aren't a nut job on a religious cleansing mission? I tried to look as mentally stable as possible and replied, "I'm not a Redeemer, I swear. I was told that you are death dealers. From the Phoenix Guild." I looked pointedly at Luke's tank top.

Darla laughed. "She's got you there." She reached behind the counter, pulled out sticks of incense, and held them up. "What do you think...?" She cocked her head to the side.

"Colina. My name's Colina."

Her lips split in a smile. "Hello, Colina. I'm Darla Cross, and that's Luke, my brother." She waved the incense sticks around. "Lavender or root beer?"

"Root beer," I answered.

She grabbed a box of matches from a nearby shelf, pulled one out, and struck it. The flame flickered wildly before she lowered it and carefully lit one of the brown sticks. After putting out the match, she held the stick up to her mouth and blew out the flame at the tip. The smoke continued to rise, curling up in swirls around her face.

"Root beer is my favorite." She smiled and placed the incense into a carved wooden holder sitting on the counter.

The sweet smell filled the room. Darla pushed the wooden holder to the side and hopped up on the counter. Once settled, she swept the mass of her hair over her right shoulder. It slid down her body like a golden river.

I wondered how long it took her to wash and dry such hair. It had to be heavy and, I'd think, very hot in the summer. I watched, mesmerized, as her nimble fingers divided the strands into three large sections. She began to braid it.

I forced my attention away from her and back to her brother. "Your uncle... When will he be back?" I asked.

Luke didn't answer. He was starting to look annoyed. I waited two beats, and when he still didn't respond, I turned to his sister.

She looked up from her braid and watched her brother for a few seconds before answering. "Not for at least two weeks. He's put us in charge of the store while he's gone."

I was desperate—no way could I wait two weeks. Chances were if I didn't get help soon, I'd be dead in days.

"Can you help me?" I couldn't keep my voice from trembling as the words came out.

This time Luke responded. "Help you learn the Death Arts?

So you can what? Take out your frustrations on the world?" He turned to Darla. "You notice that it's always the angry ones who think they can come and learn our craft?" He turned his attention back to me. "If you don't mind me asking, who's this almighty enemy who pissed you off? Ex-boyfriend? Some clerk at the local mini-mart?" His voice dripped with sarcasm.

My chin came up, and I looked him straight in the eye when I answered. "I'm not asking you to train me in the Death Arts so I can take out a busload of nuns."

This proclamation brought a half grin to his face. I wondered if he would take my request seriously. He was looking me up and down. I wore no Goth clothing, no black trench coat. I wore the uniform of the middle class in my part of town: a white and blue striped sweater covered by a sailor peacoat, a pair of faded blue jeans, and blue Vans.

I was beginning to regret the coat. The moment I entered the store, a wall of heat hit me. It was autumn outside, but someone inside liked to keep things toasty. Small beads of sweat were forming on my forehead. I considered taking my coat off, but the reception I was getting made me think I wouldn't be staying long.

I tried not to wither under his scrutiny. I knew what he saw standing in front of him—a nineteen-year-old girl with dark brown hair pulled up into a ponytail. An average-looking girl. I'm not the type to stop traffic. Thanks to my Scottish heritage, I've got a chin and forehead that are a bit too pronounced. Blunt bangs fringe my forehead, coming to rest above nondescript hazel eyes. Nothing screams, "Look at me!" I could blend into a crowd, and that's something I count on.

"I can pay." I pulled a wad of bills out of my jacket's right pocket. "I understand that you people prefer to work in cash."

The cash made him frown. Worse, it made him move from behind the big glass counter faster than I could have anticipated. I barely had a chance to take a step back before he reached out and grabbed my arm.

"Who are you?" he demanded.

He was much bigger up close. Our eyes locked, and I suddenly lost the ability to speak. He'd seemed amicable enough when I stepped into the shop, but now his whole-body language took on a more threatening vibe. Those dark eyes shone, not with anger, but violence.

Normally a big, pissed-off stranger manhandling me would have freaked me out, but I needed to be strong. After what I'd gone through—after the terrible things I dealt with —this guy couldn't scare me. I gave myself a mental shake. I was past being intimidated. Fear left the building a few days ago when bullets were flying and bloody bodies covered the floor.

I couldn't think about that now. I'd locked those images into the deepest, darkest corner of my mind, and maybe one day I would deal with them, but not today. Today I was on a mission. I didn't have a lot to lose, and this guy might be the only one who could give me what I needed most.

I pushed the money at his chest with my free hand. "If this isn't enough, name your price."

His fingers curled around the bills, and he let go of my arm and took a step back. "You're serious about this?"

"Yes. If you tell me no, I'll go find someone else," I said.

The only problem was that there weren't a lot of death dealers willing to teach outside their guild, and we both knew it.

"You think you can handle learning the Death Arts?" His voice was still low and threatening.

I wasn't sure I could handle it, but I wasn't about to admit my doubt. I kept quiet and nodded.

"Luke, you can't be serious. You can't teach her." Darla had finished braiding her hair, and her attention was now on the two of us.

"Stay out of it, Darla," he growled.

"There's no way Frank would let you do it." Her brown eyes blazing with anger, Darla jumped down from the counter and started towards him.

He ignored her and turned to me. "Have you had any training?"

I lifted the sleeve of my jacket and turned my forearm, revealing the small tattoo of a blue swallow inked into the skin just above my palm.

"You're a healer." He couldn't have sounded more shocked.

I could feel tears starting to form, but I forced them back. "I was."

"You can't learn the Death Arts. Your people would never allow such a thing." He'd looked at me first with ridicule, then amusement, and now he was watching me as though I was some kind of puzzle he was trying to work out.

It was true. I'd taken a sacred oath, and if anyone from my clan caught me learning the Death Arts, let alone using them, I'd be punished and possibly imprisoned. I knew the risk, but I didn't care.

"Will you teach me?" I knew he could hear the desperation in my voice. I felt it in the very core of my being. My hands were visibly trembling. I'd done a pretty good job of keeping it together until now, but hunger and exhaustion washed over me. I'd been on my own, trying to deal with what happened, and it was suddenly all too much. If seeing me fall apart in front of him was the only way to convince Luke of my sincerity, then I didn't care if he saw my desperation. He was my last hope. I needed to gain the dark magic. Goddess, help me. I needed to live long enough to seek vengeance.

Luke didn't answer right away. Darla stood next to him, her

eyes wide but her expression unreadable. She watched us both in silence.

As we stood there, the silence stretched on and on, and all the while Luke's unyielding dark eyes surveyed me. I pushed down the urge to shift from foot to foot while waiting for an answer. When he finally broke the silence, I physically jumped.

"Come back tomorrow night after midnight." He pocketed the bills.

"The witching hour." It was not the response I was expecting. The witching hour is a time when people sleep and the world seems tranquil, but it's really more than that. It's not truly peaceful and safe, not for people like us. For those of us who knew better, it could be wild, chaotic, and dangerous.

His eyes narrowed. "Yes, the witching hour."

A shudder went through me. *What the hell am I getting myself into?*

"There's still time to change your mind," he said.

"I know what I'm doing," I answered.

"Do you, Colina?" He demanded. "You're a healer, which means you've seen the life leave a person and watched their energy dissipate into the ether sea, but have you ever called on that same energy? Ever felt its pulse swirling around you? It's not for the faint of heart."

What could I say? He was right. I'd never called on spirits. Honestly, I only had an inkling of the type of magic his guild used. I knew it was the strongest magic. If I was going to survive—if I was going to exact my revenge—it was the magic I needed to learn no matter the consequences. I had no choice but to head down this road, but that knowledge didn't stop butterflies of panic from settling into the pit of my stomach.

I knew that, theoretically, magic is magic, but healers and death dealers were on the opposite ends of the spectrum. I'd heard that more powerful healing clans could do different types of magic, but my clan had always been just healers. In theory, I should be able to perform the basics of the Death Arts, even if I didn't have the inborn talent to become a master of them.

A phone rang before I could reply. Luke made his way back around the counter and picked up the receiver of a black phone sitting on the counter next to an old fashion cash register.

I'd gone looking for a death dealer with no leads other than an address and a brief description of the shop. I'd made it here in one piece, and someone had grudgingly agreed to teach me. It was a victory. A small one, but I'd take what I could at this point.

I realized I was standing there like an idiot, watching Luke talk on the phone when I should have been hightailing it out of there. We'd completed our business. He might have reservations, but he'd taken my money and agreed to teach me. I had no reason to linger. If I hung around, he might change his mind, yet here I was—staying and staring.

Luke was good looking, with piercing, dark gray eyes, blond hair, and a rugged jaw. He had broad shoulders, and a long scar ran down his left shoulder, the end of it lost beneath his tank top. And for a brief moment, I wondered how far down his body that scar ran. At the thought, I felt my cheeks get hot and realized I was standing there staring at him and blushing. I gave myself a mental shake and reminded myself that he was a death dealer—not someone to be trusted. I didn't know if all the rumors I had heard about his kind were true, but I did know for sure that death dealers were to be avoided. He dealt in dark magic—magic that my people both feared and hated.

I realized in horror that the phone conversation was over, and Luke was talking to me, but I had been so caught up in my thoughts that I had missed everything he said.

I felt another blush spread across my cheeks. Like an idiot, I mumbled, "Uh, what?"

"You can't go back out in the streets." He looked dead serious.

"Who's going to stop me?" I regained my composure, but my voice was more than a bit defensive.

"The Triads. I just got a call from a neighbor. The Triads are hanging out down the block." He walked around the counter until he stood in front of me. "You'll have to stay here. At least for a couple hours until they clear out."

No way was I staying, I had what I came for, and now it was time to leave. The Triads didn't scare me. I was a healer, and even they had a code against harming healers.

*But I'm not a healer anymore,* I reminded myself. I was going to delve into the forbidden magics—I would soon become someone on the fringe of society.

A wave of exhaustion suddenly hit me. I grabbed the corner of the closest table to steady myself. Making the decision to come here, surviving the last few days, convincing Luke to take me on, it all had taken the energy out of me. The anger, the desperation, the determination—everything suddenly evaporated.

"Colina, are you okay?" Darla asked, coming to my side.

My words came out in a harsh whisper, "I'm fine. I skipped a couple meals."

It had been at least three days since I'd eaten. Every time I tried to eat, the memories came, and nausea set in.

"I felt dizzy for a second. There's no need to make a fuss." My voice sounded unbelievably weak even to my own ears.

Darla's fingers grazed across my forehead. "She's not okay. Luke, bring her upstairs."

I began to slump, and Luke reached out and put an arm around my waist, supporting me.

I tried to pull myself out of his grip, but he was extremely strong. "You can let me go. I'm okay."

"Darla, lock up the shop. With the Triads out there, the best thing to do is lock up and sit tight until they get bored and move on." He ignored my protest and began to lead me behind the counter and through the doorway into a small hallway. I felt like a helpless rag doll in his arms as he moved us along the hall to the foot of a wooden staircase.

"Since you can't leave, you might as well come upstairs. We haven't had a chance to eat. We can get some food into you. Can you make it up the stairs?" The harshness had gone from his voice. He sounded almost kind.

"I'm fine. I just need to—" I couldn't finish the sentence as the world around me started to fade away.

"Hey, don't pass out on me." He leaned down and lifted me into his arms. He carried me up the stairs and delivered me across a large room onto a brown couch sitting against a brightly painted red wall.

I needed a moment to catch my breath and gather my strength. Showing so much weakness in front of strangers embarrassed me. I had been an idiot to go so long without food. Sleeping was also something I hadn't done a lot of lately. Every time I closed my eyes, nightmares rushed in. It wasn't surprising that my body suddenly rebelled and gave way. I told myself I would lie here for a minute or two, catch my breath, and then head out.

Suddenly Luke was standing over me. He had a bottle of soda in one hand and a plastic cup in the other. He handed them to me. "We've got some cheese and salami in the fridge. Darla picked up some fresh bread at the local bakery this morning."

What choice did I have? If I kept going this way, I'd end up passed out on the streets.

I looked up at him and forced a smile. "Thanks for the dinner invite. I accept."

# TWO

The food was good. I ate until I couldn't take another bite. Afterward, I leaned back against the leather cushions, my coat draped next to me, and relaxed for the first time in what seemed like a lifetime.

My gaze kept going to Luke. There was little resemblance to the imposing figure I dealt with down in the storefront. Once upstairs, Luke seemed to relax. He hadn't said much while we ate, and now he sat back in his chair, finishing a bite of bread.

Every time I glanced his way, I found him looking at me with an openly inquisitive stare.

He was not what I expected. He didn't hide like the rest of his guild members. He was wearing a phoenix on his tank top. This was not a guy trying to keep to the shadows—he lived openly in a society that deeply despised his kind. Did he feel alienated? Did he have friends outside his guild?

And what about his sister, Darla? I wondered if she practiced the arts. She sat quietly, finishing off her meal. It was hard to tell if someone possessed magic just by looking at them. Was she also a death dealer? Would the Phoenix Guild initiate someone into magic so young?

I wondered how different her life was from mine. I had become a healer like my mother and her mother before her. The path to becoming a healer started at sixteen, but at that age I had only learned about plants and making elixirs, teas, and medicine. Mama hadn't allowed me to delve into the magics that went along with healing until I turned eighteen. My training in magic started officially a year ago, and, in that time, I'd learned as much as I could, as fast as I could.

No other career choice had ever entered my mind. It had always been assumed that I would follow in my family's footsteps and, honestly, I didn't have any regrets. I love working with plants, being out in the sunshine, my hands pushed into the dirt of Mother Earth. Growing fragile things with care and love, creating medicines to heal the sick, mixing potions, learning a craft passed down through generations—there was no part of being a healer that didn't make my heart swell with joy and make me leap out of bed every morning full of excitement. The world once seemed a place of endless possibilities.

But all of that was now behind me. The path before me was full of shadows and darkness. I was going to become a death dealer, and I didn't have the faintest idea what kind of lives they led.

I took a good look at my surroundings. I was in a studio apartment, but the space was enormous. A well-outfitted kitchen with granite counters and cherry cabinets stood at one side of the room. The middle area was arranged as a living room and office. The couch I was on sat against the wall on a large, patterned rug surrounded by two oversize chairs. To the right of the couch, in front of a row of tall windows, stood a desk with a laptop computer and printer. Next to the desk was a small row of black metal cabinets. On the other side of the room were three large partitions—walls that didn't quite make it all the way up to the ceiling. Bedrooms, I imagined.

"This is a nice place." It was an expensive place. Every piece of furniture and knickknack screamed money.

"It's our uncle's." Luke leaned forward and put his plate down on the old blue steamer trunk serving as a table for our meal. "Are you going to tell us what brought you here?"

"Good food, terrific soda—what's not to like?" My answer brought a scowl to his face. I was paying for his services—I wasn't about to fill him in on the details of my life. "My understanding is that your type of work comes with a certain assurance of anonymity. Like when you pay a shrink or a lawyer."

"Client confidentiality." He leaned back in his chair and took on a thoughtful expression.

"Exactly," I answered.

He watched me in silence for a few moments. "I would like to know who pointed you to our doorstep."

Again, with the questions.

"Someone who wishes to remain anonymous," I answered cautiously. Luke could keep asking questions, and I would keep being evasive. This might be a long couple of hours.

"A lot of people know the type of work we do, but most of them, I imagine, don't run in the same social circles as someone like you."

The way he said "social circles" made it clear it wasn't a compliment.

"And what would you know about the social circles I run in?" I demanded.

Luke took his time answering, his eyes scanning slowly over my appearance. "Let me guess: your father's a plumber, and your mother's a schoolteacher."

Actually, he couldn't have been further off the mark. I forced a smile onto my face. "Do you do fortunes? Are you going to tell me my horoscope next?"

"Not something I normally dabble in, but I could if you

wanted me to." His eyes focused on me in a way I found disconcerting.

Darla spoke up, "Luke, stop being so rude."

"Why? What's she trying to hide?" Luke looked over at Darla, an amused expression on his face. "Does she have top-secret government information hidden away in the recesses of her mind?" He didn't wait for an answer, but instead got up from his chair and started clearing away the dishes.

"I'm the private 'no trespassing' type," I answered quietly to his retreating back.

He spun around so fast that my breath hitched in the back of my throat. He put the dishes down none too gently, and they rattled loudly as they hit the surface of the trunk. "What are you really doing here?"

I closed my hands around my now empty plastic cup, crushing it before taking a deep breath and relaxing my grip. This guy would not scare me off. I had food in my stomach and was feeling less shaky. I needed his help, and it would be best if I could get him to see me as strong and capable first.

I took a deliberately long pause before answering. "Paying you a lot of money."

He took a step toward me. "To learn the Death Arts?"

I could almost feel the wave of violence and intimidation wash over him. He clenched his fists and towered over me menacingly. Here I was in this stranger's apartment. No one knew where I was. At any moment, Luke could decide I was not worth the hassle and—what? Kill me? He already had my money. I'd paid him upfront like an idiot. I'd heard stories about his kind and most of them seemed outlandish, but I knew truth was buried within the tall tales. Anger I could handle, but not violence, not now, not after what happened. At the very thought of it, my stomach clenched.

I looked over at Darla. She was watching us, her expression

sullen. So far, she'd shown me only kindness. She wouldn't let Luke hurt me; I was almost certain of it.

He glared down at me, and I tried to look confident and fearless, but I didn't trust my voice not to betray me, so I just stared at him.

"Colina, why did you come here? Why are you so desperate to learn the dark magics?" He demanded.

I forced myself to sit up. I used to have a backbone, and if there was ever a time to show it, it was now. I wouldn't tremble like a scared rabbit in front of this guy. I could feel the anger growing within me. I tried to hold onto the feeling, will it along, force the flames of it to warm my blood and fuel my words. "Why does it matter? I need to learn, and a friend told me that I could find someone here who would teach me."

My reaction didn't seem to surprise him. He'd been pushing, and I'd finally pushed back.

The anger abandoned me as suddenly as it had come. "Look, you guys seem pretty open about what you do. The shop even has a phoenix on its sign. It's not like you're hiding who you are."

"I'm not ashamed of what I am," Luke said.

"A lot of people don't share that view," I said quietly.

His eyes narrowed. "Are you one of them?"

I slumped back against the pillows. "I'm the live and let live type."

His face softened, and he took a step back. "A healer."

"I told you I was." I was so tired, so sick of all the questions. All I wanted to do was go somewhere safe, somewhere I could try and get some rest.

"But not now?" He asked.

Why did he keep pushing? When I put down the crushed cup, my hands were openly trembling. "Not anymore."

"I've never heard of one of your kind walking away from the calling." His voice was softer now, less demanding.

I was anxious to change the subject. "You said the Triads are out in the streets causing havoc. Do they do that a lot?" I knew the Triads were one of the largest street gangs in the city. They're mostly mage-born, many of them vicious human beings. Part mage and a whole lot of natural-born killer types— a deadly combination any way you look at it.

"Recently more than usual," he said.

I looked towards the windows. "So it's not safe for me out there yet?"

"No," he answered.

My eyes swung back his way. His dark eyes were watching me. Once again, I felt like a puzzle he was trying to solve. "I could pay you to be my bodyguard and escort me home."

He shook his head. "It's not safe for even the likes of me out there these days."

Now that was something. I had never heard of a death dealer being afraid of anything. They're what I consider the top of the magic food chain—the hardest of the mage-born to kill.

He looked towards his sister and then back at me. "It's getting late. The streets are dangerous, and you don't look like you're up to fighting off trouble at the moment."

I couldn't keep the surprise out of my voice. "And you're proposing what? I should bunk down here tonight?"

He made a sweeping gesture with his arm that took in his sister. "We are offering a place of refuge."

Darla got up, walked over, sat down next to me, and patted my hand as if trying to offer some kind of comfort. "We're about the same size. I have some sweatpants and a T-shirt I could lend you. Luke's right, it's not safe out there. You should stay with us."

It had been a long time since anyone had offered to help me.

I wanted to say no, but it would be foolish to go out and risk my life.

I moved my hand away but gave her a smile so she wouldn't be offended. "I'll take you up on the clothes, but what I could really go for right now is a hot shower."

She gave me a smile and got up. She disappeared through one of the doors and came back, hands full of folded clothes. She handed them to me and then pointed across the room. "The bathroom's over there. You can find clean towels in the cupboard."

I walked over, clothes in hand, and opened the bathroom door. The tub was an old-fashioned one. It had a metal circle at the top that held a white and black polka dot shower curtain. A handheld showerhead hung from a long, retractable metal coil.

I slumped down on the side of the bathtub and wondered if I had the energy to take a shower. The hot water would feel good against my skin. It might clean away the dirt, but what about the guilt? Could it wash that away?

I forced my body up and got undressed. If I had any sense, I would get out of here, but I knew I couldn't. Not yet, not until I got what I needed. I looked in the mirror and shook down my hair. Now free, it came to rest on my shoulders in waves. I turned away from the mirror and stepped into the bathtub. I reached for the showerhead and held it over my head with one hand as I turned the knobs with the other. The hot water felt amazing as I sprayed it back and forth across my body. When I finally got out, I rummaged through cabinet drawers until I came across a towel and a hairbrush. I dried myself and then took my time brushing my hair. When I was done, I changed into my borrowed clothes.

Darla was wrong: we weren't the same size. She might be younger than I was, but she had a lot more curves. Everything was a bit too large. I tied the bottom of the white T-shirt into a knot and pulled the drawstring on the gray sweatpants tight. For some reason, I felt more vulnerable when I came out, even though I was fully clothed. Maybe it was because I was wearing a stranger's clothes.

I was in a strange place, with people I'd just met, and I was about to bunk down like a guest. An unwelcome guest. Even though he said I should stay, Luke did not have a welcoming expression as I came out of the bathroom.

"You were in there a long time." He was standing against the row of windows. He looked even bigger than I remembered. Was it possible that he'd grown five inches since I stepped into the bathroom? No. It was just the play of shadows against his body.

"Sorry, did you want to take one? I didn't mean to hog all the hot water."

"I usually take my showers in the morning."

He'd changed and currently wore no shirt and a pair of black sweatpants. I realized I was staring at him again and blushed like an idiot. The only thing I could think of to say was, "Oh, okay."

"Darla put an extra blanket on the back of the couch in case you get cold."

"Thanks. Where is she?"

He gestured toward one of the partitioned sections. "She went to bed."

I stood there feeling foolish, not sure what to say next.

He pointed to the couch. "The sheets are fresh, but the pillow is a bit lumpy. We aren't set up for houseguests. I'll leave the light on in the bathroom and the door open. That way, you'll have a bit of light in the room if you get up in the night."

"I'm a pretty sound sleeper." It wasn't a lie, not really. I used to be a sound sleeper until the nightmares set in. I would probably wake up in a cold sweat, trembling from head to toe. I desperately hoped I wouldn't wake up screaming at the top of my lungs.

I gave him a smile and moved past him to the couch.

He walked across the room and flipped off the overhead lights.

I settled under the covers and watched the shadows from the window play against the ceiling. "Thanks again for the food, the shower, and the place to crash."

Luke stopped but didn't turn around. "No problem."

"I like your place. It's... comfortable."

"I'm glad you approve." His voice sounded amused.

"Good night." As I said the words, I swear I heard my brother's voice whisper in my ears, *"Sleep tight. Don't let the bed bugs bite."* It had to be my imagination. Lack of sleep was starting to affect my ability to function. A good night's sleep and I'd be stronger tomorrow, and maybe ready to take on whatever challenges came my way.

# THREE

I t was the scream that woke me. I shot straight up before realizing it wasn't coming from me. Another high-pitched scream rang out, and then another, coming from the direction of the windows. Almost immediately following the screams, a loud crack of thunder reverberated against the apartment.

"Son of a—" A voice rang out in the dark, and I could hear feet hit hard against the floor. A shadow flashed across the room. It was Luke. He was out of bed and moving toward the windows.

Before I could say anything, he swung the closest window wide open and headed out onto the fire escape.

I pushed the covers off and headed toward the windows. It was raining outside. The water was coming down in sheets, and raindrops pelted my face as I leaned over the windowsill.

I could make out a group of people standing under the streetlight, surrounding a woman in the alley. The woman was lying on the ground with her hands pressed against her head. High-pitched screams were coming from her every few seconds.

Luke was going down there to confront them. Were they

Triads?

"What's happening?"

I jumped at the sound of Darla's voice. I'd been so focused on the scene in the alley that I hadn't realized she was now standing next to me. We were wearing almost identical outfits, except her T-shirt was pink.

"A woman's in trouble. I think Luke went to help." My voice came out in a rush.

I couldn't stay inside and watch something awful happen to a helpless bystander—not this time. I made my way back to the couch and flipped on a lamp on the side table. I grabbed my shoes from the floor.

"You aren't going out there, are you?" Darla sounded scared.

"Your brother might need help." Though I wasn't sure what kind of help I could be. I had learned some healing arts—practices to soothe and mend, not maim and hurt. I wouldn't be much use in a fight. Death dealers might be bulletproof, but I was not.

"Do you have any weapons?" I asked while slipping on my shoes.

"Like a gun? No, we don't have guns in the house."

"What about a knife?" I headed toward the kitchen and spotted a baseball bat leaning against a cabinet. It was better than nothing. Bat in tow, I hurried toward the windows.

"You can't go out there, Colina." Darla grabbed my arm.

"He might need help."

"Luke can take care of himself."

"Against a gang? Stay here and call the cops." I pulled away from her. Baseball bat in hand, I went out over the windowsill and onto the fire escape.

We were two floors up. The rain seemed to be coming down even harder. I made my way down the metal stairs, bat over my shoulder. If I wasn't careful, I would lose my balance on the slick surface and do a header over the rails. I slowly inched forward until the stairs ended and then made my way down the already extended metal ladder. Unfortunately, it didn't go all the way to the alley floor. There was a six-foot drop to the bottom. I let my body fall and tried to remember to bend my knees as I landed. It wasn't a graceful descent. As I hit, I pitched forward and lost my balance, ending up sprawled face first in the mud.

I scrambled up, grabbed my dropped weapon, and headed toward the alley entrance with more resolve than courage.

Luke stood at the edge of the group.

"I told you to leave her alone," Luke said, the threat in his voice unmistakable.

The guy closest to him was big, much older, and dressed in dark jeans and a jacket with an orange and black bandana tied around his right arm. The guy turned and laughed. "Or what, man?"

"I'm only going to say it one more time. Walk away now before you get hurt," Luke demanded.

"Who's going to do the hurting? You?" shouted someone else from the group.

I had no idea what I planned to do once I made it to Luke's side, but I kept putting one foot in front of the other and hoped to Goddess a police car would cruise by any second. I was surprised that they were still talking—the scene looked one-sided with Luke facing half a dozen tough-looking guys. But Luke's lack of fear seemed to confuse them.

I didn't make it far. I'd only taken a few steps forward when another guy, even bigger than the last, stepped right in front of Luke.

This was it. The fighting was going to start. My breath caught in the back of my throat, but before the guy could lay a hand on him, Luke spun around, lifted his forearm, and smashed the guy on the side of the head. The guy went down hard.

The group turned in unison, all attention now focused on Luke. The woman could have scrambled away and made a run for it now that they were ignoring her, but she lay frozen on the ground. It was then that I realized all the guys wore orange and black bandanas. Luke was facing down the Triads. The situation had gone from bad to worse. Maybe if it was a general mugging or a bunch of hooligan teenagers out for a bit of mischief, Luke might have had a chance of scaring them off, but this was an organized gang that spent most of their time looking for mayhem. From what I read in the papers, they weren't above murder.

One of them shouted, "You just signed your death warrant!"

Luke stood his ground. "Death. Now that's something I know a thing or two about."

Luke raised his hands and started to speak in an unfamiliar language—the language of dark magic and spells. Light flickered from his fingers, and his eyes shone as if lit from within. His voice suddenly took on a lower, deeper tone until it didn't sound like him at all. Then a slew of words flew from his mouth, and the light shot out towards the gang.

I watched in horror as one face formed within the lights, then another. Luke's calling on spirits. A chill ran down the length of my body. I wasn't the only one to realize what was happening.

Someone cried out, "He's a death dealer!"

Death dealers commune with the dead that have not crossed over, especially the mage dead. That gives them frightening power. It is an easy power to abuse—victimizing the dead for their own ends—and the fear that they can bind immortal souls terrifies any who see them in action.

The gang began to scatter, and I didn't blame them—lights

swirled around them in a circle, carrying whirling, formless faces. It was a freaky thing to behold. Heads and partial bodies were starting to form inside the lights. The expression on each ghostly face Luke summoned was full of pain and terror. Then the noise started: an ear-splitting screeching. He was calling up the unsettled dead—banshees.

I'd heard of banshees—they were the death dealers' most fear-inspiring magic. The rest of the magic clans and guilds viewed the very idea of them with horror, but to see these creatures shift out of the ether and take on a semi-solid form was something I never thought I would experience. They were the souls of those trapped between life and what lay beyond, ghosts that Luke had bound into a weapon. They flowed around him, blinking in and out of the material world and glittering with the dark magic that gave them form.

The hairs on the back of my neck stood up, and my arms were suddenly covered in goosebumps. I reached for the protection pouch I wore around my neck. My hands grasped at nothing but air. *Used to wear,* I reminded myself. I stopped wearing the pouch when I stopped being a healer.

The banshees began filling the alley, but there was no place for them to go. I dropped the baseball bat and took quick steps backward until I felt a brick wall behind me. They had me cornered like a rat in a cage.

The banshees moved faster and faster around the gang. The guys were fleeing, and as they ran, the lights followed, surrounding them, circling them. Voices full of panic filled the air. I looked toward the woman Luke had initially come to save. She was still on the ground, but she'd raised her head, looked at the chaos around her, and started screaming again. Her screams mixed with the shrieks of the banshees.

I should have been freaking out. I should have been shrieking in horror like the woman, but instead, I sat as though spellbound. I couldn't tear my eyes away from the scene before me.

Rain streamed down my face, and my hair clung to my cheeks and fell into my eyes. I pushed it aside and watched as blue streaks of light broke off from attacking a gang member and began heading in my direction. Within the blue lights, I could see partial forms—the unsettled spirits. I focused on the light closest to me and immediately regretted it. In its center was a shape, a form that was almost human or, rather, the forgotten memory of something that had once been human. It had long arms that ended in sharp claws and an angular face with only gaping shadows for eyes and a mouth. Its thin torso ended in shreds of mist, which trailed behind it as it flew through the air. The banshee howled as it floated my way.

*Don't ever look into a banshee's eyes, Colina.* It was a warning that had been instilled in me since childhood.

*"What'll I see if I look in its eyes, Pa?"*

*"Death. And when you look at death, child, it can take hold of you and suck you into the ether sea."*

Remembering my father's words, I dutifully closed my eyes, feeling the energy swirl around me. It surrounded me, and as it did, a loud screech filled my ears. To my horror, I realized something was touching me. I froze, filled with fear and panic. The banshee teased my hair and slid across my skin, and where it touched me, I felt a sharp pain followed by a burning sensation. It crawled across my right forearm and then brushed my cheek. I cried out. The compulsion to open my eyes and see the nightmare surrounding me was so very strong.

After a moment, the world suddenly went still. Another high-pitched, bone-chilling cry sounded, but it seemed farther away this time. More silence...another screech. With my eyes still tightly closed, I counted the seconds between the cries and willed the banshee near me to disappear.

A minute, maybe more, passed and there was no sound. No movement my ears could detect. I decided to risk it. I opened one eye and then the other. Three long, ugly scratches ran across my forearm. I lifted my hand to my cheek and felt raised welts—the banshees actually touched me. I didn't know they could do that. I'd heard tales of their soulless cries, but I'd never seen one before. If this is the type of power the death dealers wielded, it was powerful magic.

The alley was now empty except for Luke. I made out the back of the woman fleeing in the darkness through a sheet of rain. She was making her way onto a well-lit side street. The gang members were all long gone. Luke was down on his knees in the mud.

I pushed myself up and made my way to his side. "That was some show," I said, not hiding the relief in my voice.

When Luke didn't answer, I put my hand on his shoulder and watched in shock as he slumped forward.

It took my mind a moment to catch up with what was actually going on. A pool of blood was forming underneath him, streaming out onto the dirt. I turned his body over and looked in horror at the gaping hole on the left side of his stomach. I sat staring, unable to move as other images rushed through my mind.

Blood and pain-filled screams.

I covered my ears with my hands, although the screams were only in my head. My thoughts raced out of control, sending waves of adrenaline through my body.

*They're all dying, and there's nothing I can do to stop it.*

I don't know how long I stayed immobile, the images keeping me frozen, until Darla's voice broke the spell. I watched her make her way down the ladder. She was calling out her brother's name.

I sat shaking, rain pouring down my face. Luke. I had to help him. The blood had become a river, snaking its way down the pavement. He was dying, and I was doing nothing, lost in memories. I took one shaky breath and then another. With sheer will I forced back the panic, the out-of-control horror that was racing through me. This time I could do something—I would do something. No one would die while I stood by helpless again.

I rushed forward and placed my shaking hands on his wound, causing him to moan. His face was ashen, but his eyes flickered open for a moment. He could feel pain, which meant he was still alive.

I closed my eyes and took a deep breath. *Goddess divine. Mother of the Earth. Thee who brings forth all life, hear my plea. Help me.* I repeated the mantra over and over in my head, trying to push away the thoughts of doubt and fear in the back of my mind.

Nothing happened.

I could do this—I could heal him. I took a deep breath and concentrated. I waited for the familiar feeling of healing power to come into my body, a power I'd been born with and trained to use. I waited. I took another deep breath, and another.

*You can't do this. You can't help anyone anymore*, the words whispered across my mind. I knew they were true. There was too much fear, too much anger coursing through my mind and body. I couldn't find the serenity I needed in order to heal.

*You can't help him*, the words screamed inside me, but I pushed them back.

I focused and said the words out loud, this time with more determination, my voice pleading with Mother Earth to help me. Over and over, I said the words, and as I did, my mind reached out for the energy that used to come so easily to me, energy that swirled around in the ether sea. But still I was powerless. He was dying.

CHAPTER

# FOUR

T he words turned from a plea into a sob, and as I sobbed, a small tingle of energy finally flowed through my feet. It crawled its way slowly up my legs, through my body, and into my fingertips.

*Thank the Goddess.* I pushed my fingers deep into his wound. I didn't need to say the next word. Instead, it seemed to resound from the very depths of me. *Heal.* As the word grew louder in my mind and took root in my body, the small bit of energy I had summoned flowed through me and into Luke. Time stood still, and for a long moment nothing existed but the sound of his shallow breathing.

I felt something graze my cheek. I opened my eyes and realized I was lying on the ground. Luke kneeled over me, one handheld against his side. Darla was next to him, tears streaming down her face. Red slowly dripped from between Luke's fingers. It all rushed back to me.

"Colina, are you okay?" he asked.

The rain had stopped. I pushed myself off the ground.

"I thought you were no longer a healer." He took away his hand and looked down at his side.

He was bleeding, but not like before. I had stopped the gushing river of blood. He wouldn't bleed to death in front of me. I resisted the urge to slump back in exhaustion. "I'm not a proper healer. You're still bleeding."

"Yeah, but I'm alive, and that's only because of you." His voice sounded weak.

"What happened?" I whispered.

"The woman, she had a knife," he said, a grim expression on his face.

I couldn't believe what I was hearing. "She stabbed you! But you were trying to save her."

"Life throws you curveballs sometimes." He stood up and then reached down to help me to my feet. "We better get out of here before those guys decide to come back. Darla, stop crying. I'm okay."

But he wasn't. He slumped forward as he moved. Darla reached out and slid her body under his arm, but his weight was too much for her. I scrambled around to his other side and lifted his arm around my shoulder.

We staggered out of the alley and to the shop's front entrance.

"Anyone think to bring keys?" Not bothering to wait for a response, Luke pushed away from us and supported himself against the door. He leaned over, picked up a nearby rock, and broke a pane of glass before reaching in and unlocking the door. I waited for him to move, but he slumped to the ground again.

Darla and I, as if on cue, moved to either side of him and propped him up once more. Darla pushed the door open, and we made our way inside. I kicked the door shut behind me, but the broken pane provided little protection. Anyone could follow us into the store.

We eased him down to the floor.

I looked over at the broken window.

Luke followed my gaze. "Worried someone might steal something? Normally our reputation keeps people at bay." His voice was laced with pain.

Sometimes a reputation was a double-edged sword. Hatred toward death dealers was widespread. He'd almost been killed a few minutes ago because of it—the very nature of his powers horrified the woman he'd tried to rescue so much that she'd actually stabbed her savior.

Darla unwound her braid and started to wring out her hair. She was drenched, and I realized she wasn't the only one. I was shivering. We were all soaking wet, and it was a chilly night.

"We need to get out of these wet clothes." I stomped my feet a few times and rubbed my arms. I was keeping myself moving by sheer force of will. If I sat down now, I worried I would never get back up.

"I'll get blankets," Darla said, moving swiftly across the room to the doorway behind the counter.

Luke watched his sister go and then turned to me. "Do you have any medical skills beyond the magic kind?"

"Keep pressure on the wound," I said.

"We do sell some salves and herbs." He pointed toward the back of the shop.

I nodded and made my way to the back. I wandered around, picking up bottles and pouches, looking for names I recognized. There were chest ointments for colds, remedies for stomach aches, and solutions for joint pain. I found a few things I could use, but I couldn't treat a serious injury with the stuff in this shop.

I did find something I could use to clean the wound and something I could give him that might help with the pain, but what we needed was a proper healer.

A healer. I used to be a healer. A sob escaped my mouth. I

touched my cheeks in surprise and realized tears were streaming down my face.

I panicked out there. Luke almost died because I froze. I had to keep it together. I forced myself to take a deep breath. Wiping the tears from my eyes, I made my way back to his side.

I uncorked a brown bottle and passed it to him. "Drink half the bottle."

He looked at me. "Are you sure? You're not trying to poison me, are you?" His voice was weak, but he sounded amused.

"It'll help with the pain."

He drank from the bottle and nodded.

"How are you doing?" I asked.

"Still alive and kicking," he answered. His voice sounded a bit stronger.

I went to the front window and looked out. The street was deserted, and it had started raining again. We needed to get upstairs and put a few more locked doors between us and any bad guys.

Darla came bounding back into the room, her arms piled high with blankets.

I grabbed one from her, went over to Luke, and wrapped it gently around him. "Hang in there."

I looked up at Darla, who was busy wrapping herself up in a pink and white Afghan. "We need to dress that wound. What about a first aid kit?" I asked.

"I think there's one behind the counter. I'll look for it," she answered.

Luke reached out and touched my arm. "Colina, you're shivering."

I pulled my arm back. "I'm okay."

"Last thing I need is the person saving me succumbing to frostbite."

Hypothermia was a distinct possibility. I was chilled to the bone, my clothes were drenched, and I was covered in mud. I leaned over, grabbed a blanket from the pile Darla had dropped onto the floor, and wrapped it around my shoulders. "There, satisfied?" I asked, smiling at him.

"Much better." He suddenly winced and pain filled his eyes.

"We need to get you to a proper healer."

"I know someone, but we can't risk going out again tonight. That crew wasn't so happy with the way things turned out. They can be vindictive. I wouldn't put it past them to come back and hang around, waiting for a chance to get even."

"What about the cops?"

"Did Darla call them? I doubt they'll even come. This isn't their favorite part of town."

"Banshees, is that something you do a lot?"

"Not if I can help it."

I leaned down and looked at his injury. "The whole scene was pretty freaky."

"You got hurt." He touched the scratches on my arm and glanced over the ones on my cheek. "I brought them forth. I'm sorry they hurt you. I wouldn't have let them seriously injure anyone."

He was still bleeding, more than I would have liked. "Not even the bad guys?"

He kept silent and winced as I reached forward, and my fingers gently moved around his wound.

I was still trying to get my mind around the fact Luke had conjured up the unsettled dead and, even worse, had them do his bidding.

*The dead must be left alone.* It was my pa's voice this time that whispered in the corners of my mind. *Don't get involved with anyone who conjures up the Death Arts. They're wicked people, Colina.*

Luke didn't seem wicked, but what did I actually know

about the guy? He'd gone into an alley to save an innocent woman. Okay, not so innocent—she'd tried to shish kebab him —but as far as he knew, he was helping a victim. That meant he was someone with good intentions. Right?

*Only the blackest souls mess with the dead. The dead should be left alone. It's sacrilegious, the way those people call up spirits and parade them in front of their kinfolk.*

My pa's voice again. And with it, a memory...

*Pa was sitting by the fireplace. It was a week before Christmas, and most of the clan had started making their way to the winter festival. We were leaving in the morning. I was beyond excited. It would be the first time I was allowed to see the more difficult magics performed. My mother had promised that, in a few years, I would begin my healing lessons. I was young, innocent and the world seemed like a place with so many possibilities. I don't remember how the discussion moved on to the death dealers, but I remember the way my mama's face changed when she began talking about them, the look of disgust that filled her eyes at the mention of them.*

*"And what right do they have? Who made them judge and juror? How can they decide when someone should meet their maker?" my mama asked.*

My mama's whole life had been about healing. The death dealers were the antithesis of her very existence. As powerful as she was, there were those she tried to heal who were too far gone, too ill to be healed. Sometimes those dying souls would call on death dealers to help them make the transition from this life to the next. To me it seemed, at the time, a kindness to stop their suffering, but my mother corrected me, telling me it was unnatural. She warned me that they were challenging the very balance of things.

I knew those who practiced the blackest forms of the Death Arts often sacrificed animals to gain more power for their spells. But I'd also heard darker rumors. Whisperings that it wasn't just when the sick were on their deathbeds that the death dealers took a life. But those rumblings were only rumors, and it was hard for me to imagine anyone trying to practice those most forbidden magics.

*Have you ever called on that same energy? Ever felt its pulse swirling and circling around you? It's not for the faint of heart,* Luke had said. That worried me more than I wanted to admit. What I was doing was lunacy. No one stumbled into a magic shop and demanded to learn the Death Arts. Those who practice it were despised and often hated. Dark magic was something I both feared and desperately needed.

Darla knelt beside me and handed over a blue plastic box with a medical symbol on its cover. I pulled it open and started taking out bandages, tape, and a pair of scissors. "This is going to hurt."

Luke nodded and closed his eyes.

I used an antiseptic wipe to clean my hands and then got to work. I cleaned the wound and bandaged it as quickly as I could. I could tell he was in pain by the way he was breathing. Every time I came in contact with the wound, his breathing hitched or increased, and he let out a soft moan. I tried to focus on the task at hand and not the pain I was inflicting.

Darla sat beside me and quietly handed me bandages and ointments.

Finally, I had done all I could. I sat back on my knees and wiped the hair out of my face. The injury wasn't bad enough to kill him, but if left unattended for too long it could get infected and become serious.

I turned to Darla. "We need to get him upstairs."

"I can walk," he said, pushing himself up slowly, but unsteadily, to his feet.

"Last thing I need is to have you fall over and get a concussion because you're being a macho idiot," I said, giving him a hard stare.

He gave me a sheepish grin and I stood up, looping my arm around his waist.

We made our way across the room and up the stairs, Darla following closely. It was slow going. Once upstairs, I helped him into his room and onto his bed. I turned away while he finished getting undressed. When he was done and settled on the bed, I pulled a black and red striped duvet over him.

He laid his head back against the pillow. "Darla, go make some tea. It will help warm us up."

She nodded and headed out of the room.

"There you go. Snug as a bug in a rug." I leaned over and brushed my hand across his forehead. He didn't have a fever.

He smiled. "My mom used to say that to me when I was a kid."

His bedroom was bigger than it looked from the outside. He had a king-size bed with a padded headboard. On either side of the bed were two large, black nightstands, each sporting a black shaded lamp. A large black dresser stood off to one side. The other wall housed a black wooden desk and office chair.

"I bet your favorite color is black."

"Now you're the mind reader."

I looked around the room and laughed. "Call it a lucky guess."

"You need to change out of those wet clothes."

"That's the next thing on my to do list. I'll be right outside. If you need anything, just shout," I said, heading toward the door.

"Colina...thanks."

I turned back, unsure of what to say. I shrugged and smiled. "Sure, anytime."

"I'm serious. I'm glad you're here. I would hate to think

what would have happened if you hadn't been. If Darla had been alone..."

The way he was staring at me and the intensity in his eyes sent a small, delicious shiver through me. I found myself searching his face, wondering what he was thinking. It was a good face. He was a handsome guy. My glance ventured down to his lips. I realized I was staring, and I could feel a blush spread across my cheeks. I tried to keep the embarrassment I felt from my voice when I said, "Try to get some sleep." Without waiting for his reply, I walked quickly out of the room.

Back in the living room, I found Darla on the couch curled up in a big pink blanket. Her face was pale, and her hair hung down around her like a wet golden curtain.

She looked up at me. "The tea's brewing."

"Why don't you go take a hot shower? I'll stand guard in case he needs anything."

"You're staying?" She suddenly looked much younger. Her eyes were filled with panic.

I remembered that she'd just watched her brother get stabbed almost to death. I felt uncomfortable seeing the panic in her eyes and turned away.

"I don't have any place to go. Not with the bad guys out there."

"Is he going to die?" Her voice was but a whisper.

I walked over and sat down next to her. "No, he's fine."

Tears spilled down her face. "There was so much blood. I thought..."

I patted her shoulder. "He's going to be okay. He needs to see someone who can properly heal him. You can take him tomorrow. When the coast is clear."

She grabbed my hand. "Promise me you'll come with us."

"Darla, I don't know—" I started to pull my hand out of her grasp.

Her grip tightened. "Colina, promise me you'll stay until we know for sure he's going to be alright."

I had come here with a single-minded purpose: to learn the Death Arts. I'd had my fill of pain and suffering. I didn't want to become involved in other people's dramas. If I were smart, I would walk out the door and come back in a few days when Luke was all healed and the Triad chaos had blown over.

I glanced over at Darla. She looked so scared. I can't leave her, not now. Not when she's so afraid. "I promise. Now go get in the shower." I looked down at my wet, muddy, and now covered in bits of blood, outfit. "I'm afraid I'm going to have to borrow some more clothes."

"Look in my dresser or my closet. Take whatever you want."

"It's going to be okay." Even as I said the words, I knew I couldn't make that promise. I learned the hard way that the universe can reach out at any time and take away what you love most in the world. When the universe decides to mess with your life and your loved ones, you have no choice but to sit back and watch in horror as your worst nightmares came true.

# FIVE

I bolted upright and opened my eyes. It took me a few moments to realize where I was. I don't know what woke me this time. No screams filled the air. There was no commotion in the room. Everyone was sound asleep and safe for the moment. I reached up and touched my cheeks. They were wet. I'd been crying in my sleep again. It was the aftermath of a nightmare that was always the same. Most nights I woke suddenly with my heart pounding out of my chest and tears streaming down my face.

The tiniest sound came from my right. I didn't want to turn, but I forced myself to look. A large shadow loomed only a few feet away. A scream formed on my lips, but I swallowed it when the lights flickered on, and I saw Luke standing by the side table. He had one arm pushed against the back of the chair so he could keep himself upright.

"You shouldn't be out of bed." I threw off my blanket and started to get up.

He waved me back. "Stop fussing. I'm feeling better." To prove it, he straightened up and walked over to me. "I heard someone crying out. Are you okay?"

"I'm fine. It was just a nightmare."

"That must have been one heck of a dream."

I looked up at him. "I'm sorry I woke you."

"You don't need to apologize. You look shaken. Do you want me to get you a glass of water?"

"You're the injured one. I should be getting you things."

He sat down next to me. "I told you, I feel better. Whatever you gave me helped. The pain isn't as bad."

I leaned over, my hand reaching out to examine the bandage. "Is it still bleeding?"

He pushed my fingers back. "Colina, stop fussing. I'm fine. You've been crying."

Ashamed, I turned my face away from him. "It's nothing."

"Tell me what's wrong."

Even if I wanted to, I didn't know if I could. If I were able to find the right words, could I actually say them out loud?

"What trouble brought you here?" he asked, his voice soft. "Why did you stop being a healer?" He leaned closer. "What happened?"

It was unsettling, having him so close. I scooted back, putting distance between us. "You don't have to know my reasons for wanting to learn. You just have to teach me."

"I would like to know your intent."

I looked over at him. "What do you mean?"

"What do you plan to do with the abilities you get once you train and learn how to use them?" He leaned back and watched me. "Look, it's not in our nature to train people so they can go off and wreak havoc in the world. We usually know a bit about someone's background before we show them the way of the death dealers. Once they learn, they must join one of the death dealer guilds. We're open to everyone who's serious about learning and becoming one of our kind, but we try to keep from teaching our skills to those with violent tendencies or homicidal backgrounds."

"Are you worried I have a homicidal background?" When he didn't answer right away, I continued. "And what if I do? You already agreed to help me."

"I did." He nodded.

"You don't know anything about me." It was true. He didn't even know my last name.

"Only because you won't tell me about yourself." His expression was sullen.

"Then why take me on? It can't be the money. By the looks of this place, you and your family are extremely well off."

"Money isn't a problem for us."

"Then why did you agree to train me?" I demanded.

"Because you were so desperate." He inched toward me. "Because I saw something in your eyes that told me you need to do this."

I turned my face away again and said quietly, "And if the reason I need to do this is so I can go off and kill someone?"

He moved closer and put his hand on my shoulder. "Then I would be curious as to why. If we're going to take this path together, you have to trust me."

"I've said I'll do whatever it takes. Just tell me what I have to do, and I'll do it." Our hips were now touching. I could feel the heat of his body against mine.

With gentle fingers, he turned my chin toward him until we were facing each other. "That's what I mean. Why? Why are you so eager to become a death dealer and throw away the life you had as a healer?" He reached out and pushed a strand of hair from my eyes. "I don't know what it is about you, but I feel this connection."

I realized I was holding my breath. I exhaled and tried to think of something to say.

His face was just inches from mine now. His dark eyes were searching my face. "Do you feel it?" His fingers brushed against my temple, then moved slowly down my face.

His fingers touched the scratches on my right cheek. Marks left from the banshee. He gently grazed the welts. "I'm sorry I hurt you."

The breath caught in the back of my throat. His fingers lingered on my cheek. His touch sent tiny electric sparks down my skin. He was so close I could feel the heat of his whole body against mine.

*He is a death dealer!* Came a warning from within my mind. Someone I should fear, someone I should despise. Someone who should not make my pulse quicken.

He had looked at me before with both anger and amusement, but I wasn't sure what emotion now blazed from those dark eyes. They were filled with such intensity, and as he watched me, his lips slowly curved up into a smile. It was the first time I had seen him really smile. As quickly as that smile had appeared, it disappeared.

Luke suddenly pushed off the couch and moved away. When he looked back at me, I couldn't read his expression.

"I'll see you in the morning. Sleep well," he said, turning his face away.

Before I could say a word, he turned off the light and left the room.

I pulled my knees up to my chest and wrapped my arms around them. I sat on the couch looking out into the darkness, suddenly feeling very alone.

∼

THE MORNING WAS CHAOTIC. Darla rushed around, making breakfast in between fussing over her brother's injuries. The more she worried about him, the more annoyed he seemed. I didn't say much, but quietly watched the pair of them while I consumed a large plate of scrambled eggs, bacon, and two helpings of grape jellied toast.

Darla begged to come with us to the healer, but Luke refused. He reassured her that the Triads are a nocturnal group that was probably off sleeping the day away. She finally gave in and decided to stay behind. Honestly, I think he was just trying to get away from her excessive mothering.

I wore a borrowed green sweater and a pair of dark jeans that would have fallen off if I hadn't cinched them tightly at my waist with an oversize, brown leather belt. Once again, my outfit was courtesy of Darla.

Luke's long hair was tied back and he sported a black, long-sleeved T-shirt—this one minus the red phoenix and flames—along with a black jean jacket, gray jeans, and black boots. He looked a bit dangerous and girls on the street were turning to check him out as we walked by.

He was moving better this morning, but the going was still slow. We made our way to the corner and hailed a cab. A few miles later, we were out of the cab and weaving our way through the crowds. We walked for a bit along the main thoroughfare and then took a left and headed down an alley. The alley part didn't thrill me—not after our late-night adventure. I kept looking over my shoulder, worried we were being followed. Out of one alley we went and then down another until we suddenly turned a corner and found ourselves in a seedier part of town. Signs of different shapes and sizes hung over a few dozen shops lining the street. All the shops had iron bars covering their windows.

I hadn't spent a lot of time in the city, but it was easy to spot which establishment housed the healer. Going by the designs on the sign and the colorful tapestry in the window, she was a traveler. Travelers' magic is a bit different than mine. My heritage is Scottish, which means each healer in my family is part of a clan. We sometimes did magic outside the family for money, but only under special circumstances.

Travelers have a different set of rules. They work mostly for money, often traveling around, going wherever their services are needed. For the right price, they will heal you. The early travelers chose a path very different from most of the mage societies. They became nomads, never staying in one place long enough to attract attention and using weak versions of their talents to amuse the non-mages and to make themselves seem nonthreatening. They hid in plain sight, surviving over the centuries on wit and charm.

I was surprised to see that a traveler had set up shop in town. Many cities have ordinances about healers and soothsayers. Truly gifted healers in the city both clan and travelers usually work through clinics or hospitals. That made me worry, since often those who set up shop for themselves aren't the real thing. They're charlatans.

Not everyone wants to step foot into a hospital where they have to show their ID. Most of the fringe population like to stay off the radar, which means they have to use services that aren't officially approved. Using people outside the mandates comes with its own set of risks. Would the herbs they gave you cure your pneumonia and make you better? Or would you waste away in sickness and head back for help only to find that the healer had closed up shop and moved on to another location?

"Is this place for real?" I asked, quickening my steps. I wanted to get this over with.

"She's truly gifted. My guild has used her many times," Luke answered, stopping to catch his breath.

I went ahead of him and opened the door to a jingle of bells. Lavish colors covered everything, and exotic materials could be seen on the walls, pillows, and at my feet. Half a dozen different throw rugs covered the floor. The effect of one rug's zebra pattern next to another's purple circles overlaid with red stripes was dizzying. The proprietor certainly had the old-world atmosphere down to a science.

"How may I help you children?" A weathered and lined face greeted us from behind a curtain of black beads.

"Mother, we're in need of your services." Luke held out his palm, which held a small group of gold and silver coins.

The woman was dressed in a long, purple skirt and a black cotton blouse, and her hair was pulled up under a purple scarf. She motioned for us to sit down in one of the four red striped, overstuffed chairs scattered across the room. As she moved her arms, I noticed that both her wrists were covered in gold bangles.

"Make yourselves comfortable. Who's in need of my help?" She turned toward me and asked, "You?" For an old woman she moved quickly, and before I could respond, her hand reached out and grabbed my forearm. "I see much pain in you, child. Did you come to unburden yourself? I can do that. I'm not just a healer of the flesh. I can take away the pain you feel in the very depth of your soul."

The way the old woman looked at me made my skin crawl. Could she really sense my pain? The internal wounds I carried were fresh, and the nightmare I went through came buzzing to the front of my mind. I tried to push back the anguish, tried not to think of it, because I knew that if I allowed myself to fully dwell on it, I would start bawling hysterically and curl up into a fetal position on the floor.

The only thing that mattered now was staying alive, and the only way to make sure that happened was to get the dark mage who agreed to teach me healed. I pulled my arm away and pointed toward Luke. "He's the injured one."

She didn't move, but instead edged closer until her face was only a few inches from mine. "You're like me, yes? You're in the trade? I can see it on you." She reached out again and grabbed my arm and turned my wrist. Her eyes lit up at the image of the swallow. "Yes, I see you're one of us, but the pain, it's shifting your power. You've lost your balance. Let me help you regain yourself."

I let my anger show in my voice. "I'm not in need of your services. He's the one with the wound. He needs your help."

"You couldn't heal him?" she asked.

I turned my face away, ashamed. I should have been able to heal him, to close up the wound, but I hadn't been able to. I wasn't sure why my powers weren't working. I looked back at the woman. She was peering at me with open curiosity. Was she right? Had the pain, the loss, the hate, the anger—all the foreign emotions that were now swirling inside me—somehow messed up my power?

She let go of me and walked over to Luke, extending her palm. He put the coins into her hand, and they disappeared into the pockets of her purple skirt.

"Lift your shirt," she demanded. Luke obeyed. "Ah, I see." She closed her eyes and ran her hand over his side.

He flinched as her fingers made contact with the bandages.

"Whatever did this went deep. There's damage to both the muscle and tissue. Was the weapon enchanted?" she asked.

"No. It was a regular switchblade," he answered.

She nodded, walking to a shelf, and searching through bottles before returning with a white cloth and a glass container filled with orange liquid. Placing the bottle and cloth on the table in front of him, she said, "I'll use my abilities first, but afterward, you'll need to use this." She pointed at the bottle. "On the wound. Once a day. Just dab it on."

I wondered if whatever was in the bottle actually was some sort of medicine.

As the thought crossed my mind, she turned and frowned in my direction. "I'm not a fake. I'm the real thing, child."

Were my thoughts so easy to read? Had the events of the night frazzled me so much that my defenses were down? Was the old woman powerful enough to break through my mental barriers?

The woman closed her eyes and reached out, and her right hand covered Luke's bandage. Minutes ticked on, and nothing happened. Then, suddenly, a loud sigh left the woman's mouth, and as it did, a soft buzz filled the room. The drapes rustled ever so slightly as if moved by a breeze, but there were no open windows that I could detect.

The healer had some kind of medallion in her left hand. The tighter she clutched it, the louder the buzz and the more the drapes fluttered. Was the piece of metal the source of her abilities? Traveler magic was decidedly different from my clan's. We drew our energy from the earth or from the sky.

As quickly as they had started, the buzz and breeze were gone. The room stood silent. The old woman stumbled a bit as she moved away from Luke, catching her balance on the back of the chair.

She spoke without turning in my direction. "No, child, my magics don't come from any object. But it helps to focus, helps bring me focus, you understand?" She looked directly at me. "We're not so unalike, your people and mine."

She turned and faced Luke. "It will itch as it heals. The marks will close in about three days and then you'll only have a small scar. But a scar can be attractive on a man."

Luke lowered his shirt and stood up. He reached out to the old woman.

She grasped his hand in hers.

"Thank you, I appreciate your help. May you be well," he said.

"And you," she replied.

I stood up and turned and headed toward the door. I had my hand on the door handle when the old woman caught up with me, her fingers digging into my shoulder. She might be old, but her grip was like steel.

She leaned in and whispered in my ear, "Child, I know what happened and I know pain is burning inside you because of it. But if you are determined to go down this path, then your only chance at success will come if you allow yourself to trust him."

I spun around. She was talking about Luke. She wanted me to trust a guy I just met? A member of the Phoenix Guild? Tell him my secrets? I took a step back, tears of panic swelling in my eyes.

She motioned toward Luke. "If you want the power, you must tell him your story. Let him in. He has to see the very essence of you. To lead you down his dark path, he must be able to read your heart and soul. It's the only way. And, child, be careful. They're looking for you." From within the folds of her skirt she brought a red velvet pouch tied with black leather. She reached out and put it in my hand.

I was too shocked by her words to respond. I had no choice but to take the pouch as she forced it into my palm.

"For your protection. Take it. Keep it close to you." Her eyes suddenly looked unfocused. "I see you swimming on the edge of a great darkness. The awakening is coming upon you, child. It will try to consume you. The pouch, the protection, it won't be enough, but it may help."

We stood next to each other in frozen silence as the seconds ticked away. They're looking for me. For a moment, my heart stopped. I hadn't been sure they would come for me, but after what happened, I feared the worst. Now this old woman was telling me it was true. The fear burst forward again, filling my mind and body. I could hear my breath coming out in short rasps. I looked over at Luke. He was watching us. I wasn't sure if he'd overheard what she'd told me.

I took a deep breath and tried to calm my thoughts while forcing back tears. I wouldn't cry, I wouldn't lose it, not here. I looked at her and blurted out the first thing that came to mind. "I don't have any coins to pay you for the pouch."

She reached up and patted my cheek. "Don't worry about paying me. Stay alive, child. You must save yourself. And, whatever you do, don't forget who you are."

I clutched the bag to my chest and ran out the door.

# CHAPTER
# SIX

"Hey, slow down," Luke said, coming to my side. He'd followed me out of the store and had to jog a bit to catch up.

He must've been feeling better if he was running—it wasn't something he'd been able to do prior to seeing the healer.

"That place freaked me out."

"The place or the healer?"

"A bit of both," I admitted.

"What did she say to you? At the door when she gave you that pouch?"

I still held it tightly against my chest. "It was nothing." I looked over at him, and he raised an eyebrow.

"Okay, it was something. A warning. She said something about, the awakening is 'coming upon me' and that it will try and consume me."

His expression turned grim.

"What's the awakening?" I asked, not quite sure I wanted to hear the answer.

"In travelers' lore, it's considered a time when you open

yourself up to the spirits, a time when the dark magics run wild in your blood. It's part of learning the Death Arts, but that's when you need to be especially careful. The spirits and the magic can take you over, can change you."

"Swell," I mumbled under my breath. I might finally learn the Death Arts only to be consumed by them

We walked the rest of the way to the corner in silence. A cab headed in our direction. Luke raised a hand and stepped off the curb and flagged it down. He opened the cab door for me, and I scrambled in.

"So what now?" I asked.

He looked out the window. "We go back to the apartment and check on Darla."

"And after that?" I demanded.

He turned and gave me a hard stare. "You go home and then come back in a few weeks when my uncle is back, and he can get you started on your training."

I looked at him in shock. "You said you could help me."

"Colina, I know what I said."

I forced the words out between clenched teeth. "You took my money. You promised to teach me." I'd been a fool to trust him.

"I should never have promised to teach you. Only the elders in the guild can do this type of teaching—men and women who have been practicing the Death Arts for years. For me to teach you, it wouldn't be safe. The travelers aren't wrong. Dealing with the Death Arts can be dangerous."

I shook my head and tried to calm the panic I felt rising within me. "I can't wait a couple of weeks."

"Why?" he demanded.

I had started to believe I had a chance to get out of this whole mess in one piece, but now I knew I had no one to turn to, no one to help me. I was totally alone in this, and at the thought, a deep despair filled me. I turned and looked out the window of the cab and I said in a quiet voice, "You said you'd teach me."

"It's just a few weeks, and then my uncle will be back," Luke answered softly.

I needed to make Luke understand that I was out of time.

WE MADE it back to the apartment. Darla fussed over Luke, and he looked annoyed, so I tried to stay out of their way.

I was still trying to get my head around what Luke told me in the cab. If he refused to teach me, I would have no choice but to go out on my own and try to find someone else to guide me in the Death Arts. But who? Where would I go? Home was no longer an option. I could demand my money back and head out into the streets.

*You could tell him the truth*, the words whispered across my mind. I kept thinking about what the old woman said. If I told him the truth, then he'd understand why I was so desperate to learn. He might be convinced there was no time to wait; it had to be done now. I wanted to tell him the truth, I really did, but I didn't know if I had the courage to speak about what happened.

I felt cold all over. I hugged my arms around my body and walked over to the apartment's row of windows. It had started raining again. I stood looking out at the storm, watching sheets of water blown by high winds slam against the walls of the buildings and the street below.

Luke crossed the room with an easy stride. He was moving without pain now. He stood next to me and asked, "Are you okay?"

"Can you get me a glass of water?" I knew I was stalling. The last thing I wanted to do was relive it all.

He looked surprised at my request. "Sure."

I turned back to watch the storm. A few minutes later he was at my side again, a tall glass of water filled with ice in his hand. He reached out and offered it to me.

I took it and sat down on the windowsill. "Thanks." I looked around the room. "Where's Darla?"

"I don't think she's over last night's ordeal. I suggested she lie down for a bit."

If there was ever a time to clear the air, it was now, when we were alone. I didn't think I could get through it all with an audience. "The traveler said I should tell you everything."

He sat down next to me. "Tell me."

"You keep asking what brought me here, and I admit I've been reluctant." I swallowed hard. "But it's not because I don't want you to know. It's just because I don't know if..." My words faltered.

He reached out and clasped my hand. His fingers felt warm against my cold skin. I realized I felt a chill not just inside my body, but inside my soul. I gave his hand a squeeze. At this moment I was thankful for the human contact. I looked into his eyes, which were full of concern. He wasn't looking at me like a stranger; he was looking at me as though he really cared.

I forced myself to continue. "It's only by a quirk of fate that I'm even here. If I hadn't been in the pantry looking for something..." My voice broke off again. I looked out the window, watching a tree sway in the wind. "It's funny. I can't remember now what I was looking for."

I put down my water and leaned my forehead against the cool windowpane. "It was Sunday. Family dinner. We had them every Sunday. Everyone helps out with the cooking." I sat up and looked at him. "It's always been one of my favorite days of the week because we were all together." I leaned back, picked up the glass of water, and took a long sip. I put the glass back down and took a deep breath. I could do this. I could finally get it out. I just had to say the words.

I closed my eyes and took a deep breath. "My brother's name is...was...his name was James." It took a few moments for me to find my voice again. "If James hadn't been at the pantry door giving me a hard time, if he hadn't seen them..." I opened my eyes, and a sob escaped my mouth. "He didn't give me a choice, he told me to stay quiet, to stay hidden, he shoved me inside and closed the doors." My heart was pounding at the memory. Talking about it was bringing it all back. Almost like reliving the whole thing again. "My brother knew I would have left the pantry and fought by his side, but I couldn't help him because James placed a spell on the doors."

I realized tears had started rolling down my cheeks. "His last words to me were the tail end of a spell." I barely got the confession out before Luke took me in his arms. My cheek rested on his chest.

Every night since it happened, I replayed it all in my mind. It was the living nightmare that had changed my whole life—a very real, horrific moment in time I wish I could purge from my mind. I choked back a sob and forced the rest out. "The spell kept me in and kept the men who attacked us from hearing my fists pounding against the door. They couldn't hear my screams," I spoke the words against his shirt. "I watched through the door slats. James tried to fight them, but he was too late. He couldn't save our family."

A sob broke through and then another. "My people don't practice war magic. We focus on healing—keeping people alive. We learn some defenses, but nothing that would stop someone like the powerful mage who led the attackers. He blew through my father's defenses like they weren't even there. He was strong, like one of your kind." I pushed myself away from Luke and looked him in the eye. Tears streamed down my face. "He overpowered my father and he...he slit my father's throat. And then they shot my mother. The blood, there was so much blood..."

Suddenly, I was back there. I heard the screams of my family in my head. Blood poured from my father's throat and the smell of it clogged my nose and mouth. I watched the light leave my mama's eyes as the bullet tore through her head. I started to gag, and nausea rose from the pit of my stomach.

Strong arms encircled me tightly again.

"They must have known you were healers if they used guns. It would have been too great a risk to try and shoot a mage-born who wielded dark magic," Luke said. "Did you know the men?"

"I had never seen them before that day." Though their images were now forever burned into my memory.

Luke's voice turned thoughtful. "Did your father have any enemies that would go to such extremes?"

"No. My father was the strongest healer in our clan. A man who was respected and admired, but that didn't save him." I had gone over it a hundred times, trying to make sense of what happened. Why had my family been killed? I wanted to finish the story, to tell him what happened to James and about the men looking for me, but I couldn't force those words out. So instead, I sat there, embraced by his strong arms, my body relaxing against his. It was soothing listening to his heartbeat. I felt comforted and safe for the first time since the nightmare had happened.

He broke the silence. "How did you get out?"

"It took a day and a night before someone found me." I reluctantly pushed away and looked him in the face. "My family is gone, and now someone is after me."

"What do you mean 'someone is after you?"

"At the funeral, the same men, I saw them, they were there.

They came to the funeral looking for me. Three men who were dressed like funeral mourners, but never even glanced at the caskets, moved through the crowd until they stood behind me. Dark glasses hid their eyes, but I recognized them anyway. I will never forget those faces." I swallowed, my memory taking me right back to that day.

"They watched me, not the speakers or the priest. I knew they would just follow me until they could get me alone. The entire clan had gathered to bury my family and the people around me were my only protection. As the crowd began to break up, I stayed with the clan leaders until we reached the cars, and then slipped away. I stayed in the cemetery and hid behind headstones while everyone drove away. I watched the men looking into cars as they passed, turning in circles to find me—it's a huge old cemetery. After the cars were gone, they climbed into a dark sedan, arguing the entire time, and drove away."

"The only reason I got away was because they didn't want to draw attention to themselves by grabbing me in front of witnesses. I didn't know what to do. It put my clan at risk to stay around. I couldn't lose anyone else, so I just ran and kept running. Away from everyone I know, away from my home." I paused, steeling myself before meeting Luke's eyes with my own. "I have no idea why they killed my family. The only thing I can do is become powerful. I'm going to learn the Death Arts and become a death dealer. Whatever price I have to pay to get to the top of the magic food chain, I'm willing to do it."

Why were the murderers so intent on coming after me? When the men found out I was still alive, did they realize I'd seen their faces? Did they fear I could one day bring them to justice for what they did?

"I knew there was something pushing you, but I never imagined..." His voice trailed off. He reached out and grabbed my hand. "I know you're upset, but revenge isn't a reason to become one of us."

"How about survival?" I demanded. I needed to convince him to help me, and if he knew just how deep my anger swelled inside me, he might not. "I'm the only witness to their crime. My father is—was—the most powerful of our clan. If he couldn't protect us, then no one in my clan can. The only way I can survive is to become one of you."

Luke stood up with a burst of energy. "You don't want this. Believe me when I tell you this isn't something you want to bring into your life. We are hated by mages and non-mages alike. People see what we can do and how we do it, and they fear us. We take the lost souls that linger in this world and bind them to our will. We use the trauma and anger that keeps them from crossing over as a weapon against our enemies. Once you become one of us, you will never be able to go out in the world without needing someone to watch your back, because the whole world will want to stick a knife in it. You don't want to sign up for that."

"You did. You became one," I said quietly.

He glared down at me. "The guild brought me up. I knew what to expect from the time I was young. There were no surprises. I went into it with my eyes wide open. You were raised in a healer clan, and you know the way the world works, you follow the family trade."

"I know I can do this," I said, my voice filled with determination.

He shook his head, his face filled with frustration. "You don't understand. You don't even know what the rituals entail. You haven't even asked about the things you'll have to do."

"I told you—I'll do whatever I have to." I meant it. Whatever it took. Whatever trials I needed to go through; I would see my family's death avenged.

The frustration had left Luke's eyes; anger had taken its place. "You think you're willing to do anything, but you aren't."

"I can. I will. I have to. Whatever trials you send my way, I'll do them."

"Even if it means you have to die?"

I looked up at him, shocked by his words.

"Yes—die. In the first part of the ritual, the initiate has to commune with the spirits." He reached down, pulled me to my feet, and grabbed me by the shoulders. "And how do you think that's accomplished? You have to die. You have to go to the other side and be brought back." With each word, he shook me a bit harder.

I didn't try to break free. Instead, I tried to comprehend what he was saying. "Brought back? I'm dead for just a short time?"

"Yes, killed and then brought back. If we do the ritual correctly. If everything goes like it should. But if something goes wrong..." His fingers dug into my skin.

I pulled away from him and rubbed my shoulder. "Someone died and didn't come back?"

"There have been times when the ritual hasn't worked, when they lost the initiate."

"Lost. You mean..." I forced the words out. "There's no other way?"

"To wield this kind of power, you have to make a sacrifice."

I said through clenched teeth, "My family was murdered. Someone killed them, and now they're after me."

"You can get protection. Go into hiding until it blows over," he pleaded.

I shook my head.

He reached out and grabbed me roughly with his hands again. "Colina, you don't want to do this."

I forced myself back out of his reach. "I don't have a choice."

"You're prepared to die?" he demanded.

"And be brought back to life. Yes."

"I don't even know if my uncle will do it."

"I told you, there isn't time to wait for your uncle."

Luke frowned. "You can't expect me—"

"Someone is coming after me. I don't have any protection against them," I whispered.

He turned away from me. "I won't do it."

I grabbed his arm and forced him to turn back toward me. "You have to. You said you would!"

He clenched his fists. "I won't do it!"

"You said you wanted me to come back, that you were going to teach me. It would have been tonight, during the witching hour."

"I was going to scare you a bit. Scare you from going down this path, give your money back, and send you on your way. I only took the money and told you I would teach you because I saw the desperation in your eyes. I was worried you'd find someone else to teach you. Honestly, I was hoping my uncle could change your mind about learning the Death Arts. I thought that once you realized all it entails—the path you'd have to take—you wouldn't go through with it. I should never have told you I would teach you."

I couldn't believe what I was hearing. "You were never serious about teaching me?"

"No." His hands clenched and unclenched at his side. "I won't do this."

"Then I have no choice but to find someone else," I whispered.

Without a word, he turned and stormed away from me.

# CHAPTER
# SEVEN

"I don't understand. Why are you leaving?" Darla asked.

We were both standing at the kitchen counter. She was cutting up potatoes, and I was peeling carrots. Luke had made himself scarce for the last hour.

"Your brother said he can't help me."

"He surprised me when he said he'd teach you. It's not something he should have agreed to." She averted her eyes. "I know about the rituals. I haven't been through them yet, but I've watched them." She put down the knife and looked at me. "I know I'm not supposed to say it. I know they expect me to go through it one day and I will. But honestly, Colina, the things they put the initiates through..."

"Luke went through them," I said.

She went back to chopping potatoes and said in a low voice, "He did. He won't admit it, but it wasn't easy for him. He had nightmares afterwards for a long time."

Luke wandered into the room. He gave me a hard stare. "You're staying for dinner?"

"I promised Darla I would," I answered.

He nodded and picked up a piece of celery off the counter.

"Luke, convince her not to leave until tomorrow. It will be dark out soon, and that gang might come back," Darla said.

"I'll make sure she gets safely into a cab," Luke answered.

Darla dropped a handful of potatoes into a pot. "Where are you going? Home?"

I hadn't told her about my family. I would leave it to Luke to fill her in on the details of my life after I left. Maybe once he did, she'd understand why I was so desperate to find a teacher.

"I'm not sure." I turned to Luke. "If you could give me the name of someone, maybe someone in your guild?"

He shook his head. "No."

I turned back to Darla. "Do you know anyone who could help me?"

She didn't answer, but instead got busy wiping off the cutting board.

Luke watched me, his face full of disapproval, but I didn't care what he thought. If he couldn't help me, I had no choice but to move on and find another way to get what I needed.

I looked him straight in the eye and said in a firm voice, "It may take time, but I'll find someone who'll teach me."

Luke frowned and moved toward the windows.

I looked down at the carrot and peeler in my hands. "What are we making again?" I wasn't much of a cook. Mama had always done all the cooking in our house.

Darla answered. "Stew. It's my uncle's recipe—" The door flew open and slammed against the wall, cutting off her words.

Men rushed in. In a moment of pure horror, I realized I recognized one of them—the bald man with a jagged scar running down one cheek heading my way. One of the men who attacked my family. I stood in shock, utterly immobile at the counter.

Luke turned and yelled, "Run!"

His words set me in motion. I dropped the peeler, grabbed

Darla by the hand, and pulled her toward the windows. We needed to get to the fire escape.

Suddenly there were loud shouts, strange noises, and flashes of lights in a rainbow of colors. I didn't bother to turn around and see what was happening, instead, I focused my whole being on escape. We were within inches of the closest window when Darla's hand was yanked from mine.

I turned to see a huge shadow looming over us. A man over six feet tall with a large snake tattoo that curled around his forearm and disappeared under the sleeve of his black T-shirt, held onto the end of Darla's golden ponytail. He yanked on it hard enough to force her body back. His dark eyes were savage, and he bared his teeth as he dragged her away.

I reached out, grabbing for Darla. For a moment our fingers locked once again, and I pulled with all my might to try and force her free. But he was stronger, and she was soon out of my grasp. He had her now and was moving her away from me. A part of me wanted to let her go, to forget about everything but escape. A few more steps and I would make it to the window and out into the night, to safety.

Darla screamed.

I couldn't leave her. She had tried to help me and now I had to try and help her. I turned away from the windows and headed to where she was now fighting the man. He was trying to wrestle her down to the ground. I wanted to help, but I hesitated. I knew I wouldn't be able to stop him alone—he was just too big.

I turned and saw Luke standing in the middle of the room. His hands were raised in the air and lights were flinging from his fingertips. Banshees circled the room, surrounding the strangers. One lay slumped on the floor, inches from Luke. Two other men had their hands raised, too, casting spells of their own. Blue streaks of light hit a wave of purple, and the force of

Luke's magic colliding with the other mages' set off sparks of all colors.

Whatever magic Luke was commanding was strong. He'd taken one of the men down, but the others were still on their feet and fighting. Out of the corner of my eye, I saw an unfamiliar man step forward. He seemed different from the others, and he moved with a calm confidence. He was even dressed better—where the other men wore T-shirts and jeans, this man wore a dark suit.

With a determined look on his face, the man in the suit raised his hands. A flood of banshees rushed into the room to meet Luke's. I watched in horror as Luke was forced back towards the window.

Luke wasn't going to win this fight. He was going to be overpowered, and I didn't have any magic to help him. I had no war training and no weapon in hand. Luke at any moment might die before my eyes, and there was nothing I could do to stop it. Once again, I was forced to stand by and watch helplessly as people were attacked and killed.

Darla screamed again. I spun back around and saw that she was only a few feet from me. The man had her pinned down. On pure instinct I started towards her and was moving across the floor when a bright orange light flooded the room. But, unlike the other colorful lights, this one came with a punch. The air rushed toward me in a wall of crackling energy, pushing me back. I stumbled, trying to stay on my feet as it washed over me like a wave.

Luke got the worst of it. The impact knocked him off his feet, throwing him through the air, and he crashed through two windows. Debris rained down in all directions as shards of glass flew my way, and I instinctively covered my head with my hands.

And then hands were on me. Someone had me around the

waist. I fought, scratching and kicking. I swung my arms and made contact with a nose. I heard a male voice yelp out in pain. I kicked again. I screamed at the top of my lungs, beyond reason. I was about to die like my family. Any moment my throat would be slit, or a bullet would tear through my flesh. I fought harder until something slammed against my head, and a wave of dizziness overcame me. My body went limp as darkness surrounded me.

When I came to, a man was carrying me over his shoulder and out the front door of the shop. I could hear Darla's cries. I turned my head and watched as someone shoved her into a dark SUV. The SUV roared away, and another one screeched to a halt in front of us. The door swung open, and I was tossed inside. I let my body fall hard against the seat. An exclamation of pain rose against my lips, but I forced it back. It would be better if they thought I was still unconscious.

I heard voices next to me. "Where'd you put the rope?"

"Try under the seat," someone answered.

"That death dealer took out Angelo."

A loud curse filled the air. "Anyone else hurt?"

"I'll let you know when my ears stop ringing."

A phone rang, and then a voice answered loudly. "Yeah, we got 'em, boss. There was some trouble."

I opened one eye just a little. Next to me was a dark form— one of the men. He was only a few inches from me, bending over, his hand reaching down toward the floor. I inched up slowly. There was someone in the seat behind me with a black hood over their head. I scooted up a bit more until I could barely see over the front seat. The driver was on the phone, his eyes on the road, thankfully, and not the rearview mirror.

The car was barreling down the road and I realized I had one option, one crazy chance of getting away. If I'm going to escape, it's now or never. I grabbed the handle and swung the door open. Before I could change my mind, I flung myself out the door and felt my body fly through the air. Pavement rushed up to meet me as the right side of my body slammed hard against the ground. I rolled, bumping and scraping along the pavement. Every time my body hit, bursts of pain exploded inside my head. I slowly came to a stop and lay there on the side of the road, stunned. The breath was completely knocked out of me. When I could finally breathe again the first intake of air was so painful, I cried out. Patches of exposed skin were scratched and bleeding. I sat up slowly, wincing.

I barely had time to assess my injuries before the sound of screeching tires got me to my feet. I started to run, limping, before I ventured a quick look back. They were turning around, coming back for me. I forced myself to move faster, but my ankle buckled, and I stumbled. I couldn't stop, not now that I could hear the car close behind me. I sucked in one breath and ignored the pain. There was no way I could outrun them. A ten-foot chain link fence ran along the road to my right. I changed direction and headed for the fence. When I hit it, I didn't stop, I just slammed my fingers into the first openings and propelled myself up. One hand and foot at a time, I climbed, ignoring the throbbing pain in my ankle and side. I didn't dare stop or glance back. I just kept climbing. The only sound in my ears was my breath, now coming out in gasps.

I rolled over the top of the fence, catching the edge of my shirt on the sharp, twisted wires. I pulled myself free with one hand and made my way down, climbing, sliding, and finally dropping the last four feet, crying out in pain as my injured leg made contact with the pavement.

The car stopped, and the men started to get out, but as I dropped to the ground on the other side, the driver yelled, and they all got back in. The SUV spun ahead.

They were going to go around and find the first opening in

the fence or make their way up the street and around the block, circling around until they found me.

I pushed myself off the ground and ran. Every time I came to the edge of a building, I turned or changed direction. Around one building and then past another, down one alley and then up the next.

I ran until I couldn't run any longer. My chest was burning, I was gasping, and my legs refused to go on. I had to find cover. Finally, I squeezed behind a large, metal dumpster. I slumped down against a brick wall, my legs giving out. When my bruised body made contact with the dirt, I gasped in pain.

I don't know how long I stayed huddled behind the dumpsters, but when I finally emerged, it was dark and cold. I cautiously looked around the corner. No cars anywhere. The place was deserted. I had no idea where I was or if I could make my way back to Luke's.

*Luke.* A sob escaped as the image of his body flying through the air and slamming through the broken windows slid across my mind. Could anyone survive such a thing? I stood helpless as he battled for his life.

I gave myself a mental shake and forced myself to concentrate on the here and now. I have to keep moving, but my surroundings were completely unfamiliar. I had taken so many twists and turns that I was completely turned around. I wrapped my arms around my body for warmth and slowly made my way down the alley.

CHAPTER

# EIGHT

I don't know how far I walked. The miles stretched on and on as I limped my way slowly along. Every time I saw headlights or heard the roar of an engine, I ducked behind the corner of a building or dove behind the closest telephone pole. I didn't know if the men were still out there searching for me.

Somehow, I found my bearings and eventually made it back to the magic shop. When I got there, I saw that the door had been smashed in. I made my way cautiously inside. The place was a mess. Every piece of glass in the room was broken. Items once neatly stacked on shelves now covered the floor. Ripped books lay piled all around.

It must've taken a brutal streak of violence to tear the place up like this. As I stood in the middle of the wreckage, my thoughts turned to Luke. *Please, Goddess, let him be okay, let him be here, please, let him be alive.* I prayed under my breath as I took the stairs two at a time.

I rushed into the main room, and there he was, sitting in a chair, with his head laid against his folded arms.

I was so happy to see him that I cried out his name. "Luke!"

He looked up and leaped out of the chair. We came together, our bodies slamming into a hard embrace that made me gasp in pain.

"You're alive," I whispered.

He tightened his grip. "So are you."

We stayed like that, entwined in each other's arms, until he slowly pulled back and asked, "Where's Darla?"

"I don't know—" My voice broke. "They still have her."

He pulled me into his arms again. "How did you get away?"

"I jumped from the car."

He took a step back and looked me over. "Are you hurt?"

I held out my arms and turned them over, "I've got some cuts and bruises, and I twisted my ankle, but I'm alright. Are you okay?"

"The railing stopped me from going over into the alley. I hit my head." He reached up, touched the side of his head, and winced. "I must have been unconscious for a while. When I woke up, it was dark, and you were both gone." His voice was full of anguish now. "I didn't know where to start looking. I know people hate our kind, but I never imagined they would raid the house and try to kill us."

I had to clear my throat a few times before I could get the words out. "Those men weren't after you. They were after me."

"You recognized them?"

I had recognized two of the men. I was so full of guilt; I couldn't look at him. I was the reason he'd almost died and why Darla was now in danger. "I'm so sorry. I should never have come here," I whispered.

He came up behind me and rested a hand on my shoulder. "We need to find Darla."

I spun around. "Your family can help us find her and bring her back."

"My guild, my family, everyone, they're all on the retreat.

They're up in the mountains. It's remote and cell phones don't work up there. Darla and I were the only ones who stayed back to watch the store. There's no one to help."

"But you said your uncle would be gone for weeks. Does that mean no one will be back for weeks?" Panic filled my voice.

He nodded his head. "Darla's not dead. I'd know if she—" He stopped and took a deep breath.

"How do we find her?" I whispered.

"We don't. You do," he answered.

I looked at him in shock. "I don't understand."

He had such an odd look in his eyes when he said, "Your family was murdered by these people."

I just looked at him, still not understanding.

"Maybe your family went into the light or maybe their spirits still linger," Luke said, watching me closely. "If they are still here, they might be able to tell us something about the men that killed them. Something that can help us find Darla."

"Still linger..." And then it dawned on me what he was talking about. He was saying my family might be spirits trapped on this plane. Souls trapped in between. My blood chilled as one thought rang through my head—death dealers can control spirits.

"Can you call on my family's spirits?" Even as I asked the question, I knew I didn't want to hear his answer. I knew he could conjure the dead. If my family was "between"—their spirits in an eternal state of unrest—would they be like one of Luke's banshees? I didn't know if I could stomach seeing Mama's face filled with that level of pain and anguish, I'd seen on those terrifying banshees faces that Luke had raised.

"If they were going to contact me, they would have when you first showed up. Spirits decide who they visit. They didn't come to me, but I'm betting they'll come to you."

"You want me to call on my family's spirits?" My voice trembled.

"Yes, but to do so..." He looked hesitant for a moment before straightening his shoulders and continuing, "You'd have to become one of us."

I couldn't believe what I was hearing. "You said you wouldn't teach me."

"There's no choice now." He turned and started pacing. "I don't want to do it. You don't understand how hard it's going to be. For you to become one of us... I don't know what'll happen if we do it this way. But these people killed your family. They have Darla."

He's going to teach me. I was going to get what I wanted. I should have felt triumph, but instead I only felt fear and a sinking feeling that, maybe even now, it was too late to save his sister.

He grabbed my arm. "We need to find somewhere safe to go. It'll be light in a couple hours. We can do it tomorrow at the witching hour—we can perform the first ritual."

"How many rituals are there?" Darla's words came back to me. Whatever these rituals were, they weren't going to be easy. They were something she was afraid of.

There was an intensity in his eyes I'd never seen before when he answered, "Three. Normally candidates perform the rituals over a full year, sometimes longer. People learn to wield their power slowly, gradually building up until they're in true possession of their gifts, but we don't have that kind of time." His grip tightened on my arm. "We can do the rituals over the next three nights. It's crazy, and as far as I know, it's never been done, but we don't have a choice."

"And if they hurt Darla before I finish the rituals?" I was suddenly afraid to hear his answer.

"I looked up your family's death on the internet."

I gave him a hard stare, confused about the change of topic, and quickly put two and two together. While we were making dinner preparations, he'd been surfing the net, looking for more info about my family. Didn't he believe me when I told him what happened?

He waited for me to say something, but when I stayed silent, he continued. "It wasn't hard to find. Mass murder makes headlines. But those men, the ones who attacked us today, when I fought them, I could tell that most of them were just minor mages. They had some power, but it wasn't strong enough to overtake me. Anyone can learn magic, but the most powerful mages are from the clans or the guilds. Most of these guys were too weak for that, but one of them, his power was like mine."

I gasped. "He was a death dealer?"

Luke turned his face away. "He was, but stronger than anyone I've ever seen. To be that strong, he has to have been doing things—certain rituals—that are hundreds of years old. Things that are no longer done. Things my people now condemn. Listen, it probably didn't mean anything to you at the time, but they killed your family on the night of a full moon. The timing of the murders, I think it was a sacrifice."

I could feel the blood draining from my face. A cold seeped into my body and chilled me to the very bone. "A sacrifice..."

"A human sacrifice. They slashed your father's throat, right? It was most likely with a knife specially prepared for the ritual. Some of the stronger dark magics need a blood sacrifice to power them. The more powerful the sacrifice, the more powerful the spell. That might explain why they're hunting strong mages, like your family. Maybe they're trying to create a powerful dark forbidden spell."

My father was a human sacrifice. I was horrified at Luke's explanation. I stood staring at him, speechless.

"If they are grabbing people to sacrifice, if that's why they took my sister..." his voice choked up. His expression was now one full of anguish. "If they plan on hurting Darla, plan on using her, it's not the right time to perform any ritual. There are six days until the next dark moon. Power can be drawn during a full moon, but even more power comes with a dark moon." He reached out and grabbed me by the shoulders. The expression in his eyes was one of desperation. "Colina, we have time to save her, but I can't do this alone. I wasn't strong enough on my own. You saw what happened. If you become one of us, you may be able to help pull some of the focus from me when we find her, so I can try and work more powerful spells. We may be able to hold our own long enough to free Darla even if you aren't at full strength. With your help, we might have a chance."

I looked around at the wreckage. Furniture had been over-turned and smashed and there were burn marks on the floor and rug. "Do we perform the rituals here?"

"No. They might come back here. We need to leave and go somewhere safe. Somewhere we can rest and get ready for tomorrow night." He reached out and grabbed me, hugging me tight again. "Darla will be okay. We'll get her back. Everything will be okay."

I wanted to believe it, I really did, but in the depths of my soul, I didn't.

# CHAPTER
# NINE

Luke decided it was too dangerous to travel at night. We didn't want to risk running into anyone looking to cause us trouble or harm, so we settled upstairs and wrapped ourselves in blankets, waiting with trepidation for the bad guys to show up. In theory, we would sleep in shifts, ready to flee out the window and down the fire escape at the slightest sign of danger. But in reality, I couldn't sleep; I lay next to him and stared out into the dark, playing the events of the day over and over in my head.

When I saw Luke fall through the window, I was sure I'd never see him again. And then I made my way back to the magic shop, and our eyes locked. We both realized we were lucky to be alive and rushed into each other's arms. He held me tight, and, in that moment, I was so happy to see him. My mind had only been full of thoughts for Luke. For a moment I had forgotten entirely about Darla. Is Darla still alive? I prayed she was, and that Luke was right, that we had time to find her.

Luke had agreed to put me through the rituals. I was going to get what I had come here for, what I wanted most in the world at the moment, but instead of feeling triumphal I was terrified. My mind was spinning with thoughts of those dark rituals. Could I, would I, survive them? And if I did, what would I become? There had never been a healer turned death dealer before. My parents would have thought such a thing an abomination. But here I was, willingly walking down this path. And once I become this mythic being—this abomination—will anyone accept me? The woman in the alley stabbed Luke just because his people communed with the dead. Once I became one of his kind, what would the superstitious populace try to do to me?

That last thought made me shiver violently.

"Can't sleep?" Luke asked. It was his turn on watch.

I rolled over and looked up at him. "I just keep wondering what tomorrow will bring."

"I'm thankful we're both still alive, which is no small miracle." He reached down and his fingers brushed the hair back from my face.

My skin flushed at the contact.

"You need to sleep." Those gray eyes watching me were filled with so much intensity I found myself looking away in embarrassment.

I pulled the blanket tighter around me. "I don't know if I can."

His fingers slid across my forehead and through my hair. "Whatever happens tomorrow, we'll face it together. Close your eyes."

I sighed out loud with pleasure and felt my body begin to relax.

"Just sleep," he whispered as his fingers stroked my hair.

I woke up to light streaming through the windows. We had survived the night. I sat up and looked down at Luke's who laid next to me still asleep. Gone from his expression was the usual anger and intensity. Sleeping Luke had a slight smile on his face which made him look younger and more vulnerable. I found myself suddenly hesitant to wake him. The moment those gray eyes opened the horror of his sister being kidnaped would settle back into them.

The enormity of what we were about to embark on chilled my blood. Off to parts unknown to rest up so I could participate in some horrific dark ritual. I know it was what I wanted most, but the thought of wielding that same dark magic that I had witnessed Luke use to battle those men was terrifying.

I forced myself to stop thinking too much about the rituals and instead to focus on what needed to be done next. I got up quietly and made my way around the broken mess strewn across the floor. The kitchen that had been turned into a disaster zone. I found the coffee pot still on the counter and working, and after some searching, I came across a bag of coffee grounds in the cupboard. I was filling the coffee pot full of water when I hand settled on my shoulder. I jumped and spun around spilling water all over the floor.

Luke gave me an apologetic smile. "Sorry, I didn't mean to scare you."

"I thought I would make some coffee."

"Darla bought a carton of two dozen eggs yesterday." The moment his sister's name was on his lips that smile disappeared. He looked at the fridge now wide open, most of its contents emptied and smashed on the floor. They had destroyed so many things in the apartment and smashed up most of the contents of the magic shop below. If they could do this much violence for no reason, what might they do to poor Darla?

I reached out and touched Luke's arm. "We will find her."

He put his hand over mine and we stood there staring at each other in silence for a long moment until he lifted his hand and gave a long sigh and then motioned towards a small set of doors next to the fridge. "I think the best I can do is some toast. Toast and jelly if the bastards didn't destroy everything in the pantry."

I started the coffee brewing and then busied myself clearing the kitchen table. Once the table was clear I went in search of plates and mugs. I found some plastic plates in a bottom cupboard and two cups that had survived. I sat down at the table and looked over at Luke. He was moving around the kitchen, his stride both graceful and powerful. But as he moved, I realized there was also this undeniable air of 'dangerous and ferocity' he wore about him— reminded me of a panther on the prowl.

Luke had fought to save us last night. The aftermath of that fight was all around us—broken furniture scattered on the floor, a crystal lampshade shattered over the desk, and across the walls and floor odd, shaped dents and scorch marks as if they had been set ablaze. My eyes swung to a corner of the room where lay a fist sized pool of dried blood. Trailing from it was reddish-brown smeared drops that tracked all the way to the front door.

When I was in the SUV the man on the phone had said Luke had taken some of the men out. I knew Luke's power was strong, but was it also deadly? Had Luke killed last night in our defense? If he had been forced to take a life, it was all my fault. Luke and his sister would have been safe had I stayed away. Somehow those men had followed me to the magic shop. It was because of me that Darla was now in danger and the guilt I felt over that was almost more than I could bear.

Luke gave me a questioning look and I did my best to

compose myself. I tried for a reassuring smile, but I'm not sure if I pulled it off. I turned and peered through the windows to the empty streets below

"What time is it?" I asked.

"Close to 6," He answered. "The shops will start opening in a couple hours."

Outside everything had been washed clean by the torrid rain last night. Everything looked so calm and peaceful.

Luke brought over a plate stacked with toast slathered in jam. He slid half the toast on my plate, and we began to eat.

When the coffee was finished brewing, I got up and filled our mugs. "Hope you like your coffee black," I said sitting back down and sliding one of the mugs his way.

Luke's gaze swung to the kitchen floor. A bowl of sugar lay in pieces near the open fridge where milk still dripped from the shelves "All my life Darla and I've been warned to be on our guard when we go out. There have been small acts of violence against our kinds over the years, but never have I heard of anything like this happening."

"It's all my fault," I whispered. "I brought this trouble to your doorstep." If I had never come here, none of this would have happened. Darla would be at home safe, not out there in the hands of those mad men. My eyes began to brim with tears, and embarrassed I turned away.

I heard the chair push back and then suddenly Luke was there kneeling down on the floor in front of me. His fingers came up and he gently lifted my chin until my eyes were level with his. "This is not your fault," Luke said.

I wanted so desperately to believe him. "Do you really think Darla is still..." my voice choked on that last word.

He gave me a ghost of a smile. "My sister is still alive. I would know if something bad had happened to her. Ever since we were kids, we have had this connection. When she fell off her bike and badly sprained her wrist, in that moment my wrist also throbbed in pain. I've always known when she was hurt or injured. I know within the very depths of my soul that Darla is alive." His fingers came up and wiped away a tear. "We should get ready to go. It would be better if we left while the streets are still empty." He stood and offered me his hand.

I took it and in one firm motion, he pulled me to my feet. He was stronger than I imagined, and as he pulled me up and forward, I stumbled into him. Instead of moving quickly back, I found myself resting my head against his chest. Those strong arms wrapped around me. I closed my eyes and I listened to his heartbeat, and I reminded myself to breath. I wasn't alone in this. I had someone to lean on, someone to help me. Together we were stronger. Together we would do whatever it took to save his sister.

For a long while we just stood there in each other's embrace, until finally, reluctantly I moved out of his arms. I stood back and looked up at him. He was staring at me with such intensity, but this time I forced myself not to look away, this time I didn't blush in embarrassment, this time I just stared back at him.

He gave me a slow smile.

I could feel my pulse quicken as I smiled back.

A horn blared somewhere down in the streets below and I jumped and spun around at the noise. When I realized it was just a passing car and not danger headed back our way, I turned back and gave Luke a sheepish grin. I wondered if my life would ever go back to normal, if I would ever be able to just exist without so much anxiety, so much fear.

Luke reached out and put his hand on my shoulder. He gave me a nod then turned and started walking towards his bedroom. He called over his shoulder as he went, gesturing towards Darla's bedroom. "There should be a suitcase somewhere in Darla's closet. Make sure to pack some sweaters. It can get cold at night where we're going."

I walked into Darla's room and started to rummage through her drawers and then her closet, pulling clothes from both and throwing them into a pile on the bed. Eventually I came across a pink suitcase at the bottom of the closet and started shoving clothes into it. I had no idea where we were going, honestly, I was only half conscious of what I was grabbing, what I was doing. My mind was so a buzz with worry and random flash-backs about all that went down last night that at some point I realized my hands were trembling and my legs felt weak. I slowly slide to the floor, my arms wrapped around my legs, and I rocked back and forth.

It was Luke's voice calling out to me that set me back in motion. I forced myself to my feet. Standing in front of the mountain of clothes I grabbed some sweaters and a pair of shoes and stuffed them into the case before zipping it up and heading out of the room. In the living room Luke stood with a green duffel bag slung over his shoulder.

"Ready?" he asked, turning, and heading towards the door, not waiting for my answer. It wasn't until he was all the way across the room, his hand on the doorknob that I finally found my voice.

"What's stopping them from following us?" I finally asked the question that had been consuming me all morning. I thought I'd been so careful when I escaped the funeral and I had been so sure no one was following me as I made my way to the magic shop. How could I have been so wrong?

He looked off towards the windows and then said quietly, "They are not close by."

I moved towards him. "You know that for sure?"

"Yes." He sounded so confident. "Last night as you slept, I

put up a protection spell around the neighborhood. If they were near, I would know."

He said he put a spell up not around the shop, but neighborhood. I realized I was gaping at him, trying to take in just how much power his kind possessed. His kind. Soon to be my kind. I would wield this power if I survived the rituals.

He reached out his hand. "We should get going."

I found myself walking towards him on unsteady legs, but when I reached out and put my hand in his I suddenly felt stronger, more ready to face what was outside that door.

He squeezed my hand and gave me another smile. "There are some things I need to get from the shop for the spells we will be doing."

We made our way down the stairs. If I thought upstairs was a disaster zone, I had forgotten how much energy they had put into destroying the shop and all its contents.

Luke's face looked like a dark storm about to break loose as he wandered around the torn-up store, searching through broken bottles and ripped books, looking for the things he needed. Eventually he seemed satisfied and with the green duffel bag now stretched full, we headed out to the street. I was surprised to see a cab waiting at the curb. He must have called for it when he was packing in his room.

He opened the door and got in and when I slid into the seat next to him, I finally asked, "Where are we going?"

He gave the cab driver instructions then looked my way. "My cousin Pagan's place. She's out of town, but she won't mind under the circumstances, and I know she'll have everything I need for the rituals."

I remembered we'd also taken a cab to the healer's place. "Don't you own a car?"

"One of my cousins borrowed my truck for the trip. They take a lot of tents and camping equipment and I'm the only one with a truck in the family. My uncle took his car, and Darla can't drive yet. Uncle says he's going to get her something old, reliable, and built like a tank for her sixteenth birthday which is next month." At the mention of his sister, his eyes filled with an incredible sadness.

The rest of the cab Luke seemed distracted. He spent most of it looking out the window. When he talked to me, I could see the lines of worry etched on his face. He might be speaking with me, but his thoughts were clearly with his sister. I reached out and took his hand in mine, trying to offer what little comfort I could. I knew there was nothing I could say to make the situation better.

My other hand slid across the material of the seat and my fingers grazed across something sticky. I had a moment of regret about leaving my car behind, but there was a possibility that the people after me knew my car by sight, and I hadn't wanted to make the job of tracking me down any easier. But it hadn't mattered. They had somehow found me anyway.

I turned and watched the passing landscape through the window. We were heading out of town, past the suburbs and into the country. "Your cousin, she doesn't live in town?" I asked, my voice full of surprise.

"No, she refuses to be a city girl. She's an architect. She converts old barns into houses."

It wasn't abnormal for a mage to live in isolation. Many still preferred the privacy of the countryside, a throwback to the hundreds of years that our kind spent hiding from the world. Like most people looking for open space, many of them ended up in the vast, unpopulated territories of the West.

One of the things I learned as a child was the history of our people. I knew mages used to live as an accepted part of the population—they were the shamans and healers. This arrangement continued for millennia, with the mage-born living among their more mundane brothers and sisters. But the whole thing fell apart, at least in the Western world, with the rise of the church. The church saw village wise women as a threat to its power and authority and declared them heretics. Church zealots hunted all mages, killing many and driving the world into its long Dark Age. Because of the need to go "underground," so to speak, the mages formed their own isolated communities, clans, and guilds. They banded together for safety as the world changed around them, happy to be forgotten and live in peace. They worked in this isolation, developing unique skills and powers, and eventually becoming the clans and guilds of today.

I belonged to a clan, a group of people that pledged to protect me and shelter me, but I knew they weren't strong enough to stand against the men who were after me. My clan's magic wasn't much use in combat. All they could do is die by my side. I couldn't take that danger home—I wouldn't let any more people I cared about die. But I couldn't help wondering what the clan would think of me once they found out what I was doing.

We drove and drove some more. I lost track of time. The farther we went, the more rural the countryside became. Fences lined the road, cows grazed in pastures, and farmhouses and barns riddled the landscape. It was beautiful landscape and at another time, I would have enjoyed exploring the countryside, but I was bruised, scared, and tired. I tried to keep my mind focused on the passing landscape, but thoughts of the rituals kept searing across my brain. Would I survive the first ritual? And if I did, what were the other rituals I would have to endure? A part of me wanted to demand more details from Luke, but knowing brought fear, and I didn't want to be afraid. I wanted to have the courage to go through with them.

The cab turned off the main highway and headed down a

dirt road. We passed a creek and a few rolling hills, until the cab finally came to a stop in front of a large, red barn.

I grabbed my stuff, and we got out. Luke paid the driver, and the cab took off.

"Pagan keeps a key in a fake rock. My cousin loses her keys a lot." Luke gave me a ghost of a smile. "She left her car behind. The keys for it have to be inside somewhere."

I nodded my head and followed him up a gray brick path.

Luke retrieved the key to the house, and we walked to the large, white framed door. When he opened it and we walked in, I was speechless. The place was breathtaking. The barn looked like the others we'd passed on the road, but his cousin had converted it from a home for animals to a luxurious living area. It was a big, wide open space with high ceilings.

My eyes wandered around the living room. A sizeable gray carpet filled the area, and the biggest leather L shaped couch I had ever seen dominated the space. Antiques were scattered around. A humongous stone fireplace covered one wall. On the other side of the room, a rustic dining table that looked like it could seat twenty people stood next to an old-fashioned kitchen with a large, red stove.

"This is unbelievable," I said.

Luke looked around the place with pride on his face. "One day I plan to have her convert one for me. When I'm older, settled, and married."

I could picture Luke and his future wife moving into their converted barn. My stomach turned. The thought filled me with unexpected envy.

I had dreams of a future once. But all those dreams died with my family. Now the only path before me was full of darkness.

I was silent too long—Luke was giving me an inquiring look. I tried to force a smile on my face, but I couldn't quite pull it off. "And this older you, is he going to run the magic shop?"

His voice was serious when he answered. "No, that's my uncle's place. He doesn't have any kids, and I know he'd like to leave it to one of us, but it's not the kind of thing I can see myself doing forever. Darla loves the shop. I wouldn't be surprised if she ends up running it one day."

"If you're not running the shop, what'll you do?"

"This older me? I'm not sure." He gave me a smile. "How about the older you? What plans do you have for her?"

The words "be a healer" started to come out of my mouth, but I stopped them. I wasn't sure I could heal again. Was the traveler, right? Had the pain of losing my family shifted my powers? I had no goal now but revenge. And what will I do if I fulfill that one destiny? There would be no going back to the clan once I became a death dealer. No one would welcome me with open arms once I was part of the Phoenix Guild and that was assuming the guild let me in. Would the Phoenix Guild even want me? And even if they wanted me, could they accept me? If they did, what kind of wrath would having me around bring down upon them?

Healers lived by the mantra, 'Do no harm', it was part of the sacred oath, and once you were a healer, you were one for your entire lifetime. No one ever turned their back on the profession. Healers had an easier time living in the non-mage world, working in the medical community where they could use their powers without drawing attention. The clans lived almost in plain sight in larger cities. We were taught only a few defensive magics and were protected mainly by the good will of whatever communities we served. If I could learn to heal again, I could go someplace far away and start my life over.

I could change my name and go underground, but what did I know of living on the fringe of society? I'd always had a stable, loving home. My family wasn't rich, but I'd never gone without food or a roof over my head. I was young and resourceful—I could get a job in a clinic or a hospital. I could make enough to support myself. But that could only happen if I walked away from the dark path I had started down.

I knew for sure none of my kind had ever dared to do something stupid like ask to be trained in the Death Arts. A healer using dark magic would be a threat to the entire clan. And what would my clan's reaction be once they found out what I had done, the lengths I had gone to for my revenge? I would be shunned at the least, and most likely imprisoned.

But maybe I didn't have to worry about any of this at all, maybe I wouldn't make it.

If the first ritual doesn't kill me, the men after me just might.

Luke, still waiting for my response, saw my shiver. "It's cold in here. I'll get a fire going."

All I knew for sure was that right now, at this moment, I was glad to be by Luke's side. I took comfort in the sight of him. Maybe together we could pull it off; save his sister and survive. What else could we do but try?

"Are you hungry?" he asked.

"Starved." Coffee and toast hadn't come close to curbing my appetite.

"I'll work on the fire. Can you see if there's any food in the house?" Luke pointed across the room. "Try the cupboards and see if you can find us anything to eat."

The fridge was empty except for a large container of ketchup and mustard. The cupboards were mostly bare, but I found a half dozen tins of ravioli and jars of green olives in the pantry.

Luke joined me in the kitchen after ten minutes. "I got the fire started. It should start to warm up soon. There's no central heat, and it looks like it'll be a chilly night." He reached around me and opened the nearest drawer, pulling out a can opener. "The plates are in the cabinet next to the stove."

I nuked the ravioli in the microwave while he set out dishes on the long, polished wood dining table. I set down the plate piled high with food in front of him before sitting down, too.

He took the plate and nodded his head in thanks. "Pagan's been out of state doing some work. I don't think she was expecting company. I found the keys to her car on a nail by the phone, so tomorrow morning we can drive to the local market and get some supplies."

I sat down and started eating. We ate in relative silence, accompanied only by the crackle of the fire. When I finished the last bite on my plate, I asked, "Are we doing the ritual here?"

"Not the first one. We have to do it in a place just over the pasture on the other side of the creek."

Pastures and creeks. We were definitely in the boondocks.

"And we do it during the witching hour?" I asked. Outside, in the cold, at night—I was not looking forward to whatever was going to happen.

He didn't meet my gaze. "After midnight. I know you didn't get a lot of sleep last night. Neither did I. I think we should try to get some sleep now. It's going to be a tough night."

I asked the uppermost question on my mind. "The rituals, are they really that bad?"

His expression was grim. "I never wanted you in this situation." Luke reached across the table and grabbed my hand. "They're not easy, but my family's been doing them for centuries."

His hand held mine, his gaze never wavering as he watched me across the table. Whatever happened next, Luke would be by my side. "And lived to talk about it?" My voice trembled as I asked the question.

"Mostly."

Mostly. I don't like the sound of that. "You did it," I whispered.

He let go of my hand, turned his face away, and said in a quiet voice, "I did." He picked up our empty plates and headed toward the kitchen. "We should get some sleep. You're going to need all your strength."

"I'd like to take a hot shower."

He motioned toward the other side of the room. "The bathroom's over there. We never tended to your scrapes, did we? I know Pagan has some bandages around here somewhere. While you're showering, I'll see what I can find to bandage them up."

I TOOK A LONG SHOWER, allowing the hot water to run down my body. And after the shower, I rummaged through the suitcase and found a long black flannel shirt to change into. The shirt once on hung almost to my knees. When I came out of the bathroom, Luke was sitting in the living room on the sofa with a box of bandages, hydrogen peroxide, and cotton balls on the coffee table in front of him.

"Sit down. Let's get something on those deeper cuts," he said.

I sat down next to him and held out my arm. He rolled up my sleeve, and I winced as he dabbed some of the peroxide on the cut on my elbow.

"Does it hurt?"

"It stings."

He nodded his head and gently put a bandage across the gash. "Anywhere else?" he asked.

I pointed to my calf and turned so he had full access to my

leg. He bent down and dabbed a few cuts on my calf and knee, then covered them in bandages.

"Your shirt was torn last night. Is that scrape on your shoulder bad?" he asked.

I know he was just helping me, but there was something in the way his eyes were now roaming across my body that sent a hum through me.

Self-conscious, I slowly unbuttoned my shirt and lowered it off my shoulder.

When his fingers touched my skin, I couldn't help it, I shivered.

"Does that hurt?" he asked, his voice low.

"No, it doesn't hurt." It was just the opposite. It felt so delicious to have his fingers on me. Where those fingertips slide along my skin, I could feel this heat, this almost electric energy.

He moved closer and I could feel his breath on my neck. He was so close now if I turned my head just a bit our lips would brush against each other. That one thought raced through me and without really thinking, just reacting in that moment, I turned and pushed my lips against his.

I was kissing him and for one brief second, he didn't react at all. I realized in a moment of pure panic he was not kissing me back. Mortified over what I'd just done, the way I had pushed my attentions on him when clearly, he was not interested, I started to pull away. But as I did, he began to move, to reach out and suddenly he pulled me back against him and his lips crushed against mine.

He kissed me. His hands came up and tangled in my hair and our kiss deepened. My whole world suddenly became focused on *Luke*. Focused on the feeling of his body against me, the taste of him, that velvet tongue that now slid so deliciously along my lips. We kissed and kissed again. And then he began to fall back against the sofa, and he pulled me with him. My whole body lay against his, as our kisses grew deeper still.

I felt bewitched, exhilarated, felt suddenly on fire in a way that I'd never felt before. He began to lift me, and in one incredibly physical move he rolled me until my body lay beneath his. His body for a moment was entirely against mine and the weight of him crushed all the air from my lungs. He then lifted himself and hovered inches above me as his lips found mine again. We kissed and kissed some more. I honestly don't know how long we lay there together until suddenly his lips broke away from mine and his body moved and I realized I was lying on the sofa all alone. I lay there, my thoughts still fogged by desire and my body still humming with excitement from his touch. My lips still quivering with delight from those kisses, and my heart pounding so hard I could still hear it ringing him my ears.

I turned my head and realized he was standing a few feet away. He was just standing there, his hands balled into fists, watching me. There was a scowl on his face.

I sat up confused. "Did I do something wrong?" I whispered.

"Colina, I can't do this." His expression was now one of anguish. "There is too much at stake —" He turned away and when he turned back his features were more composed. "We need to stay focused on the ritual." He motioned towards the bedroom. "You need to go and get some rest. You can take the bed and I'll stay out here."

I sat stunned, not sure what to say.

When he spoke again his voice was more commanding, "Go get some sleep. I'll get the suitcase from the bathroom and bring in some extra blankets. It can get cold in that bedroom."

"Okay," I finally said and realized I was grasping my fingers tightly together. I forced myself up and without another word I made my way across the room into the bedroom.

I RESISTED the urge to slam the door behind me and instead closed it quietly. Then I stood there just staring at the door. Luke was right, we needed to focus on the ritual, on helping me gain the dark powers. A part of me wondered if he had felt the same wild abandonment when our bodies crushed together, when our lips locked. Had he truly pushed himself away from me out of concern about the ritual or was it just an excuse? I had been the one who had kissed him first, but he had reached for me when I pulled back. He had kissed me, not just once, but again and again. He did have feelings for me, it was not just something I was imagining.

I realized my hand was on the doorknob. I shook my head and let out a loud sigh. I spun around and took in my night's lodgings. Pagan was definitely a romantic. In the room was a four-poster bed with white, sheer material draped across the top and dangling partway down the sides. Against one wall stood a large white dresser with painted flowers on the front. Against another wall sat a smaller matching dresser sporting a large, gilded mirror. A bay window held drapes touching the floor, which were covered in the same flowers as the dresser.

I made myself comfortable on the edge of the bed and sat there staring at the wall for, I'm not sure how long, when there was a knock on the door.

"Come in," I shouted.

The door swung open, and Luke stood in the doorway, his arms full. "I brought you some clean sheets and blankets." He walked quickly towards me. He put the suitcase on the bed and then pushed the bedding into my arms before making a quick retreat.

"Good night," I called to his back.

He lifted his arm in acknowledgment but didn't turn around. I watched him close the door behind him.

Light was streaming in the window. My body ached. I knew I needed sleep, but my mind refused to turn off. The look on Darla's face as the man grabbed her and pinned her to the ground kept popping into my head.

The room was chilly, so I opened the suitcase and pulled out a blue sweater and put it on. I changed the sheets and forced myself to lie down and pulled the large, fluffy white comforter over myself. I closed my eyes, but as I did, more images started to fill my mind.

My father lying dead on the floor.

My mother's lifeless eyes staring up at me.

It didn't take long for me to get out of bed, needing to escape the horrific images. I wrapped my arms around myself for warmth as I made my way back into the living room.

Luke was lying on the couch under a red blanket.

"Are you asleep?" I whispered.

"No." He sat up. "What's wrong?"

"I don't want to sleep alone. I'm still kind of freaked out." I was scared, as much as I hated to admit it.

His eyes widened for a moment, and then he pushed his covers off and got up. He was shirtless in a pair of gray sweatpants.

"I'm sorry I woke you up—"

He interrupted me before I could continue. "It's still too cold in here. Go back into the bedroom. I'll be there in a second. I'm going to put another log on the fire."

I made my way back into bed, and a few minutes later he came in and settled down next to me. I turned toward him, and he opened his arms. I laid my head down on his chest, my fingertips resting on his skin. An unreasonable desire to trail my fingers across his chest and down his stomach filled me. I swallowed hard and resisted the temptation this time.

We needed to only focus on the dark rituals. And if I survived them and gained the dark powers and used those powers to help save his sister . . . What then? What might be possible between the two of us once Darla was safe back home? It was a question I wanted to ask, but honestly, I wasn't sure what to ask. How do you ask a guy who was just passionately kissing you an hour ago, what his intentions are without sounding ridiculous?

Luke's hands started to caress my hair, interrupting my embarrassing train of thought. "Sleep. I'm here. Everything is fine. Go to sleep."

I dutifully closed my eyes, pushing back my questions, and fell asleep listening to the sound of his heartbeat.

CHAPTER

# TEN

When I woke, Luke was coming back into the room, a cup full of something steaming in his hand. His hair was wet and slicked back.

"What time is it?" I asked, holding back a yawn.

"It's almost eleven. We should get ready to go."

I looked out the window and was surprised to see it was dark out. "Eleven at night?"

"You slept for twelve hours."

I'd actually slept soundly for the first time since this whole nightmare had begun. "Did you get any sleep?"

He took a sip from the cup. I noticed he looked tired. "Some," he answered. "Do you want to eat something before we go?"

I shook my head. I was too nervous. The very thought of the ritual made my stomach queasy.

"It's cold out, wear something warm. It'll take us about fifteen minutes to get to the cemetery."

I sat stunned at the word 'Cemetery'. *We're doing the ritual in a cemetery.*

"Are you okay?" he asked.

I forced myself to sit up and swung my legs over the bed. "Yeah, just great."

His eyes narrowed. "Colina, you don't have to do this."

I raised my chin and looked him in the eyes. "We both know I do."

He gave me a brief nod. "Don't take too long getting ready. We need to be out the door soon."

"The ritual begins at midnight?" I asked, trying to keep the fear I was feeling from my voice.

"Yes, but we have to get there and get things set up." He was watching me, his expression one I couldn't read.

I forced a smile onto my face. "I won't be long."

He nodded again and headed out the door, shutting it softly behind him.

Once he left, the tears started sliding down my face. I raised trembling hands to my temples and tried to force myself to calm down. *I want to do this*, I told myself. I'd gone to the magic shop to be trained as a death dealer, but it terrified me that I was actually about to go through with it.

I straightened my shoulders. Doing the ritual would keep me alive and hopefully help Luke save his sister. I took one deep breath and then forced myself to take another. I could do this. I had to be brave and face it head on.

*He's going to kill you.* The words seared across my brain.

*But he'll bring me back.*

*I trusted him to bring me back.*

I forced myself to my feet and started to get ready.

WE WERE in the middle of the cemetery, standing at the edge of a very old, very creepy grave. No one was around but us and the dead. I looked at the tombstone standing beside me.

Etched on its surface were the words MATHEW SMITH, 1805–1850.

It was hard to believe we'd trekked to a cemetery in the middle of nowhere in the deep of night. We'd crossed pastures and even splashed through a stream to get here.

Overhead, the moon cast long shadows over the rows of marble headstones. The cemetery looked like something right out of a horror movie. The gravesites themselves were a combination of patchy dirt and grass, and I could make out shapes above the headstones. A handful of life size angel statues were scattered around, appearing to move with the shadows. And beyond those were a few larger monuments, above ground tombs that were the resting places of the truly wealthy. Inside the wrought iron fence surrounding the cemetery were only a couple of planted trees. It was fall, and although the trees around the countryside had changed color and started to drop their leaves, these trees were bare, their limbs gnarled and twisted. I couldn't fight the feeling that Luke and I were being watched. I turned back to where Luke was working.

A dozen candles now lined both sides of Mathew Smith's grave. On the marble headstone was a box, and at the foot of the grave sat a bottle full of a red liquid that looked like blood.

"You need all this to do a spell?" I asked. The act of healing came from within. It was true that healers often used herbs, salves, and elixirs in combination with their magic, but for the most part healers stayed away from all the trappings that came with spell magic.

Luke started lighting candles. "I do. Spells are about focusing your abilities and calling on the forces of nature."

"Why this graveyard?" I asked.

"Because graveyards are a doorway to the other side. Think of them as a portal to the dead—a place where many spirits are closest to the earthly realms and easier to contact." Luke looked around and made a wide sweeping gesture with his arm. "We've buried the members of our family in this particular graveyard for generations." He pointed down at the grave. "We could do the spell on any grave, but one of the strongest mages in our family line is buried here."

I looked down at the grave and tried to quench the fear rising inside me. "What spell are you doing tonight?"

"It's the first part of the ritual. It's called the passage—the passage into the magics of the death dealers. Your spirit has to commune with the other side. You have to touch the hereafter and see death firsthand in order to wield its power."

I straightened my back and tried to feel brave. "So I do have to die."

He looked up at me and nodded his head. "It's the way my guild has guided students into the Death Arts for centuries."

"You plan on killing me. Then what? You'll bury me and bring me back up like a voodoo zombie?" I couldn't keep the sarcasm out of my voice.

"No. There's no voodoo involved and no zombies." He went back to lighting candles.

I watched him work for a few minutes in silence. He pulled something out of a black duffle bag he'd brought—a glass jar full of black powder. He started sprinkling some on the ground around the gravesite.

"Luke, I trust you," I said quietly.

His expression turned sullen.

I knew about death. I had watched Mama bring people on the brink of it back with her healing. But whether she could bring them back or not was never a certainty. Death had its own rules: when it decided to claim someone, its grip could be stronger than a riptide.

Luke walked forward until he stood in front of me. "I've been by my uncle's side when he's done this. I've assisted him in the ritual, but I've never done it myself. It's not something you're allowed to do until you're older, until you truly master your power."

"You can do it. I have faith in you."

His eyes filled with anger. "And if you're wrong? If you trust me and something goes wrong?"

I shrugged my shoulders. "Then game over. Look, everything in life is a risk—a gamble. I'm here, and I'm throwing the dice." I didn't want to ask the next question. It had been haunting me ever since he'd told me about the ritual, but now, standing here in the cemetery, I had to know. "How are you going to do it?" I whispered.

"Strangulation is easiest." His voice was suddenly void of emotion.

I looked at him in shock. I had assumed he'd give me a potion. I'd drink something, slowly fade out, and then be given an antidote to undo the spell.

"I'm going to put my hands around your neck and squeeze the life out of you. You have to experience the pain, experience your death at the hands of a death dealer. It's the only way the ritual works." Fear—there it was again in his eyes. "You don't have to do this. It's crazy we're doing this."

I took a deep breath and stepped toward him, even though my body screamed at me to run away from all this. "You know we don't have a choice. If you want to save your sister, you need my help. I can't help you as I am. I need power." It was true, I wanted to save his sister, but I also wanted to exact my revenge.

He stood looking at me for a long moment, then turned and walked over to the bag. He pulled out a handful of black feathers. "Raven feathers." He started scattering them about. "I'm about done with the preparations."

"What do you want me to do?" I asked my voice and hands trembling as I said the words.

He pointed toward the ground. "Lie down on the grave."

*This isn't happening. I'm in some bizarre nightmare, and I have to wake myself up.*

He didn't look at me when he spoke this time, "Make sure to lie on your back. I need to see your eyes."

I got down on my knees, then slowly turned over and lay down against the damp grass. I tried not to think about the skeleton lying a few feet beneath me.

Luke was suddenly straddling me. "There's still time to change your mind."

*Yes, yes, get out of here!* the voice in my head screamed.

"Do what you have to," I whispered.

I flinched when his hands circled my neck. They seemed somehow bigger, rougher, and the panic I felt rise from the pit of my stomach was almost more than I could stand.

"Last chance. You don't have to do this," he said. The fear was back in those gray eyes.

The images of my father's broken body flashed through my head. I had no choice; I had to keep going.

"Do it," I said between clenched teeth.

His hands tightened. The pressure on my throat slowly increased and my lungs began bursting with the need to breathe. I looked up into his eyes. The expression on his face was one of blank concentration.

*He's killing me.* And in that moment of sheer terror, I changed my mind. He needed to stop. I couldn't go through with this. My hands came up and clawed against his fingers, but he was too strong. I had to stop him from strangling me. I struggled, I twisted, but he was too big and too heavy. The pressure on my neck increased even more. There was a blinding pain as I felt my throat being crushed. My hands gave up on his, and I reached up to claw out his eyes. He anticipated my move and raised himself up until his face was out of reach.

*You're killing me!* I tried to plead with my eyes. He had to see the expression in them and know that I wanted him to stop. But he didn't.

The pressure increased.

There was a burning in my chest and my eyes clouded with tears—the desire to breathe, to live, was so strong I could feel it pulsating through my whole being. But there was no breath, no air. My lungs, my heart needed oxygen to survive, and without it, I began to die.

# CHAPTER
# ELEVEN

The beating of my heart slowed. My thoughts turned to the terrible burning that was consuming my body. I could feel his hands crushing my neck. My eyes unfocused, my vision went gray, and a sudden darkness beckoned.

Then there was nothing. No pain. No graveyard. No Luke. Just a vast emptiness surrounding me.

Without warning, I wasn't alone. I realized in a moment of horror that I sensed something nearby. Not the living, but something else. Spirits? At first, I couldn't hear or see anything in the darkness, but then a black cloud and a rush of noise surrounded me.

*Is that screaming?*

Someone was shouting—another voice was praying. Slowly, one face formed in front of me and then another, until I was surrounded. But these faces weren't flesh and bone—they were ghostly images, flickering in and out of the darkness. Thin, transparent lines of gray came and went like someone was turning a light switch on and off. More noise, this time someone was yelling in pain. Something held me immobile in this place.

*Where am I? How do I escape?*

The faces and voices began to move closer, and I felt nothing now but fear.

And then a loud, male voice boomed from within the darkness. "You are not of my blood, but my blood brought you here. What is it you're seeking?"

"Seeking?" I asked. No—I didn't ask... I wasn't really there, was I?

"Come, child, there isn't much time. What is it you seek?"

*Revenge.* The word blazed across my mind.

"So be it," the voice said, and the world around me went silent.

No more ghostly images. No more sound. Now just a vast, gray space stood before me. Lighter gray wisps floated in the darkness toward me, like fog on a moonless night, and I was overcome with panic and claustrophobia. The dark mist closed around me and my blood chilled at the thought that any number of monsters could be in it with me. But I seemed to be alone, and I drifted in the darkness for what felt like an eternity, unable to tell up from down, all scale and substance lost in the darkness. I could feel my arms and legs, though they seemed distant and numb, and when I touched my face with my hand, my skin felt cold and stiff.

*Am I caught somewhere in between the real world and the afterlife? Is any of this real?*

I drifted forever, trapped out of time and space, and terror overcame me. I screamed and cried, but no one came to help. I was stuck here and feared I might never escape. Finally, my panic began to subside. I picked a direction and tried to swim through the smoky darkness. The mist or smoke or whatever it was, swirled around me, but it didn't feel like I was moving. I struggled for a while, until I finally gave up.

I screamed in frustration, wishing—no, demanding—to be

somewhere else, and finally the mists began to move. I felt more than saw the fog swirl around my face. In the far distance—or perhaps not far at all, it was hard to tell with no frame of reference, I saw what I thought was a flicker of light.

Gathering my will, I drove myself toward it, and it either slowly moved closer to me, or I moved closer to it.

And then I noticed something else.

A growl, a snarl. Small, red eyes peering at me from the darkness. The eyes blinked, and I felt stunned. What was this new horror? More ghosts? No, something different—something worse. I knew it deep within my very core.

I'd been frightened when confronted by the ghostly images and strange cries, but now something inside me, something more primitive, was screaming at me I was in danger. Whatever was out there was far worse than anything I'd experienced so far. It was evil. It was dark and sinister.

*It wanted me.*

The eyes were moving closer. The snarling was louder now. I felt a terror rise within me that I had never felt before. There was nowhere to go, nowhere to hide. The thing in the darkness would consume me.

And then something else drowned out the frightening noises. I felt the panic leave and a calmness overcame me. Familiar voices were coming from the light far away in the darkness.

My family was calling to me to join them.

They were there, in that light, waiting for me. The pain of their absence was no more. Life and its struggles were past me. There was nothing now but my family and the light. I willed myself closer, expecting any minute to see the face of my mother, of my father, but instead it was my grandmother who welcomed me. She stood as if bathed in sunlight. She was wearing her favorite blue dress, the one that matched the color of her eyes. Her hair was wrapped in a tight bun.

A look of bewilderment crossed her face. "Child, what are you doing here?" She reached out her hands and then pulled them away. "No, it's not your time, you shouldn't be here. You have to go back."

As soon as she said, "go back," I heard a familiar voice shouting at me from a great distance. The sound was muffled; I could barely make out the words.

It was Luke.

"Do you see the light? Do you hear the voices?" he cried.

I should have felt relieved to hear his voice, but instead I felt panicked.

*Yes, I hear you,* I wanted to respond. *Go away. Let me go to the light. Leave me to my peace.*

And then, suddenly, there was only pain and a rush of noise and sensation. The burning in my chest, the pounding of my heart—my mouth opened, and oxygen rushed into my lungs.

I struggled against the pain. I fought to go back to the light. I wouldn't leave my family. I refused to let them go without me again. My body jolted as something rammed into me. More pain. More burning. A jolt again and—

I was back in my body. In the world.

Luke's mouth was covering mine. Blowing air into me, I realized. And his hands were on my chest. *CPR. He's doing CPR.* My brain fed me words as I began to think through the fog.

His mouth lifted from mine. He looked terrified. More scared than I had ever seen him. He begged, "Stay with me, Colina!"

I tried to talk, but I couldn't. I coughed savagely. My throat was raw and on fire.

He forced me up into his arms. "Drink this. It will take the pain away."

Liquid ran down my throat. I choked and coughed, but the pain slowly ebbed away, and I could breathe. I could swallow. My chest felt bruised, and my throat felt sore, but I was alive.

Luke was still hovering over me. His face was close to mine. I needed distance from him, and with all my strength I pushed myself away.

He backed up. "Are you alright?" he asked.

I couldn't meet his eyes. This guy killed me. What was I supposed to say?

"No." My words sounded guttural.

He stretched out his hand to help me stand. The desire to push it away was so strong, but I reminded myself that I asked him to do it, to kill me and make me a death dealer. I took his hand, and he pulled me up into his arms.

The strong hands now resting on my back were the same brutal hands that had taken my life. It was more than I could handle. I struggled against his embrace.

Luke tightened his hold. His voice was soothing, "It's okay. You're safe. Everything is fine." His hands began to move up and down my back in a gentle motion.

A cry broke from my lips, and I leaned my forehead against his shoulder. His head came down and rested against mine. "It's okay."

It wasn't, though, and never would be again. Tears ran down my face. I couldn't stop the emotions I'd been holding in so tightly from breaking free.

I was all alone.

My mother, father, and brother had not been in the light with my grandmother, which meant they were in between. Would I ever see them again?

My sobs were louder and harder now.

Luke began to rock slowly back and forth. I felt like a tree in the breeze. The motion was soothing.

"You're safe," he whispered the words against my cheek.

My sobs slowed and eventually stopped. "You can let go."

He pushed back and looked down into my face, his hand raising my chin and forcing me to look into those dark eyes. Concern and something else I couldn't quite make out filled them.

"You killed me." My voice was unsteady.

He held me close again. "I brought you back."

"Please tell me we only have to do that once."

He whispered against my ear, "I swear I won't kill you again. Cross my heart and hope to die."

It was a bad joke.

"Come on. We're done for tonight." Luke started to move away. "We need to get out of this cemetery quickly, before any spirits—"

We both froze as the ground gently shook beneath our feet. I looked at Luke. "Did you feel that?" I whispered.

Luke looked down at the grave. "I did."

There it was again, a loud thumping noise. The ground beneath our feet moved again, this time harder.

We both stood there, watching the ground, waiting for I wasn't sure what. The seconds ticked on, and nothing else happened.

Luke looked over at me and said, "Whatever that was, it was not part of the ritual." He turned and started to walk away, and I slowly followed.

I couldn't help it, every couple of steps, I looked back over my shoulder, expecting to see something following us.

THERE WASN'T a lot of conversation as we walked back from the cemetery. I was still trying to process everything that had happened to me. My mind and body were very aware, not in a pleasant way, that Luke was only a few inches from me. When he held me in his arms before, my body hummed everywhere he touched me. Now all I could feel when he was near was uncontrollable fear.

The logical part of my mind knew it was crazy to fear him. Luke had never shown any violent tendencies toward me, not even when I first approached him about learning the Death Arts. He'd acted intimidating, but he never laid a hand on me. He'd shown me only compassion since I'd told him about my family. He'd only ever tried to help and comfort me since we had been thrown together. And yet, another part of me couldn't get the feeling of his hands around my throat out of my mind. I forced the image away.

*I asked him to do it, to teach me the Death Arts,* I reminded myself. The death dealers were feared for a reason, their rituals were barbaric, their magic powerful. No one should mess with the spirits of the dead. My shaking hand went up to touch the tender bruises at the base of my neck.

We crossed the stream. I could see the lights from Pagan's house ahead of us.

"Are you alright?" Out of nowhere, Luke stopped and turned toward me.

"I wish you'd stop asking me that." My voice was still coming out in a rasp.

"The ritual can be terrifying."

"Was it for you?" I asked.

"It was something I'll never forget. A moment like that never leaves you."

"And the person that did it to you, do you still see them?"

He nodded his head. "Yes. He is my mentor."

"How can you forgive him for what he did?" I demanded without thinking.

I hurt him with that question, I could tell. His eyes filled with a look of remorse when he answered. "By facing what happened and realizing it wasn't personal. He wasn't trying to hurt me. It was a necessary evil. I asked to be initiated into the Death Arts, and I had to accept all that came along with it." He looked up at the stars. "There's no good or evil to magic. Each person brings their own intentions, wishes, and dreams to it. Use it for the wrong purposes and it can become dangerous. It can get out of control; it can consume you in a way that you can't stop."

"And do you know this from personal experience?"

He looked at me again. "No. I never headed down that path. I always wanted to use my gifts to help people."

"Use death magic to help people?" It was a crazy notion.

He nodded his head. "Yes, it can be used that way." He abruptly changed the subject. "Now that you've done the first ritual, you'll be able to contact the dead, but killing you and bringing you back was only part of the ritual to claim your power over death. Next, you have to commune with the dead; the second ritual is possession."

"What do you mean...What will I have to—" I swallowed, unable to get the words out.

"Don't think of it now. We need to go back, and you need to rest. To get your strength back," he said.

I took a deep breath and then another. *Possession.* The word blazed through my mind.

His expression turned grim. "This next ritual is a hard one. It won't be pleasant or easy."

I couldn't keep the horror I was feeling from showing on my face. *And dying was what? The easy part?*

# TWELVE

The clock on the nightstand blinked 3:00 a.m. Two hours had passed since we made it back to Pagan's house. Conversation had been minimal. I told Luke I was tired. It wasn't true—honestly, I didn't know what to say to him, and I was having a hard time meeting his gaze.

My body trembled every time he walked close by—and still not in the good way it had before. A fear was now rooted deep within me. Fear of a guy who never wanted to hurt me.

I kept telling myself that it was only part of the ritual. Neither one of us had a choice—we had to go through with it. I hoped if I repeated that fact enough times in my head, I would stop being afraid of him.

Luke had offered to sleep next to me again. I'd declined in a way that was not so gracious and obviously hurt his feelings. I could see the pain I was inflicting by shying away from him, but I couldn't seem to stop myself. Coming so close to death and seeing the other side had unnerved me in a way I couldn't really put into words.

I had hoped that by shutting myself away in Pagan's bedroom, I would be able to close my eyes and convince myself it had all been an unpleasant nightmare. But I lay there in the dark, tossing and turning, unable to fall asleep. Every time I was on the verge of sleep, I felt the sensation of his hands grasping my neck, tightening slowly and painfully. Each time it happened I bolted upright in bed, my heart pounding and tears streaming down my face.

Finally, I decided to give up on sleep. I wrapped a blanket around my shoulders and headed toward the kitchen. It would be daylight in a few hours. We would go to the market and get supplies and then spend the day resting before the next ritual. The next ritual. At the thought, my trembling hands tightened around the blanket.

Light from the fire cast shadows around the room. I could just make out the living room furniture and sidestepped my way around the couch and into the kitchen. I opened the nearest cupboard and pulled out a tall plastic glass, then moved to the sink and filled it. I was raising it to my mouth when a hand suddenly reached out of the darkness and grabbed my shoulder.

The glass dropped and bounced against the floor as I spun around, panicked. The overhead light flicked on. It was Luke standing beside me. At the sight of him, I instinctively took a step back.

"Sorry, did I wake you?" I asked, my breath coming out in a rush.

Luke moved toward me. "Another nightmare?"

I took another step away from him. "No. I couldn't sleep."

One more step in my direction and he had me cornered against the counter. My heart pounded in my chest.

His hand reached out, and he gently brushed a tear from my cheek. "I'm sorry I hurt you."

I tried not to shy away from him this time. I took a deep breath and met his gaze. "It's okay. I'm fine."

He squeezed my arm. "You're not fine."

"I am. I wish you'd stop fussing over me."

"You know I would never hurt you on purpose." His voice was low, and concern filled his eyes.

"I know you wouldn't," I answered, trying to keep the fear from my voice.

"But you're afraid of me?" Anger now filled those dark eyes.

"I don't want to be," I whispered.

He turned and started to walk away, but then spun on his heels and reached for me. He pulled me hard against him. His lips crushed down on mine.

For one moment the fear inside, me was replaced with something more powerful. A need, a desire filled me, and as he kissed me again, I found my lips answering his. I hadn't meant to kiss him back, but once I started, I couldn't stop. My arms came up and encircled his neck. The kiss deepened. His tongue was like velvet against mine. It felt so good to be in his arms. His hands came to rest at my back, and he pulled me closer.

We kissed again and again. His mouth broke away from mine, and his lips trailed down my neck. His right hand came up and glided down my throat, gently following his lips. Strong fingers brushed against the raw bruises on the surface of my skin.

*He killed me. He strangled me!* the words screamed across my brain.

Luke was unaware of the panic that began to fill me. He brought his lips back onto mine and kissed me again, but instead of kissing him back, I pushed hard against him. He stopped and took a step back, but he was still too close. I reached out and shoved his body back farther.

"Don't touch me," I said, my breath coming out in a harsh gasp.

Luke's eyes filled with confusion and then with realization. I expected him to get angry, but instead he looked helpless. We faced each other for several long minutes. Then he gave me a ghost of a smile, shrugging his shoulders before turning and walking away.

I was left alone in the kitchen. I suddenly felt extremely cold, but my body still burned everywhere that his skin and lips had touched mine.

I made my way back into the bedroom, tears streaming down my face. Tumbling back into bed, I wrapped the comforter tightly around my body and lay there sobbing, my body shaking as both fear and anger raged inside me. When I thought I couldn't shed another tear, my body and mind shut down. Finally, I was able to drift off to sleep.

But I was restless. I tossed and turned. Nightmares and horrific images of my family and Darla suffering kept jarring me awake.

A pounding at my door forced me upright. Light streamed through the windows. The clock on the bedside table now showed 1:00 p.m. I had slept ten hours, but I didn't feel refreshed. I felt physically and mentally exhausted.

The door slowly opened to reveal Luke in the doorway, a plate in his hand piled high with pancakes and bacon.

"Hi," he said, stepping into the room, his expression guarded.

"Hi," I answered back.

"You can sleep more if you like. I just wanted to check on you." He lifted the plate. "I thought you might be hungry since you didn't eat last night."

"I am."

Instead of handing me the plate, Luke walked over and put it on the dresser. He returned to the open door and stopped just inside the doorway. "I went to the market earlier. I didn't want to wake you. Did you sleep well?"

"Not really, but I'm okay."

He nodded but didn't move or say anything else.

I felt self-conscious as I got out of bed and got the food and then settled back on the edge of the bed.

He still stood there looking at me in silence.

I took a bite of bacon and mouth still full mumbled, "It's good, thanks."

I could tell by his expression there was something he wanted to tell me, but he just stood, silent, watching me. What is he waiting for me to do? Probably scream at him to get out and close the door behind him.

*He didn't want to hurt me,* I reminded myself yet again.

I forced a smile onto my face. "So, what's the plan for the day?"

"When I was at the market, there was talk..." He hesitated.

"Talk about what?"

"A girl was drowned a few days ago in a lake not far from here. We could go check it out."

I stared at him in shock.

"It's not Darla," he whispered.

"If Darla is alive and we are on a mission to save your sister, shouldn't our focus be on the rituals?" At the last word, my hand unconsciously reached up to touch the dark bruises on my neck.

Luke's eyes followed the movement. At the sight of the bruises, he flinched and looked away. "Yes, but the other night when those men attacked us, there were spirits in the room."

I nodded my head. "The ones you called, the banshees? I saw them."

He took a step forward. "No, not the spirits doing my bidding. There were others—spirits full of unrest called out to me. They were tied to the attackers. They were calling for vengeance. They whispered of murder, of being bound and then drowned."

"Bound and then drowned? You mean like the people the Redeemers have killed?" I was truly shocked by what he was saying. If he had felt these other spirits and they had told him things about the men that attacked us, why hadn't he mentioned it? Why was he just telling me all this now? "You think those men are Redeemers? You think they killed my family? Killed all those innocent people?" But they couldn't be Redeemers, it didn't make sense. "The men that attacked us were mage-born. No way could they be involved with the Redeemers." He knew as well as I did that the Redeemers despised anything to do with magic, which meant they hated all mage-born with a deep passion.

Luke's expression turned grim as he answered. "I don't know what's going on, but we can't do the next ritual until the witching hour, and the lake is only a short drive from here."

"You want to go investigate? And what, hope to see the spirit of the dead girl?" I asked, afraid to hear his answer.

He nodded. "If she was murdered and is wandering the ether sea in a state of unrest, there's a chance she'll come to me."

"And if she does?" The idea of calling on spirits still made my skin crawl.

"Maybe we can get some answers."

I didn't want to go, but what was my other option? Sit around all day feeling scared and freaked out as I waited for the clock to tick away until midnight? There was another nightmare ritual heading my way and the last thing I wanted to do was sit around and dwell on it.

I raised a piece of bacon and tried to give him a smile. "I'll finish eating and get ready."

But the moment Luke walked out and closed the door, my

appetite vanished. I put down the plate, got up, and started pacing the room.

Now that I had seen the other side, did that mean I could communicate with the dead? I tried to imagine driving to the lake and seeing the dead girl's ghost pop up. I shuddered at the thought. Dealing with spirits was no big deal to Luke, but the only spirits I had ever seen were the banshees he had summoned. Luke said the next trial was "possession." It made sense; the whole point of me dying and coming back was so that I could communicate with spirits. But I didn't know if I was ready to face the spirit world.

I stopped pacing and looked out the window, closing my eyes and taking a deep breath. What if my family came back to me and they had faces like Luke's banshees? I tried to shake the image of my mother's eyes filled with suffering and pain.

I clenched my fists and forced myself to think of the men who killed her. They needed to pay for destroying my world and killing my family. Revenge. It was what I wanted most in the world, and if it was going to happen, I needed to stay strong. I opened my eyes and straightened my shoulders.

I had died and come back—I could talk to spirits. I could do this.

*I can do this.*

I turned and headed toward the closet. I needed to get dressed and prepare myself for what came next. As I started to pull out clothes to wear, I whispered to the empty room, "Undead, unsettled...ready or not, here I come."

# THIRTEEN

The lake was bigger than I'd imagined. I could see wood cabins hidden amongst the trees around the lake. The lake itself was crystal blue. Small waves floating across the surface sparkled in the sunlight.

It was a beautiful fall day. The trees around us were all shades of red and orange. They'd started shedding their leaves, and I shuffled my feet through the colorful foliage on the ground as I followed Luke toward the water.

"The spirit is here. Can you feel it?" Luke asked. He was standing a few feet from the water's edge.

There was something out there—I could definitely feel it. The hair on my arms stood up, and a chill ran down my neck. "Yes," I answered, taking an unconscious step closer to him.

He turned and grabbed my arm. "Try not to concentrate on her."

I resisted the urge to pull out of his grasp and instead demanded, "I thought you wanted me to commune with the dead." Wasn't I supposed to talk to spirits? Hadn't that been the whole reason I went through that first horrendous ritual of his?

"You will, but not like this. Not yet. You aren't ready." He started to edge closer to me but seemed to change his mind and instead let go of my arm. "You don't know how to handle spirits yet. Until you're ready, it's too dangerous. A spirit can take you over." He took a step closer to the water. "Try to fill your mind with other things."

Like what? At the thought I felt a sudden chill run down my arm and a strong breeze whistle past my cheek.

Luke spun around. "Colina, listen to me. You have to focus on something else!"

At his words, I could feel pieces of my hair lifting in the breeze. But not all of my hair—only a piece here and there. I looked over at the nearest tree, which stood only a few feet away. It wasn't swaying in the wind—its leaves and limbs were still. Whatever was happening to me wasn't natural. It was a spirit.

"A childhood song," Luke said. "Think of a song you sang as a kid."

I closed my eyes and tried to remember the words to a song my mother used to sing when I was young. I tried to focus on the tune and ignore the breeze now blowing across my arm.

Luke suddenly looked up into the sky. "I hear you. Come closer. I can help you."

I hummed to myself as I watched him. His gaze became fixed to his left, and his head tilted as though he was listening intently to something. Or someone.

I heard him mutter, "What's your name?"

And for a moment I could have sworn I heard another voice on the wind. A girl's voice, just off in the distance.

But just as I tried to focus in on it, Luke turned to me and frowned. "The song. Keep filling your mind with the song."

I nodded and took a few steps away from him. I turned my back and studied the countryside. I loved how the trees changed color—deep red, orange, and yellow. Fall used to be my favorite time of year.

When things were different. When my family was still alive.

I turned my thoughts from my family and forced the words of the song back into my head. My mind slowly began to wander, this time my thoughts turning to Luke. My emotions were in turmoil. A part of me was attracted to him, even as another part of me trembled in fear every time he came close. I hadn't been afraid of him before the ritual.

No, that's not true, I admitted to myself. I'd been scared of who he was from the first moment I walked into the magic shop. Death dealer. Banshee wielder. A mage who performed the dark magics.

Even as I watched him now, I could feel my pulse quicken, but not with fear—it was something else. I wanted to reach up and brush the hair from his eyes. Wipe the frown lines off his forehead. My fingertips reached up to my lips at the memory of his kisses. I abruptly turned around, so he wasn't in my view anymore. This was crazy. I felt two opposite emotions toward him at the same time—desire and fear.

A hand reached out and grabbed my shoulder. Startled, I spun around.

"Sorry. I said your name a few times, but you seemed lost in your thoughts," Luke explained.

"The spirit?" I asked.

His expression turned grim. "She came to me. She was murdered by a group of men. Men who possessed magic."

I gasped in shock. "But the way she was killed—that's how the Redeemers have been killing. Drowning. None of this makes sense. They can't be Redeemers. How could they be? Redeemers hate anyone with magic. They would never allow a mage into their cult, but if it's not them, who is it?"

"Someone trying to cover up the murders by making it look

like the Redeemers did it."

"If it was truly men of magic who killed her, does that mean —" I took a deep breath, my voice shaking. "Was she mage-born? Was she a sacrifice used to power a spell? A sacrifice like my father?"

"She was a mage, but she wasn't killed on a full moon or a dark moon," Luke answered.

I gasped again and grabbed his arm. "That means Darla isn't being kept for a spell. That means they could hurt her at any time. That means she could already be dead."

Luke's eyes darkened. "Darla is still alive. I would know if she..." His words faltered off.

My fingers dug into his skin. "The spirit, can she help us find Darla?"

Luke's eyes suddenly had an odd, faraway look. "The girl, her name was Sarah. They wanted something from her, something she couldn't, or wouldn't, give them. And when she refused them, they killed her."

"What did they want?" I whispered.

His attention focused back on me. "I don't know. Spirits don't always talk in straight lines. When they're murdered, the very essence of them is forced suddenly from their bodies and there's a lot of confusion."

As I listened to him, the image of my brother, James, popped into my mind. No knife or bullet had touched James's body. Instead, it had been something far worse. Something I hadn't been able to tell Luke about. Not yet.

Luke continued. "Communicating with spirits can be some-what cryptic. The things they tell you, they often talk around things or in a way that's hard to immediately understand." Luke looked around as if trying to find the right words. "Think of it as pieces of a puzzle you have to put together in order to see the whole picture."

"This girl, Sarah, she gave you some pieces to the puzzle?"

He nodded. "Not a lot, but she talked about the ones that killed her. About the place where they kept her. She stayed there —was held there—for days before they killed her. I think it might be where they're holding Darla."

"Where is it?" I demanded.

His eyes filled with sadness. "That's the problem. I don't know. She didn't communicate enough about the place. She said it was big. It was dark when they took her there. She seemed more focused on the men. It just happened, her death. Sarah doesn't fully realize that she's dead. Her spirit is a jumble of emotions and confusion."

"And will that change?" I asked, worried the answer would be no.

He took a deep breath and looked up into the sky. "It does for some, as time passes. They realize they've passed. But Sarah's spirit won't find peace until the men who killed her are brought to justice."

"Sarah can't help us find your sister." And where does that leave us?

Luke's eyes met mine. "It doesn't look like it. Our best bet is still your family. Once we do the second ritual, you'll be able to communicate with them. That is, if they come to you."

I shuddered at the thought. "But, Sarah, are you sure she can't help us? If she's confused, can't you help her? Can't you just tell her to go to the light or something?"

"No. Some spirits can cross over on their own, but Sarah's spirit is looking for justice. I could make her come forward again, but I'm not sure how useful it will be. Until her soul finds justice, she's bound to the ether sea," he answered.

"But you can bring spirits forth? Like the banshees?"

He nodded. "Yes, I can make spirits do my bidding."

A shiver went through me as I thought of my family. "You

force them? Force them to do your bidding?" My voice trembled.

He turned away from me. "It's hard for you to understand now. It will make more sense to you later."

Horrified, I reached out and grabbed his arm and pulled him back around. "You're forcing these poor souls into doing your bidding!"

"Colina, the souls are restless, they can't go to the light. They're stranded in the places between and nothing I could do would set them free."

"So, you use them?" I said, my voice full of anger.

"Yes," he answered quietly.

"And force them to do whatever you ask? To hurt people?" I demanded.

"To protect myself. To protect my family."

That part I could understand, using whatever tools you have to protect the ones you love, but another part of me was outraged. "And when I become a death dealer, you'll expect me to bind spirits? To force them to do what I want?"

He looked away and said quietly, "You'll do it."

"And if I won't?" I demanded.

He looked back at me. "There's no choice. It will be something you have to do as a death dealer." Luke's voice grew softer. "You have to understand, often they can't move on. It's like an empty hole they have within them that someone else has to fill in order for them seek the light. Getting vengeance for their murder, for example, or finishing something that was left undone. For those that can't move into the light, at least this way they can be of some use."

I thought of my family's souls. Of their souls forever chained to a death dealer. Their anguished faces full of pain. Forced into our world, becoming a pawn in some mage's twisted game. I felt unexpectedly cold. If I didn't get vengeance for my family, they may never find peace.

CHAPTER

# FOURTEEN

When we got back to Pagan's house, we once again went our separate ways. Sleep was out of the question, so I spent the rest of the afternoon holed up in Pagan's bedroom, pacing the floor, my thoughts full of terrifying images of banshees and the undead. I now regretted every scary movie I had ever watched.

I wasn't sure what Luke was up to, but at some point, he pounded on the bedroom door, and when I answered, he shoved a plate and a mug into my hands. The plate held a ham and cheese sandwich and a large portion of potato salad, and the mug was full of hot chocolate. I wasn't hungry but knew I needed to eat. It would be foolish of me to face whatever challenges the night would bring on an empty stomach. I choked down the food and barely noticed the taste as I finished off the hot chocolate.

As the afternoon went on, the room became chilly, cut off from the main source of heat. I went through Pagan's closet and borrowed a heavy gray sweater. And then I began to pace again.

I walked, lost in my thoughts as shadows slid across the wood floor. Soon the room became so dark I had to switch on a light. I looked over at the clock and realized in a moment of panic that it was almost eleven o'clock at night.

I would be doing another terrifying ritual soon.

I made my way to the bathroom and splashed cold water on my face. I stared in the mirror; I could see the edges of dark bruises peeking above the sweater's high neckline. I pulled back the collar and studied my neck. Most of the soreness was fading, but dark purple and red marks still lingered at the base of my throat. I looked closer and realized they were in the shape of fingers. Luke's fingers. Marks from where his hands had encircled my neck and squeezed.

I closed my eyes and tried to quash the panic rising from the pit of my stomach. In the first ritual, he killed me. Strangled me. And now we were about to embark on the second ritual. *What horrors would this trial bring?* My hand moved across the surface of my neck. I flinched in pain.

Possession. Communicating with the spirits. Darla had said each ritual was worse than the last. Each one was a terror that caused her brother nightmares for months.

*How bad is it going to get?*

The old traveler had warned me. She'd told me that the protection pouch would help me. Where was it? Had I brought it with me, or did I leave it back at the magic shop? I scrambled to the closet and pulled out Darla's suitcase. I rummaged through the case until my fingers brushed across velvet material. There it was, at the bottom of the suitcase. I pulled it out. I untied the leather wrapped several times around the top of the pouch and looped it around my neck, tying the ends together so the pouch hung down against my chest. It would protect me. I suddenly felt more at ease.

I physically jumped when the door suddenly burst open. Luke stood in the doorway, a grim expression on his face. He held up a white dress. "It's time. You need to put this on."

I stood, arching an eyebrow at the garment in his hand. "You want me to wear that?"

"Yes, you need to wear this for the ritual." His eyes went to my neck. He pointed at the pouch. "You can't wear that."

My hands wrapped protectively around it. "Why not? The traveler gave it to me. She said it would keep me safe."

"It's blessed in a way that protects you, yes. You can still hear the spirits and communicate with them, but it gives you a layer of defense against them."

"Defense against the spirits sounds like a good idea."

"To truly communicate with the dead, you need to be wide open. You have to be vulnerable. The whole point of this next ritual is to blow all those doors that are normally closed in your mind wide open. Doors that most people want to stay closed."

I nodded, and with trembling hands, untied the pouch and let it drop to the bed.

Luke looked at me, his expression full of regret. "I'm sorry. You know this isn't easy for either one of us. I understand if you've changed your mind."

I couldn't back out now that I was aware of the spirits but unable to control them. Spending the rest of my life at their mercy was not an option.

I held out my hand. "Let's get this over with."

He handed me the dress. "I'll be in the living room. Everything is just about ready."

"I won't take long. I'll be out soon. And Luke," I straightened my shoulders and met his gaze square on, "I'm ready, I truly am. I'm ready for whatever comes next."

He jerked his chin down in semblance of a nod and left.

I stood, staring at the closed door. *I am ready.*

But was I really?

# CHAPTER
# FIFTEEN

I 'd changed my clothes and now wore the white shift dress. The material was thin and even though a fire blazed in the hearth, I still felt cold.

Luke had rearranged the living room and pushed all the furniture to the sides of the room. A wooden chair surrounded by burning black candles stood in the center. On one side of the circle of candles was a pile of thick rope.

"I don't quite understand what's going to happen," I whispered.

"We are calling on the dead."

I couldn't keep the discomfort I felt from showing on my face. "And my outfit?"

"Part of the ritual. It's tradition. Goes back hundreds of years. Something along the lines of a virginal journey into the underworld."

Like a bride. It sounded twisted. You'd think a guild of people who wear mostly black would be the last group to sport white, the color of purity. But what I was doing was far, far from anything pure—far from anything that came from the light.

Luke stood in front of me. "I know traditions sometimes

don't make sense, but the elders have done it this way for centuries. Look, if you're uncomfortable, go back and change into something else."

He'd taken my silence for disapproval, but I was willing to follow his direction. "No, I don't want to buck the system. If this is how it's done, this is how we'll do it." Honestly, the outfit was the least of my worries—what concerned me most was the rope he bent down and picked up. "You aren't planning on hanging me, right?"

He ignored my question and started to walk around the chair. "Now, after the cemetery ritual, you're wide open for the dead. Think of yourself as an empty vessel. Like water pours into a cup, a spirit will pour into you." He continued. "That's why we aren't doing this ritual at the cemetery—there are too many souls there waiting to be set free, clamoring for the use of your body. It could overpower you forever. There are maybe one or two spirits roaming close by this location."

At the words *a spirit will pour into you*, I felt my blood run cold. "And what happens to me?"

"You're still in there. Your spirit and the dead will share the same space. One of the things you'll learn, with training, is how to stay in control. To make sure the spirit doesn't overpower you."

I did not like the sound of this. "If that's something I'll learn, that means this time the spirit will overpower me?"

He nodded. "Yes."

"And the rope?"

"The rope is to keep you safe. I have to tie you to the chair, restrain you. As you train and learn you'll be able to decide which spirit you will allow to possess you. They're always around, forever floating on the ether sea. When you call them to you, you don't know who'll show up, it could be something with good intentions or something evil. As you get more practice, you'll be able to figure out who's around you, and you'll be able to choose whom to let in."

"Since I can't choose, something might come and possess me that's evil?" I said my eyes going to the rope again.

He studied me before answering. "It's possible." Luke tried to look reassuring. "By tying you to the chair, I'm keeping us both safe."

"How much control will this spirit have over me?" I asked, afraid to hear the answer.

"At first it will be able to overpower you and push the very essence of your being back. It will be able to control your mind and your limbs. It will speak through your lips. It will move using your body."

"Terrific," I muffled. Being tied up was starting to sound like a good idea. "How will I make the spirit go away?"

"You won't be strong enough yet to do it all on your own. That's why I'm here to guide you through the ritual. I'll be able to help you banish the spirit."

"And if you can't?" I asked.

He gave me a reassuring smile. "Don't worry. I can."

I was starting to understand why so few people went into the Death Arts. You had to be more than a little bit insane to agree to be killed and then possessed.

I looked over at Luke and wondered why he'd chosen this life. "You never had the urge to turn your back on the family tradition and become a baker? Or a mechanic?"

A ghost of a smile flashed across his face. "Never."

"How did your first possession go?" I asked. I realized I was bidding for more time before I had to start the ritual. But honestly, I was interested in what happened to him when he went through the same thing.

His expression became more intense. "It was like swimming

in the sea against the current. It's not painful, if that's what you're worried about."

My fingers drifted again to the bruises on my neck.

He noticed my reaction. "Those bruises should be gone in a day or two. I promise, you can count on me. I'll keep you safe."

I sat in the chair, and he tied my hands behind my back with a length of rope. The rough threads cut into my flesh. He pulled gently on the knot. "It needs to be tight enough to hold whatever may come through, but if it's too tight, let me know."

Next, he tied each of my legs to a chair leg. And last he attached a length around my waist. He tugged on all the ropes again. Satisfied, he moved back in front of me. "How are you doing?"

I shook my hair out of my eyes with a toss of my head. "Go ahead. Do it. Let's get this over with."

He walked over, opened the drapes, and then slid open the window. Next, he flicked off the lights. The black candles glowed in the dark. He took out a piece of red chalk from his pocket, leaned over, and began to draw a symbol on the floor around me. It was a pentagram surrounded by a triangle. At each point he drew words I didn't recognize.

He looked up and saw me watching him. "Latin. I'm not sure what'll be coming through. It's getting closer to a dark moon and that sometimes makes the spirits stronger. I want to be prepared for whatever comes."

"You're drawing a protection circle?"

"Not just for protection. It also amps up my abilities. Focuses them, allows me to be at my strongest." He went back to drawing. He finished the circle and then slowly etched out a phoenix to one side of it. "Ready?" he asked.

No. I would never be ready to be possessed by spirits. But we were here, and I was committed. Or should be committed, I thought wryly. This was crazy. I took a deep breath. "Let's do it." *Goddess protect me.* I said the prayer under my breath.

He picked up a leather-bound book, flipped it open, and looked at me. "Here we go." He started to read from the book. Latin flew from his mouth.

I recognized some of the words. I'd been given some lessons in Latin but had forgotten most of them, except the ones dealing with plants and flowers. And yet, words seemed to whisper in the corner of my memory.

"Animus," Luke said the word for spirit. He raised his arms and shouted out, "Ex vita abire!" That was something about death. As the last word left his lips, a light began to form by the window.

At first, I thought it was a trick of the eye—perhaps the shadows from the candles flickering against the ceiling and the floor. But these shadows were moving independently. They were coming at me. I didn't bother to stifle my horrified scream as the shadows stretched out and rushed toward me.

I was drowning. It felt like my mind was being sucked down into a whirlpool of darkness. The worst part, I suddenly realized, was that I was not alone. There was something there in the darkness with me. I could feel its presence. It was close, watching and waiting. I tried pushing myself to the surface of consciousness, and for a brief moment, I broke free and felt myself rising up. Then something grabbed me and started to pull me back down. I kicked and struggled to no avail. The grip of whatever held me was too strong.

Then all movement stopped, and I found myself in a small, gray place. I couldn't feel my body, but I could hear voices. My ears strained to make sense of the words.

The conversation was garbled at first, but then it became clearer. I realized in horror that it was my voice speaking. But then again it wasn't my voice—it didn't sound like me at all.

There was sound coming from my lips, but only because something had possession of my body, possession over my lips and vocal cords. At this realization, I felt myself fall further into the oblivion.

"Good evening, death dealer."

Luke's voice answered. "Who are you?"

"You want to know my name? We both know there's power in a name."

"Who are you?" This time Luke's voice was louder, more commanding.

"I'm Wanda Branston. There, you forced it out of me. Aren't you proud? What a nice looking young man you are. I'm sure we can come to some kind of arrangement. If you let me keep this one, I promise to do your bidding."

"You will leave her when I tell you." Luke sounded angry.

"Will I? Do you think you're strong enough to make me go?"

"Colina, can you hear me?" Luke's voice called out.

I could hear him, but I couldn't respond. I was in this small, dark place, alone and frightened.

"Colina, you have to fight, bring yourself to the surface."

"Is she strong enough to fight, boy?" Wanda's voice spoke. "Do you really think this youngling is going to break free?"

"Colina, focus on my voice. Center all your thoughts on my voice. I know you're feeling fear right now, and that's what the spirit feeds on. Break the fear and find yourself again, and you'll regain control."

As Luke said the last words, I felt the presence move closer to me and heard a wicked giggle.

It's all in my imagination. I'm not in this small, dark space —I'm tied to a chair in a room.

I tried to force my panic and fears away, or at least gain control of them.

*I'm not afraid. Luke will make sure I'm not hurt.* As the words echoed in my mind, I felt the presence edge farther away.

*I can do this. I can break the surface and regain myself.*

I struggled, and then struggled some more. It felt like I was wrapped in cotton candy.

Luke's voice spoke out again. "Is there anything you want to tell me before I banish you, spirit?"

Wanda answered with a cackle. "What? Kind words for my loved ones? Maybe a secret I could share with them or you? Is that what you think I'll do? Be grateful to you for passing my words onto the living and then leave quietly? That's what you hope for, isn't it, boy? But I won't go. I won't, do you hear me! I'm here, breathing this fresh air. Smelling the . . . what's that? Yes, jasmine in the air. I love the smell of jasmine. And watching the stars, the way they glimmer in the night sky. I miss living."

"You can't stay. You can't have this body," Luke said.

"But why not? I beat others to get to it. Finders, keepers. It's a strong body, a young body. It's mine now, and I won't give it up!"

"You don't have a choice." More Latin words. Luke was working a spell.

"Stop! Stop, I say! You can't make me go!" Wanda screamed.

Suddenly in the darkness around me was a small glimmer of colored lights. The lights expanded, and as they did, I tried to reach out to them. But before I could, the presence was there beside me again. It spoke not from outside my body, but from inside, this my small, dark place I seemed to be stuck in. "I won't go. You hear me, girly? I'm not leaving again." As the voice spoke, I realized in horror that there wasn't just one presence near me. I felt other things. There was no sound or physical shapes, just movement and gray swirls of—

*What is that?*

Something in the blackness was near me. I suddenly felt like a deer in the woods being hunted by wolves. There was something out there worse than Wanda. Something out there, waiting, and hungry. I was so small and vulnerable and any moment it would reach out and grab me.

And there was nothing I could do to stop it.

Fear raced through me. A panic I had never felt before gripped me, and I tried to cry out.

"Colina!" Luke's voice again. "You have to break free. I can't do this without your help."

If he couldn't do this, would I be stuck forever in this small corner of...there was only darkness and emptiness.

*Is this hell? Is this the ether sea?*

Wanda's voice inside my head cried out, "No, girly, this isn't the other side. And it ain't heaven, neither. No loved ones surrounding you here. I've tried to go to the light, I have, but I can't seem to get there. It beckons to me, but every time I move its way, it disappears. So here I am, floating around. But now I have a chance. I have you. You've given me a chance to be alive again. To live in the outside world. You just be a good girly and stay put."

*No.* The word resounded inside me. I wouldn't be forced into this corner of darkness forever. Luke was waiting for me out there.

*You won't hold me here. I'll break free.* As I said the words in my head, I felt the panic and fear start to ebb away.

Luke said fear fueled the possessing spirit. The more scared I was, the stronger it became. I had to be brave. I had to trust that he could get me out. I could do this. I forced myself to concentrate on the lights again. I reached out with my mind and my whole being.

*I can do this. I will do this.*

"You can't—stop fighting. Just give in and let me stay." Wanda's voice sounded weaker now.

*No!* This time when the word echoed through my mind, I felt myself rise. I felt the presence shrink back. Wanda was no longer controlling me. But as she left, I felt the other presence move in to take her place. The bigger and darker presence that seemed so much worse than Wanda. It had no voice, no personality trying to overcome my own—just desperate anger. It seeped inside me, a cold anger filling me up. I again felt like I was drowning. I fell back into that small, empty place again, but this time there was a light, a bright light that seemed to be coming not from outside, but from within. The light began to dim, and I reached out to it desperately. It grew brighter, and suddenly it was like I was pulled from the dark waters. I broke the surface and gasped in a breath of air.

I was back in my body. My head was throbbing, my chest was pounding, but I was back in the chair. I felt the ropes digging into my flesh. I felt a cramp in my left leg. I let out a cry of relief and Luke was beside me.

"Colina?" he whispered, looking into my eyes.

"It's me." The words came out in a sob.

He nodded, untied me, and then reached out and pulled me toward him. I was wrapped up in his arms.

I should have felt comforted to be free—to be standing in his embrace. I should have felt safe, but I didn't. Everything looked different. The room, his face, even the air around me smelled different. It was hard to explain. Had I truly come back? Was this really me? Or was a part of me still in that dark corner? I could feel the material of his shirt pressed against my cheek.

I was me, but somehow, I was not the same. And the thought terrified me.

CHAPTER

# SIXTEEN

An hour later I stood in the bathroom and looked at myself in the mirror. I no longer recognized myself. Something about me had changed. My face was my own, yet it wasn't. What had the rituals done to me? I continued to study my reflection. It was almost as though I was seeing the shadow of another face on top of mine. I wiped a hand over my face. No, it was definitely my reflection looking back at me in the mirror, but something was off. It was something in my eyes, in my expression—it wasn't just the way I looked, I felt different.

Darkness now filled me.

I felt as if my soul had been torn from my body and not fully replaced. I was not myself. I had been shattered. The world looked bleaker, grayer. And in the place where there was normally fear, I now felt anger. It burned through me like a great flame fueling my blood.

I was invincible.

Before I'd felt powerless and helpless, but not anymore. I was ready and willing to fight, and I felt a sudden desire to inflict pain.

*Inflict pain.* The thought stopped me cold. It was true; I felt an odd desire to hurt someone, which was not normally in my nature. I had wanted the men who killed my family to die, but I had never really thought about actually killing them. Their deaths were more of an abstract thought. I'd been brought up as a healer, to care for people and take away their pain. This newfound desire to see someone cower before me, to feel their fear, was so strong I could almost taste it.

The awakening was dangerous, the traveler had said, and now I fully understood what she meant. I felt as though I stood at the edge of a great abyss, a sea of darkness reaching before me. Farther within the darkness, nameless, faceless voices and shadows called out to me, enticing me to come join them.

The thought of what those men did to my family filled me with a swell of violence. As it consumed me, the hatred roared through my body and my blood. If I could wrap my hands around the necks of the men that hurt my family, I would strangle them with my bare hands. I would make them suffer, like they made my family suffer. Slit their throats and watch the blood ooze from their gashed necks. Watch bullets tear into their flesh.

The thought brought me a feeling of glee.

Was I actually feeling gleeful about inflicting gruesome pain on human beings?

I looked again at my face in the mirror. It was contorted in rage and hate. Violence gleamed out of my eyes, and my hands reached toward the reflection in the mirror.

*Who was this girl?*

*Darla. You must save Darla,* whispered across my brain. I had forgotten about her. My lust for vengeance had filled me in a way it never had before, and that terrified me. I was changing that was true, but I told myself, I was becoming whatever I had to in order to survive.

I EXITED THE BATHROOM, glancing at the mussed sheets on the unmade bed before heading for the dresser. I'd finally slept—no tossing or turning this time, but I woke with a heaviness that seemed to fill the air around me. My brain wasn't working at full speed. I felt slowed down, both mentally and physically drained by last night's activities. I should be thankful I'd survived another one of the rituals, instead, a feeling of foreboding filled me.

I picked up Darla's suitcase and put it on top of the bed. I needed something to wear. I held up a yellow top and threw it back down. I couldn't bring myself to put on such a cheerful color. It didn't match my current mood. I'd woken up in a funk. Bright clothes no longer seemed appropriate—the darkness had touched the very essence of my being and changed me. I held up another brightly colored top and realized I wanted to dress in a way that matched how I felt inside.

I rummaged through Pagan's closet since she wasn't around to protest and hit pay dirt. I shimmied into a tight black dress that flared out around my knees and threw on a dark gray and black striped sweater over the top of it for warmth. A pair of black tights and black lace up chunky boots finished the ensemble.

In the bathroom, I helped myself to a drawer full of makeup. I normally didn't bother with the stuff, but today was a day for something different. I lined my eyes with thick black eyeliner and opened one lipstick, and then another, until I came across a deep purple. I took my finger and ran it over the surface of the lipstick, then leaned forward and carefully smeared the purple over my lips. My hand reached up and touched the hair hanging in gentle waves to my shoulders. In another drawer, I found a straightener. I took my time taming my wavy hair until it was straight and sleek. Finally satisfied, I took a step back for a closer look at my image in the mirror.

Gone was the middle-class girl who'd stepped into the magic shop days ago. In her place stood someone who now looked more dark and dangerous. I stared at my reflection for a long time. I had always been an optimistic person. I had always been surrounded by happy people.

But that part of me—the part that considered the glass half full—now seemed very, very far away.

When I was done, I made my way into the kitchen.

Luke was pouring himself a glass of orange juice. He slowly took in my appearance. There was an appreciative gleam in his eyes. "New look?"

I shrugged my shoulders and tried not to feel self-conscious. "I guess." I opened a loaf of bread sitting on the counter and slid two pieces into the toaster.

"How are you feeling this morning?" he asked.

I shrugged my shoulders again. He looked at me, waiting for an answer. When I realized, he was not going to let it go, I finally admitted out loud, "I don't feel like myself. It's hard to explain."

His expression changed and turned more serious. "It happens after the rituals."

Here was someone who had gone through the exact same thing I did. If anyone knew how I felt at the moment, it was Luke. "Did you feel different afterward?"

He nodded. "I did."

"In what way?"

"I became..." He turned and stared out the window for a few seconds before answering. "Stronger. Harder."

Last night, after I broke free of the possession, I no longer felt the panic or fear that had been constantly swirling inside me. That fear had been my steady companion since watching my parents' murders. I now felt a new sense of... It was hard to put into words. Violence? Hatred? Whatever it was, it seemed to be coursing through my veins and warming my blood.

When I first met Luke, I had sensed an overwhelming violence radiating from his whole being. Was that a product of the rituals? As I continued forward in the process, would I keep changing? Morphing into someone different? Before I could voice my questions, I found that I suddenly felt very odd.

A tingling at the base of my neck slowly spread and radiated down my spine. The room turned cold. We weren't alone. I tilted my head and looked over to the far corner of the kitchen. Something was there.

Something not of this world.

I looked over at Luke and realized he was staring at the same spot.

"There's a spirit. I can feel it."

Here was the power I had begged to learn. The Death Arts—magic at the upmost top of the magic food chain. I could now feel spirits. At that realization, I felt shaken to my very core.

Being possessed, having my very essence forced into the dark recesses of oblivion, had been a terrifying experience. I hadn't been in control of my body. Something else had looked out of my eyes and spoken with my vocal cords. Something else had been inside me, and I was freaked out at the prospect of it happening again.

I stood frozen, unable to tear my eyes away from the corner, horrified that at any moment I would see a rush of dark shadows coming toward me again.

"Tell me what you see," Luke said, coming to my side. He put his hand on my shoulder.

For the first time since the night in the cemetery, I didn't recoil at his touch. Instead, I had a strong desire to throw myself into his arms and beg for protection. I didn't want any part of the thing in the corner, didn't want to deal with whatever restless soul was lingering around the ether sea, waiting for the opportunity to jump into me again. At the thought, I wrapped my arms around myself.

But this is what I wanted, I reminded myself. I was getting my deepest desire, and if we were going to save Darla, I had to face down my worst fears.

I took a deep breath and tried to focus on the corner. "I don't see anything."

"You're not looking hard enough."

I glanced around the kitchen. As my eyes passed over a small mirror hanging from the wall near the fridge, I could have sworn I saw a shadow move across its surface.

"By the mirror?" I asked.

"Yes," Luke answered. "Now try communicating with it."

I shook my head and took a step back. "But what if...what if...it takes me over?" I forced out between clenched teeth.

"This spirit is someone I've dealt with before. I promise he won't hurt you. You don't have to be afraid. Just open yourself up and communicate with him."

"How?" I asked, my hands now trembling.

Luke's voice was calm and reassuring. "Reach out with your mind. Focus all your energy in the direction of the shadow."

A wisp of breeze when I knew there could be none rustled the window coverings, and the room grew even colder. I could actually see my breath.

Luke was suddenly behind me. He leaned against me and whispered in my ear, "You can do this. Trust yourself. I'm here to help you."

The image of darkness filled my head—those swirls of gray floating around me, hungry things, awful things, that I could feel coming near me. The cackle of Wanda's voice inside my head. As the memories rushed in, I felt panic rise from the pit of my stomach.

"Where is he now?" Luke asked.

I took another deep breath and forced myself to look around the room. A knock sounded at my right. I physically jumped at the sound.

"Steady." Luke's arm encircled my waist.

Another knock, this time closer.

"There." I pointed across the room by the dining room table.

"Yes. The spirit is there. Now, make contact."

I can do this. Luke is here. I am not alone. I focused on the spot above the table and an image slowly began to form. A white, shimmering light began to waver in and out, and ever so slowly an outline came into focus. A face—there was a face. I could just make it out as it flickered in and out of the sunlight streaming through the window.

I tried to erase the panic from my voice. "It looks like a child."

Luke's arm tightened around me. "Good."

"He's small, maybe ten or eleven years old."

"Ask for a name. Ask out loud."

I licked my lips, they felt so dry and chapped all of a sudden. "What's your name?"

"Thomas." The word floated past me as if carried on the wind.

"He said his name is Thomas."

The presence moved toward me, and I instinctively began to back up.

"Stand your ground. Don't be afraid," Luke said. "Trust me. It's okay, you're not in any danger."

The shadow continued forward until it was directly before me. Then I felt the sensation of small fingers caressing my arm.

"Colina." The childlike voice said my name.

CATRINA BURGESS

"He just said my name."

"Good. Ask him what he wants."

I spoke again, but this time my voice was stronger and calmer. "What do you want?"

"I have a message for you." The words were there again, and with them a warm tingle of air fluttered against my cheek.

"What's the message?"

This time the words slid through my mind. *He's coming for you.*

Small, invisible fingers ran down my hand.

"Who?" I asked, trying not to freak out and pull my arm back.

"The one you've been seeking." There was a light giggle and then, "He doesn't like it that you got away. You're the one that got away." I felt a tug on my hair. "It won't be long now. He'll find you."

A cupboard door banged open and shut once. Twice.

"Who will?" I demanded.

"Are you ready for judgment day?" the boy whispered, and then he vanished in front of me.

I shook my head, trying to make sense of what the child had said. I raised trembling hands to my face, turned, and looked at Luke. "The boy, Thomas, he didn't try to possess me."

"Most won't. They want only to be seen and acknowledged." His hand came up and gently brushed my hair out of my face. "The ones that possess have a powerful need. They weren't ready to die and will do anything to try and make it back into this world."

"And what happens when they take over a person and you can't get them out?"

"Usually, it's when they jump into someone who has natural abilities, but no idea how to use them. These people are unprepared for the assault, and when it happens, they're pushed back and left helpless. Trapped."

A shiver ran down my spine at the very thought. "And the spirits stay inside them forever?"

His expression turned grim. "The spirits use these unsuspecting people, these vessels, to make their way through the world. How long they stay depends on how strong they are." Luke's fingers wrapped around mine. "Your hand is freezing. When spirits come forth, they tend to bring down the temperature. How about some hot chocolate or tea to help warm you up?"

I didn't want him to move away. It felt good having his body close to mine. I gave him a smile. "Tea sounds good."

He let go of my hand and made his way back into the kitchen. I followed behind.

He grabbed an electric kettle off the counter and started filling it with water from the sink. "And those that don't have full control of their faculties," he said abruptly. Luke turned off the faucet, plugging in the now full kettle before pointing toward the cupboard. "Grab a couple mugs, will you? Spirits can possess people who don't have full control of their conscious mind. Those folks are always on the edge of reality anyway. And those who are on the edge can be easily manipulated by the dead."

I opened the cupboard and pulled out two red mugs. "How can you tell if you meet someone who's possessed? Someone who has a spirit commanding them?"

He pulled out two bags of tea from a canister on the countertop. "You can tell sometimes, but not always. You can feel the wrongness inside them. You feel it in your gut."

I set the mugs down in front of him. "But this spirit, the one that just came to me, you've met him before?"

"He's a young child whose family used to live here." Luke

pointed toward the floor. "Not in this barn, but on this same piece of land years ago, before a barn was here. He died of a fever. He's bound to this particular spot."

"And he can't go to the light?" I asked.

Luke shook his head. "No." Luke gave me a wry smile. "We share our space with spirits all the time."

I looked around the room, a feeling of dread filling me. Would another spirit pop out at any minute? "Do they always contact you when they're around?"

He shook his head. "Not always."

"But you know when they're around? When they're in the room?" I asked as I scanned the kitchen. It was no longer cold, and I felt normal.

"Yes, I can always feel their presence," Luke said.

For the rest of my life, I'd be bombarded with spirits. I was having a hard time wrapping my mind around it. "And what do you do if you don't want to communicate with them, but they want to talk to you?"

He put a tea bag in each mug, reached over, and grabbed the kettle. He slowly filled each cup with hot water. "You learn how to tune out, how to sort of turn it off. That works in most cases, but if a spirit is strong enough—desperate enough—to communicate with you, it will."

My hands went to my head again. I'll be like this forever. Any place I walk into now, I'll see spirits.

My life just turned into a new type of nightmare.

Luke turned and gave me a reassuring smile. "I promise it gets easier with practice. It's something you grow accustomed to."

I looked at him like he'd lost his mind. I couldn't imagine ever getting used to talking to the dead.

"Have you felt anyone from your family since last night?"

His question caught me by surprise. "No."

"It's easier at night, when the world is quiet and people settle down, to hear spirits. We'll see if they come to you tonight." He handed me a mug.

I wrapped my fingers around it. It was warm and felt good against my cold skin. I took a sip and looked at Luke over the rim. "And if they don't?"

He leaned against the counter. "I have to believe they'll come to you. It's the only way we'll find Darla." He sounded so sure of himself.

"And the last ritual?" I whispered.

He gave me a look devoid of emotion and said, "I'm working on it."

"We can't get it done tonight?" I wanted to get it over with as soon as possible.

"I don't have what I need for it yet, but I will soon."

I wanted to ask him what he was waiting for, what new, horrifying situation I was going to find myself in, but I couldn't force the words out.

"Before I forget." Luke put his mug down, reached into his pocket, and pulled out the traveler's pouch. The last time I'd seen the pouch, I was setting it on the bed after he told me I couldn't use it to protect myself during the possession. Why did he have it now?

"Until you learn how to protect yourself, this will keep you closed off. It will keep anything from trying to possess you."

I reached for it, but he pulled it away. "The thing is, we want your family to contact you. You need to stay open, so I don't want you to use it yet." He put the pouch down on the counter. "But later I'll need you to carry it with you."

"What's the plan for the day?"

"We're heading to the hospital." Luke said.

I stared at him. "Are you okay? Are you feeling sick?"

He gave me a reassuring smile. "I'm fine. There's just an

errand I have to run and someone I have to see. Drink your tea, it's getting cold."

There was something off about his expression when he answered the question. I'd been with him long enough now that I was able to read his body language and moods. I had the strongest feeling he wasn't telling me the whole truth.

# SEVENTEEN

The rest of the morning was relatively normal. No spirits showed up. No ghostly boys dropped by to give me more messages. Luke spent most of the morning on the phone. Whatever he was planning, he didn't want me within earshot of his conversations. Every time I wandered his way, he'd make a none too subtle move to another room. If the guy wanted to keep secrets, so be it. He couldn't leave me in the dark forever. Not if he wanted my help.

Sometime after three o'clock in the afternoon, Luke announced that it was time to head to the hospital. I grabbed a short black coat from Pagan's closet and found a pair of elbow high, black and white striped fingerless gloves. The weather outside had turned chilly.

Storm clouds were gathering overhead. When Luke opened the front door and we stepped out, I could see my breath. I stood in the doorway and buttoned my coat.

Luke came to my side. He was wearing a black parka. He reached into his pocket and held out the pouch. I took it from his hand but didn't hide the surprise I felt. "I can have it now?"

He nodded his head. "You'll need it where we're going. Ready?"

"Yes," I answered, but for what, I had no idea.

Inside the car, Luke turned up the radio, which made conversation impossible. There were so many questions swirling around in my head.

*What's with all the mysterious phone calls? Why are we going to the hospital? What does the last ritual entail?*

I looked over at him. He seemed relaxed. He was singing along to a song on the radio, but there was an apprehension about him, a radiating tension, a look in his eyes that set my nerves on end.

When we finally pulled into the hospital parking lot, the anxiety building inside me was almost unbearable.

*What the hell are we doing here?* I wanted to shout at him.

Luke shut off the car and turned toward me. "The pouch. You should wear it around your neck. It'll give you the best protection that way."

I took the pouch out of my pocket and set it in my lap. I slowly started to unwind the leather wrapped around the top of it.

He slid closer to me. "Here, let me help."

I handed him the pouch and lifted my hair off my neck. "How long are we going to be here?"

"Not too long." He lifted the pouch and wrapped it around my neck. He slowly tied the two pieces of leather together. His fingers lingered for a moment.

Delicious sensations ran across my skin where his fingers grazed my neck.

Luke edged his body closer.

My breath hitched in the back of my throat. He's going to kiss me again. At that thought, my heart began to beat faster. That night we kissed on the couch I'd surrendered to the feelings swirling inside me. But then after the first ritual when he kissed me fear rushed in and forced me to push him away. If he kissed me again, would I still feel that same panic and fear?

No. I was no longer scared of him. That irrational fear that consumed me after the first ritual was finally gone. But in its place, I felt this anger, this all-consuming rage. Emotions so foreign to my being that I didn't feel at all like myself.

I might not feel like myself, but I couldn't deny that my body still hummed when Luke was close to me. His arm rested against mine. I could feel this electricity slid across my arm where his skin touched mine. I turned toward him and now his face was just inches from mine. I wanted him so badly to take me in his arms again. I wanted so badly in this moment to forget everything that had happened to me and just sink into him.

Those dark eyes were watching me closely. "There's something you have to know," he said, his voice low. He reached out and took my hand in his. "Now that you're one of us, the hospital..." He seemed to be searching for words. "It's not an easy place to be. There are a lot of souls passing, a lot of spirits lingering around."

While I was sitting there like an idiot hoping he would kiss me, he had been solely focused on the business at hand.

My hand went to the pouch around my neck. "But this will keep them from bothering me."

"Not entirely. They won't be able to possess you, but protection magic isn't strong enough to keep them completely at bay. You'll be able to feel them around. You'll be able to sense them, and maybe see and hear them."

I couldn't keep the horror I was feeling from showing on my face. That was not what I expected him to say.

He reached out and grabbed my hand. "I wouldn't have brought you here, not so soon after the first two rituals, but we're running out of time. You have to get used to dealing with spirits. You have to learn how to trust and use your new abilities. We can't take things slow. Normally you'd be eased into dealing with the spirits and you'd have time to adjust to your new abilities, but we are out of time..." He looked away.

I squeezed his hand. "It's alright. The only thing that matters is getting your sister back." I said it out loud, but I knew as the words left my mouth that it wasn't true. Finding the men who killed my family and making them pay was the one thing keeping me going.

He let out a sigh and looked back at me. "Whatever happens, remember I'm here with you and I won't let anything happen to you."

I nodded.

He reached out and his finger gently brushed against my cheek. "Just remember to breathe."

"Breathe. Got it," I whispered.

We made our way across the parking lot and went through a pair of sliding glass doors.

*Remember to breathe*, Luke said.

Easier said than done, because the minute I walked into the building, the breath was knocked right out of me. It was as if a wave of static electricity slammed into me. It buzzed against my skin. I stood there, trying to get my bearings, when a cold draft rushed by me. And then another. I heard a whisper of voices on the wind.

*We weren't alone.*

I felt like I was in a crowded room. I tried to take a breath but couldn't. I was claustrophobic and suddenly it was as though there wasn't enough oxygen. Everything began to close in on me. I felt my knees start to buckle.

And then Luke was in front of me. His eyes were filled with concern. He reached out and put his hand on my shoulder.

"It's okay. It'll get better in a minute. Try to concentrate on me."

I looked into his eyes. The feeling of panic, of claustrophobia, started to ebb away.

I took one breath. And another.

"Keep your focus on me. Focusing on the living helps."

I nodded my head and looked around at the hustle and bustle of the hospital. Plenty of living roamed the halls. I just needed to keep my focus on them and away from whatever lurked in the shadows.

Luke took my hand, and we headed through a waiting room and into a wide hallway. We walked up and down a maze of halls, pushed open a door, and headed up a flight of stairs. We were entering another wing of the hospital. In this section, rooms were full of patients. As we passed open doors, I could make out shapes lying in bed. Many of the people were hooked up to machines. Beeping filled the air. There were fewer nurses in this section of the hospital. One glared at us from behind a desk.

Luke abruptly stopped and dropped my hand. He pointed to a group of chairs over in a corner. "Wait here. I'll be right back."

At the loss of physical contact, I felt a moment of panic. My hand came up and grasped the pouch. I settled into a chair and watched Luke head down the hallway.

He stopped in front of one of the rooms. A woman came out and greeted him. They shook hands. I watched them, and then realized someone was talking to me.

"I know you can hear me."

I turned and looked up, expecting to see someone standing over me. No one was there. I was alone.

But I wasn't.

"See. I knew you could hear me."

The hairs on the back of my neck stood up.

The seat next to me rattled. "Listen to me. I need you to listen to me. My son, he needs to know about the ring, I meant to tell him, I thought there was still time."

A spirit was talking to me. I should have felt petrified, but instead I leaned forward to hear the voice more clearly. I felt a tug on my arm and found myself on my feet, heading toward a room.

I stood in the doorway. There was an elderly lady lying in one of the beds. She was hooked up to machines and a mask covered her face. Tubes protruded from her arms.

"I'm no longer in that body, those machines are keeping my heart beating, but it is a heart that no longer holds my soul."

I could feel a breeze slid across my arm. "Tell him I put the ring in a blue box in the back of the closet. My hiding place in case someone robs my house."

I noticed other people in the room. A man and woman were sitting in chairs in the corner by the window. They were holding hands. Sadness filled the man's face.

"He's going to marry her. He told me last week that he was going to propose. He asked me for the ring, but before I could give it to him..." The voice trailed off.

Luke had said spirits are often confused and talked in puzzles. This old women's voice held no confusion. She knew exactly what she wanted from me. She was demanding I tell her son about the ring.

This was crazy. What was I going to say to the couple? I shouldn't be here. I shouldn't be interfering in these people's lives, not when they were dealing with something so personal, so sad.

I started to back out of the room, but there was a tug on my arm again. "You have to tell him where to find the ring."

And if I didn't help her, would that mean that something left undone would force her to roam the ether sea forever as an unsettled spirit? Was this one request she had of me the thing that would allow her to move into the light? I would move heaven and earth to help my family find the light.

I had to say something. I had to try and help this spirit.

I opened my mouth and the words rushed out. "Excuse me, sir."

The man looked up at me. Grief filled his face.

"Your mother wants you to know..."

He rose from his seat. "Are you a friend of hers?" He put out his hand. "I'm sorry, I don't know all her friends."

I took a step back and shook my head. I felt a nudge at my shoulder as if someone was giving me a gentle push.

The voice again, this time more insistent. "Tell him about the ring. His grandmother's ring."

"Your mother wants me to tell you that she left the ring in a box. A blue box in the back of her closet."

"The ring?" The man looked confused.

"Your grandmother's engagement ring."

A light of understanding came into his eyes. He turned and looked at the woman. "Oh... The ring."

The voice whispered in my ear, "tell him not to worry. I'm going to a better place."

"Your mother, she says not to worry. She's going to a better place."

"I don't understand." His face suddenly filled with fear. "Who are you?" he demanded.

I couldn't believe his reaction. Here I was, trying to help him, and he was looking at me like I was dangerous. My hands clenched into fists, and I felt a strong, irrational urge to hit him. This man was losing his mother. I should have been feeling sympathy for him, and instead, I only felt anger towards him.

*What is happening to me?*

I took a step back. "I'm sorry. I didn't mean to intrude."

I turned and rushed out the door. I headed down the hallway and ran into Luke.

Luke held up his hands. "Whoa—I was looking for you. Is everything okay?"

I couldn't get the image of the man's expression out of my head. I'd told him something only his mother's spirit would know. The only people who talk to spirits are death dealers. It only took him a moment to realize what I was. That look of fear and repulsion that came over his face was one I now recognized — I was a death dealer now; people would look at me like that for the rest of my life.

I averted my eyes from his. "Yes, everything's fine."

Luke grabbed my hand. "I'm done. We can go."

I started to walk away.

The voice whispered after me, "Thank you. Thank you for telling him."

This was my life now. Dealing with spirits. Despised and feared by people. What had been done to me could never be undone. I had opened the doorway to the spirits, and now I would spend the rest of my life passing on messages from the dead.

CHAPTER
# EIGHTEEN

When we returned to Pagan's place, Luke announced that he had some research to do before the next ritual. He grabbed a half dozen books off various shelves scattered around the room and piled them onto the dining room table.

He met my offer of assistance with a half-smile and a "No thanks, I've got this."

Left to my own devices, I paced around the living room. Waiting for my family's spirits to appear meant that I was more than a bit on edge. Every noise had me jumping. When I grew tired of pacing, I spent a long time flipping through magazines I found on the coffee table. An hour passed...then another.

Nothing happened.

I wondered what Luke was doing and why he didn't want my help. He'd been distant since we left the hospital. I guessed that maybe he was just lost in thought, but now, as I sat alone in the living room and time ticked by, I had to wonder what was running through his mind. I knew he was worried about the last ritual, and he wasn't the only one. Another ritual. I sighed. Another chance of losing myself even more to the darkness.

Thunder rumbled overhead. A storm had been brewing outside, and it was finally making its appearance. The dark clouds opened up, and rain slid against the windows. I sat watching the trees blow back and forth in the wind. The temperature in the room dropped, but this time the chill was nature's doing. It was getting quite cold outside.

It was also chilly inside. I rubbed my hands together and looked over at the dying fire. A stack of wood leaned against the wall, so I got up and threw a couple of logs on. I spent quite a bit of time sitting in front of the flames, stabbing at them with a long, black fire iron.

More time passed. How long will I have to sit here? I wondered impatiently. I was bored and extremely hungry. I hadn't eaten breakfast or lunch, and when my stomach growled for the second time, I dropped the fire iron and headed into the kitchen. It was time to make myself something to eat.

I passed Luke sitting at the table bent over a book. Whatever he was reading had captured his full attention.

I stopped and sat down in the chair next to him. "How's it going?"

He didn't look up. "Fine. Everything's fine. Any contact from your family yet?"

"No, no spirits," I admitted. All he cared about was my family coming to me. He didn't ask me how I was feeling or what I'd been up to. I watched his eyes scan the pages of the book in front of him. I knew he was trying to do whatever preparation he had to for the next ritual. Deep down, I knew he wasn't ignoring me on purpose—or at least I hoped he wasn't.

Another book lay open on the table in front of me. I took a closer look. It was big and covered in brown leather, the pages yellow with age. Intricate drawings done in black ink covered the pages. I leaned closer and studied a picture of a man standing before a big block of stone, a dozen faces floating around him. Those must be banshees. Other things surrounded the banshees—bigger, darker things. I wondered what they were.

"How's your research going?" I reached out to tug the book closer.

Luke grabbed my hand and pulled it back. "Don't touch the books."

"I just want to take a look. I'll be careful."

His expression was serious. "I'm not worried about the books. I'm worried about you." He held up the book he'd been reading. "These have power. You're still untrained and wide open. There's no telling what could happen."

I yanked my hand away and pushed my chair back. Talking to the dead was more than enough for me to handle at the moment. The last thing I wanted or needed was more freaky and scary in my life.

I waved my hand at the table. "Does this stuff have something to do with the last ritual?"

He closed the book in front of him. "Not this one." He pointed to another book. "That one has the spells I've got to do for the ritual."

"Spells? There's more than one?" I didn't like the sound of that.

He ran his hand through his hair, looking tired. "It's a complicated ritual. I told you before, I've never done them—I've only watched others do them. But this last one, it's very tricky, and I've only seen it performed a couple of times."

"But you can do it?"

He looked away for a few moments before answering. "I think I can."

His reluctance didn't make me feel any better.

"Did you get what you needed?"

He gave me a questioning look.

"At the hospital, did you get what you needed to do the spell?" I asked.

He replied in a low voice, "We can do the last ritual tomorrow night."

*Tomorrow night.* I was going through the last ritual tomorrow night. I wondered how bad it was going to be and if Luke would give me some kind of warning at the last minute—a speech like he'd given me before the first two rituals about how things didn't always turn out well, and how the people who'd messed them up weren't around anymore. I gave myself a mental shake. I'd survived the first two rituals. I could survive this last one.

"And until tomorrow night, what's the plan of action?" I took a few steps back. Better to give the books some distance. I didn't like the idea that they had spells swirling around them.

"We wait for your family to contact you."

"And if they don't?" They hadn't so far. I was starting to wonder if they ever would.

He looked at me in silence for a long moment and then said, "They will." He sounded so confident. He turned back to the table, grabbed another one of the books, and started flipping through the pages. "We need to know where they're keeping Darla. Without that, putting you through the last ritual will be pointless. Once we find out where she is, we can make plans. Then we can go through the last ritual so you can have some magic of your own to help me and protect yourself."

Luke seemed more stressed and preoccupied with this ritual than any of the others. *Why is this one so different?* I wanted to ask, but I swallowed my question. *Did I really want to know?* First, I'd been strangled and then brought back to life. Then I'd had a spirit possess me. Goddess only knew what this next trial would entail. But we weren't doing it until tomorrow night. The more I knew, the more time I had to worry about what might happen.

"I'm going to make myself something to eat. Are you hungry?"

He looked up and gave me a smile. "No, but thanks for asking." He motioned toward the books. "I'm just going to get back to this."

"Okay. Good luck." I didn't know what else to say. I couldn't exactly demand that he stop working and pay attention to me. That would make me sound like a whiny girlfriend.

*Girlfriend.* Had that word really just popped into my mind?

In a moment of utter embarrassment, I realized I was literally standing there, gawking at him. He was poring over books, trying to figure out how to do the last ritual, worrying over his sister and what was I doing? Just standing there like an idiot, wondering if he would ever pay attention to me again.

All of a sudden, the room felt stifling. I quickly turned and made my way into the kitchen.

I hunted around the cupboards and the fridge. If we were going to stay here any longer, we would need to get more food. There weren't a lot of choices grub wise. I poured myself a glass of milk, slapped together a couple of peanut butter and jelly sandwiches, and then, food in hand, made my way back to the living room.

I ate in front of the fire. When I finished, I decided to lie down and close my eyes. There was no reason not to take a nap. Nothing pressing had to be done. If my family wanted to contact me, they would. There wasn't anything I could do to speed up the process.

A blanket lay on the back of one of the chairs. I grabbed it and pulled it over me as I settled down on the couch. I closed my eyes and tried to empty my mind. After a while, I drifted off to sleep.

And the dreams began.

I was back in the pantry. James closed the doors in front of me and whispered the spell that locked me in. I watched in horror as men surrounded my family. My father fought. He struggled hard, using magic to keep the men at bay, but the defensive magic of a healer is no match for the physical and magical forces he was facing. They quickly overpowered him, grabbed him from both sides, and forced him down to his knees.

A man I didn't recognize pulled out a knife and raised it high in the air.

"Join us and live, or refuse us and die," the man demanded.

"Macaven, I'll never be a part of your madness!" my father yelled.

Before I could cry out, the man brought the knife down fast and hard against my father's throat. Blood gushed out. Desperation filled my father's eyes as he struggled to get free. The more he struggled, the faster his blood spilled. It ran down his shirt and splattered onto the floor. Gradually, he stopped resisting. His body went limp. The men let go of his arms, and my father fell forward, crashing to the floor.

I cried out. I screamed. I pushed and shoved against the pantry doors. My fingers bled as I clawed at the wooden slats, trying to force my way through. But I couldn't get out.

I watched the man holding my mother throw her across the room. She fell to the floor, and then she was up on her feet and started running. But she only took two steps before her body lurched forward. A bullet tore through her and embedded itself into the wall. A red spot appeared on her forehead as she twisted around and fell backward. She slammed into the wall and slid to the ground.

I closed my eyes, covered my face with my hands, and screamed "No!" over and over. I slumped forward, tears streaming down my face. I was crying so hard, I could barely breathe. I don't know how long I was there, on the floor. There was only grief and pain filling my mind and body. Time seemed to stand still.

I kept telling myself that this wasn't happening. That it was a nightmare I would wake from any moment. That's when I heard James's screams. I sat up and forced myself back on my feet. I made myself look again through the wooden slats.

James stood on the other end of the room, his hands raised in the air. Magic flowed from his fingers, but it wasn't enough. The powerful mages' magic came crashing down around him and forced him back. Another scream ripped from his throat.

I watched in horror as they scooped James's spirit from his body.

It was some sort of magic I had never seen before; magic that skipped the step of murder and went straight to stealing the victim's soul. They tore James' soul from his body. They forced it out and cast it into the sea of unrest. I could hear James's anguish as his spirit left this world and was sucked into the ether. His screams lingered until I didn't think I could take it any longer.

I clamped my hands over my ears, praying to wake from this horrible nightmare.

And then my eyes opened.

Luke stood over me, gently shaking my shoulder. "You were crying out in your sleep."

"I was?" I touched my cheeks, which were wet with tears, and sat up. "What time is it?"

He sat down next to me. "It's late." He reached out and took my hand in his.

Even through the shock of reliving my family's death, I felt cold rage wiping away the fear. "Luke, his name is Macaven— the guy who ordered my family's murder."

Macaven. I savored the name, tying it to the hate that had been driving me. How had I not recalled it before? I finally had someone to hold accountable for my family's death. I would make him pay for what he had done, and for what he was making me now become.

I turned until I was facing Luke and looked into those dark eyes. He never wanted to hurt me. I'd begged him to lead me down the path of the Death Arts, and he'd done it, but the whole time he'd feared for my safety. He cares about me.

He let go of my hand and reached up to my face. His fingertips glided softly across my cheek as he wiped away the tears. He whispered my name. "Colina." Those dark eyes were full of emotions. Emotions that I was sure were mirrored in my own eyes.

Luke was not evil. He was a death dealer, and yes, there was darkness inside him, but now that same darkness was inside of me.

He took a deep breath and got up off the couch. When he looked back at me, he was more in control, more composed. "You were calling out in your sleep," he said.

And all I could think as I stared at him was, *why don't you take me in your arms again.* I felt suddenly cold without those arms around me.

"Colina, did your brother's spirit come to you?" he asked.

"No," I answered.

"But I heard you calling out his name."

"It was just a nightmare about what happened to my family." The same nightmare I'd had so often since my family was killed. Now I felt the anger and frustration I saw in Luke swirling inside me. My family's murderers need—no, Macaven needs to pay for what he's done. No matter the price.

Luke looked grim. "There's been no contact with your family?"

"None," I whispered.

Luke's fist came down hard on the coffee table. "It doesn't make sense!"

"Maybe they went to the light."

"Maybe." He didn't sound convinced. He turned and watched the fire. "But their deaths were so sudden and unexpected." He turned back to me. "The way they died, so violently, I was so sure they'd come to you."

Images rushed into my mind again, those last terrible moments of my family's lives forever embedded in my mind. I tried to force the horrific memories away.

We watched the fire for a while in silence.

"There's something we can try. It's not something I would normally even think about doing because it is dangerous, but we're running out of options."

"More dangerous than the rituals?" I whispered.

"Have you ever used a Ouija board?"

At his question, I sucked in a breath. I was brought up to fear things like Ouija boards. "My parents never allowed one in the house."

"My kind doesn't need the boards to communicate with those on the other side. You're almost one of us—since you've gone through the first two rituals—you can contact any spirit that wants to communicate with you. But since they aren't coming to you, there's a way we can persuade them to communicate."

"Force them like you force banshees?" The notion of binding my family like that made me ill.

His voice was low. "This is different. The banshee is a spirit that willingly comes to you. Once you're in contact with a spirit, you can bind it to you—make them do your bidding. You create the banshee. If your family is out there and their spirits are unsettled, we can use the board and do a spell that will call them to you. Forcing a spirit forward isn't something we normally do. When spirits come to you this way, they can get angry and upset."

Upset, angry spirits. Not something I wanted to deal with. Ever.

"Spirits do have power. They can hurt you physically," Luke said.

I touched the marks on my arm. They were scabbed over now. "Like the scratches I got from the banshee." I couldn't imagine that my family would ever hurt me, even if they were in spirit form and angry that I had called them forth.

"If they're angry enough, they can touch the living and manipulate objects."

I jumped to my feet. "You mean move things?"

He nodded his head. "Knock things over, throw things."

I didn't like the sound of that. I didn't like the idea of seeing my parents as spirits. I longed to see them again, but not as wisps of their former selves, not knowing they were tortured by the horror they'd been through. Were they still reliving those awful moments over and over? Would their faces be full of that pain when I looked into their ghostly eyes? I turned away and walked toward the fire. I stood there watching the flames for a long while before asking, "We do this spell, and my parents will come?"

Luke came to my side. "If they're around, yes."

"And then what?"

"Then we try to get any information we can that will help us find Darla." He put his hand on my shoulder.

I turned and looked at him. "Okay, let's do it."

He looked surprised at my answer.

I shrugged. "We don't have a choice, right? Without their help, we've no idea where to start looking for your sister." I didn't want him to go through the same nightmare I had. I didn't want him to lose those he loved. If it was in my power to spare him that torture, I would.

He looked around the room. "Pagan has a Ouija board somewhere. We can use it—the board is a catalyst to the other side on its own. The spell just amps it up and focuses it and sort of pings the other side. Puts out a call, beckoning whatever spirit you're searching for to come to you. If they're around, they'll make an appearance. They've no choice." He looked more than uneasy. "Unfortunately, if something else is out there, it might also try to break through. This could get a bit tricky. We have to be on our guard and keep anything unwanted from answering the call we put out."

I didn't like the whole idea of "something else" breaking through. I imagined dark things, like what I'd felt when my control had been shoved aside during the possession. "How many times have you done this?" I hoped to hear "a zillion."

"A few."

*Terrific.* I sighed out loud and stared at the wall in silence for a long moment. Then I looked back at him and asked, "What do we need for the spell?"

"Some candles and a medallion."

"Like the medallion the traveler used to heal you?"

"Yes. There are different kinds of focus items. You can fill them with spells, give them power, and then release that power when you need to."

We were about to mess about with Ouija board. Communicating with spirits was considered unnatural...something evil. But, then again, spirits would communicate with me now whether I wanted them to or not. Did it really matter how I talked to them?

# CHAPTER
# NINETEEN

The books had been cleared from the dining room table and in the center sat the Ouija board. Four white candles surrounded it, and outside the candles lay a black bag and two small bowls—one black, the other red.

Luke had a large metal amulet hanging from a thick, silver chain around his neck. The amulet had a black phoenix etched into its surface.

We sat across the table from each other.

I looked at the board with trepidation. It was only another way of communicating with the spirits, right? I kept telling myself that and tried to believe it, but there was something ominous about the board. It felt wrong. Evil.

The wooden board had a polished surface that made it shine. Letters and words gleamed against the grain in sharp contrast.

I leaned in to get a better look.

In the top left corner was the word yes. In the top right corner was the word no. Below these two words were all the letters from the alphabet arranged in two rows, and each row was arched in a way that created a half circle. Beneath the letters were the numbers one through nine. There was no number ten, but there was a zero to the right of the number nine. And below the numbers was the word goodbye.

A pointer sat on top of the board—a heart shaped piece of plastic mounted on three felt tipped legs. At the tip of the pointer was a transparent circle that showed the selected letter or number beneath.

"We both place our fingers on the planchette," Luke said.

"The what?"

Luke pointed at the white plastic pointer. "It's called a planchette. We ask questions, and the spirits answer by moving the planchette back and forth around the board."

*Sounds easy enough.*

"But before we begin, I have to do a few things." He rose and took out a green bundle of herbs about four inches long from the black bag on the table. He saw me watching him. "Rosemary." He took out the lighter and lit one edge of the bundle, letting it burn for a few minutes, before blowing out the flames. With the fire gone, the bundle emitted a thick, smoke. "Rosemary cleanses the atmosphere."

I watched him make his way across the room. He held the rosemary up high and waved it as he walked back and forth. When he was done, he came back to the table and dropped the smoking bundle back into the black bowl.

He then took the lighter again and lit each of the candles. Reaching into the bag, he pulled out a bottle full of red liquid and slowly poured the contents into the red bowl. Next, he pulled out two raven feathers and placed them on either side of the board. He placed two fingers from his left hand into the red bowl, closed his eyes, and wrapped his right hand around the medallion.

Luke said a few words in Latin, slowly withdrew his fingers from the bowl, and then spread them across the board, smearing reddish black slime. When he finished, he sat and wiped his fingers across his arm.

He held out his hands across the table. "Now, we say a protection prayer."

I stretched out my arms and put my hands in his. Whatever was about to happen, I was glad Luke was by my side.

There was a grim expression on his face as he looked down at the board and then back up to me. "You should never use the board alone. It's best if you use it with two people."

I gave him a nod and then silently vowed to myself; *I'm never going to use this thing again if I can help it.*

Luke tightened his fingers around mine and closed his eyes. "Let the flames of the candles protect us. Let the candles bathe the four corners of this room in light and force out negative energy. I invite spirits to come through who are helpful. Let those helpful spirits harm none." He opened his eyes and let go of my hands. "I need you to take a moment and think about your family."

I closed my eyes and thought of my mother, my father, and my brother. I tried to recall happier times. I held a picture of them in my mind for a few seconds before opening my eyes.

Luke gestured to the planchette. "We both put our fingertips on the pointer."

The thought of touching the board sent panic racing through me.

"Colina, it's alright. No matter what happens, I'm here."

I took a deep breath and placed my fingers carefully.

"Make sure your touch is light."

I nodded. "What do we do now?"

Before I could finish my sentence, the pointer started to move across the board.

I cried out in surprise and snatched my fingers to my chest. The pointer stopped moving.

"It's okay, it's supposed to do that. Put your fingers back. Trust me."

I looked at Luke and forced my fingers back onto the pointer.

As soon as I made contact, it began to move again. It circled around the board in the shape of a figure eight.

"We'll start out asking yes or no questions," Luke advised.

"Terrific," I mumbled under my breath.

"Do you want to start?"

I shook my head.

"Think of your family again."

As I did, I felt a chill settling in the room. *Something's here with us.*

Luke closed his eyes and spoke in a loud voice, "Spirit, are you here?"

The pointer slowly moved until the word yes could be seen through the transparent plastic circle.

Luke opened his eyes and looked down at the pointer. "Thank you, spirit." He looked at me. "The spirits like to lie. And they aren't the best spellers."

I couldn't help myself I laughed.

He shrugged and gave me a half grin, then looked back at the board. "Spirit, do you have a message for us?"

The pointer moved slowly to yes again.

"What would you like to tell us?" Luke asked.

The pointer stopped moving.

"Spirit, are you still here?" Luke demanded.

Nothing. The pointer didn't budge.

The flames on the candles began to flicker. At the same time a prickling feeling crawled down the back of my neck.

Luke looked around the room and took his hands off the pointer.

I lifted my fingers. As I did, the planchette started moving on its own. It slowly weaved into a figure eight again.

I looked at the board in shock and whispered, "Is that normal?"

Luke frowned. "No."

The pointer started to move faster. And faster still. It spun around the board in figure eights.

There was a whooshing sound and the flames on the candles suddenly rose. The room filled with noise. It sounded like someone was humming. The humming grew louder. Another whoosh. The candle flames went even higher.

I was glued to my chair, too afraid to move. I kept looking back and forth from the racing pointer to the candles. "Is this the 'something else' you were worried about?" I shouted to be heard over the racket.

Luke's right hand was wrapped around the medallion and his lips were moving, but I couldn't make out what he was saying.

There was a loud thump from underneath the table. I scooted back in my chair. The thump came again, and this time the board rose off the surface of the table a few inches.

I looked over at the mantle where the travelers' protection pouch lay. I had taken it off earlier, when we'd returned from the hospital, so I would be open to the spirits. I sorely wished I had it on now.

"Should I be worried?" I yelled.

Luke didn't answer. His full focus was on the board as his lips moved faster.

A book flew off the bookshelf. And then another. There was a loud knock on the wall, and the whole table jumped. All four legs actually came off the ground. I shot out of my chair and stood, not sure what I should do or where I should run.

Luke stood, raised his hands, and shouted, "Be gone!"

The Ouija board flew off the table and slammed into the nearby wall. As it hit the floor, the room went silent. There was another loud whoosh.

Then the candles went out.

We stood in the dark. The only sounds were my heavy breathing and my heart pounding in my chest, which sounded like a jackhammer in my ears.

I heard a clicking sound.

Luke's lighter flared to life in his hand. He went over to the candles and relit each one.

I said, "Let's not do that again."

He walked across the room and picked up the board and the planchette and put them both back on the table.

He glanced at me. "Are you ready?"

I took a step back and looked at him in shock. "You want to do that again? Seriously?"

"I'm not sure what came through, but whatever spirit that was, it was dark and angry. It was not your family." His face was void of expression. "Which means we have to try again."

That was the last thing I wanted to do. A better plan was to take the board and throw it directly into the fire.

Luke sat in the chair, quietly watching me.

Some evil spirit had just jumped into the room and thrown things around. What if Luke hadn't been able to force it back? And now he wanted to try again? I stood there looking at him. I didn't want to touch the board, but we had no leads, no idea where to look for Darla. This might be our one chance at finding the answers we needed.

I took a deep breath, walked back to the table, and sat down. "I'm ready."

Luke got up from the table and relit the rosemary. He walked around the room, waving it back and forth again. When

CATRINA BURGESS

he was done, he put the rosemary bundle into the black bowl. He sat back down and held out his hands.

I put my hands in his, and once again he said the opening prayer. Then he lifted his fingers and put them on the planchette. "Think of your family."

I closed my eyes and brought back the memories of my family. When I opened my eyes, I slowly forced my trembling fingers back onto the pointer. I took a deep breath and nodded.

Luke asked the room, "Spirit, are you there?"

The pointer moved slowly to YES.

"Spirit, do you have a message for us?"

The candles flames flickered.

*Here we go again.* I braced myself. Any minute the planchette would start doing wild figure eights and crazy humming would fill the room.

The pointer moved around the board and then stopped. As it did, I noticed a light in the corner of the room. A shimmering light, fading in and out. Shadows from the candles?

"Colina." The word was but a whisper on the wind.

I sucked in a breath in shock. My voice cracked with emotion. "Mama?" I was up out of my seat and halfway across the room.

It was my mother. The outline of her body floated in the corner; I could see through her to the bookshelf on the wall.

"Mama," I whispered.

My mother's gaze focused on me. "Colina, you're alive." Her head turned from left to right. "Your father...? Your brother...?"

A tear slid down my face. I forced myself to say the words aloud, "Dead. Mama, they're both dead."

She let out a loud, anguished cry. "No. He took them. Where are they? Why can't I see them?"

"Mama, we need your help. Do you know who hurt you? Do you know how to find them?" I wanted to find the strangers

170

who hurt my family so badly. I wanted them to pay for what they'd taken away from me. I looked at Luke. "They have Luke's sister. He needs to find her before they hurt her, like they hurt you."

"He took them from me. He took them from me," my mother sobbed in anguish.

"Mama, can you help us?" I begged.

My mother's image flickered in and out. Her sobs grew louder, and the windows shook.

Luke was beside me. He grabbed my arm. "She can't help us. She's too far gone in her grief. It's all she can focus on. She can't help us find Darla."

"But if I talk to her..."

He shook his head. "Her spirit might stay like this forever, focused on her loss. She may eventually move past it, but how long will that take? Years? Centuries?"

*Centuries. My mother's spirit, forced to roam the ether sea for centuries?* My stomach dropped at the thought. I took a step forward, my arms outstretched. She had to move on. I couldn't handle the thought of my mother stuck forever in the abyss of in between.

"Mama, you've got to go to the light. Mama, do you see a light?"

A crack of lightning lit up the dark sky outside. A few seconds behind it came a loud roar of thunder.

My mother looked at me, her eyes filled with sadness. "Colina..."

"Yes, Mama. I can hear you." Tears streamed down my face.

Panic filled my mother's face. "Colina!"

"Mama, I'm here. I'm right here."

My mother turned away from me, and her image flickered. When she turned back, fear blazed from her eyes. "Baby girl, listen to me, they're coming for you. They're right outside."

Another crack of lightning lit the room, and my mother's image started to disappear, but her voice rang out, "Run, baby girl. Do you hear me? Run!"

"Mama!" My hands reached for where her spirit had vanished but only caught empty air.

Luke grabbed me. "We have to go."

I didn't care about anything but seeing my mother again. "Mama," I sobbed.

"We have to get out of here!" Luke's arms circled my waist, and he dragged me from the living room. He pulled me into Pagan's bedroom and slammed the door.

I was crying. My whole body shook as tears streamed down my face.

Luke opened the bedroom window, then picked me up and carried me out and over the windowsill. He lowered me gently to the ground beside him.

I was frozen, unable to move or think. Images of my mother flashed through my mind—the gun aimed at her head, the bullet tearing into her skull, her blood bursting against the wall behind her. Those lifeless eyes staring into me as she fell to the ground.

"Mama," I whispered.

The slap came hard and fast across my cheek.

My hand came up to cradle my face. I stood stunned.

Luke pulled me hard toward him. "Colina, we have to get out of here. There are men. I saw them out the window when the lightning flashed. Three, maybe four of them, advancing on the house." He let me go and looked frantically around. "We need to get out of here. Now."

The wind blew my hair around my face. Rain fell hard from the sky. The men who'd killed my family, Macaven's men, were inside Pagan's house. The last thing I wanted to do was run. I wanted to rip out their eyes. I wanted to see them bleed, and I wanted them to die.

He pointed into the dark. "I know this area. We can go across the field. Find a place to hide."

I heard crashing and loud banging from inside the house and turned back. I had no plan in mind. I was just filled with rage. Anger I could no longer control took over.

Luke grabbed me and shoved me in the opposite direction, away from the house.

The sounds from within grew louder. I struggled against him. I didn't want to run—I wanted to stay and fight.

"What are you doing?" he grunted, trying to control me.

"Those men killed my family!"

"It's suicide to go against them now. You haven't finished the rituals. You have no power."

Somewhere through the red haze pounding in my head, Luke reached me. He was right. I didn't want to die senselessly. I wasn't even sure these were the right men. Had they even had a hand in my family's murders, or were they just Macaven's lackeys? I needed to think, to plan, to make sure I made the right people pay—which meant that right now, I needed to stay alive.

I followed him, stumbling as we hurried across uneven ground.

Glass broke behind us. I turned and watched lights crisscross through the overgrown field.

Luke's voice was low but urgent. "They're coming. We have to hurry."

More lights appeared, but these were colorful, and they moved above the ground. They floated up into the sky and swirled around. Then in a flash they streaked across the night—in our direction.

Luke let go of my hand. I stopped next to him.

He shoved me forward. "Colina, run."

"I'm not leaving you."

"Run," he demanded. "Get moving!"

He had magic. I could see spirits, talk to them, but that was all I could do. I didn't have any way to protect myself, not yet. No way could I help him in a fight.

They were coming. Luke was going to stand against them, and there was nothing I could do to help.

Lightning illuminated Luke's face for a split second, and in his eyes, I saw the same fear that was present during the first ritual.

"Run." This time he pleaded. On an impulse, I reached up, touched his cheek, and then rose onto my tiptoes to kiss him. His lips were soft against mine. I forced myself to move away. He turned to face the house. His hands clenched into fists.

I couldn't help him. I turned and looked into the darkness.

I ran.

# TWENTY

I pushed past bushes and stumbled through tall grass. Even after crossing several fields, I could still hear voices shouting behind me. The rain poured, and lightning streaked across the sky. I had no idea where I was going as I made my way in the dark, and every time lightning flashed, I tried to take in as much as I could of the landscape. I climbed over a wooden fence, crossed another pasture, and kept moving forward.

Luke stayed to fight, to face men who had already overpowered him once back at the magic shop. He'd barely made it out of that fight alive. What were his chances this time?

A noise sounded close by, and I dove behind a bush and threw myself to the ground. I held my breath, waiting to be captured.

Nothing.

No sound of footsteps, no sign of flashlights. The night was now silent except for the occasional crash of thunder overhead. I didn't know how far I'd gone, but I was sure I wasn't far enough from the house to be completely safe.

I forced myself back to my feet. The rain was coming down

in sheets. Drenched, I pushed my hair from my face and wrapped my arms around myself for warmth. I was cold, scared, and worried about Luke.

Is he still alive?

An image of Luke flashed before my eyes—of his body lying lifeless on the ground. I shook my head and forced the dark thoughts away. He would survive. I refused to consider any other possibility.

More lightning raced across the sky. I pushed through a thick row of thorny bushes that scratched my face and arms, and as I ran into another pasture. The ground suddenly disappeared from under me.

I reached out, grabbing for anything, but there was only empty space. I fell a long way down, knocking my arms and legs against something hard before slamming against the surface of water. I plunged down into the cold, wet darkness and the shock of the cold forced the oxygen from my lungs. My momentum had carried me down and I no longer knew which way was up, back toward the surface. I kicked my feet, my lungs near bursting for air, but my clothes and combat boots only dragged me farther down. I struggled, finally clumsily kicking off the heavy boots and began to rise. I kicked harder, forcing my body upwards.

When I didn't think I could survive a moment longer, I broke through the water's surface. I can breathe. I sucked in oxygen—sweet oxygen—and frantically moved my arms, trying to stay afloat.

I looked up and saw lightning zigzagging across the sky.

How far had I fallen? Ten feet? Twelve feet? I kicked forward, reached out, and felt smooth stone. I slowly swam, my fingers in constant contact with the stone surface.

A perfect circle—I'd fallen into a well. My arms and legs were bruised. I'd hit them against the wall on my way down. I looked up at the sky again as I searched the smooth rock with my fingers. There were no handholds. No way to climb up and out. The water was so cold, I began to shiver. Would I die down here? No one knew where I was. I forced down my panic and tried to stay calm.

I sensed something.

An unnatural chill ran down the back of my neck. A breeze moved past me. I had the feeling that whatever hovered near me wasn't of this world.

I heard a whisper. My ears strained to make out the words, but there were none—at least, none I could decipher. More noises that didn't sound human echoed in the small space.

I spun around in the water. "Who are you?" My words were forced out between chattering teeth.

Another growl, this one louder and closer.

"What do you want?" I desperately continued treading water, trying to keep my head above the surface.

"You," echoed in the darkness, and as it rang out, something grabbed my foot and yanked me under.

*No!* the word screamed inside me. I kicked hard, forcing myself back up. I broke the surface and sucked in a mouthful of air only to be pulled under again. Whatever had me was strong. I kicked and struggled, frantic to break free from its grip. I couldn't breathe. I did a couple of hard scissor kicks, and for a moment my head bobbed above the water again. I sucked in another lungful of air before it dragged me back under.

Whatever had me was going to drown me, just like that girl in the lake. Suddenly the image of Luke standing at the edge of the lake filled my mind. His head had cocked to the side as he listened for the murdered girl. What was her name? Sarah.

As soon as I recalled her name, I heard a small voice in the corner of my mind say, *I'm here.*

I opened my eyes, and in the dark water I saw a flicker of

light. A face appeared before me—the face of a pretty girl about my age.

"I'm here." The words were louder this time. As I heard them, a light expanded and encircled me, suspended in the water. I felt warmth fill my body. With it came a surge of strength.

I kicked powerfully and suddenly I was free. My arms moved like windmills as I frantically forced myself up to the surface. I gasped and sputtered for I'm not sure how long before I heard another growl. Fear ran through my body. I knew the thing would try and drown me again.

I had nowhere to go, nowhere to run.

Then a voice shouted my name. "Colina!"

I realized the sound came not from within the well, but from above.

The voice grew louder. "Colina!"

I looked up—lightning lit up the sky around a shadow this time.

*Luke.*

I frantically shouted back, "I'm down here! I can't climb out!"

"They're coming. Hide and stay quiet, I'll come back and get you out when they leave." Luke spoke in a harsh voice, almost too soft to hear in the echoing darkness of the well. His silhouette hung above me for a long second. Then he disappeared.

"Luke," I whispered. There was nothing but silence.

I kept treading water, so cold now that I could no longer feel my face. My limbs were frozen, and I was having trouble forcing them to cooperate. But I had to keep moving. *I have to stay afloat.*

I heard a sudden commotion overhead, loud voices shouting. I was about to shout back when I realized it wasn't Luke speaking. A flashlight shone down against the wall of the well a few feet above me. I watched as the circle of light started to slide toward me, illuminating everything in its path.

*I've got to hide.*

I knew what I had to do, but oh, I didn't want to. My mind and body rebelled against the idea of forcing myself back down into the dark water. The light was only a few inches above me now. I took a deep breath and allowed myself to sink.

I kept my eyes open, searching for—what? To my surprise, I realized I wanted to see Sarah's reassuring face, but there was nothing but inky blackness before me. I held my breath. I had to stay under as long as I could, but I felt so cold I didn't know if I'd be able to move my limbs again to swim to the surface. My thoughts began to slow down. My lungs burned. I felt as if I were huddled in a cocoon or wrapped in bubble wrap. It would be so easy to just let the water in and end it all.

*Just let the water in,* a whisper suggested in the corner of my mind.

Horrified, I realized the thought hadn't come from me. Something else was talking to me, trying to lull me into doing the one thing I shouldn't do. It wanted me to die, but I refused to give in. Luke needed me. Darla needed me. I forced my legs to move, to kick and I pushed through the water with my hands, willing the surface to appear. One more stroke, another kick. I was almost there.

Finally, I broke the surface. I looked up into quiet darkness. Only thunder rumbled in the distance.

I treaded water and waited. Luke will be back soon. He will save me.

The cold was seeping into my limbs and making my thoughts sluggish. In a moment of delusional panic, I wondered if it actually had been Luke calling my name, telling me to keep quiet. Had I really seen him? Or had it been wishful thinking?

Time passed, and my whole existence narrowed to how cold I'd become. I'd never felt so frozen.

There was a loud splash, and then something brushed against the back of my head. I immediately thought of whatever had pulled me down earlier and envisioned it touching me. I cried out in panic.

But then I spied a figure standing above. "Grab the rope," Luke called down.

I turned and reached for it. Or at least, I tried to. "I c-can't climb up...t-too cold...I'm s-so c-cold," I barely managed between shakes.

"Tie it around you!" he shouted.

I knew about knots. My brother James had loved to rock climb. He'd taken me with him on a few adventures over the years. Thanks to him, I knew how to rappel down a cliff.

*I can do this.* I grabbed the rope, but I could barely feel my hands. My fingers fumbled; it took me a half dozen tries before I got the rope around my chest and made a decent knot.

"I'm ready!"

The rope jerked, and slowly I began to rise.

When I approached the mouth of the opening, Luke rasped, "You have to climb out the rest of the way."

I grabbed at the dirt and grass, pushing with my feet against the stone. Somehow, I pulled myself out of the well and collapsed.

Luke fell next to me, breathing hard. He touched my shoulder. "Are you alright?"

"I'm...c-c-cold," I said between tremors. The shivering had grown worse, far more violent now that I was out in the open air.

Luke rose to his feet and pulled me up into his arms. "There's a barn about a quarter mile from here. It's where I found the rope."

I tried to walk, but my legs wouldn't work.

Without warning, Luke swung me into his arms. "I've got you."

Warmth wrapped around me. It felt good to be in his arms again. I rested my head against his shoulders, closed my eyes, and let him carry me toward shelter.

It was dark inside the barn, so dark I couldn't see my hand in front of my face.

Luke gently lowered me to the ground. "Give me a minute." He muttered a few words, and the barn became dimly illuminated. A bluish light glowed at his fingertips.

"Handy trick, becoming a human flashlight—" My words ended in a long, harsh cough.

Luke moved around the barn. At the far corner, he came across boxes piled against the wall. He rummaged through them and held up an old lantern. "This will work."

He lifted off the glass covering and placed a fingertip inside. When he touched the wick, it burst into blue flame.

The lantern and its unnatural glow lit the entire room. "I don't have a match," Luke explained. "This won't last long." He walked toward me.

I finally saw his face and gasped. There were bruises on his cheeks, blood oozed from a gash on his chin, and a deep burn mark was seared across the right shoulder of his shirt.

Before I could ask any questions, he gestured upward. "There."

There was a loft maybe ten feet above us. I could see stacked bales of hay.

Luke walked to a wooden ladder. "I'll be right back." He quickly made his way up and out of sight.

I sat on the floor, shaking, and shivering with cold. I heard movement overhead—the sound of grunting and things being shoved around. I closed my eyes, hugged my knees, and tried to think about anything other than the terrible cold piercing through me. I imagined sitting in front of a roaring fire.

Luke was beside me again and he gave me a reassuring smile. "Do you think you can make it? I'll be right behind you."

I gave him a nod and took his hand, and he pulled me up. I moved on unsteady feet toward the ladder, grasped the wood railings, and started up, one foothold at a time. It was slow going. My body didn't want to move, and I had to force myself forward. Luke climbed the ladder behind me.

The shaking grew uncontrollable, but I kept going, climbing until I reached the top. I let go of the ladder and stumbled to the floor of the loft.

He motioned to a pile of hay spread out on the floor. "I know you're freezing. I think we should lie on the hay and huddle together for warmth. My magic can make light, but I can't make a true flame, so I can't start a fire. I'm soaked through from the rain, and you're drenched. We need to get out of these clothes."

I started to take off my sweater. My hands fumbled—my fingers were frozen and not working properly.

"Here, let me help." Luke pulled off my top and helped me wiggle out of my skirt and leggings. I stood in my bra and underwear.

Luke started to undress. He pulled off his shirt and jeans and stood in front of me in a pair of gray boxer briefs.

I lowered myself onto the hay, and he laid down next to me. "I have to get you warm." He opened his arms, and I rolled into them.

I rested against him, my head just below his chin as his

hands rubbed up and down my arms and my thighs. "Better?" he whispered in my ear, his breath tickling my neck.

"Yes," I answered enjoying the feel of his hands sliding across my skin.

He pulled me closer and wrapped his arms around me and ever so slowly that terrible chill that consumed my limbs and mind finally began to fade away as his body warmed mine. I nestled against his body and a sigh of contentment escaped my lips. It felt so good to be in his arms, to be close to him. With that thought a desire to be even closer filled me. I found myself turning over until our faces were just inches apart.

Those dark eyes were watching me, so full of concern.

"I'm okay," I said. My fingers reached up and gently touched his bruised cheek. "I thought I'd never see you again."

His fingertips slid across my lips. "Colina," he whispered my name. There was such longing in the way he said my name.

I felt it too, this undeniable longing to be next to him. A wanting, a need to feel his lips pressed against mine again, to feel those hands slide across my naked flesh. I have never felt such a longing, such desire to be with someone like this before. Whenever I was this close to him, my mind, my whole being become only focused on *him*.

We had almost lost each other tonight. He could have been killed in the battle and I could have been drowned by that monster in the well. We had been lucky once again to find ourselves alive and back in each other's arms. But when would this luck of ours run out?

We were here now together. Safe for the moment with no idea what tomorrow would bring. All I could think of was that I wanted to be with him.

I pressed my lips gently against his.

We kissed and kissed again, each kiss became deeper and more demanding.

Another kiss and then another still, and his lips began to slide down my naked shoulder. Those strong fingers moved along my arm and across the curve of my breast. Those delicious lips of his peppered kisses on the swell of my breast just above my bra as his fingertips glided, teased across the wet fabric, sliding back and forth, the friction from his fingers making my nipple go rock hard and my body arch with bliss.

"Colina," he whispered my name again. "I want to bring you pleasure," he said as his hands moved across my naked flesh.

This storm of emotion was carrying me away. "Oh yes," I cried out.

Goddess, surrender never felt so sweet as he coaxed one bosom free and then the other until his hands cupped my naked breasts.

That clever tongue took full advantage. Pink-tipped nipples hardened as he tasted and teased. He sucked gently and then harder and all coherent thoughts left my head.

Each breath now raced with his very touch. My body arched as though it suddenly had a will of its own. My heart began to pound wildly in my chest and my legs began to tremble.

His right hand moved roughly down the length of me. He raised himself up and then moved me below him and those clever fingers began to slide down my inner thigh and then moved upwards in slow torturous circles eventually finding the soft, sensitive skin at the edge of my panties.

The breath caught in my throat as he suddenly pushed them aside and a finger slid inside me. I gasped, he pushed in farther, deeper. His mouth closed on mine. I gasped again but it was lost within our kiss. Those fingers delved deeper, and my body bucked, once, twice and he began to match his movements with mine. His finger moved in and out, harder, faster, pushing back and forth as I squirmed and gyrated in slow, insistent movements beneath him. First one then two fingers pressed deep inside my pussy.

Pleasure ripped through me. I thrashed and moaned. I was no longer in control of my body. I was like a possessed woman, writhing beneath him. But he took no mercy. I came and came again. Each cry of pleasure captured within his kiss.

When his lips finally lifted from mine, and those soft lips moved down to capture a harden nipple once again, I whispered, my voice ragged, "I need you inside me."

Those lips crashed down on mine again. The kiss between us so hard and savage I tasted blood when he pulled away.

His face was inches from mine. "Tell me again what you want."

I begged him, "I need you to fuck me."

Suddenly he was over me and as our eyes locked. Ever so slowly my panties were pushed aside and he guided himself inch by incredible inch inside me.

The sensation of his hard shaft, sliding against the wetness of my flesh, made the breath catch in the back of my throat.

He watched me, his eyes never leaving my face as his movements were slow at first, then harder. Slow again and then harder he plunged into me. He drove in again and again, until he pulled himself back, leaning all his weight onto one arm. A finger slid into the deeper heat within me. Fingers searched, explored, until they hit upon a spot that made me gasp out loud.

It was too much. I felt another orgasm building inside me. My breath was now quick and shallow. The movement of his hand, of his hard shaft thrusting into me, forced my body into a frenzy. I was tortured over and over until finally I found release in a sudden violent shudder.

My body rocked and I cried out his name.

As his name left my lips, he convulsed against me, and, for a moment, his body became dead weight against mine. We lay against each other breathing hard, covered in sweat. He slowly rolled off me and lay next to me.

I looked up at the ceiling of the barn and raised a hand to my chest. I could feel my heart still pounding hard. I was a great fan of sex, but what had just happened between us was something different than I'd ever felt before.

Strong arms pulled me back into an embrace. I felt the warmth of his body as he pulled me close. There was an emotional void inside me since my family's death, a loneliness that had permeated every moment of my life since they were taken from me. But now I realized this man whose arms I was lying in had somehow filled that vast emptiness inside my shattered heart.

THE BLUE LIGHT from the lantern had long ago burned out. We lay together in the dark holding each other tight. My head resting on his chest. Listening to his heartbeat was so incredibly soothing. I just laid there enjoying the moment, wanting so desperately to forget everything else that was going on around us. I imagined what it would have been like if we had met at a different time and a different place.

What if we meet not as healer and death dealer, but just as two people that bumped into each other one day on the street. I allowed myself to daydream this alternative reality where we came together, fell in love, and had a normal life. One day married, one day having children of our own. One day living in that converted barn that Luke's cousin Pagan built for us. For a moment I just allowed myself to drift and float around in this impossible glorious daydream. But that's all I allowed myself, one moment of silly what ifs.

If my family was still alive there was no way in any circumstance Luke being a death dealer would have been okay with my family or my clan. A relationship between a healer and death dealer would have been forbidden. Their children despised and feared. My hand grazed across my stomach. We had come together last night, made love for the first time, but I was not worried about any accidently pregnancies. The special tincture I took to prevent such things wouldn't be wearing off for another couple weeks.

I was no longer a healer. I was something else entirely different now, morphing into possibly something monstrous, on this road to completing the last ritual. Once I went through with the third ritual and gained the dark magic, I would be one of the dark mages, a death dealer, a person feared by everyone. This was my reality and the weight of all of it settled back onto my shoulders.

Those men had come after us. It was the second time they found us. They were determined to do what? Capture us? Kill us? When Luke faced them last night, I was so certain they would kill him. But he had somehow fought them and survived.

"Luke, how did you get away?" I asked.

He was silent for a long moment and then he said, "I wouldn't have survived if not for your mother."

"My mother?" I gasped in disbelief.

"Her spirit came to me, and she helped me. When they had me overpowered your mother's voice suddenly shouted out your name and then a brilliant blast of white light exploded around me, a light so strong it pushed back the banshees attacking me. It was a distraction that allowed me to slip away." His arms tightened around me. "Without her help, I'd never have escaped. Your mother must have had extremely powerful magic when she was living."

"She is...she was one of the strongest healers my clan had

ever seen," I whispered. My mother's spirit was still out there, reeling in despair over the deaths of my father and my brother. When I finally found the men responsible for my family's death and killed them, would that bring her the peace she needed to cross over to the other side?

His hands began stroking my hair. "When I was looking for you, there was something that drew me to that well, but it wasn't your mother's spirit..."

"Sarah," I whispered into the dark. "The girl murdered at the lake, she was in the well with me. But there was something else..." I shuddered at the memory. "Something down there with me. It tried to drown me. Sarah saved me."

He pulled me closer. "You're safe now."

He didn't seem surprised by what I said. Was it normal to have fucked up evil spirit things inside wells? This new world I was now a part of was terrifying. "Where do we go now?" I whispered into the darkness. Macaven's men were out there. We couldn't go back to Pagan's house.

"We'll find somewhere safe to stay," he said.

"And your sister?" Darla had been taken three days ago, and the dark moon was only two days away. We were running out of time. If they were saving her for a sacrifice, we had to act soon.

Luke sighed. "I haven't given up hope." We lay there in silence for a long while and then he softly said, "Close your eyes. See if you can get some sleep. It'll be light soon."

What else could we do but wait for dawn? Hopefully, some brilliant idea that would help us locate Darla. I closed my eyes and focused on the warmth of Luke's body pressed against mine.

# TWENTY-ONE

A whisper disturbed the small peace that sleep had granted me—a whisper that washed into my dreams and took them over.

"There is something you need to see." Unconsciously I recognized the spirit's voice—Sarah. She saved my life in the well and earned my trust. I relaxed, following where she led, and found myself in a moonlit forest.

A loud crack sent me sprawling to the ground. Not a gunshot. A tree branch snapping? Another crack, this time closer. I pushed myself out of the dirt and ran. Ignoring the branches tearing at my face and hair, I kept running. My chest burned, my heart pounded in my ears, but I pushed on.

Just when I thought I couldn't go a moment longer, the dark waves of the lake glittered in the moonlight. I'd made it. There were cabins nearby—cabins with people in them who might help me.

Finding help was my only thought. I started to run faster but then tripped and fell. I scrambled up, but it was too late, people now surrounded me on all sides.

How many were there? A dozen? How had they found me?

A flashlight switched on and pointed straight in my face. I raised a hand to shield my eyes, and rough hands grabbed me. Before I could protest, a body pinned me to the ground. I opened my mouth to scream, but they stuffed something into it.

The light turned away, and someone crouched down next to me. A face appeared inches from mine. A small, dark man with cruel eyes came close, his foul breath washing over me.

I tried to scoot away, but I couldn't move. The heavy weight on top of me made it hard to breathe.

The small man whispered, "Now, now, no screaming. We wouldn't want to wake anyone. They might ruin all our fun." He stroked my cheek and I recoiled as far as I could. "Don't worry. It will all be over soon. No use fighting and making it harder on yourself."

The man stood up and turned toward whoever was holding the flashlight. As he turned, I saw the silhouette of a long, thick rope. He gestured with the rope toward the dark lake. "Let's get her ready."

When he turned back, the light bathed him full in the face. Insanity blazed from his eyes. Terror filled me, and I began fighting desperately to escape.

He jerked me to my feet, forcing my arms behind my back and binding my hands together. The rope dug into my flesh.

I struggled, and as I did, someone hit me on the side of the head. Dizzy, I slumped forward, half conscious. I was barely aware when they tied my legs together. A slap in the face brought me back, and I blinked to see the water's edge nearing.

They dragged me closer. From behind me, a man said, "It's your lucky day. Not everyone gets the chance to be tested."

They pulled me upright by the rope and one man held me by my feet, the other by my shoulders. They swung me back and forth and then flung me through the air. The moment before I slammed into the water, someone from the shoreline yelled, "Welcome to judgment day."

I sank. I struggled to get free, but the rope bound me too tightly and my clothes weighed me down. I felt myself sinking farther into the cold, dark water. The desire to scream, to open my mouth and shout, was strong, but I held my breath. I kicked desperately, chafed my wrists until they burned trying to escape the thick rope. I began to panic. There was no one to save me. No one to come to my rescue.

I was going to die.

I couldn't hold my breath any longer. I opened my mouth and choked on the black water as it poured down my throat. I was drowning. I frantically looked out into the murky darkness. Nothing but blackness stared back at me.

*I'm dying!* I tried to scream, but there was only silence.

I came back to myself. I gasped, my mind racing, and looked around. I was in a dark place. In a void. There was movement in front of me and then sound.

"I can help you find her." A voice filtered through the dark.

"Sarah?" I asked. *Wait, I know where I am...* I was in that place—that dark corner of oblivion I'd inhabited when Wanda had taken over my body.

Sarah voice was suddenly full of pain and torment. "They killed me. This is what they did to me."

It was Sarah's death I had just witnessed in my vision, my dream. She'd been chased, captured, tied up, and then thrown into the lake by a group of madmen. They drowned her.

Her voice whispered, "But before they hunted me down, they took me somewhere. Held me prisoner. She is there...his sister...I'll show you where to find her."

Images flashed through my mind.

I was Sarah again.

I stood in front of a big house. No, not a house, a hotel. I could just make out water sparkling in the moonlight a long way below. We weren't far from the lake; we were on the mountain above it. My hands were bound behind my back, and I'd been forced to my knees in the gravel. Hands grabbed me and dragged me up the driveway. I couldn't scream past the gag in my mouth.

I looked around for help in desperation. Lights blazed from within the hotel. Loud noises came from the open front door. Around it, a group of people mingled, dressed in long, dark cloaks. The people turned in unison, quieting as they watched the men drag me.

No one stepped forward to help.

No one protested.

They just stood there, watching in silence.

The crowd parted as I was tossed onto the front steps. They pulled me to my feet, shoved me through the front door, and then to a doorway that led down into darkness. I tottered on the top step before someone pushed me, and down I went. I tumbled down the stairs and bounced off the stone wall, wrenching my shoulder. I didn't stop until, finally, with a loud thud, I hit hard against the ground below.

I lay there, stunned. The pain from my shoulder shot through me. I heard the sound of heavy steps on stone as my captors followed me down, laughing harshly. I moaned and struggled to rise, but before I could make it to my feet, rough hands pulled me up and dragged me down another hallway. They shoved me through a set of large wooden doors that slammed loudly behind me.

The room was dark. I slumped to the ground, trying to catch my breath through the white-hot pain in my shoulder. I took one deep breath before I sensed another presence. My eyes grew accustomed to the darkness, and I made out forms huddled nearby.

"This is where they took me, held me prisoner before they let me loose and hunted me like an animal," Sarah voice whispered in the darkness. "This is where his sister lays and others they hold captive. Bound and gagged on the dirt floor like I was. This is where she will stay until they decide to hunt her."

With a rush of color and sound, I felt my perspective changing again. I was no longer in the basement, but back underwater, trapped in the dark liquid of the well, drowning all over again.

"They killed me. They will kill her. You must hurry..." Sarah's voice wailed.

The cold surrounded me, my lungs seized, and my body sank farther down.

There was a rush of light and a pain so strong it made me gasp. Air rushed into my lungs as strong arms pulled me from the water—no, from my dream.

Soft light streamed in through the weathered boards of the old barn.

Luke leaned over me, his face hovering just above mine.

"Colina." He caressed my face.

"Wha—?" My throat burned. I tried again. "What happened?"

"You were choking. I tried to wake you, but I couldn't. You were struggling like you couldn't breathe."

*I was drowning.*

I sat up.

"Take it slow." He wrapped an arm around me.

"It was Sarah. She came to me. She showed me what happened to her. I was her...I became her..." My words came out stilted, "I died."

"You relived her death?"

"I did. Men chased her down and threw her in the lake."

His hand reached for mine. "Did you see the men? Did you

see or hear anything that would help us identify them? Help us track them down?"

"Luke, I saw everything. Macaven, he killed Sarah. She showed me where they took her. I know where he is holding your sister."

# TWENTY-TWO

I must have fallen asleep again. When I woke this time, I was all alone. I pushed off the hay covering my body. I shivered hard in the chilly morning air dressed only in my underwear. My clothes lay in a pile on the loft floor a few feet away. They were still wet and cold, and I couldn't bring myself to put them back on. I carefully made my way down the ladder and stood in the middle of the barn, dressed only in my underwear and unsure of what to do next.

I rubbed my hands up and down my arms for warmth. Where the hell was I? I didn't know the area—the last thing I wanted to do was start wandering around in the light of day half dressed.

The barn doors gave a loud creak as they swung open. I spun around, not sure what I was about to face, and found Luke standing in the entrance. His arms were full—he was now wearing an oversize blue and black flannel shirt and a pair of faded jeans.

He gave me a wide smile "I have supplies." He walked over and laid his bounty on the floor in front of me. "I found some clothes." He rifled through a couple of plastic bags, pulled out a black T-shirt, and handed it to me.

I pulled the shirt over my head—it came all the way down almost to my knees.

Luke handed me a blue flannel shirt. I put the flannel on over the T-shirt. It felt so good to be warm again.

"How...?"

"I broke into a house not far from here. I took what I needed. Desperate times call for desperate measures, right?" He handed me an orange.

I was starving. I quickly peeled the orange and shoved a piece in my mouth. It was sweet and delicious. I ate half and handed Luke the other half. "You stole all this?"

He nodded his head, making short work of the rest of the orange.

"Was the house empty?" I asked.

He pulled out a half loaf of French bread from one of the bags. "No, but I got in and got what I needed without anyone spotting me. It was early and the family was still sleeping." He tore a large piece of bread and handed it to me. "I'll go back later and leave money to pay for all this. It's just some clothes and a bit of food. They won't miss what I took."

I gasped. "You could've been shot."

"Bullets don't work on us." He tore a chunk of bread for himself and started eating it.

I just stood there looking at him in amazement. I've heard the rumors, but are they really true? "Death Dealers can't be shot?"

"We are bullet proof. Way back when guns were first invented, they seemed like magic on par with the Death Arts. The guilds feared that any non-magical person could take down a mage, so now all-powerful death dealers learn to block bullets early on. Death dealers all learn combat magic, to keep us safe.

I'm not quite good enough to bounce bullets back boomerang style, but I'm not in any danger from guns."

"Is this something I will learn?"

"Someday. There's no time for you to learn the spell now, so if we get shot at be sure to stay behind me." He pulled me into his arms and leaned back to study my face. "I'm sorry I left you, but you were sleeping so soundly. Are you okay? You didn't have any more bad vision or dreams?"

"No visions or dreams," I answered, looking up into his eyes.

His arms tightened around me. "I shouldn't have left without telling you. Figured I'd scout around." He stepped back slightly with a half grin, and his hand reached up and brushed the hair from my eyes. "Now eat the bread before I try to talk you into giving me your piece. I'm still starving." He leaned in and gave me a quick, gentle kiss.

I finished off the bread and watched him as he rummaged through the bags.

My upper body was nice and toasty thanks to the flannel I was wearing, but a breeze was making its way around my legs and up under the T-shirt. I looked down at my bare knees. "Any chance you found a pair of jeans for me?"

He shook his head. "I just grabbed what I could and got out of there before someone woke up."

"You didn't see the men from last night? Macaven's men?"

"No, but they might still be around."

My stomach grumbled. Half an orange and some bread barely made a dent in my current hunger level. I sorely regretted not eating more yesterday.

Luke pulled out a half gallon plastic jug of milk from the bag. He took a drink and motioned with it in my direction.

I took it from him and gulped down a couple swigs before passing it back to him.

"The question I keep coming back to, is how are these guys finding us?"

"No one followed me when I came to the magic shop. I was careful," I said.

"They have to be using magic to track us. It's the only thing that makes sense." He took a swig of milk and wiped his mouth with his sleeve. "If it's magic, it's a powerful spell. I put up protection spells around Pagan's place. They shouldn't have been able to break through it, but they did. Whatever magic they are using it's not something I've seen before."

If Pagan's house was now off limits, where did that leave us? We couldn't stay here in the barn without any supplies. "So where do we go?"

"I know this area. I spent a lot of time here as a kid. There's someone I know about two miles from here. If we can get to his house, he can help us. He's not one of us—not from the guild. He's a friend I grew up with. Not mage-born, but he can lend me some money, maybe loan me his car." Luke watched me, his expression turning serious. "You said last night that you know where Darla is. Are you sure you can recognize the place?"

I nodded. "Sarah showed me in my dream." I shuddered. I didn't want to go through anything like that again. Reenacting someone's death.

Forget reenacting, more like reliving her death.

I'd felt everything Sarah did—her terror, fear, and pain as she was first hunted and then killed. I remembered the horror I'd felt as I was drowning. No, as she was drowning. It was a terror I hoped never to feel again. I glanced at Luke. He was watching me, concern in his eyes.

"They held Sarah captive for a few days before they killed her. A big place above the lake, surrounded by trees." I tried to focus in on the images of the property from the vision. "It looked too big to be a house. More like a hotel?"

Luke moved away from me and started to pace, lost in thought.

I stood by quietly, watching him.

Seconds dragged into minutes, and then he spun around and said, "There's an old resort that was popular in the twenties. The Freemont. It's big, very old school money. It's the only place I can think of that would pass for a hotel up here." His words came out in an excited rush. "It's surrounded by ten acres of private woods. You could do anything up there without people knowing about it. The closest neighbor is miles away. It has to be the place." He looked down at my bare legs. "We need to get more supplies and get you some clothes."

"All of which your friend can help with?" A friend who wasn't mage-born, Luke had said. "Can your friend help us go after Darla, too?" I asked.

Luke frowned. "He can help with supplies, but he can't help us rescue Darla. It'll just be the two of us."

"The two of us going against how many?" I demanded.

Luke didn't answer.

"When those men attacked us back at the house, I had no way to help you." I didn't want that to happen again. I looked at the bruises still visible on his face. He barely escaped with his life. The next time we were in danger, I wanted to stay by his side. "Can you teach me some of your spells?"

He shook his head. "Spells take time." He reached out and grabbed my hand. "Even if I started teaching you some spells today, it would be months before you could properly perform them."

"Then I don't understand what I can do to help when we go after Darla."

His fingers tightened around mine. "You can finish the rituals. Then you'll be able to wield banshee magic."

Banshees. I took a step away from him. "You want me to force someone's spirit to follow my orders?"

"To do your bidding, yes." Luke's voice was low. "It's a powerful magic, controlling the dead. If you had banshee magic, it might be enough—it could be the tipping point to help us save my sister. You'll be able to control banshees after the third ritual."

The time had finally arrived—the final ritual. First, I had to die, then I'd been possessed. What would I have to do in this last one?

"Tonight, we'll do the last ritual." Luke wouldn't meet my eyes.

I didn't want to know, I really didn't, but I couldn't help myself. "What do I have to do?" I whispered.

His expression was grim when he answered. "You have to take a life."

We left the barn and walked down the country road in silence. Eventually we left the dirt road, crossed a pasture, and then went over a small hill. On the other side of the hill sat a white farmhouse. Luke pointed at it. "There. It's not far. How are you doing?"

"I'm fine. About what you said...the last ritual." I swallowed thickly. *Take a life.* I'd heard the words, but my mind refused to fully comprehend what he'd said. As a healer, my path had always been one of helping others. Luke said that his kind no longer performed human sacrifices, that those kinds of things were no longer allowed and hadn't been for centuries. "You aren't seriously saying you want me to kill someone?"

"I want you to help someone pass over to the other side. Someone who's sick and in pain," he answered.

I froze at his words. "But I'm a healer."

He stopped walking and turned towards me. "You were a healer. Now you're a death dealer."

I shook my head insistently. "I can't do it."

"You have to," he said quietly.

"I can't kill someone," I whispered.

"Colina." He moved closer, grabbing my arm.

When I tried to pull away, his fingers tightened. "It has to be done. You aren't killing them. You're helping them move from this plane to the next."

I couldn't do that—I couldn't help someone die, not when everything in me would be screaming for them to live.

He was watching me closely. "I found someone who needs our services. The family called yesterday."

"When we were at Pagan's someone called?"

"There aren't a lot of death dealers. Those who know about us can find us if they need help to end the suffering of a family member who's sick and in pain." His grip on me relaxed, and his voice turned persuasive. "They ask for help for those who no longer have hope, whose existence is filled with suffering."

I couldn't believe what I was hearing. This was something his guild did on a regular basis? "Have you ever done it? Helped someone to the other side?"

His expression was solemn. "Yes. We all have to. It's part of the ritual."

"You can't ask me to do this!" My voice was louder this time, a bit more hysterical.

"Colina, you're stronger than you know. You survived the first two rituals. This is the last one—the last bridge that has to be crossed for you to be initiated as a death dealer."

"But I can communicate with the dead already. I can talk to them now whether I want to or not."

"Yes, you can communicate with spirits, but you can't control them. Not in the way you need to in order to—"

I interrupted him. "—bind them to me?" I pulled my arm out of his grasp. "And by murdering someone I'll gain this power?"

Luke was getting angry; I could see it in his eyes. "It's not murder. Death dealers assist those who need to cross over. We do not kill to gain power, we do not murder people to steal their souls. I told you that kind of behavior has been condemned for centuries. This is the kind of bigotry is what makes it impossible for my people to walk the streets safely."

"Tell that to the men holding your sister," I shouted.

His anger boiled over this time and his voice came out in a low growl. "The mages involved in this have crossed the line. They've gone down a path of forbidden magic. Macaven will be brought to justice for what he's done."

If there was any true justice in this world, I would see them dead. "You want to see them imprisoned and punished for their crimes? They murdered people. They are still out there killing people even as we stand here."

"My people won't let Macaven get away with the things he's done. I promise you, Colina, there'll be a reckoning."

But how many more would die before this justice came about? His people weren't around. There was no one to stop this madman but the two of us.

He was watching me. "This last ritual won't be easy, but I know you can do it. You have to remember that the family requested our help. They're asking, begging for our help."

I didn't know what else to say, so I stayed silent.

Luke started walking again. What choice did I have but to follow?

We made our way down to the farmhouse, and Luke pounded on the front door. After a while it opened, and in the entrance stood a good-looking guy about our age with dark, disheveled black hair cut short and spiky, and wearing a shirt that was only partially tucked in. He was a bit taller than I was, blocky and muscular, and built like a football player. When he saw us, a huge grin spread across his face.

"I heard you were back." He swung the door open wide and waved us in.

Luke stepped inside, and I followed close behind him.

"Freddy, this is Colina."

Freddy took in my outfit and then Luke's. "You show up at my house at the break of dawn, what's up? You staying at Pagan's place? Have car problems or something?"

"We're in trouble," Luke answered.

Freddy's expression turned serious. "Okay. Fill me in, but can you do it while I make some coffee? You know how I am before I have my first cup of java." Freddy started heading out of the room, Luke on his heels, but he stopped abruptly and turned back toward me. He gestured to the couch. "Sit down. I'll turn up the heat. You look cold. Make yourself comfortable."

I looked around the room. I'd never been in a farmhouse before, but it looked like I'd imagined one might. The furniture was mostly older and worn, but clean and comfortable. Antiques were scattered around. Overstuffed cushions on the blue couch beckoned me to relax into the security and warmth of the old house. I gave in, sank into the cushions, and curled up on the couch, wondering if it was possible for me to ever feel truly safe and relaxed again.

I don't know how much time passed as I stared out the window, lost in my thoughts. It took me a minute to notice Freddy standing in front of me. He handed me a cup of coffee and put a pair of gray sweatpants next to me on the couch.

"Luke filled me in."

I wrapped my fingers around the hot cup and took a sip. The heat felt good against my cold fingers.

"Where is he?"

Freddy sat in an old armchair across from me. "He took the car. Said he had to get some things."

I felt my anger rise out of nowhere. I couldn't believe Luke left me alone with a complete stranger. Then I felt a rush of anxiety—Luke was out there alone. Are they still looking for us? What if they spot him? The alarm I felt must have shown on my face.

"Don't worry. He told me to tell you that he won't be long. Do you want something to eat? I have cereal."

I forced a smile. "Cereal sounds fantastic."

Freddy pointed at the closest doorway. "The kitchen's through there. Come in whenever you're ready."

"Thanks," I said.

Freddy got up and left the room.

I took my time finishing the coffee. When I held up the sweatpants, I found they were far too large. I stepped into them anyway and pulled the string as tight as it would go. They still weren't tight enough; on my first step forward, they started to fall down. I grabbed one side of the pants with my left hand and made my way into the kitchen.

Someone liked the color yellow. It was everywhere, from the walls to the utensils and even on a kettle on the stove.

Freddy was rummaging through the fridge.

"Cheerful kitchen."

"Thanks." He pulled out a jug of milk.

There was a box of cereal, a bowl, and a spoon already set on the table. I made my way over and sat down.

"Sounds like the two of you had quite a night." He placed the milk on the table in front of me.

"I'm just happy to have survived it."

Flopping down, he sat across from me. "So you're becoming a death dealer."

"I am." I poured cereal into the bowl, avoiding his stare.

I seemed to have Freddy's full attention.

"Something you're doing by choice?" he asked.

"It is." I chose this path—this crazy, twisted path that was now heading in directions I'd never imagined. But now that I was on it, I didn't have any choice but to follow it to the end.

He leaned back in his chair. "It's just that you don't hear of many people choosing to go into something like that. Usually you're born into it."

Freddy seemed nice enough, but I wasn't about to pour out my soul to someone I'd just met. I wondered how many questions he had. I guess I'm about to find out. He didn't look like he planned to leave the kitchen anytime soon.

I poured milk over my cereal and didn't say anything, but my silence didn't seem to deter him.

"Luke said you used to be a healer." He leaned forward, and a frown formed on his brow. "I've never heard of a healer becoming a death dealer."

"Neither have I," I answered honestly.

Whether possible or not, the rules against it were clear—my clan would either shun me completely or lock me away for even trying to gain dark magic. It occurred to me that it had to have been tried at some dim point in the past and gone badly enough that a rule became necessary. Will I turn into something more hateful to my clan than death dealers?

The thought unsettled me, but I tried to keep the alarm off my face—apparently without much success. Freddy had a questioning look in his eyes, and I explained. "If my clan finds out what I'm trying to do, they would at the very least shun me. Going home is not really an option for me anymore."

"You don't have to worry. Your secret is safe with me. Luke

and I've been friends since we could walk. Our parents have known each other for years."

My surprise must have shown on my face because he continued. "I know his kind usually stick to themselves, but our fathers grew up together. They aren't related by blood, but they were raised together like brothers." Freddy's expression changed, he looked angry. "Luke says someone has Darla. Someone's holding her hostage. I told him I want to come with you guys and help."

We could use all the help we could get, but it wasn't my call to make. "What did Luke say?"

"That I'm not mage born, but that doesn't mean I can't be useful. When he comes back, will you help me persuade him to let me come along? I can't just sit by and do nothing while Darla's in danger."

Luke made it pretty clear he didn't want Freddy coming with us. I doubted anything I said would change his mind. I shrugged my shoulders. "I'll try."

Freddy nodded and got up from the table. "Help yourself to as much cereal as you want. There's orange juice in the fridge."

"Did Luke say when he'll be back?"

"Nope." Freddy gave me a smile. "Luke's always been a bit mysterious." His eyes filled with amusement. "Don't worry. Our boy will be back soon, safe and sound."

I took a spoonful of cereal and tried not to worry, but my thoughts kept going back to the last ritual. Every time I heard Luke's say "take a life" I couldn't help but shudder. If I do this awful last ritual, what does that make me?

A murderer?

CHAPTER

# TWENTY-THREE

L uke came back at dusk. He offered no apology for leaving me behind with a stranger and forcing me to worry about him for hours. By the time he walked through the door, I was more than a bit pissed off.

Luke smiled as he walked into the room. "Hi." He was now dressed in all black— black sweatshirt, black jeans, black combat boots.

"Hey," I answered from the couch, continuing to flip through shows.

Luke had a gray duffel bag in each hand. He walked over and put them down in front of me before joining me on the couch. "How are you doing?"

"I'm great... Been here all day, watching TV and eating cereal." I turned and gave him a glare. "How's your day going?"

"I went back to Pagan's."

I gasped. "You didn't. We decided it wasn't worth the risk."

"I know we did, but there were things I need for the ritual that I can't get anywhere else. Not out here." He frowned and ran a hand through his hair. "There was no one around. They've trashed the place but didn't take anything as far as I could tell.

They just went through the place and smashed stuff everything for the fun of it."

*Just like they had done to the magic shop.* Pagan's beautifully converted barn, ruined. "Did you find everything you needed?"

"I did." He gestured toward one of the duffel bags. "Just about everything. I stopped and did some shopping." He took in my clothes. "I figured you might want to wear something that actually fits." He looked around the room. "Where's Freddy?"

"Upstairs," I answered.

"We should get going soon. There's something else I need to get, and it may take a bit of time."

"Freddy wants to come with us," I said. "He wants to help."

Luke shook his head. "It's a bad idea."

"I know he doesn't have any magic, but—"

"I'm going to help get Darla back." Freddy's voice sounded from the stairs.

Luke stood up. "You are not coming with us."

Freddy walked down the stairs and over to Luke until he stood toe to toe with him. "I've known Darla all my life. If she's in danger, I'm not just going to sit here and do nothing." He looked over at me. "If nothing else, I can hang back and be a lookout. Or be backup. If you two get caught, someone has to be around to tell your family where to find you."

Luke's expression turned grim. "If we get caught, we'll probably be dead by the time the family comes back."

Freddy crossed his arms. "All the more reason you need my help."

"The magic they have is powerful," Luke said.

A stubborn expression crossed Freddy's face. "I'm willing to take the risk."

Luke didn't say anything for a moment. "Okay. You can help when we go after my sister. But you can't come with us tonight."

Freddy started to say, "But you might need me..."

Luke held up his hand and stopped him. "What we're doing tonight isn't something you can be a part of. We've put you in enough danger by coming here. Somehow, they keep finding us, and the longer we stay, the more likely you'll end up on their radar."

The two of them stood glaring at each other.

Freddy was the first to break the silence. "You promise you won't head off to save Darla without me?"

Luke nodded. "I promise." He reached out, and Freddy took his hand. "Thanks again for letting us use the car."

"You know whatever you need is yours," Freddy answered.

Luke turned toward me. "Are you ready?"

I nodded.

Luke picked up the bags and headed out the door.

Apparently, we were leaving. Why the rush? I had no idea. Luke didn't give me a chance to question what he was up to, nor was I going to get a chance to change my clothes. Wherever we were going, we were in a hurry. I stood up and grabbed at the sweatpants before they fell straight to the ground. With a fistful of material in one hand, I headed toward the door. Halfway there I stopped and gave Freddy a half smile. "Thanks for everything."

Freddy smiled back. "Anytime. Hey, good luck."

We need all the luck we can get. I straightened my shoulders and headed out the door.

I sat in the backseat of the car, attempting to wrestle into a pair of black jeans. Dressing was easy when you could do it standing up. Dressing in a moving vehicle, on the other hand, took agility and balance. They should turn this into a competitive sport, I thought, groaning as I tried to twist my leg up high enough to get it into a pant leg.

"How are you doing back there?" Luke asked watching me in rearview mirror.

"I'm doing just great." I finally wiggled into the jeans. My outfit now matched Luke's—black sweatshirt, black jeans, and black boots. "Where are we going?"

"There's a certain plant I need for the ritual. Well, not the plant, actually, but an ointment that's derived from it. A woman who lives out here makes a lot of ointments, teas, and tinctures for the magic shop."

I slid over the front seat and settled in next to him. I knew a lot about plants. Mama used to make her own ointments and teas for the sick. I had learned how to make most of the popular ones. "What are we after?"

"Devil's berries."

I gasped. *A nightshade plant.* One of the most toxic plants found in the Eastern Hemisphere. "Poisoning someone..."

He held up his hand. "This ointment isn't for the person you're helping."

"Then who is it for?" I demanded.

"It's for you."

*What the hell did he mean it was for me?*

"Have you heard of the twilight sleep?" he asked.

I nodded. "Something they did in the 1800s. A way of 'putting you under,' except you weren't really under—you were still conscious. They used it during childbirth. If it worked and didn't kill you, it helped fight the pain and then dimmed the memory afterward." I stared at him in shock. "Using devil's berries to bring on the twilight sleep is crazy. They're too unpredictable." I searched my memory everything I had learned about the nightshade plants. "They can cause vivid hallucinations, delirium—"

He interrupted me, "—paralysis, convulsions, and even death. I know what can happen when you take the plant, Colina."

"And you still want me to use it?"

He took his eyes off the road for a moment to glance over at me. "I do. You'll have to trust me. It's part of the ritual." He turned his attention back to the road. "I went by the place earlier, but she wasn't there. There was a note on the shop's front door that said she'd be open again after dinner."

I studied Luke's profile. He said I should trust him. I did, but I was more afraid of the third ritual than I wanted to admit. Death, possession, spirits...I'd survived all these wild things. I'd gone through each trial in hopes of gaining more power, but so far, I couldn't do anything more than talk to ghosts.

And now I was heading down another dark path—murder and poison.

WE PULLED up to a cottage set back in the woods. The whole place was painted purple. There were twinkly white lights—the kind people usually put up for Christmas—wrapped around the porch, blinking on and off. A pink neon sign flashed open from one of the windows. Over the front door hung a wooden sign with a blue swallow painted on the front.

"I think I'll wait in the car, if that's alright." The blue swallow told me that the healer who owned this place was one of my kind. I didn't know if I could stomach coming face to face with a healer, not when I was just hours away from committing the last ritual and sealing my treason.

Luke didn't look surprised by my request. "I won't be long."

*Murderer.* The word whispered in the corners of my mind. I would be taking a life. The antithesis of everything my family had taught me. But I have no choice. I wondered if I would start believing that if I repeated it enough.

"Murderer." This time the word came on the wind. A breeze moved across my hands. I looked around, waiting for a face to pop out or a voice to speak up.

There was nothing but silence.

Deep down, I doubted I could go through with the last ritual. If I refuse to do it, if I turn my back and walk away... what will the consequences be? Luke would be left alone against a slew of men. The odds wouldn't matter—I knew he'd take any risk, pay any price to see Darla returned unharmed.

When Luke finally came out of the store, he had a small, brown paper bag in his hands. He slid into the driver's seat, put the bag between us, and started the car.

I looked down at the bag, afraid to touch it. "You got what you needed?"

He nodded.

"So where to now?" I looked out the window and wished as hard as I could that his answer would be something trivial. Hey, want to see a movie, want to run away and forget all this madness? A part of me wished we were back in that haystack in the barn, huddled together, making love. Would we ever have a chance of being together again, of finding happiness in each other's arms?

Each ritual held a possibility of something going wrong. And after each one, more darkness filled me. Even as we sat here, killers were looking for us.

Instead of hearing my thoughts and coming up with something not related to dark magics, he answered, "The hospital."

My heart sank. The hospital. A place full of sick and dying people. I should have realized earlier that the errand to the hospital had to do with the person I was going to kill.

*It's not killing, Colina. It's mercy...* I remembered the people I saw as I walked down the hospital hallways—patients lying in beds, hooked up to machines. Weak, sick, and full of pain, but striving to survive, desperate to stay alive. It's how I always viewed illness as a healer. The fight against death. Death was the enemy of my kind.

A single tear ran down my cheek, the start of a breakdown I struggled to control. I turned my head before Luke could see me crying. I can't do it. I can't take a life. No matter how much I tried to rationalize what needed to be done, deep down I was still a healer. I wanted to keep people alive. I didn't want to be the one ending their lives.

We drove on for a long while until finally the car came to a stop, and Luke glanced at me. "We're here."

My heart thumped hard in my chest. "But it's not even close to midnight."

"This ritual doesn't have to be done during the witching hour. We're not worried about making the veil between the living and dead as thin as possible so you can have an easier time contacting spirits." His hand came down and rested on the bag. "This time we have the ointment, and you're closer to the spirit world now."

"I don't know if I can do this," I whispered. My hands trembled as I wiped away the tears.

Luke reached out and grasped my fingers in his. "What you do tonight has to be done of your own free will."

"And if I decide not to go through with it? If I've changed my mind?"

His fingers tightened. "I won't lie and say I don't need your help. I do. But if you've changed your mind, Colina, you can walk away. I'll find another way to save Darla without you."

He looked so earnest, I almost believed him. Almost. I could see a muscle in his cheek twitch ever so slightly and feel the tension radiating off him. If I left him on his own, his chances of surviving—and of Darla surviving—was slim.

I took a deep breath and let it out slowly. "I'll try."

He wiped a tear from my cheek. "If at any time you want to stop, we will. I can take over. I can finish what needs to be done."

Even if I didn't do it, Luke would. No matter what, this person's life would soon be over.

Luke reached into his pocket and handed me the traveler's pouch. I tied it around my neck.

*Murderer.* There was the word again, blazing across my mind. I slowly opened the door and got out of the car.

Luke followed, pulling two duffel bags out behind him. "Ready?" he asked, swinging the wide straps of both bags over his shoulders.

I nodded.

We went into the hospital, and like before, a myriad of sensations rushed in on me. They knocked the breath right out of me. Static electricity slammed against me, frantic whispers buzzed around my head, and a cold breeze crawled across my neck.

Remember to breathe, Luke had told me the first time I came here. I forced the claustrophobic feeling away and concentrated on controlling my breathing. I tried to focus on the living—the people mingling around the hallway in front of us. I desperately tried to ignore the dark shadows that kept creeping into the edge of my vision.

We headed down the hospital hallways, but this time people didn't ignore us—they stared openly. I could hear people whispering as we passed by, and out of the corner of my eye I saw people pointing in our direction.

"Do we have death dealer tattooed on our foreheads? How do they know who we are and why we're here?" I whispered.

"Word spreads quickly in places like this," Luke said quietly as he picked up the pace. "It's better if we don't engage anyone. If we keep to ourselves, no one will bother us."

I squared my shoulders and followed him.

We took the same path we'd taken the day before. As we came through a pair of double doors, a fifty something brunette walked out of a room close by. She was dressed like a visitor, not a doctor or nurse. She saw us and gasped out loud, her hand going to her chest.

"Death dealers." She said the words as if she were cursing. Her face twisted into a look of deep hatred. "You're not wanted here."

Luke pointed down the hallway, where a small group of people were gathered outside a room. "They called and asked for our help."

"What you do is sacrilegious." She stepped into our path.

*Is she going to physically try and stop us?*

Luke grabbed my hand. "We mean you no harm, but we will pass." His voice was low and threatening.

The woman's eyes widened, and after a moment, she stepped aside. As we went by, a string of curse words flew from her mouth.

*Death dealer.* I was almost one of them now, despised and feared by many. Someone in the family must have talked. These people knew what we were going to do, the hate and fear that followed the death dealers everywhere they went had bloomed into the threat of open violence.

Down the hall we went. The small crowd parted as we came close. An older man with a brown beard stepped forward and extended his hand. "Thanks for coming." He gestured toward the room. "We've all said our goodbyes. Are you sure I can't be there when it happens?"

"I'm sorry, but this is something that must be done by us alone," Luke said.

The man sighed. "I understand."

Luke walked into the room, and I followed.

There was someone in the bed, hooked up to half a dozen machines. The only sounds I could hear were the steady beeping and my heart pounding wildly in my chest.

"Close the door," Luke said without turning around. He walked up to the bed and dropped the bags to the floor. His whole attention was now focused on the person in the bed.

My hands trembled as I grasped the door handle. I looked out into the sea of sad, worried faces and slowly closed the door.

Luke looked my way. "Colina, lower the blinds."

I nodded and followed his orders. Close the door, lower the blinds and when he says to kill, will I just blindly follow along? Blinds closed, I took another deep breath and forced myself to move to the bed.

The slight form resting on the sheets barely resembled a body at all—she was more like skin and bones. I looked closer before recoiling in horror.

"It's a—a—child." I could barely get the words out.

Luke walked over to the edge of the bed, gently reached out, and touched the child's forehead. "Her name is Anna. She's ten years old, and she has cancer." His eyes met mine. "There's nothing they can do for her."

# CHAPTER
# TWENTY-FOUR

The little girl twitched suddenly.

"She's in pain—constant, excruciating pain." Luke pointed toward one of the IV bottles. "The doctors can give her morphine, but it's not enough. It doesn't dull the pain." He looked at the closed door. "Her family wants to help her move on. She could stay like this for days, weeks, but there's no hope. With our help, she'll move directly into the light. We can help her spirit pass through this life and into the next."

She was a child. He was asking me to take the life of a child. I stumbled back, my head shaking violently back and forth. "No, no, I can't do this!"

"If you close your eyes and concentrate, Colina, you can see that her spirit is on the brink." His voice was low and soothing. "You're not killing her. Her spirit is already almost to the other side. She just needs our help to get across."

"I can't..." My hands went to my face. "You want me to murder her." My cheeks were damp. I hadn't realized I was crying.

"It's not murder, it's compassion."

"But I'm doing this so I can gain power. I'm not doing this

to help her. I'm doing this to avenge my family, to help you save Darla."

"Do your motives really matter? Her family has asked for our help. We're here. Does it really matter why? She needs to move on. By helping her, you're also helping yourself. Is that so wrong?"

Tears ran down my face. "I can't do this."

"Yes, you can. You're strong. Look at what you've survived. You lived when the rest of your family died. You're still here, and so is Darla. But for how long?" Anger blazed from his eyes. "How long until those men kill my sister? They killed Sarah, they murdered your mother, your father, and your brother." He unclenched his hands. The anger left his face, and he reached out to me. "We're the only ones who can help this girl and her family. They asked for our help. If we walk away, she'll continue to suffer. Her family can only sit and watch. Do you really want that?"

I didn't move.

He lowered his hands and said in a gentle voice, "Sit down." He gestured to a chair in the corner. "I'll get everything ready for the spell. You just sit down and keep breathing. Okay?"

He was talking to me as though he thought I was going to bolt out of the room at any minute. He wasn't wrong. Every cell in my body shouted at me to get out. To walk away. But instead, I sat in the chair.

I watched him move around the room. He placed five black candles at the foot of the bed.

I looked at the girl. Her name was Anna. I wondered if I'd ever be able to forgive myself for doing this. Killing, even in mercy, went against everything I believed in, against the very essence of the person I was.

*Used to be a healer*, a voice whispered in the corner of my mind. But I was no longer a healer. I had slowly morphed into a death dealer, and now I was about to become a killer.

Luke took a small volume bound in black leather from one of the bags and gestured for me to join him.

I didn't think I could get out of the chair. My hands were trembling so hard, I had to clench them together in front of me. It took every ounce of willpower I had to force myself to my feet. I have no choice; I have to do this. I took one step after another until I stood by Luke's side.

He pointed towards my neck. "The protection pouch. You need to take it off."

I hesitantly took off the pouch and handed it to him.

He took it, then leaned over, unzipped one of the duffel bags, and dropped it inside. I watched him pull out the small, brown paper bag the healer had given him earlier. He withdrew an orange plastic tube.

"Is that the devil's berries ointment?" I asked, my voice shaking.

He nodded, flipping it open. He leaned over me as he squeezed the tube. I watched as a thin line of white cream spread across the back of my left hand.

"Rub it in," he commanded.

I didn't move.

His voice was gentler this time. "Colina, I can't touch it. You have to rub it in."

I took a deep breath and began slowly rubbing the ointment into my skin. It felt cold and sticky against my fingers.

When I was finished, Luke handed me the book.

It vibrated slightly in my hands. He'd said books like this had power, had spells surrounding them. I looked down at the pages. They were yellowed with age. "I know some Latin, but mostly for plants. I can't read this," I said, holding it out to him.

He gently pushed the book back into my hands. "I'll help you pronounce the words."

Before I could answer, the door burst open. A woman rushed into the room, tears streaming down her face. In her hands she held a gold necklace with a tiny heart dangling from it.

"I forgot to give her this," the woman said, making her way to the bed. She fastened the necklace carefully around the girl's neck. "There. She loved my necklace. There's a picture of her inside from when she was a baby." The woman reached out and brushed the hair from Anna's face. "They said you won't cause her any pain. Promise me my baby won't be in anymore pain."

"I promise," Luke said, his voice low.

The woman's eyes were bleak. "I don't know what else we can do. The doctor gave her as much morphine as he could this time. She's unconscious, but I know she still feels the pain. Her body twitches, her face shows it." The woman's voice came out in a sob. "She's in so much pain. We just want it to stop."

She leaned over and kissed Anna on the forehead. "Goodbye, my angel. Mommy will see you again. One day I'll be with you on the other side. Wait for me in peace, my love." With those words the woman took a step away from the bed.

She started toward the door, but then stopped and turned back toward the bed, reaching out as though she wanted to move forward and embrace the girl again. But instead, she shook her head, and another sob escaped from her lips. "You promise there's no pain?" she whispered, looking at us, her eyes wide and full of...what was that emotion?

I recognized the look. I'd seen it enough times in the mirror since my family's death.

It was grief.

Luke looked over at Anna. "I promise she will have no more pain."

The woman shifted her eyes between us and then word-lessly walked out of the room. She didn't look back as the door closed behind her.

Luke turned to me. "Her mother wants us to do this. She's begging us to end Anna's pain."

He was right. A part of me wanted desperately to get up and walk out the door, but instead I stood there, ready to do whatever he told me. I couldn't find the words to answer, so I just nodded and looked down at the book.

Luke came to my side and read the first word. I repeated each one, trying to articulate them the exact way Luke did.

I focused on my pronunciation, not on what I was doing. If I stopped and thought about what was about to happen, I might not be able to continue.

Minutes passed. My body started to get hot, feverish. I felt a warmth rising up through my limbs, crawling slowly up my neck toward my face. Something's not right. I felt strange. The room suddenly seemed too bright, and the words began to blur on the page. I blinked and blinked again, trying to clear my vision, but the words began to move, sliding down the page. They inched toward the edge of the book and, ever so slowly, began to fall like a small waterfall onto the floor. Where they landed, a pool of black ink formed. It expanded as more words fell and began to quiver. Before my very eyes, the ink pool stretched and changed. It morphed into the shape of a long, thin insect, like a caterpillar.

I shook my head, trying to clear my thoughts. *Am I hallucinating?* The black caterpillar rose up onto its legs, crawled across the floor, and disappeared under the bed. I turned toward Luke. *Did he see it? Was it real, and if it was, what kind of spell was this that changed words into bugs?*

Luke's eyes never left the book. He repeated another word, and I tried to open my mouth and copy what he said, but nothing came out. I opened my mouth again, but my throat was suddenly incredibly dry—so dry the words couldn't escape. My throat constricted, and with the loss of breath I began to panic. My heart pounded in my chest. Fear raced through me, and pain simultaneously burst out from the center of my forehead. It spread, white hot, through my skull. It was so intense I dropped the book and fell to my knees. I instinctively cradled my head. Gray shadows edged in, and my vision blurred.

That's when I heard the laughter.

I looked up, seeking the source of the sound. Anna was standing by the bedside. No, wait, that's not her. It can't be her. I looked back at the bed. She was there, hooked up to the machines. I could hear them beeping.

The laughter again. My eye swung back to the girl standing by the bed. It was Anna, but she was strong and healthy. Her hair hung in red curls down her back. She gave me a wide smile and tried to step away from the bed but stopped. A frown crossed her face. She seemed unable to move, frozen in that one spot. That's when I noticed a glowing, silver cord between the two bodies. It ran from the center of the healthy Anna into the middle of the bed-stricken Anna.

The smiling Anna tried to move again, and as she did the silver cord flexed and stretched but then bounced back, intact.

"Colina, can you hear me?" Luke's voice came from somewhere far away.

I tried to answer, but no sound left my lips.

"You have to help her move on. Do you see the connection? The cord stretching between Anna's body and spirit, the cord of life?"

"I see it." I shouted the words, but I had no idea if he could hear me or not.

Luke's voice sounded urgent. "You have to sever that cord in order for Anna to move on. Look inside yourself, to the place where your power is hidden, burning like a banked fire waiting for you to blow it to life. Do you see the fire?

It was there, a small flame burning in the darkness of my mind.

Luke's voice whispered across the darkness. "You need to make it higher, hotter."

I concentrated on the flame inside me. It wavered slightly before sparking up and expanding. With it, my body began to burn. The fire slid up and down my limbs, and flames flickered off my skin.

"Now send it toward the cord. Focus on the connection and burn it through," Luke's voice commanded.

The flames grew hotter, and I became alive with fire. It pumped through my heart, ran through my veins, fueled my blood. On instinct I reached up and was astonished when flames shot from my fingertips.

Orange and red fire encircled the silver cord. It burned brighter and brighter until the cord was sizzling. Finally, it broke.

Anna's spirit was free.

The healthy Anna leaped away from the bed. I heard a loud shout of excitement and singing filled the room.

Without warning the world spun around, and I felt myself being dragged down against my will. I shouted in fright as something pulled me into a dark abyss. When my vision focused, I found myself standing at the mouth of a great stretch of darkness. Within it, things called out to me.

I was in that place again. Oblivion.

"There you are girly. I've been looking for you." I recognized a familiar spirit's voice close by... Wanda?

Questions shot rapid fire through my mind—How is she here? Does she have some sort of tie to me because of the possession ritual? I didn't have much time to speculate. I felt Wanda's presence edging closer.

"You thought you could get away from me, but I found you," Wanda cackled. "I knew I would if I kept looking hard enough. I've always been a wily one, alive or dead. Anything I wanted bad enough, I would and could get. And, girly, I want to live again!"

She can't have me... "No."

"Now, don't be difficult. No one's here to help you this time. It's just you and me, girly. And that's the way it should be."

"Leave me alone!" my voice commanded. My words shook through me, and I felt myself rise up. I wouldn't stay in the shadows. I refused to be forced into that dark place again.

As quick as I could blink, I felt Wanda's presence surrounding me, tightening like a vise around my mind. I fought against her insidious will. She seemed to be everywhere, grasping with clinging hands, but I held my ground. We grappled silently for a few moments, and I felt myself weakening, being forced back. Then, like a candle lit in a dark room, I felt a new strength rise to my call. Desperate, I grasped at the power and pushed Wanda back with a force of will that I didn't know I possessed. I knew without thinking that it was a strength I'd never had until this moment. I tried to focus on it, let my mind swim in it, use it to force her away once and for all.

She wasn't deterred. "You owe me a new body, deary." I felt a mental pressure as Wanda renewed her efforts, driving at me with the desperation of a drowning woman who, in her panic, was unintentionally dragging down the lifeguard.

I blocked out every other sensation and turned inward, gathering my new strength to me. With a grunt of effort, I cut away the bonds Wanda tried to place on me. They snapped easily, as if severed by a blade. She howled in frustration and fled into the darkness.

Wanda's presence shrank back, but the great expanse of inky blackness was still spread before me, its depths roiling like smoke. This time I heard a growl, and my skin broke out into a cold sweat. There's something else out there. I felt it slowly coming my way.

I steeled myself for another fight and waited for words to form or a voice to say something to me, but there were no human sounds that I could distinguish. The noises were unearthly—snarls and snaps, as if from dogs or wolves. And then an awful sound. A dragging, slinking, thumping. I felt myself shiver in fearful anticipation. My instincts were screaming at me to back up and flee, but there was nowhere to go.

The otherworldly thing was coming closer. I felt certain it came out of the very depths of hell. I shook violently when its presence rushed toward me, unable to follow my instincts and flee. The abyss seemed to become even darker, and though I couldn't see it, I knew it loomed over me.

The darkness slid inside me when it made contact. "No, leave me alone!" I protested, panicking, but it was too late. I felt the blackness ooze into my veins and move into my blood. I knew without a doubt I had felt this thing's dark touch before —it had reached out for me during the second ritual. Now its anger and hunger spread through me, and I felt its darkness settle into my bones. When it spoke, the sound came from inside me.

"Revenge can be yours, but we will demand a price." The words vibrated through me like the echo of corruption.

"What price?" I called out. "What do you mean?" I asked, but immediately knew that the answer didn't matter. I'm willing to pay whatever price to avenge my family's death. I'll do whatever needs to be done to see the men who killed my family brought to justice.

"So be it," called out the voice, and then it withdrew, laughing wickedly.

"No!" I cried out in horror. "I didn't agree to anything!" But in my heart, I knew it was a lie.

I screamed, "No! No!" As my words echoed, flames rose around me, and I was on fire again. The flames inched higher until they consumed me. Red heat blazed up against the blackness.

Then I opened my eyes.

I was on my feet, but barely. Luke's arms supported me, holding me tight.

"Are you alright?"

I couldn't speak. I was so relieved to be away from the darkness that I just sobbed.

We stood there together for a long time.

I took a deep breath and pulled away from him. I looked over at the bed. "Anna?" I whispered.

"She moved on. You helped her move on," Luke said quietly.

I walked over on shaky legs and looked down at Anna's body. Her eyes were wide open. Sky blue, filled with emptiness. She exhibited no signs of life.

I killed her.

I waited for dread to fill me. I waited to feel the pain of killing someone seep into my soul. But I looked down at Anna's lifeless body and felt nothing. I was completely numb. I should've felt...what? Sadness at the girl's passing? Happiness that I'd helped her pass on to a better place? Anger at the injustice of her death?

Instead, I felt absolutely nothing, and that frightened me even more than the darkness of oblivion.

# TWENTY-FIVE

I stood silent in the corner watching Luke pack away everything back into the duffel bags. I'd survived the three terrifying rituals. They were finally over. Am I relieved? I wasn't sure what I felt. Before I could delve too deep into my current emotional—or was it more accurate to say emotionless—state, Luke slung the straps of the bags over his shoulder and motioned for me to follow as he walked out of the room.

Anna's family greeted us in the hallway. Her mother's eyes were full of tears. "Is it—is she—"

"She's passed on to the other side." Luke's voice was full of compassion.

The family, their faces stricken with grief, made their way into the room and left us on our own in the hallway. We stood for a moment before I realized we weren't entirely alone.

A group of people mingled at the other end of the hallway. In the midst of the group was the woman who'd confronted us earlier. Just as I recognized her, she spotted us and pointed in our direction. I couldn't hear what she was saying, but I could read the expressions on the faces around her.

Whatever was about to happen was not going to be pleasant.

"It might be a good idea if we found another way out. I don't like the look of that crowd," Luke said, reaching out and taking my hand.

The crowd, which was starting to look more like a mob, began to move in our direction. Luke pulled me with him, and we hightailed it down the hallway in the opposite direction. We picked up speed as we went, and by the time we hit the flight of stairs, we were jogging. At the bottom of the stairs, we went through another set of doors and Luke halted.

"We're in the basement," Luke gestured to the left, "right next to the parking lot. Once we're out the door, we'll only be a few feet from the car."

I nodded and sucked in a lungful of air. I hadn't been prepared to run a marathon around the hospital.

Luke started down the hall. "Wait here—I'm going to check to make sure there isn't another welcome party waiting for us outside."

I sagged against the wall after he disappeared, watching, waiting for him to let me know it was safe to leave.

I didn't recognize the noise at first.

It wasn't until the buzzing sound increased a few notches that I noticed it at all. The sound was coming from a room to my left. My legs started down the hallway. My mind caught up with what I was doing, and I found myself standing in front of a set of large metal doors. Above the doors in bold, black letters was one word—morgue. Before I could truly process what was going on, I'd pushed through the doors and gone into the room.

*Why had I come into the morgue?* I could speak to spirits now —the last place I wanted to be was in a room full of dead bodies. I looked around, expecting a face or voice to pop out at me at any moment. The air was chilly—cold enough that I could see my breath. The space was enormous. Dozens of small metal doors with metal handles lined one wall. I was looking at the drawers where they kept the dead bodies.

*What the hell am I doing here?* What strange urge propelled me through those doors? I should turn around and march out, I thought, but my feet seemed glued to the floor. I twisted around and took in the rest of the room.

Against another wall was a large sink. I shuddered at the visual of what might go down that drain. Blood? Human tissue? I forced myself to look away. Shiny, black tile covered the floor, and four metal tables about waist high stood in the middle of the room. White sheets covered two of them, but they weren't lying flat against the tables' surfaces.

Something was under each sheet.

Dead bodies. Dead bodies were on the tables.

It shouldn't have been a surprise—I was in a morgue—but as I realized that bodies lay just a few feet away from me, I felt a totally irrational urge take over.

*I have to see them.*

I don't know why the thought crossed my mind, but once it did, I felt compelled. I took one step at a time toward the tables. I wasn't full of dread or fear. I should have been, but instead, I felt empty.

I'd seen dead bodies before—my mother had been a healer after all. In the past when confronted with the dead, I felt sadness—a heavy mourning for the loss of life. The person that passed no longer had the chance to feel the breeze on their face; they would never again hold a loved one in their arms. Death, loss, sadness, all these were things that I had been trying to come to terms with as I took on the role of a healer. All my life I'd watched my mother fight against death—do battle to save her patients' lives. And just moments earlier I had helped someone die. I'd forced Anna to the other side. I kept waiting for remorse to set in, kept waiting to feel regret, but I didn't. I just felt numb.

Well, not completely numb. An undeniable urge to see what lay under the sheets washed over me. The urge was so strong, I wondered if something was controlling me. The thought seemed to melt away as my hand reached out and grabbed a corner of the material. One hard pull, and the cloth partially fell away.

It was a man. I couldn't tell his age. Something had crushed part of his skull. On one side of his head was a gaping hole—a mess of protruding white bone and red tissue. The other half was still intact. I could make out a straight nose, a wide mouth with pleasantly shaped lips, and one good eye. The sheet lay bunched up against his stomach, but from what I could tell there were no other injuries—at least, none that I could see. His arms, his hands, and his chest seemed fine. Whatever trauma had happened to him only impacted his head.

*How did you die? Was it fast? Did you have time to realize what was happening?*

As the questions popped into my head, my body inched forward.

I don't know why I did it, but I couldn't seem to help myself. My hand acted almost of its own accord. My fingers brushed against cold, clammy skin. As I made contact with him, an orange light exploded around us. The light was so bright I was momentarily blinded. With it came a rush of sound and a barrage of images. I stumbled back, almost falling to the ground.

The room quieted.

I steadied myself. *What the hell just happened?* I looked around for any answer, then glanced at the table and shrieked, "Goddess!"

The dead man was slowly sitting up.

I blinked, trying to take in what I was seeing—my mind was reeling with panic.

*This can't be happening. How is this happening?*

His head slowly turned toward me—his head with its gaping wound and exposed skull—and his lips began to move. "Girly, where am I?" It was Wanda's voice. Wanda's voice was coming out of the mouth of the corpse on the table.

"What's going on?" The corpse's hand lifted and began to frantically wave around. It gasped with realization. "I made it. I'm back with the living again!"

I backed up and spun around, knocking into the other table, and falling flat against the second body. I scrambled away, but as I moved, part of the sheet came with me. My hands grazed across a cold patch of skin.

Light exploded again with another rush of images and noise.

The second body was a woman. Her head was all there, but she was missing an arm. It looked like it had been ripped off— the edges were jagged, and pieces of flesh hung down. I watched as her eyes popped open. Her mouth moved, opening wide, and she let out an otherworldly scream.

My hands flew to my ears. I backed up frantically until I fell against something solid. I screamed.

Strong arms circled me, and Luke's voice spoke into my ear, "What have you done?"

Me? I haven't done anything. I'd just walked into the room. I'd looked at the bodies, but barely touched them. Whatever was happening had nothing to do with me.

The woman's body was rising. She was getting up off the table, stiffly. The sheet dropped into a pile on the floor. She was completely naked. A large, jagged, open wound ran down her left leg. The cut was so deep I could see all the way to the bone. Pieces of tendon flapped, dangling down. Her dead eyes focused on us, and she let out another eardrum busting screech. She took an awkward step, her good arm reaching out toward us.

And there was Wanda's voice again, moaning from the man's body on the floor. "Girly, what have you done to me?" The body was moving, inching forward, trying to rise. I could hear fingernails scratching against the tile.

Both bodies were intently focused on us and moving in our direction. Could they hurt us? I didn't want to stick around long enough to find out.

Apparently, Luke felt the same. He shoved me behind him and yelled, "Move!"

We both scrambled out the door. I stood in the hallway, not sure which way to run, and that's when the mob of angry people appeared around the corner. They must have been searching for us throughout the hospital. By the looks on their faces, they weren't about to give us a warm reception.

At the end of the hallway was a sign with the word exit in large red letters. I started toward it, Luke close behind me. I couldn't help but look over my shoulder, and what I saw made me stop in my tracks.

The mob was following us, but as they passed the morgue, they ran smack dab into the dead bodies. High pitched screams were followed by a frantic scrambling for weapons. A handful of mob members began wailing on the dead bodies with IV stands and oxygen tanks.

I could hear Wanda's yells of "Help me! Get off me, you idiots!" echoing down the hall.

I don't know how long I would have stood there, looking on in astonishment at the ruckus, if Luke hadn't grabbed my arm. We both ran flat out down the hallway and out of the hospital. I came to a halt only when my fingers gripped the handle of the car door.

Luke opened the driver's door, unlocked the passenger side,

and we both slid in. Before I could speak, he had the car started and we were moving down the street. We zigzagged up and down side streets for a while, and then Luke suddenly pulled over and turned off the car. I expected him to say something, but he just sat there in silence.

"What happened back there?" I asked, still breathless.

Luke didn't answer.

I spoke louder this time. "I wasn't hallucinating. You saw it, right?"

Luke turned and gave me a brief, anxious look. "Why did you go into the morgue?"

I sat staring out the window, trying to make sense of what I'd just seen. "I don't know. I felt compelled to go in."

"Was anyone else in there?" Luke asked.

"No, the place was empty except for the bodies."

"You didn't feel any spirits?"

I shook my head. "No, I didn't. I just felt this urge to go in and then, I had to see them—the bodies." How could I explain it? "I didn't mean to lift the sheets. I didn't mean to touch them."

"You touched them, and they came alive?" Luke sounded shocked.

We'd been through a lot together, Luke and I, but up until this point, even with all the strange stuff that had happened, nothing had fazed him. His shock meant that whatever had just happened was unexpected.

"I recognized the voice coming out of the dead man's mouth." I paused and took a deep breath. "It was Wanda, the spirit who possessed me during the second ritual."

Luke shook his head. "Impossible. Restless spirits possess the living, not the dead."

"It was her." I'd never forget her voice or that terrifying

moment when she'd whispered to me in the darkness. It was Wanda; I was sure of it. She even called me "girly."

In a rush I said, "It was the same spirit from the second ritual. Wanda. I thought spirits were bound to the place they died?"

"It's not that simple. They can be bound to objects and death dealers can bind them, but..." He took on a puzzled expression. "I've never heard of an unbound spirit following someone around."

"All I did was touch the body." Whatever I had done was unintentional. I didn't mean to raise the dead. I wasn't thinking at all when I went into that room. I was feeling an urge, one I couldn't ignore. And now dead bodies roamed the hospital hallways.

"I heard the scream—that's how I found you." Luke looked in the rearview mirror.

Does he think they're following us? Could they? "That scream sounded like one of your banshees."

"Those bodies were dead. All you did was touch them. You didn't say any words? You just touched them?"

"No words. I barely touched their skin and then I saw a bright, orange light. And there was noise. I saw things rushing by in my head, but I'm not sure what the images were. It all happened too fast."

"A bright, orange light?" Luke demanded.

I nodded my head. "So bright, it blinded me."

"That sounds like death dealer magic. But how can the dead come alive?"

I realized Luke wasn't asking me; he was asking himself. I answered anyway. "They weren't alive. They were possessed."

"I just don't understand what happened," Luke said.

We sat there, neither one of us talking for a long time.

When Luke finally spoke, he said, "I remember my grandfather talking about an old folktale." He tapped his finger on the steering wheel. "What was it? The old man used to tell us stories, bedtime stories to scare us... Oh!" He slapped the steering wheel. "It could be a draugr!"

I raised an eyebrow and waited for him to continue.

Luke turned and looked at me. "The Vikings believed draugrs were ghosts that animated dead bodies. They could roam around. They devoured human flesh. Anyone who hung around them for too long would go insane. It's not exactly what happened, but maybe what happened is the truth that they're based on."

This time I was the one sounding shocked. "Could they be zombies? Maybe they were bit by something before they died? They have something like that in voodoo culture, too, don't they?"

"There is no such thing as zombies," Luke answered, though he didn't really sound too sure.

He could say that all he wanted, but I'd just watched a guy with a gaping hole in his face crawl across the morgue floor. "And spirits can't possess the dead, yet I swear Wanda was in that man's body." What happened to them after we left? "Should we have left them there?"

"What would you suggest we do with them?" Luke asked sarcastically.

"I don't know. Buy an axe, go back, and chop off their heads? That's what they do with zombies in the movies."

Luke's expression turned serious. "I've never seen or heard of this kind of magic. I don't even know if they're draugrs. Draugrs are just something old people tell children to keep them from roaming the streets at night; bedtime horror stories they tell to scare and entertain gullible children." He looked thoughtful for a moment and then shook his head, as if the notion that a draugr might be real was ludicrous.

"But those bodies were dead, and now they're crawling and walking around. You were there. You saw the same thing I did—I wasn't hallucinating."

I wasn't seeing things, not like before in Anna's room. That devil's berries ointment had done a number on me. It set my body on fire and filled my head with visions.

Could this have something to do with the devil's berries? Maybe it had something to do with the last ritual.

Dead bodies walking around. This wasn't something that would go unnoticed.

"That mob was fighting them, Luke. Those people saw us coming out of the room ahead of those things."

As I spoke, a look of horror filled Luke's face. "They know we're death dealers. They'll blame us for what happened." He reached out and grabbed my hand. "We have to figure out what happened. If you did do something, what was it? And how did you do it?" His grip tightened. "We already scare the general populace. They know we raise spirits, and we have banshees do our bidding. Those things alone scare them enough to treat my—our—kind with disgust. But this..." His voice broke. "If they think that we can raise up the dead, if they think we can create walking corpses...draugrs... whatever those things are, people won't just despise us. They'll start to hunt us."

# TWENTY-SIX

H e turned away and looked out the window. We sat in silence for a few minutes before he spoke again. "There has never been a healer turned death dealer. At least, I've never heard of any." He looked back at me. "I knew that you had some magic of your own—that you could heal—but I never imagined what your natural abilities combined with the power you got from the rituals might create." He let go of my hand.

"You think I can raise the dead?" If I can raise them, does that mean I can destroy them?

"The people in my family I could ask are at the retreat." He shook his head slowly back and forth. "I should never have tried to teach you. Maybe when I did the rituals, I messed them up. Maybe I did something wrong."

He looked so distraught that I put my hand on his shoulder. "You didn't mess up—I survived, didn't I?"

"You did." He leaned forward until his face was inches from mine. His dark eyes were staring at me with smoldering intensity. "And for that, I'm very thankful." He leaned back and his fingers reached out and caressed my cheek. "But..." He left the thought hanging.

Suddenly I could read what he was thinking on his face. "But what if you turned me into some kind of monster?" I moved back away from him.

"That's not what I was going to say." His voice was soft.

"And what if you did?" I demanded. I looked down at my hands. "I did it, didn't I? I touched the body, and Wanda somehow jumped into it."

"You're not a monster," he said, pulling me into his arms. "You're brave and strong and, I think, pretty wonderful."

I pulled back and looked into his eyes. He looked directly at me and gave me a reassuring smile. "We'll get through this together."

I wanted so desperately to believe him. The desire to drive away from this place, and to keep driving, putting all this madness behind us was so strong for a moment it sucked my breath away. I forced myself to focus on Luke. My hand reached out and took his, our fingers intertwined. He was right, whatever happened next, we would handle it together.

I took another deep breath and closed my eyes, I went through the whole crazy scene in the morgue again, trying to make sense of it. One question kept coming back to me—if Wanda jumped into the dead man, what jumped into the woman? She screamed like a banshee.

I opened my eyes and said, "Tell me more about banshees."

"The spirits we bind for banshees are spirits who have been around a long time. People who were murdered, died tragically, or died suddenly. Their spirits are unable to come to terms with their deaths. They can't move to the other side. After years of roaming the in between, they go a bit mad."

"You only bind spirits of the dead who have been around for a long time?" I asked.

He nodded. "It would be wrong to take someone who just died. They need a chance to come to terms with their death. They need a chance to move into the light and over to the other side."

"If my mother, if she stays like she is—" My voice choked up.

He pulled me into his arms. "She won't stay like that. She'll eventually get over her grief. One day she'll find her way to the light. I'm sure of it."

How could he be so sure? He told me that many spirits he came across never found the light. My mother was out there now, wandering the in between, mourning the loss of her family. I would avenge my family's deaths. Hopefully my mother would then be able to move on. If that didn't give her enough peace to cross over, I'd try to find her, communicate with her, maybe I could help her find the light.

We held each other in silence for a while.

When he finally pulled away, he said in a quiet voice, "We need to go back to Pagan's place."

I didn't bother to hide my shock. "But you said they trashed it."

Luke turned the car back on. "They did, but the books I need to try and figure out what's going on are at Pagan's. They didn't destroy everything. They ripped pages out of some books and smashed anything breakable."

"But it's not safe. They found us there before."

"I still don't know how they did that, but we have to risk it. I have to see if I can figure out what you did in the morgue."

"And those things we left?" I asked.

Luke's expression turned grim. "We can't go back there. Not until we know what we're dealing with. If we go back now, they'll string us up without asking any questions. My magic is pretty strong, but no one can fend off a mob."

239

"What about Darla?" I demanded.

"We will go after her, but we need to figure out how to focus your magic. How to make sure that when we face them, you have power you can use. There are two days until the dark moon. I know she's still alive, I can feel it. If they haven't harmed her yet, they won't. Not until the dark moon."

"Freddy said he'd help us." Three of us against who knows how many.

"I won't go back on my promise. I said Freddy could come, and he can."

"So we go after Darla in two days—the day of the dark moon?"

He pulled the car back on the road. "I'm not waiting that long. Tomorrow night we go. I know that doesn't give us any time to check out the layout of the hotel, but I know the place. I've been there once before." He looked over at me for a brief moment, before turning his attention back to the road. "I figure we can go up and see if we can get her out. If it's too heavily guarded or not safe enough, we'll regroup and try the next night. But if we wait until the night of the dark moon..."

I finished his sentence. "It might be too late."

"These lunatics are making human sacrifices. Whatever they've planned, whatever spell they're trying to power—it's old. I found some references in Pagan's books to the type of rituals they might be trying to perform when I was studying the spells for the last ritual." His voice turned angry. "Whatever spell they're planning has to be something truly dark and powerful. Something that hasn't been seen in a hundred years. If they succeed, I don't know if even the eldest in my guild could fight the type of magic they might raise."

"We save your sister and then what?" I whispered.

"We wait until my guild comes back and take on the whole pack of bad guys."

"But other people are being held there. Sarah showed me in my dream. If we rescue your sister, what's stopping them from sacrificing the others?"

Luke's hands tightened on the steering wheel. "There's no way the three of us can save a whole group of people. If we get lucky, we sneak in and get Darla out without anyone finding us."

When I didn't say anything, his voice turned persuasive, "We go back when we have reinforcements. We make a stand against Macaven's men with my guild. We take these guys out and stop them from ever doing this again."

"But your guild won't be back for another week." We had no idea what Macaven and his men were planning. If we didn't know what spell they were trying to power, how would we stop them? If Luke's guild came back, would they keep me out of the fight? How could I be sure they would make my family's murderers pay? "What if they release this terrible spell before your family gets back?"

"Colina, we can't stop these men on our own. We need to see what they're doing, get as much information as we can, and then regroup so we can figure out how to go about stopping them." His voice was calm, he was trying to reason with me. "I swear to you, when my family is back in town, we will go back and save everyone."

"Save everyone who's still alive, you mean?" I was mad. Anger flowed through my veins. Why didn't he understand? "If they're responsible for all the deaths—if they've been posing as Redeemers—then they've already killed five people. Six including Sarah. How many more will die in a week? And why are they doing it? Why would they kill these people under the guise of being Redeemers?"

"To keep the guilds from realizing what they're doing. They had to hide the human sacrifices, had to keep the fact that

241

they're doing forbidden magic from the others. If the guilds had found out, they would have put a stop to it before now." He turned and gave me a measured look. "There are only three of us. What do you think we can do?"

"Fight. Save everyone."

His anger was back, but this time it was directed at me. "You're being unrealistic. I have power, but Freddy isn't mage-born."

"And I'm without any real power." I could apparently create zombie like creatures, but could I do anything that might help us?

"You do have the power to bind banshees now." He lifted his hand before I could interrupt. "I can show you how. It's powerful magic."

"You want me to make slaves out of lost spirits?"

He raised his voice. "I told you before, you're a death dealer now. Binding banshees is part of the magic we wield."

I crossed my arms in front of my chest.

"You don't have a choice!" He slammed his hand down on the steering wheel. "I don't know what you expect me to do. We have a slim chance of getting Darla out—an extremely slim chance, but I'm willing to take that chance to save my sister. You, of all people, should understand."

I did. I'd have done anything to save my family. I'd have given my own life trying to protect them, but I couldn't stop thinking of those innocent people being held against their will, waiting to be slaughtered by Macaven.

I knew Luke was focused on getting his sister to safety, but my goals were not his. There was no saving my family—I could only avenge their deaths. The men who killed them needed to pay for what they'd done. I wanted them to rot in hell.

I suddenly felt exhausted. I'd survived the rituals, apparently raised the dead, and now had to learn to create banshees so I could storm a hotel against an army. The chances of surviving this ordeal were less than slim.

I looked out the window in silence for the rest of the drive.

We finally pulled into Pagan's driveway and Luke turned off the engine.

I turned to him and demanded, "When do we start the binding banshees leassons?"

"We need to get some food in us and then get a few hours' sleep." He glanced over at me. "Colina, you've been strong through this whole thing. This won't be bad, I promise. It's not as bad as you think."

He really believed I could do this. I knew he was counting on me. He said binding banshees wouldn't be that bad.

Goddess, I prayed he was right.

# TWENTY-SEVEN

Pagan's house was in shambles. Shattered glass and shredded papers covered the floor. Someone had taken a knife to the couch and pulled most of the stuffing out through the long, jagged slits in the leather. The dining room table was turned over, and some of the wooden chairs looked like they'd been slammed against the ground until parts of them had finally flown off.

What was the point of all the destruction? Had they been searching for something?

Luke picked a book up off the floor. Someone had ruthlessly vandalized the once ornate cover and ripped out a handful of pages. He flipped through them. "This is one of the books I need. We need to find the missing pages."

He's got to be kidding—he wants to stay here and go through this mess? What if those maniacs come back? What'll they do to us if they were this violent to inanimate objects?

"It's cold in here. I'll start a fire." He scanned the broken furniture before giving me a half grin. "Shouldn't be hard to find kindling."

He's making jokes? I expected Luke to be enraged at the destruction; instead, he seemed cool and collected.

He gestured toward the kitchen. "Can you see if they left anything for us to eat? I don't know about you, but I'm starving."

I made my way into the kitchen. All the cupboard doors were wide open. Anything breakable was in pieces on the floor. I stepped carefully over broken glass and looked through the cupboards. There were a few tins of food. I found more on the floor by the back wall. I ran my hand down the wall, which was now covered in dents—they must have flung the cans at it. That was the only way to explain all the divots. I leaned over, picked up a can of chili, and found a couple of pots a few feet away. When I left the pantry, glass crunched under my foot. If I was going to try and cook anything in here, I had to clean up. I found a broom and dustpan in a closet. By the time Luke came into the kitchen, I had most of the mess swept up.

I pointed at the cans sitting on the counter. "There's some chili and a can of corn."

"Great. I have the fire going. I found about half the books I was looking for." He had one under his arm that seemed to have made it through the attack unscathed.

"Find anything about your draugrs in those books?"

"A couple references, but nothing that will help us."

I started opening one of the cans, a hot and spicy southwestern chili. "You still think that's what those things were?" I poured the can's contents into a pot and turned on the burner.

"Draugrs are the only type of magical creature that comes close to what we saw." He reached over and handed me the other can. "I got the fire going. I tried to clean up a bit in the living room, but the place is still a disaster."

I looked out into the living room. "They did a number on this whole place."

245

Luke ran a hand through his hair. "I just don't see the point. Why trash it?"

I remembered what they had done to the magic shop. "For the fun of it?"

"Who are these guys?"

"A bunch of murdering crazies," I muttered under my breath, opening the can of sweet corn.

Luke nodded, staring pointedly at the pot of chili. "How long until we eat?"

I poured the corn into another pot and turned on the burner. "Not long. It should take about ten minutes to warm everything up."

Luke opened the book in his hands and looked down at the pages. "Sounds good. I'll keep searching for the other books I need."

Snapping the book in his hands shut, Luke headed off to search, looking desperately for answers to all the questions swirling through both our heads. What type of magic had I wielded at the hospital? I raised the dead. I couldn't be the first to have done so. What evil spell was Macaven and his men trying to perform? Did Luke's books speak of the forbidden magics?

We were flying blind and about to head off into the unknown against a group of men we knew very little about. There wasn't much else to do other than barrel ahead and hope that, whatever happened, we would all survive it. I turned my attention back to the stove and our dinner.

We ate sitting in front of the fire on the floor. It had been no small job sweeping up the living room. Debris now lay in a pile in the corner.

"It's too bad about the couch." I looked over at a pile of white stuffing Luke had swept against the wall.

Luke's expression turned grim. "Pagan picked out all the

furniture herself for this place. She's going to be devastated when she sees what they've done to her house."

I leaned closer to the fire, watching Luke pick at his food. He'd been distracted ever since we got back. And what about me? I wasn't sure how I felt. I should've been scared or panicked at the thought of dealing with banshees, but instead I felt numb.

Luke looked over at me. "We should try and get some sleep."

"I'm not tired. If we're going to do this banshee binding thing, I'd rather do it now." I was sick of waiting. It seemed better to just get it over with.

Luke put down his bowl, reached over, and threw another log onto the fire. He picked up the black fire iron and fiddled with the coals for a while before turning back and asking me, "Are you sure you feel up to trying it tonight?"

Whenever we'd talked about creating banshees, I'd always argued with him. To me, binding spirits seemed just plain wrong. Luke, on the other hand, always defends his people's practice. I could tell by the way he was looking at me now that he anticipated another argument. I guess I should've fought him about it, but I honestly didn't feel anger. I didn't feel anything.

"I'm guess I'm ready," I said.

Luke got to his feet and left the room. When he came back, he was carrying all the things he'd used when he performed the spell to call on my family's spirits: candles, bowls, a bottle of red liquid, raven feathers, and the Ouija board and planchette. Around his neck hung the medallion. He walked over to the table and laid everything out. The Ouija board now sat in the center of the table, and on top of it, the planchette. Luke gestured for me to join him.

I sat down across from him. The last time we'd used the

board, something not so pleasant had shown up, and so had my mother.

Luke lit the candles. He did everything exactly the way he had the first time: he poured the contents of the bottle into the bowl, placed his fingers in the liquid, closed his eyes, and hung onto the medallion. He opened his eyes again, said a few words in Latin, and spread his fingers across the board, smearing the red liquid against the surface of the polished wood. He then reached across the table. I placed my hands in his.

Every time he touched me, my skin seemed to come alive, I could feel an energy, an electricity every place his skin touched mine. I looked into his face. His expression was one of concentration. We were about to perform another spell, but all I could seem to do was wish we were sitting in front of the fire, wrapped in each other's arms instead.

"Now the prayer." He evoked the prayer, saying each word slowly, before letting go of my hands.

I started to place my fingertips on the pointer.

He stopped me. "This spell is a little different than the last one we did. We're going to call on the dead like we did during the second ritual."

"You're not going to tie me to a chair or make me wear a funky white dress, are you?"

He laughed and shook his head. "This time you have more power, but you still don't have any training in the arts, which makes you vulnerable. I'm hoping a spirit will show up who you can control." He lifted the medallion over his head and handed it to me. "Take this."

I reached out and took the medallion from him. The metal felt cool against my skin. I looked down at the etching, my fingers tracing the outline of the phoenix.

"It'll help you focus your abilities. Hold it tight in one hand and put your other hand on the planchette."

I grasped the medallion, reached out, and gently put my fingertips on the pointer.

"Okay. This time close your eyes," he instructed. "I need you to focus your thoughts on the room. Only think of this room and what you can feel within it."

I closed my eyes, but this time I didn't feel freaked out. There was no fear racing through me—instead, I felt a deep calm.

"That's it," Luke said in a soft voice. "Focus on the room. See the walls of the room in your mind."

I took a deep breath and tried to imagine Pagan's ruined living room. As I did, I felt the now familiar sensation of something rushing toward me.

"There's a spirit here," I whispered.

"Ask for a name."

"Who are you?" I spoke out, and the pointer started to slide. I opened my eyes and followed its journey across the board.

It stopped on T, then slid to the letters H, O, M, and A. It finally came to rest on the letter S.

Thomas. The boy I'd felt the other day in the kitchen. I looked over at Luke. "It's Thomas."

Luke looked pleased. "Good, good. Now I want you to reach out to Thomas with your mind and your spirit."

A cold breeze blew across my face. I tilted my head as the tail end of a whisper floated past my ears. I concentrated harder, trying to make out the raspy whisper. "I can hear him, he's close by, talking to me."

Luke put up a hand. "This time, Colina, I need you to do more than just listen to Thomas. I need you to focus your thoughts toward him, reach out to him." He paused as if trying to find the right words. A few seconds passed, and then he continued. "I need you to imagine the very core of your being moving forward, making contact... Think about that part of you where your power resides, the center of your being reaching out toward Thomas."

I tried to do what Luke asked. I didn't have a clue what I was doing, but I tried to focus all my thoughts—my whole being—on Thomas. At first nothing happened. I could only hear the sound of my own heart beating in my ears. But then a breeze rustled the drapes in the living room. The windows were closed, so I knew it was Thomas—he was here, I was sure of it. I could hear his small voice chattering in the distance. I couldn't quite make out what he was saying, but he was talking to me.

I tried to imagine Thomas, but I had no idea what he looked like—there was no photo to go on. Before, when I'd seen him in the kitchen, he'd only been a ghostly outline of a boy. There hadn't been any distinct shapes or characteristics on his face— at least, not any I could truly recognize. I closed my eyes again.

*Thomas, what do you look like?*

As the thought appeared, an image started to glitter in the dark recesses of my mind. It was the face of a boy. Suspenders hung from slight shoulders, and a cap sat tilted at an angle upon his brown, ruffled hair. It was a style of clothing I'd only seen in movies. Historical movies.

There was a loud bang and my eyes popped open in surprise. One of the candles had fallen off the table and dropped to the floor. Luke quickly got up from his chair and extinguished the flame. An open candle and a wood floor were a dangerous combination.

Suddenly I saw—it wasn't sickness that took Thomas's life. Luke was wrong.

Thomas died in a fire.

I saw the flames flickering around the room, climbing up the walls, rushing across the ceiling. The smell of smoke was so strong, I raised my hand over my nose and mouth. I looked over at Luke. Doesn't he see what I'm seeing? I blinked, and the flames disappeared. But I knew I hadn't imagined them. There had been a terrible fire here. Well, not here in this house, but in a house that had once sat on this very spot a century ago. Thomas's home.

Thomas's image was no longer just in my mind—he was now standing only a few feet from me. His body was translucent. I could still make out the furniture behind him. He looked at me with a questioning expression. I didn't feel any fear, but rather a strong sense of curiosity. How long has he been bound to this place? Was he destined to roam in between forever?

Thomas began to sway, first to one side and then the other. The image of him flickered in and out in the candlelight. Then, before I knew what was happening, Thomas rushed forward. I instinctively raised my hands to defend myself as I felt his spirit crowding in on me.

Luke shouted, "Force the spirit back! You're strong now. You have the power!"

I tried to do what Luke said, I tried to will Thomas's spirit back. I could feel sweat form on my forehead as I strained to stay in control.

Luke was by my side, his hand on my shoulder. "That's it. Push him back. You're stronger than he is." Luke's grip tightened. "Now focus all your energy on Thomas again and, quickly, repeat these words: Constringo Constrixi Constrictum."

I spoke the words, and a loud screech filled the air.

Luke's fingers dug into my flesh. "Concentrate! Say the words again!"

I spoke them louder this time, and the screeching intensified.

Thomas's spirit swirled around me. Goose bumps rose on my arms, and the hairs on the back of my neck stood up. The ungodly screeching was still going on, but now I could hear

Thomas's voice in my head. He was shouting out in pain. Whatever I'm doing is hurting him!

"Say the words again," Luke demanded.

I shook my head. No. I tried to scoot back in my chair, but Luke's hand moved from my shoulder and came down hard on my arm. "You can't stop now. You have to bind Thomas to you."

What am I doing? Thomas's screams intensified. The spell's causing him pain! I don't want to hurt him. I never wanted to bind the spirit of this innocent young boy.

Things started falling from the nearby shelves as if someone was tossing items randomly across the room. One of the bowls on the table suddenly flew and slammed into the wall. A stereo in the corner turned on and off and then on again. When it came back on, the volume increased. Loud music filled the room. The screeching, Thomas's cries of pain, the music booming and vibrating through the air—it was all too much. I shook off Luke's hand and came to my feet. I had to stop this madness.

Luke rounded on me, his expression one of anger. "You can't stop now. You're almost there," his voice raised above the music. "You have to trust me—you're a death dealer. This is the only way for you to truly wield your power. Don't you want to avenge your family's death? Colina, this is the only way!"

Everything I had been through, all of it would be for nothing if I didn't do this. Without the banshee power, I'd be useless by Luke's side when he attempted to save his sister. When Macaven came after me again and I knew that it was just a matter of time until he did—I would be helpless. My only option would be to run again.

I was tired of running.

The power Luke offered was the sole reason I'd shown up at his doorstep. It would mean I'd finally be able to stand and fight. I'd be able to defend myself. I'd have a chance to live, and hopefully one day see the men who hurt my family pay for what they'd done.

I shouted out the words again. "Constringo Constrixi Constrictum!"

All sound stopped.

A bright light appeared.

I turned my head toward it. Is this part of the spell? In the light, I could see shadows, shapes, and human forms. It was as if they were standing in the doorway of a strongly lit room. There was a woman—I could feel her presence. I could feel sorrow, a longing for something lost, radiating out from her.

Then I heard the voices.

There was no more screeching, no more sounds of pain. These new sounds were words of comfort and love.

It's Thomas's family.

They were standing in the light, beckoning for Thomas to come and join them. The woman was his mother, and she was desperate for him to come to her. Thomas was still there in the room—his spirit was only a few feet from me, flickering in and out. He was facing me, and I realized he didn't see the light. He wasn't reacting to the pleas of his family. Instead, he focused only on me.

I thought of my mother, her spirit roaming the world forever in unrest. A sudden desire filled me—I wanted more than anything for Thomas to move toward the light. I wanted this little boy, who died so suddenly and tragically, to be reunited with his family. I wanted to call out to him, to somehow comfort him. The healer inside me was still there, that part of me still alive in a small corner of my being. The awakening of my inner death dealer had pushed it aside, and I had changed. I wasn't the girl I used to be, but deep inside, a part of me wanted so desperately to help instead of harm.

I looked again at the light, and as I did it swirled out toward me, circling me. Without thinking of what I was doing, I raised my hands and willed it toward Thomas.

He turned. He could see it. His expression changed, and his arms rose. He could hear the voices of his family—he could hear them calling to him. The light engulfed him and then flared, glowing so brightly that I raised a hand to shield my eyes. I could hear cries of joy—a feeling of love and contentment filled the room.

I reunited him with his loved ones.

The light dimmed. I turned and looked over at Luke.

His expression was one of shock. "What just happened?" His eyes searched the room. "I don't understand. You did the spell to bind him. Thomas should be bound to you."

"He's not here." I watched the remaining light slowly fade away. Thomas was finally back in the arms of his family.

Luke frowned. "I don't understand."

My eyes met Luke's. "His family was calling to him." I wasn't sure how to explain what had just happened.

Luke was silent for few minutes and then he said, "You set him free? You sent him into the light?" An odd expression crossed his face. "No one can do that. No one can set a spirit free."

"Thomas wanted to go."

"For over a century Thomas has been stuck here. His spirit was unable to move on. I know because Pagan and I tried to help him years ago."

I gestured toward the other side of the now empty room. "But he went into the light."

"You somehow forced him into the light," Luke said in a low voice.

"But that's a good thing, right?" I couldn't understand why Luke looked so upset. "All spirits want to go to the light."

"They do, but when they can't, no outside force can help

them cross over. What you just did, it's never been done before. I've never heard of anyone doing something like that before."

"Someone in the past must have been able to do it."

"Not in any of the books I've read. Not in any of the spells I've heard or been taught." He looked at me, his eyes filled with awe.

Whatever I had just done was something he hadn't expected, and it seemed to excite him. Did this mean I had other powers that I might be able to use against Macaven's men?

I waited for him to continue, but he turned away from me and started clearing off the bowls, candles, and Ouija board.

Am I really doing things no one else can? It meant that I did have power, of a sort.

I could raise the dead, and now it seemed I could also set them free.

# CHAPTER
# TWENTY-EIGHT

Pagan's room was the one place out of the whole house that had seen the least damage. Someone had torn down all the sheer white material hanging around the bed and pulled the drawers out of the side tables and dresser, strewing clothes across the room. I'd spent some time folding and putting them away, but I still wasn't tired.

Thomas had moved on. He'd crossed over and was now with his family. I should have felt joy, but I didn't. I should have felt guilty that I hadn't done what Luke wanted. I had no banshees, no real power of my own to help Luke when he needed it most. When I helped Thomas cross over, I hadn't been thinking of Darla, I hadn't been worried about my own safety, my own need for magic—all I cared about at that one moment was seeing Thomas go into the light. Now that it was over, I had to face Luke knowing that I let him down when he needed me most. I felt no fear, no joy. Just a crushing indifference, a cold numbness that seemed to spread through my body and mind.

*What's wrong with me?*

Luke knocked on the open door. He held a blanket in his hand. "I thought you could use this."

We were both dressed in black sweats, but he, as usual, was not sporting a top.

Doesn't he get cold when he sleeps? I couldn't help myself—my eyes traveled down his chest and across his stomach. I waited for the usual hum, the wanting, the desire that filled my body and mind whenever I was this close to Luke, but there was nothing. Just that same cold void where my emotions should be. "Thanks."

He stepped closer. "Are you okay?"

After the second ritual, I felt different. Anger seemed to fuel my blood, but somehow the third ritual had washed that all away. Had it washed away all of my emotions? Was this unfeeling creature I'd become, the one who could raise the dead, all that remained?

My eyes met Luke's. "I feel numb inside. It's hard to explain. After what happened with Anna..." I shied away from saying the words after I killed Anna. "I felt this emptiness inside me, that has been getting stronger and stronger. Right now, I don't feel scared, or anger...I feel just...nothing."

Luke took step after step until he was only inches from me. His hand reached out and caressed my cheek. His fingers slid down my neck. He looked at me as if asking a question. He pulled me gently toward him. His lips pressed against mine. Heat spread across my body at his touch. My blood was on fire again, but not from anger this time.

He pulled away. "Did you feel that?"

"Yes," I whispered.

The blanket he held dropped to the floor, and he pulled me against him. We kissed again as he lowered me slowly onto the bed. Our bodies moved together as we fell against the thick white covers. We lay there together, his lips still on mine. My body tingled as his hand slid down the length of me. His fingers were in my hair, then running down my back.

The kiss stretched on, and with it came a heat that spread through my entire body. Each kiss became deeper, more desperate. I tried to pull him closer. I needed to feel his full body against mine. I no longer felt numb. Instead, desire, excitement, and overwhelming happiness—now swirled through me. I felt suddenly overheated, feverish.

Luke's fingers ran across my leg up until they slid against my naked stomach.

I shivered at his touch.

"See, you can still feel," he said suddenly pushing his thigh up between my legs.

There was this heat, this wanting, this desire that was making my pussy throb and when his thigh pushed farther up and farther still until it pressed against that throbbing center, I cried out and began to ride him. My legs wrapped around him, my fingers pressing into his back. Bucking, arching wildly against him, I rode that rock hard thigh again and again, crying out each time it pushed against my soaked panties. Moaning out each time it parted my wet pussy until finally a wave of pleasure came cresting over me and I found sweet relief.

"Did you enjoy that?" he whispered his hot breath tickling my ear.

"Yes," I moaned my legs still tight against his, my muscles still trembling.

"God, I love feeling you lose control." His lips pressed against my neck. "But I'm nowhere close to being done with you. I want to feel you come again," he growled.

My shirt was lifted off, my nipples puckering in the cool air. My panties were pulled off and then his body hovered over me. His lips lowered and taunted my nipples then made a slow path across the exposed skin of my stomach. But he didn't stop there. His mouth kept moving, down, lower, and then lower yet, until I could feel his hot breath against my inner thigh.

Strong fingers pushed inside me. Faster, harder pushing inside of me until those fingers were replaced with the heat of his mouth. The thrust of his tongue against the lips of my pussy forced the air from my lungs. I sucked in harsh and uneven breaths. All thoughts were seared from my head.

Pleasure rolled over me as his mouth suddenly sucked hard against the center of my mound. I needed to let go. I was desperate for release, and he was in no hurry to give it to me.

My hands began to glide across my skin. Down they went, across my neck until they found their way to my breasts. My fingers grazed across my nipples, and I began pulling and tweaking the hard rounded rose tips. But it was not enough. I lifted a finger to my mouth and licked it before lowering it again and rolling the wet skin across a now pebbled hard tip. I rocked against him my hands pleasuring myself—frantic fingers plucked and pinched my own nipples trying to bring myself over the edge while his mouth slowly pleasured me.

Small and then larger tremors glided across me. I undulated and I whimpered. My body tried to wrench itself free, but strong hands suddenly surrounded my ass and forced my pulsating core back against his mouth. He was relentless—his tongue tasting every part of me, his mouth seeking the very core of me.

My body could not take anymore. My hands went into my hair as I was forced into a violent arch and the word 'Goddess' was torn from my mouth as an earth shuddering orgasm ripped across my body.

Small explosions of pleasure still vibrated within me when he began to move away from me, and I started to cry out, but then he was over me again. He hard shaft entered me. Nothing about this was slow and gentle. He fucked me hard, and harder still. He pushed himself deep inside me. My fingernails dug into his back as I cried out, "Fuck me harder." I begged again, "Harder, fuck me harder!"

And he did. Our stomachs smacked together from the force of each penetration. Sweat now streaked our bodies. My whole being was focused only on the wave of passion that was building inside me. Those waves of ecstasy making me call out his name, again and again, until finally we came together in one earth shattering climatic moment.

I lay there underneath him, not wanting him to move, not minding that he was crushing me. The tremors of pleasure still slid across my skin as we lay there together.

We were here together. I didn't care about tomorrow. Now, right now, being in his arms, having him inside me was everything.

I woke to light streaming through the window. Luke lay beside me on the bed, the blanket wrapped around his chest. I sat up in bed and looked down at his sleeping face. The urge to run my fingers over his back was so strong that I pushed myself off the bed and walked over to the window. This guy was making me feel things I had never felt before. My body had trembled under his touch. The passion I shared with him last night both thrilled and terrified me.

I looked at him lying there, the sheets tangled around his legs. He looked so innocent in his sleep, and I wondered, Do I really know him? Who is this guy who stepped into my life just a few days ago? How did he suddenly become so important to me? I had so many questions racing through my head, but the answers, those would only come with time.

That last thought stopped me cold. Time. Did I want to stick around and find out what kind of relationship we could build together? If I didn't stay, was there a place for me to go? I could not go back to my clan. I had no home or family that would welcome me with open arms. I was alone in the world.

But that's not exactly true. I looked down at Luke.

I'd lost so much already. I didn't know if I could allow myself to care for someone so deeply ever again.

If I opened my heart again, allowed myself to love someone, there was too much at stake. I could lose Luke. If that happened, I might finally lose myself forever in a cloud of grief and sadness. I might become so lost, I may never find myself again. Never be able to walk through this word happy again.

A part of me wanted, more than anything, to go back to bed, lay my body down next to his, feel his skin against mine, and have his lips kiss me again.

I want to love him. As those words echoed through my mind, I froze. This had all happened too fast. I hardly knew him. Circumstance had thrown us together. The heightened emotions constantly swirling around us were to blame.

I was falling hard and when I finally hit the ground, I might shatter into a million pieces.

Luke's eyes opened. He gave me a wide smile. "Good morning."

I was having a hard time meeting his eyes. "Morning," I answered before turning away and looking out the window.

"What time is it?" I heard him sit up behind me and stretch.

"A little after nine o'clock."

He got out of bed and came to stand next to me, wrapping his arms around me. "Do we have anything to eat for breakfast? Anything besides chili and corn?"

I closed my eyes and leaned my head back against his shoulder. "I'm afraid the cupboards are bare."

"We can get dressed and go out to the market. Maybe even stop someplace for breakfast," he whispered in my ear.

"Do you think that's a good idea?" I whispered.

His hand reached up and brushed a strand of hair behind my ear. "If they were after us, they would have found us by now."

"You don't think they're looking for us?" Why would they stop? They cornered us at the magic shop, they tracked us to Pagan's, and they chased us into the night and across open fields. They seemed pretty determined. It didn't make sense for them to just stop.

Luke spun me around, his face inches from mine. "I have no idea what they're up to. I just know that last night they left us alone, and for that I'm grateful." He kissed me.

I kissed him back for a long moment, enjoying the feel of his lips against mine. Then I moved back. I needed to keep my head —we still had big problems to deal with.

He looked puzzled for a moment but then smiled. "I call first dibs on the shower. I know the cupboards are bare, but please tell me there's some coffee left somewhere in this house."

I couldn't help it—I felt myself grinning. "I'll go check if you promise not to use all the hot water."

WE WENT to the market and bought enough groceries to last us a couple of days. When we arrived back at home, I found myself looking down at the bag full of food sitting on the counter and wondering if we would make it back after tonight's excursion. Did Luke purposely buy more food than we needed as a way of proclaiming to the universe that we would return? Would we be sitting down to a spaghetti and meatball dinner tomorrow night?

I hoped so.

I put the groceries away and walked into the living room.

Luke was building another fire. A cup of coffee and a muffin on a plate sat on the floor by the couch. Both were mine. We hadn't stopped for breakfast—instead we'd hit the local coffee shop on the way back to Pagan's.

I sat down on the floor and took a sip of coffee before asking the question that had been uppermost on my mind all morning. "Do we have a game plan for storming the hotel and saving Darla?"

He stuffed some shredded paper between the five logs stacked in the fireplace. "Nothing concrete. I figure we go, case the place, and see if an opportunity comes up."

"So...we're totally winging it?" I couldn't keep my voice from sounding annoyed.

"I don't see what choice we have. We don't know what's going on up there. We don't know how many bad guys we'll be facing. I was hoping you would have some power we can use when we go against them, but you couldn't bind any banshees. You have no magic you can use to defend yourself. Do you have a better suggestion?"

Luke's plan sounded like insanity to me, but I honestly didn't have a better idea.

Luke lit the fire and then sat down next to me. "I want you to stay with me after this is all over."

I couldn't believe what I was hearing. I was worried about surviving the night, and he was talking about a future we might never see.

"You've got to be kidding," I blurted. Why did his words surprise me? Earlier I'd had the same thoughts—I'd wondered about our future and if we had one. I'd wondered what might happen if we lived through all this.

He looked at me. "I'm not."

I turned my face away. "I can't stay with you," I mumbled. "What would your guild say once they find out what I can do?

You know they won't just welcome me with open arms. They won't accept me."

His fingers reached up and touched my cheek. "You're a death dealer now. You're one of us. You can be part of our guild."

At his answer, I laughed harshly. "But I can't." I shook my head slowly back and forth. "I'm not one of you. You've seen what I can do. You don't know what the magic is that I'm doing or how I'm doing it. You don't know what I've turned into. I don't even know what I am anymore."

He reached out and grabbed my arm. "You're someone I care about. Someone I want by my side."

I pulled my arm away. "You say that now, but in a few months, or in a year, how will you feel then?"

His voice was angry now. "The same."

I spun around and confronted him. "You don't know that. You can't say that for sure."

The anger faded, and his expression turned serious. "I know how I feel about you. I don't want to lose you." He took a step toward me. "I know you have feelings for me."

I took a step back. "I don't know what I feel."

His anger was back, blazing from his eyes. "When everything is all over, you can't just run away from this...from us."

I couldn't stop myself from saying, "There is no 'us.'"

"There can be if you have the courage to face your feelings."

I felt cold and wrapped my arms around my body. "You don't know what you're talking about."

His voice turned low and persuasive. "I know you lost your family. I know you're still grieving for them, but you can't throw what's between us away because you're scared."

"I'm not scared. I'm realistic. I don't belong in your world."

He reached out toward me. "You do. You can make a place for yourself with my people."

I didn't move. "I can't go around helping the sick die. I can't spend my days roping in spirits so their living relatives can have a conversation with them. I can't live this life of yours."

Luke's arms dropped by his side. He looked hurt. "What'll you do?"

"I don't know," I whispered.

"Where will you go?"

I shook my head. "I'm not sure."

His exasperation showed on his face. "Look, this is crazy. I'm not going to let you walk out the door when all of this is over. I care about you, whether you want to hear it or not. And I know you care about me."

"Stop saying that!"

"I won't let you go."

I laughed suddenly, but even to my own ears it sounded hollow and forced. "You plan to force me to stay with you?"

His voice was low. "You know that's not what I meant."

Neither one of us said anything for a few moments; we just stood there staring at each other. I finally broke the silence. "You don't want me. You don't have feelings for me. You can't."

"Don't tell me how I feel." He was angry again.

"We barely know each other." I could feel tears forming but blinked them back.

"I know all I need to. I want to be with you."

"You can't mean that, we barely know each other." A single tear slid down my face. "I can't do this."

A voice called, "Is this a bad time?" Freddy stood in the doorway with a large, black duffel bag over one shoulder.

I wiped my tears away and greeted Freddy quickly, "Hi, Freddy. There are some muffins in the kitchen if you want one."

He glanced from me to Luke. "Thanks, but I've already eaten." He set the bag down on the floor. "Is everything alright?"

I waited for Luke to say something, but he just stood there silently, frustration apparent in his eyes as he watched me. I forced a smile onto my face. "What's in your bag?"

Freddy crouched down and opened it. He started to pull out items. "Duct tape, some rope, a small axe, basically anything I could think of that might help."

That was the problem—none of us knew what type of situation we were walking into. It was foolish and reckless for us to head up there and try to save Darla without a plan, but that's exactly what we were going to be doing in just a few hours.

## CHAPTER
# TWENTY-NINE

J ust after the sun set, we climbed into Freddy's car and started heading up to the hotel. Instead of focusing on what we were about to do, I kept going over the conversation I'd had with Luke.

Luke confused me—the way he made me feel when I was around him was something I'd never felt with anyone before. My head kept telling me that this thing between us was all happening too fast, that I couldn't trust the emotions swirling inside me. But did I mean all those things I had said to him? I wasn't sure.

I couldn't see myself fitting into the life of a death dealer. I feared the reaction I'd get from his guild when they found out what I could do. Luke seemed to think they would welcome me with open arms, but I doubted it. I remembered the look on his face when I'd raised the dead and the terror that filled him when he realized the mob at the hospital would connect us to the undead rising. People had feared Luke and his guild before, but now they might be hunted.

If the death dealers became targets, it would be because of

me. If the general public started hurting or killing their kind, how could the guild ever forgive me?

I looked over at Luke. He was behind the steering wheel, his full attention focused on the road. I sat in the front seat next to him. He hadn't said anything to me since we got in the car.

I regretted our fight. We didn't know what we were heading off to face, and we didn't know if we would be coming back. What if those words said in anger were the last words, we ever spoke to each other? I reached over and touched his arm. Luke glanced at me; a questioning look on his face. I gave him a smile. He smiled back.

Freddy began telling yet another story from the backseat. Luke had been quiet, and I'd been lost in thought for most the drive, but Freddy had been a nonstop chatterbox.

Apparently, Freddy was the type to talk when he was nervous, so for a solid twenty minutes I heard stories of Darla, Luke, and Freddy growing up together. I now knew why Luke had a small scar on his elbow. At age seven he fell out of a tree and broke his arm. It probably hadn't helped that Freddy dared Luke to climb the tree in the first place, or that after Luke scrambled up, Freddy started throwing rocks at him just for "motivation." I found the stories charming and funny. Knowing where we were going and what we were about to try and do, they were distracting, and that was a good thing. Freddy started another tale, this one about the time he and Luke prank called Darla when she was babysitting. They freaked her out by imitating weird, scary voices over the phone.

Luke interrupted him. "Freddy, enough with the stories."

He pulled the car over onto a dirt road and stopped.

I looked out the window. The headlights shone on dense trees and foliage, but outside of the glare of the headlights, it was pitch black.

"Where are we?" I asked.

"About half a mile from the hotel. This is an old logging road. I figure we can make our way on foot to the edge of the property and hopefully not be seen by anyone." Luke gestured to the left. "If we kept to the main road for another few minutes, we would've hit the main gate. Then, through the gate, it's about a mile up a winding driveway to the front entrance."

"We hike through the woods and scope out the place?" Right now, it was the only plan we had.

"That's the idea. We get as close as we can and do some reconnaissance." Luke looked over at me. "We'll see how well they're guarding the place. Maybe we'll get a glimpse of how many people are there. If we get lucky, we'll stumble across Darla and get her out."

And if we get unlucky, we'll end up dead. I didn't say what I was thinking out loud, but Luke seemed able to read my mood.

In a defensive voice, he said, "If anyone has a better idea, speak up."

When neither Freddy nor I said anything, Luke turned off the headlights and ignition. He opened the car door and got out. "Freddy, hand me one of the flashlights you brought."

Freddy reached into his bag and pulled out a small light.

Luke turned it on, aiming the light toward the ground. "Darla, Freddy, and I hiked up here quite a few times when we were kids. There's a favorite picnic spot with a view of the lake not far from the hotel property. We should be able to make our way through the woods without too much trouble."

And when we get there? I hadn't been able to bind Thomas to me. I had no banshee magic to wield against the bad guys. Freddy brought his bag with the axe and duct tape. How either was helpful was beyond me, but at least we had another body helping out. Three against a dozen? Two dozen? I shook my head and tried to push away all my doubts. We were here now. It made sense to check the place out.

We hiked through the dark woods, me trailing behind Luke. When he suddenly stopped, I stumbled against his back.

He turned the flashlight off. "You see the lights up ahead? We're close."

He moved forward and I followed. Now walking in complete darkness, I stumbled on a rock.

Luke reached out and grabbed me before I fell. "Careful, the ground ahead is uneven."

"How can you see where you're going?" I whispered.

"I've always had good night vision. Put your hand on my shoulder."

I did as he said, and we made our way slowly through the trees and underbrush toward the house.

The hotel was bigger than I imagined. We were facing the rear. Tiki torches lined a back courtyard. There was some kind of event going on. People were gathered in small groups, scattered around the grounds.

Are they having a party? It didn't look like a celebration. There was no food or drink.

I moved closer and observed that the people were all wearing masks. A ritual? A gathering of the clan? This was not what healer clans did when they got together. Healer clan gatherings were under the sun, and food and drink were abundant. They often played games and put on events showing off feats of strength and skill in magic. People wagered over the games, and everyone laughed and talked.

There was no loud laughter or loud speaking going on, but people were talking—I could tell by the way they huddled together, heads almost touching. Whispering.

Masks and near silence.

What are they doing?

So far, we hadn't stumbled across any guards or security. The property had been easy enough to breach. They oddly didn't seem worried about keeping people out. Darting from shrubs to trees, Luke, Freddy, and I slowly made our way closer. When we were on the very edge of the grounds, about ten feet away from the closest group of people, a trumpet sounded. The crowd, which had been quiet until now, broke out into loud shouts and cheers.

What the hell is this about? Everyone turned in unison and started to make their way back to the hotel. There was an arched doorway leading inside. The group closest to us started to follow the herd, but one person lingered. The person stopped, pushing back the cloak and pulling down the golden mask hiding the top half of their face. It was a woman. She was leaning over, moving aside the hem of her cloak to adjust a strap on her fancy footwear.

I looked down at what I was wearing. Black jeans, black boots, and a black jacket. If we wanted to get in, we needed one of those cloaks and a mask. I didn't have a real plan in mind, and I was as surprised as anyone when I started moving forward. Luke reached out as if to stop me, but I sidestepped his grasp.

My whole focus was on the woman. If I can somehow get close enough. I reached down and picked up a fallen tree branch. Just a little closer now and I'd be within reach. One more step.

The woman spun around. Her eyes registered surprise and then outrage, and she sucked in a breath to shout an alarm. I raised the branch, and without even the slightest hesitancy, brought it down on her head.

The woman dropped to the ground.

I stood, almost as stunned as she was. I looked at the branch in my hand and let it fall from my grasp. The woman was lying on the ground with a large gash on the side of her temple. Blood began to seep from the wound.

Oh, Goddess. I killed her. I hit her over the head and killed her.

I began to panic. I couldn't believe what I had just done.

But then, to my surprise, the woman's head began to move back and forth. She moaned softly. My knees almost buckled with relief.

She's not dead. She's alive!

Luke was at my side, grabbing my arm. "Are you crazy? What are you doing?"

I raised a trembling hand to my forehead. "We need her cloak to get in there." I was still having a hard time wrapping my mind around the fact I had just walked up and clubbed some innocent woman.

*Not so innocent,* a voice whispered in the corner of my mind. She was one of the bad guys, and I had to admit to the rush of adrenaline I'd felt when I brought that branch down on her head. A part of me wanted to see her suffer for hurting my family. It was not like me. I was not a violent person.

But I had changed.

The rituals changed me, and I was morphing into someone else. Someone who seriously scared me.

Freddy was suddenly in front of us. "Whatever the two of you are doing, I suggest we move. We're sitting ducks out here. One person turns our way, and they'll see us."

I leaned down and grabbed the woman's right arm to pull her toward the shrubbery. I looked up at Luke. "I need your help —she's heavy."

He frowned, but without a word reached down and grabbed her other arm. Freddy picked up her feet, and we carried the woman into the bushes.

Once under the cover of the foliage, I squatted down beside the woman. She moaned, but her eyes stayed closed. I didn't know how much longer she'd be unconscious. Whatever I was going to do, I needed to get moving. I opened the front of the cloak and eased it off her, then made a grab for the mask. I put them both on and turned toward the hotel.

Luke blocked my way. He stood arms crossed at his chest, a determined look on his face. "No way you're going in there by yourself."

"This was your plan. You said if an opportunity came up to save Darla, we should take it." I lifted the mask. "This is an opportunity."

His eyes narrowed. "You're not going in there without me."

"Find another way in." I looked over at Freddy. "You guys can scout out the rest of the hotel. This is a gargantuan place, there has to be some side door or servants' entrance you can get through."

"Luke, it's not a bad idea," Freddy said, coming to my side.

Luke's eyes filled with concern. "Colina, I'm not letting you out of my sight."

"This was your plan. We have a chance for me to go in and see the layout. Try to find where they're keeping Darla." I could see by his expression that I wasn't changing his mind, so I tried again. "I'm in a cloak and mask surrounded by a couple dozen people dressed the exact same way. No one will recognize me. I can blend in and move around unnoticed."

Luke shook his head. "It's a bad idea."

I pulled the mask down and started forward. "I'm doing it, and I don't need your permission."

Luke put his hand on my arm as if to stop me, but I shook it off and kept moving.

His hand came down hard on my shoulder this time, and he spun me around. "I know we fought earlier. It was a stupid fight."

"I'm sorry about the things I said." I looked over at Freddy, who just stood there watching us. I reached out, grabbed Luke's hand, and pulled it into mine. "I'm not going to do anything stupid."

He squeezed my hand. "Promise me you'll just take a look around. If you see Darla or any of the guys who tried to grab you at the magic shop, you won't do anything. You'll wait for us."

"I promise," I whispered.

He took a step forward and lifted the mask off my face. Before I could say anything, he leaned in and pressed his lips against mine. It was a soft, gentle kiss. His fingers came up and brushed against my cheek. "We're all going to get out of this in one piece. We just have to play it smart."

I didn't know what to say to that. A part of me wanted to push myself into his arms—to feel his warm, solid body against mine, but I held myself back. If I hugged him now, I may never let go. I forced myself to release his hand and take a step back. Then I gave a half wave, turned around, and made my way to the hotel.

I knew he was watching me. I desperately wanted to turn around, to see him one last time before I headed off into Goddess only knew what. What dark and creepy things would I run across in there? I squared my shoulders and lifted my chin. I could do this. I had to do this.

I quickened my steps and headed toward the unknown.

CHAPTER

# THIRTY

I was running out of time. Most of the crowd had made their way in. I hurried my steps toward the large archway. A man, also dressed in a cloak and mask, was closing two exceptionally large, ornate wooden doors about ten feet high.

I spoke up. "Wait, wait. I'm coming."

The man swung the door open.

I put on my best smile, remembering a second later that I was wearing a mask. "I'm sorry, I had a problem with my shoe."

The man nodded without any sign of suspicion, and I slid by him.

I was finally inside. Now what? They were holding Darla somewhere inside, but where?

I made my way down a hallway and into a big room. Mirrors covered one of the walls. The floor was wood, but not any kind I had seen before. Different colored, exotic looking wood panels created elaborate patterns and designs across the surface of the floor. Three large, crystal chandeliers hung from the ceiling.

I expected to see a crowd, but the space was empty. I moved

across the room and through another set of doors. This hallway was smaller than the last and entirely red: red paint covered the walls and ceiling, and red carpeting lay on the floors. Hues of red, yellows, and oranges covered the half dozen paintings on the walls. I made my way down the hall, and at the end I stopped in front of another large door.

I was reaching for the doorknob when I felt a chill running across my arms. There was another breeze across my face and a whisper, and I knew I wasn't alone.

I felt a tug on the cloak and then another, and the words "This way" echoed through my mind. It sounded like Sarah's voice. It was then I noticed the large red and gold tapestry hanging on the wall to my right.

I walked over to the tapestry. This way? There was no door, at least not one I could see. I was starting to turn away when something pushed hard against my back, and I stumbled forward. I reached out to catch myself, but instead of falling against the wall, I fell through the tapestry.

I came down hard on my knees on a stone floor. A secret room? I looked around. It wasn't a room, but another hallway. This one was barely wide enough for a single body to move through. Light flickered from somewhere down at the other end. I got to my feet and made my way down the small passage-way. My hands trailed against the cold stone wall as I walked. The passage slowly opened up into a small room that was only a few feet long, and on the other side was a gray stone staircase winding into a spiral, heading down. Old fashioned light fixtures lit the walls, and I could see light shining up from wherever the staircase led.

So far, I hadn't met anyone. No one had demanded to know where I was going, and up until this point, if I ran across some-one, I could claim to be lost. But if I came across someone now, how would I explain my descent through the dark, winding staircase?

I held my breath as I made my way down the stairs. I got lucky—there was no one to greet me at the bottom. I now stood in a hallway that ran in two directions.

I was looking right and left, trying to decide which way to go, when I heard Sarah's voice again. "Close," she said. Pieces of my hair gently lifted on the left side of my head. Decision made. I turned left and started down the hall.

I don't know why I stopped—no voice sounded this time; no invisible hands were guiding me. Doors lined the hallway, but for some reason one particular doorway brought me to a dead halt. I tried the doorknob. It turned easily enough, but the door still wouldn't open. Looking up, I saw a padlock and hasp near the top of the door. I put my ear to the thick wood—there was a noise. Another. Muted voices on the other side?

It was a crazy thing to do, but I knocked on the door and said softly, "Darla?"

Silence answered my question.

I tried again, this time louder. "Darla, are you in there? It's Colina."

I waited a few seconds. I was starting to walk away when I heard the tap. It was coming from the other side of the door.

"Darla? Is that you?"

Two taps this time.

It's her! I was sure of it. Darla was on the other side of the door. I rattled the door handle in frustration. "Darla, hang in there. The door's locked. I have to try and find something to get it open. Your brother's here. Freddy's here. We're going to get you out."

Two more taps. Was it truly Darla behind the door, just unable to speak? No one had jumped out to grab me, so it wasn't a bad guy. I wanted to believe with all my being that it was Darla.

But if it was and I'd found her, how was I going to get her out?

I made my way back up the stairs, down the passage, and through the tapestry, retracing my footsteps. And then I paused, confused for a moment about which way I had come. All of the doors looked the same, and Sarah seemed to have gone quiet. I went through the door at the end of the hall, trusting luck to lead me out. My only thought was getting back outside so I could find Luke and Freddy. We had to come up with a plan to get back inside and open that door.

I was expecting to walk into another empty room, but this time the room was full. It was identical to the other. Mirrors hung from one wall, wooden patterns ran across the floor, and glass chandeliers hung overhead. But the chandeliers weren't lit. The room was mostly dark except for the glow of candles. A dozen large, black candelabras circled the middle of the room, and each held six lit red candles. The flames from the candles created eerie shadows that danced across the mirrors.

Everyone was dressed in cloaks and masks. Those closest to the door turned when I entered. I had no choice now but to join them and try to act like I was supposed to be there. I nodded my head while walking into the room, and as I did a loud voice boomed overhead, "The time is finally here!"

A man stood on a platform in the center of the room, surrounded by the candelabras. He wore a red robe, and a bright orange mask covered his face.

The man raised his hands and his voice. "Everyone, everyone, thank you for coming!" He made a sweeping gesture with his arms. "I know you're as excited as I am that the time is upon us. We've waited so long for this day."

I immediately recognized his voice.

It was Macaven, the man who murdered my father.

At first, I felt astonishment. Here was the man who killed my family. Then, that shock was replaced by a cold rage. I wanted to rush forward, to attack him and claw at him with my bare hands. My fingers trembled and tears swelled in my eyes. I tried to calm the raging emotions swirling through me.

People began to move forward, and I moved with them. Silence fell over the crowd and bodies pushed in. Everyone's attention was on the man in the red robe.

Someone led a white sheep with large horns up onto the platform. It struggled to get free, bleating loudly, but was held tight. Someone lifted it and put it next to Macaven. It was only when Macaven took a step forward that I saw the stone altar. They tied the sheep to it.

They were going to make a sacrifice. An animal sacrifice.

A large knife was handed to Macaven. He held it high in the air with both hands. The knife came down fast and sliced across the sheep's throat, silencing its frantic bleating.

Applause sounded from the crowd, and they began to chant the name "Macaven" as blood gushed onto the altar.

I felt my whole body begin to tremble.

He killed the sheep just like he killed my father.

Macaven raised a hand in the air, and everyone fell silent. "I know we've waited so very long for this day. Many of you have newly come into our fold to be a part of this fantastic journey we're about to embark on." He wiped the blade of the knife across the sleeve of his robe. "As you know, I'm Donald Macaven, grand master of the Garuda Guild. For one hundred years, the rest of the death dealer guilds have forced our people away from the past traditions that made us one of the strongest guilds. It was a vain attempt to gain favor with weak souls unfit to lick our boots."

"For one hundred years, we've stood by and watched as

other weaker guilds used small, minded rules to steal our power and influence. They outlawed sacrifices, which are the path to true power. Our weakness forced us into submission, but no more. No more will we follow the ways of others. We've been and always will be the true leaders of our kind. Magical royalty pumps through our veins."

He began to walk around the stone altar. "With the traditional sacrifice of a ram, I call this convocation of the Garuda Guild to order. With this sacrifice we commemorate the greater sacrifices that have made this day possible and ask the blessing of the dark powers in our great working.

"I know many of you who have entered our fold over the last year are not blood kin." He raised his hand again. "But that doesn't mean that you're not family to us. You're all closer now than blood could ever be, for you've helped shed blood in our name, for our cause. You've done what had to be done in order for us to raise ourselves back up toward greatness. Without your help, we wouldn't be here now on the precipice of a new age."

"I know there were some who refused to be a part of this great adventure. I think we should take a moment and bow our heads in silence for those lost to us, for those poor souls who could not—or would not—see the way to true enlightenment."

Everyone around me bowed their heads. I did the same. What the hell is going on? Who are all these people, and what is this "enlightenment" he's talking about? I have to get out of here and find Luke and Freddy. I had never heard of the Garuda Guild, but, then again, I wasn't that familiar with death dealer guilds.

I started to take a step back, looking for a way back outside, but before I could move away, Macaven lifted his head. He raised the dagger high in the air and swiftly brought it down into the middle of the now dead ram. He slashed across its midsection. Blood and guts started to ooze out onto the stone's surface.

He shouted and raised his arms. "We call on you, dark powers beyond, the forces that can show us the way to the true calling!"

The ram's blood and entrails poured down onto the altar, and a swirl of orange began to form above the stone. Faces slowly surfaced within the orange cloud—faces with expressions frozen in torment and pain. Macaven was calling on spirits. As these spirits opened their mouths, wild, terrified shrieks filled the room. Banshees. He's raised banshees.

I began to move back in earnest but was only able to take one step before a shock of recognition ran through me. One of the faces in the mist looked familiar. There was something about the nose and the lips. *Oh, Goddess, how can this be?* I watched in absolute horror as the spirit of my brother, James, floated past.

"James," I whispered. The moment I did, my brother's spirit changed direction and headed toward me.

I took a faltering step forward, my hand outstretched. "James."

Before I could move, arms grabbed me roughly from behind. A hand covered my mouth, dragging me back into the shadows. I struggled against my assailant, but he was stronger. I was shoved to the back of the room. I broke free and twirled around, my hands forming into fists. I started to take a swing, but then froze when I grasped that it was Luke glaring down at me.

He had on a black cloak, and a golden mask was pushed up onto his forehead. "Are you insane? You can't confront a banshee. It's suicidal."

"It's James, my brother—did you see him?" My words came out in a rush.

CATRINA BURGESS

Luke stood looking at me, his expression one of shock. "One of the banshees is your brother?"

I nodded. A tear slid down my face.

"Colina, how did your brother die?"

I turned away, unable to answer.

CHAPTER

# THIRTY-ONE

Luke grabbed my arm and pulled me out of the room, through the door, and into the hallway. He stood behind me, his voice low. "Tell me what happened to your brother."

I swallowed thickly. "He was there and then he wasn't. They did something to him. I didn't understand it at the time. I could hear his screams even after his body fell to the ground."

As I began explaining to him, the horrible memory flashed across my mind. I tried to calm my racing thoughts, but for a moment the images overwhelmed me.

James tried to fight, raising magics designed to heal and using them in ways that I never thought possible. He was older and fully trained. He had an arsenal of spells in his repertoire that I hadn't even begun to learn. I might not have been able to cast the spells, but I recognized them when I heard them. He manipulated a spell used to slow poisonings and two of the men bent over, vomiting violently. I heard him shout the words for a spell that Mama often used to anesthetize patients for surgery—another man collapsed onto the floor. But there were

283

three more mages, and they were unaffected as James threw attack after attack at them.

But it was Macaven who advanced on James slowly, the air around him crackling with discharging energies. He paused to kick one of the vomiting men out of his way, sending him sprawling into a pool of his own sick. Macaven laughed cruelly at the miserable man, stepping around him to stand in front of my brother.

James gathered his power and fired a spell at Macaven. It was a simple spell—one used to break up blood clots in stroke victims—but James fueled it with all of the power he possessed. He released it at Macaven, but to my disbelief, the dark mage calmly clapped his hands together and the spell rebounded back onto James. The light around the magic changed color and expanded. The spell my brother cast was somehow morphed; Macaven had turned it against him.

When the ball of light hit James, he collapsed to the ground like a puppet cut from its strings. He lay still for a moment, then rolled onto his side, coughing heavily. Red blood sprayed the floor in front of him. He rose slowly to his knees, his breathing loud and labored, and began to crawl away from Macaven—and toward me, hiding in the pantry. His face rose to meet mine through the slit in the pantry door. I screamed at the sight of blood pouring from the inner corners of my brother's eyes like tears. Blood slid out of his ears and nose. An alarming volume flowed down his chin, splashing onto the floor in a rapidly spreading pool.

I shrieked, but they couldn't hear me.

Even as he started to die before my eyes, James's spell bound me to the pantry, kept my presence hidden, kept my cries blocked from the outside world.

His eyes locked onto mine for a second. I was still cowering in my hiding spot, and I saw the awareness dawn in his bloodshot eyes that he was leading Macaven straight to me. He stopped crawling, a look of calm resignation on his face. He turned, trying painfully to rise to his feet as Macaven strode up to him. Macaven reached out a long finger and placed it on the center of James's chest.

In one final act of defiance, James spit a mouthful of blood into Macaven's face.

The dark mage didn't even blink. His lips moved in a spell I couldn't hear, and James started screaming. Macaven pulled his finger back, and I stared, horrified, as my brother's soul came with it. He screeched as if he was being shredded from the inside out. After a few more moments of painful wailing, James's body collapsed to the floor, his mouth slack and unmoving—but still the scream went on, roaring through the air as his spirit was torn from his body and thrown into the ether sea.

My eyes never left my brother's face as all the blood left his body, forming a large puddle around him. My mother and father died brutal deaths, but their ends had come mercifully quick. Not James. James died painfully, horribly. His was a death I couldn't bear to think about.

When I finished, the expression on Luke's face was full of tortured grief.

"I'm so sorry," he whispered as he wrapped his arms around me, trying to shelter me from the horrible memory I'd described.

I realized I was breathing heavily, my heart pounding in my chest. Tears streamed down my face. I forced the image of my brother's empty eyes, of his crumpled body covered in blood, from my mind, and I was finally able to slow the out-of-control memories that raced through me. I leaned against Luke, feeling my pulse return to normal in the warmth of his embrace.

When I found my voice again, I asked, "Does that mean

Macaven bound James's spirit?" I held my breath, hoping his answer would prove my worst fears wrong.

"It makes sense. Macaven could have bound your brother's spirit. If he did, James is one of his banshees now."

At Luke's words, a desperate anger filled me. "No! We have to help him." I started toward the door. Voices could be heard shouting from the other room.

Luke pulled me back. "We have to save Darla. Now that the ceremony has distracted everyone, we can search for her."

"I know where she is."

Luke's fingers dug into my arm. "Where?"

I pointed toward the tapestry. "Through there. There's a hidden passage and then a set of stairs, and at the bottom of the stairs are rooms. I think she's in one."

More shouts could be heard from the other room. Luke looked from the door to the tapestry. "We have to get her out. Our best chance is now, while everyone is busy."

"But James—"

Luke interrupted me. "Your brother is dead. But Darla is alive." He reached over and pulled up my mask. "I'm sorry, Colina." He brought his face close to mine. "James's spirit can't come to you. Macaven has bound him."

"Is that why when I called my family, I could only make contact with my mother? But what about my father?"

Luke turned away.

I gasped. "You know something about my father?"

He turned back toward me. "There's no time for this. We have to go after Darla."

"What did that madman do to my father? Tell me!"

Luke didn't say anything for a few seconds. He just stood there, looking as though he were trying to decide something. A grim expression crossed his face when he finally spoke. "When I was researching what ancient spells they could be trying to do, I came across one that involved a dagger. When we were in there, I got close to the platform, and I got a good look at the knife." He sighed. "I think it might be the same one they used to kill your father."

I let out a quiet moan.

Luke reached up and wiped away a tear from my cheek. "If I'm right and Macaven's using the same ceremonial knife, the one I recognized from the books, then your father's soul became trapped in the dagger."

"I don't understand."

"Macaven needs magic to power the old spells. He wants to create something—something that can wield power. Something bigger, something not of this world. From what I heard people saying in the crowd, tonight he's making preparations for an old and powerful spell. He's trying to bring forth—" He stopped.

"A spirit? Like the banshees?"

"No. Something far worse." A look of fear crossed his eyes. "A demon."

Another burst of sound came from the room. Whatever they were doing in there, they were enjoying it. The crowd had looked on with enthusiasm as Macaven killed the ram. What will they do when he starts sacrificing people? The thought sent chills down my spine.

Luke must have been thinking along the same lines—an expression of fear and then outrage crossed his face. He looked at me and said in an angry voice, "A demon isn't a spirit, not in the strictest sense. It's a combination of spirits, of their essence, it makes something bigger, darker. For this spell Macaven would have had to kill a lot of men who had evil in their hearts."

His words shocked me. "My father was not evil." My voice was full of outrage.

"No, but he was powerful. Once Macaven had a collection of

souls, the essence of those souls would give the demon enough power to cross over. But it's not enough just to gather the souls. Macaven would have to form some sort of gateway, a dark door to bring it into our world. And to do that, he'd need power. Lots of power."

"And you think that's why he's been killing people?"

"Right now, we have to save my sister. I heard them say they're going to do more sacrifices at midnight. We don't have a lot of time."

"But James..."

Luke raised his hand and stopped me. "First, we free my sister. Then we will find a way to help your brother."

Everything Luke said made sense. The reason my father's and brother's spirits had never tried to contact me was because Macaven had bound them. Now they were both part of his sick and twisted plan.

I had to find a way to set them free.

# THIRTY-TWO

L uke turned toward the door. "Freddy's still in there, on the other side of the room. We split up. We were keeping watch for you."

"How did you get the cloaks and masks?"

He touched the silky black material. "We came in a side door. They had these all laid out on a table for people to take." He took a step and put his hand on the doorknob. "I'll go get Freddy."

I started to follow.

He pointed toward the tapestry. "You wait in the hidden passage. I promise I won't be long."

"We should stick together." If he was going back in there, I was going with him.

"From the sounds they're making, who knows what kind of twisted magic they might be doing. I've got a better chance on my own." He turned and faced me. "Colina, I promise we will find a way to help your brother once we get Darla out."

James's spirit is in there, bound to that madman. "Can you make someone release a banshee?"

Luke put both hands on my shoulders. "No. You have to kill

the mage. As soon as a mage dies, all the spirits bound to them are released."

I clenched my fists. "If I kill Macaven, my brother's spirit goes free?"

"It's not as easy as it sounds. Macaven is a powerful mage who's been practicing ancient spells. He's more powerful than anyone I've ever come across."

"And my only powers are raising the dead and helping spirits cross over." I grabbed his arm. "Do you think I could force my brother's spirit to the other side like I did with Thomas?"

Luke shook his head. "Not while Macaven has him bound. His magic would hold your brother's spirit here. You'd have to somehow break his spell to release James."

"If I could get the dagger, I could slit Macaven's throat like he did to my father." The violent words that came out of my mouth surprised even me.

Luke's fingers dug into my skin. "That's your anger talking. It's an enchanted dagger. Killing Macaven with it, you don't know what that might do, what spell or thing that might set free." He let go of me and said in a soft voice, "Trust me, we'll find a way to release your brother, but right now we have to get my sister. Stay here. I'll get Freddy."

Without another word, Luke walked through the door and shut it quietly behind him.

I stared at the closed door. I could free my brother by killing Macaven. I wanted to kill Macaven as vengeance for my family. But even if I wanted to, how could I kill a powerful mage? I made my way behind the tapestry, into the passage, and stood at the top of the staircase, waiting.

Minutes passed, and there still no sign of Luke or Freddy.

I was starting to seriously worry when I heard footsteps

coming down the passage. There was no place to hide, no place to duck into. If it wasn't Luke and Freddy, I was in real trouble.

I heard a familiar voice call out. "We come in peace." Freddy wore a black cloak and held a mask in one hand.

I gestured down the stairway. "I think Darla is in a room at the bottom, but I couldn't get in. There's a heavy lock on the door."

Freddy opened the cloak and revealed the bag hanging over his right shoulder. He patted it. "No worries, I brought a few things that might help."

We made our way down the stairs and stopped in front of the door.

Freddy took off his cloak and put the bag on the floor. He opened it and rummaged around, withdrawing a bizarre assortment of implements. A hammer was followed by a can opener, then a bundle of bungee cords and a box of cookies. He swore quietly and shook the bag around to peer at its contents before finally pulling out a pair of bolt cutters.

"What didn't you bring?" Luke asked.

Freddy smiled up at us. "Like the Boy Scouts, I'm always prepared." He reached up with the bolt cutters, and after a few tense moments of wrestling, broke the lock.

I didn't have any proof that Darla was in there, only a gut feeling. We had no real idea what we were about to walk into.

Luke took the lead and leaned his hand on the door. "Stay behind me."

Freddy passed me a flashlight. "I'll stay out here as a lookout."

The door swung open, and I followed Luke inside, moving my flashlight in a wide arc. It illuminated the room, showing two dozen bodies sitting and laying on the floor. Some turned to look at us as we entered, their eyes flat and hopeless, but most didn't even react to our presence. Their captors had placed tape over their mouths and bound their hands and feet with thick rope.

As I shone my light across fear-stricken faces, I came to the conclusion that these were the ones who'd refused to join Macaven's ranks. How could someone round up innocent people to be sacrificed? How many have they already killed? I could feel the anger building inside me.

I finally came across a face I recognized and gasped. There were bruises on Darla's face, and her mouth had been taped over. Someone had blackened one eye, and there were bruises on her face, but that wasn't the worst part.

They had hacked off her beautiful hair.

Where golden strands once fell almost to the floor, her hair was now short. It was chopped hazardously around her head above her ears. Her eyes were locked on us, and she tried desperately to rise despite her bound hands and feet. Luke rushed toward his sister. He pulled out a pocketknife and started to cut the ropes binding her hands.

I reached up and touched her face, which was wet with tears. "Darla, what did they do to you?"

Luke reached up and grabbed one edge of the tape covering her mouth. "This is going to hurt."

Darla nodded her head, and Luke yanked.

A cry of pain escaped Darla's mouth. Her now free hands reached up and touched her brother's face. "You found me. I knew you would." They embraced.

I didn't know how much time we had, but there were a lot of people to untie. I moved to the body closest to me and started to work on the ropes when I heard Freddy's voice. "Someone's coming. There are lights coming down the staircase."

Luke's large hands grabbed at me. "We have to get out of here."

"But we can't leave them," I said, looking around at the

people that filled the room. Eyes pleaded with us to save them. The looks on the faces, the fear in their eyes. We couldn't just leave them.

Luke pulled me roughly to my feet. "We can't help them if we get caught. We have to get out of here now."

I wouldn't leave them to be slaughtered like my family. I fought against him, but Luke pushed and shoved me out of the room. Freddy supported Darla as Luke roughly shoved me down the passage.

At the end of the hall was another set of stairs. We didn't have a choice—we headed up. We went through another narrow passage and came to an exterior door.

Luke opened it and stuck his head through. "It's clear."

We made our way out of the hotel, across the patio, and back into the bushes. Darla rushed into Luke's arms as soon as we were a reasonable distance from the hotel. Luke held his sister as she cried softly into his shoulder.

Freddy dropped his bag and went over to join them. The three of them stood there, huddled together.

Freddy spoke up. "There were a couple dozen people in that room. Why have they taken so many people hostage?"

"So Macaven can kill them," I answered.

Luke held his sister at arm's length, examining her, and then drew her close again. "Not everyone Macaven has taken is dead. My guess is that he's building some kind of coven. And they're recreating the spells of old. The girl from the lake—Sarah. She said they gave her a choice, and she refused to give them what they wanted, right? I'm betting they wanted her power, whatever it might have been. They wanted her will given over to the group."

I was trying to understand what he was telling me, but none of it made sense. "But why?"

"So, they could combine and become more than just themselves. Groups are dangerous. My people never combine our magics. We're a guild, true, but everyone wields their own power separately. Centuries ago, there were covens—groups of magicians. The problem is that the leader of the group defines what that magic is like, its flavor, you could say. They take over the coven's free will. Everyone in the coven becomes like the banshees, in a way, a living person magically bound to the coven's leader. Bound to do their bidding."

"Macaven is trying to form a coven with the strongest mage members he can find? And if they won't play along, he kills them?" I shook my head. "But they didn't sacrifice Sarah. They just killed her."

Luke's eyes met mine. "There are tales in the old books about covens hunting people for pleasure. For the thrill of killing. The violence inside them takes over in a way that's dangerous. The power that runs through the blood of the mage-born is addictive. Macaven could lose control of them at any moment; but from what we just overheard, he's close to letting the demon out."

"And if he does?" I demanded.

Luke frowned. "Demons haven't roamed the earth for a hundred years."

Demons. Luke is talking about demons. A shiver went down my spine at the thought of such an evil creature set loose on the world. "How do you stop a demon?"

"There were people trained to kill them, to force them into oblivion, but those arts have long been lost." Luke slowly shook his head back and forth. "There are no demon killers in this day and age."

"The demon would have free reign, and Macaven would control it?" There will be no one to stop him, I thought immediately. But Luke said Macaven was still preparing for the spell, which meant we still had time to stop it. "How will he raise the demon?"

"If he has enough people in the coven, they'll help him generate the power he needs," Luke answered.

"And my father, you think his spirit is in the dagger?" I asked.

He looked away. "Your father is gone." Luke left Darla's side and came to mine. He reached over and grabbed my hand. "It's not like your brother. Your father's spirit, his very essence has combined with the others who were sacrificed with the knife."

"Combined with the evil ones?" I said through clenched teeth.

Luke's voice was grim. "The darkest hearts and souls."

I couldn't believe my father would be trapped forever in the dagger, turned into the power source for some evil spell. "There's no way to release him?"

"None that I know of," Luke answered.

"We have to stop Macaven." We couldn't let that madman go through with his plans. How many had he killed, and how many more would die at his hands if he raised a demon? We'd left all those people. All those people in the basement were going to be slaughtered, killed brutally just like my family. The image of the bullet tearing through my mother's forehead flashed before my eyes. I could still remember the smell of my father's blood as it gushed from the wicked gash across his neck.

Everyone bound and gagged in the basement of the hotel was going to die, and we hadn't done anything to stop it.

Luke looked over at his sister and then back at me. "Soon they'll figure out Darla's missing and start searching for her, searching for us. We need to head back to the car and get out of here as fast as we can." He put his arm around Darla and started urging her away from the hotel.

I walked over to Freddy's bag and started rummaging through it, looking for a weapon I could use. I pulled out the axe. It was heavy, but light enough for me to swing. "I can't leave those people to be killed by Macaven and his insane followers."

"You saw how many there were. We're outnumbered," Luke said.

"We can't just turn and run," I cried. James's spirit was still bound as a banshee. My father's spirit was lost within the dagger. I believed they both could be saved—there had to be some way to free them. I wasn't going to run away again, not this time.

Luke's eyes met mine. "Our guild will be back next week. When they come back, we'll make sure Macaven pays for what he's done."

I couldn't believe what I was hearing. "By next week Macaven will have freed the demon. Your said it yourself: there are no more demon killers. You said there isn't anyone strong enough to stop him. Macaven is powerful now, but with a demon at his side, he'll be invincible."

Luke's arm tightened around his sister. "Colina, it's suicide to go back in there."

"I can't leave those people. I won't leave those people. I won't leave James," I said through clenched teeth. I swung the axe. It sank a good inch into the solid trunk of the nearest tree.

Luke was starting to get angry. "What do you think you're going to do with that? You think you can take on dozens of mages with your little axe? You aren't thinking straight. You have a right to be upset about your brother and your father, I understand—"

I cut him off. "You don't understand." I pulled the axe out with a violent tug. I watched helpless as my entire family was taken away from me. My brother's soul was bound to a madman, my father's soul possibly imprisoned in an evil dagger. I couldn't walk away. I had to make Macaven and his coven pay for what they did.

"We have to play it smart and wait for backup." Luke's eyes were now pleading with me.

"You don't have any banshee power. You don't know any spells. We go back in there and we are all dead."

I knew what he was saying was true, but I didn't care. A red-hot frustration burned inside me. I was past reason. The only thought pounding through my head was revenge.

I looked at him and said, "I'm going back in."

Luke made a grab for me, but I pushed him away. I started running back toward the house. What I was doing was suicide, but I didn't care. What if by the time we came back with his guild, the coven had all disappeared? Once they left, it might be impossible to find them again. I knew where they were now, and I wasn't going to lose this chance to try and stop them. With their deaths, dozens would be saved.

This was my last chance before Macaven became untouchable, too powerful for anyone to stop.

I ran toward the hotel. Luke started to follow but tripped over a branch and hit the ground hard. By the time he got up and started after me again, I was already at the door. I slipped inside.

Anger fueled my blood and violence radiated out of me. The powerful darkness coursed through my body giving me power and I could feel sliding down my limbs and tingling from my fingertips.

I'd find a way to balance the scales. These madmen would pay for what they did with their lives.

# THIRTY-THREE

This time there was no one standing watch over the archway. I had no plan of action. I wasn't thinking now, only reacting. My heart pounded in my chest; I could hear it roaring in my ears. An image of the dagger flashed before my eyes. If I could get my hands on the dagger, I could stop Macaven from creating the demon. I'd freed Thomas, hadn't I? I could find a way to use my new abilities to free my father. Kill the mage and the banshees go free. If I could kill Macaven, my brother's spirit would be released.

I needed to get my hands on the dagger and thrust it through Macaven's heart. If only I could create some kind of distraction and get close enough to the altar. I could wait until they weren't paying attention and make a grab for the knife. If I could get near Macaven, I might just be able to pull it off.

And once I did? How would I get away? How could I possibly escape? I pushed those thoughts aside and kept moving.

I went through one room and into the hallway. I was jogging now, trying to get back to the convocation before they moved on to human sacrifices. I didn't know what time it was, but, come midnight, Luke said they would move from killing livestock to killing people. They would start murdering the hostages held down below. Once I killed Macaven, I'd try to find a way to help the others escape.

No more innocent people would die, not if I could help it.

I came up to the door into the main room. I could hear people cheering on the other side. An image of Luke flashed through my mind and my fingers hesitated on the doorknob. There was a good chance I wouldn't make it out of this alive, and there were things left unsaid between us. I'd never told Luke how sorry I was about the stupid fight we'd had. How, the more I thought about it, the more I realized I did want to stay with him after this was all over. If his guild wouldn't accept me, maybe the two of us could go off together on our own. Luke said he wanted to be with me. If he cared about me, he might be willing to leave his guild to be with me.

I shook my head. If I did this—if I went through the door—I was risking everything to try and save the innocent lives of the people Macaven held hostage. But more importantly, I was getting vengeance for my family's death. My brother and father were dead, but Macaven still held their spirits. I had to try and release them from the dark mage's hold.

A sob escaped my mouth, and my hands trembled. I had to do it. I would fight this time, I would save what I could of my family.

I had to try.

I took a deep breath and let the anger run through me like a fire. It was what I needed now—the anger, the violence—that made death dealers so effective. I might not have spells, but Luke was wrong. I did have some magic.

I could raise the dead.

So what if I couldn't bring forth banshees? All I needed was a dead body or two, and I could create the distraction I needed.

My mind didn't even shy away at the thought of killing some-one. I was no longer the weak, helpless healer who'd stumbled into the magic shop. I'd been through the rituals and survived them. I watched my family be slaughtered, and I was still func-tioning. I'd been tested by fire and come out stronger. The fire turned me to steel.

I pushed open the door and walked into the room. Macaven was still by the altar, but this time instead of a ram lying across it, there was a teenage boy. The boy's hands were tied to either side of the stone surface as Macaven stood over him.

Everyone in the room except Macaven was swaying back and forth. As I passed a group of people, I realized no one in the crowd seemed aware I was there. They all were in some kind of trance. Macaven held a black book in one hand and the dagger in the other. He was reading words from the book in Latin with such intensity that he didn't notice when I entered.

I moved forward through the swaying crowd, weaving my way around black capes and making my way toward the altar. I pushed back my cloak, gripped my fingers tightly around the base of the axe.

Someone bumped into me. I turned. This guy didn't have a glazed expression on his face. He looked pissed. His hands came up and he started to make a grab for me.

He said, "Got her!" and I realized he was talking into an earpiece.

More guards were closing in on me from the back of the room. The coven had me trapped. I didn't doubt for a minute that they would kill me.

I didn't realize I'd lifted the axe until I saw it swinging down toward the man's head. It smashed into the side of his temple and stayed embedded as he fell to the ground. Blood spurted everywhere.

Adrenaline pumped through me. A part of me couldn't believe what I'd just done.

A cold breeze swirled around my neck, and the words "They're coming for you" whispered past my ear. Sarah was still with me.

I shook my head and looked across the sea of bodies. No one close to me seemed to notice what I had done. They were still swaying and chanting, their eyes glazed over. I could see movement, though—three or four men were making their way slowly around and through the crowd. I dropped to my knees next to the fallen guard. He was dead, I was sure of it. There was no spark of life in his eyes.

Before I could stop and think about what I was doing, I reached out with my hands and touched his face. A bright, orange light exploded, and there was a rush of sound and images. I sat back on my heels and watched as the dead man sat up.

"Girly, what've you have done to me now?" It was Wanda's voice. "You left me to that mob in the hospital. They tore the body I was in limb from limb, but it wasn't until all the parts started rotting that I was finally free, and now look what you've done!"

I closed my eyes and focused on Wanda's voice. I tried to reach out with my whole being and touch her spirit. I slowly spoke the words Luke had told me when I'd tried to bind Thomas's spirit. I didn't have a Ouija board or any of the other props, but I had to try something. "Constringo Constrixi Constrictum." I pointed toward the men coming my way and commanded, "Stop them."

I had no idea if it would work. I was reacting on pure instinct, but if I could create the undead, then maybe, like a banshee, I could bind them and control them. I held my breath and waited. Ever so slowly, the dead man rose to his feet, the axe still embedded in his head. He started walking toward the back of the room.

"What the hell is—I don't want to go this way. Why am I moving?" Wanda's voice cried out.

The dead man's arm reached up and pulled out the axe. He started to swing it in the air at the crowd as he moved.

I just raised the dead and released this thing, this zombie into the crowd. A zombie swinging an axe. How many people will that thing kill?

I'd wanted a distraction, true, but I had just committed murder—a healthy person this time—and now I'd set a monster onto the crowd. A part of me was crying out, screaming in my head that what I was doing was insane, but the anger in my blood was roaring so loud that I was having a hard time focusing on anything but the red rage washing over me in waves.

I watched Wanda stumble through the crowd, axe swinging clumsily back and forth through the air. The clumsy swings did little damage for the most part, but here and there the edge cut into a dazed follower. The axe came down into someone's arm and blood spurted out in a gush, but the trance was so deep that the man didn't even seem to notice. He swayed back and forth until his body slowly slid to the floor. Wanda the zombie was hurting people. Wanda the zombie would probably kill people.

I should have stopped her.

Instead, I turned and looked for Macaven.

He was still at the altar. I shoved my way through the crowd. The people around me were repeating each word that madman was saying. He was using the magic and the will of his coven to power a spell, but If Luke was right, Macaven would wait to release the demon under the dark moon tomorrow night.

If Macaven isn't releasing the demon, then what spell is he trying to work?

Screams began to ripple through the crowd behind me. Would Wanda's violence be enough of a distraction to unravel the spell? I turned and saw that she'd cut a path most of the way across the room. Bodies littered the floor behind Wanda and blood blended with the dark robes in the candlelight. I watched as Wanda approached a wide-eyed guard. He pulled a semi-automatic weapon from underneath his robe and began firing.

The bullets passed through Wanda, but it didn't stop her. Several more guards revealed weapons and opened fire, trying to bring Wanda down with the sheer weight of all that lead. The stream of bullets passed into the crowd, and more of the coven fell. Wanda wobbled and collapsed behind a tall man. It was as effective as putting on a bulletproof vest: the bullets hit the man and zinged off, bouncing in every direction. I knew powerful death dealers could deflect bullets, but actually seeing it was something else. He didn't seem to be doing anything special, and he looked as surprised as anyone else at the chaos around him. He smiled in macabre pleasure as bullets meant for him cut down those who stood near him. Around the room, the most powerful mages became islands amongst the carnage.

More bodies dropped—those who weren't so powerful or lucky. In moments, dozens lay dazed, dead, or screaming in pain on the floor. The firing slowly stopped as the guards fell to their own bullets bouncing back at them.

I'd wanted a distraction, but what I set in motion was more along the lines of mass murder.

People are dying. I shook my head—bad people are dying, people who committed murder themselves. These were not innocents; these were the ones who agreed to follow Macaven. These were people trying to release a demon into the world.

The innocents were down below, helpless, in danger unless I did something to save them.

Macaven had stopped to watch the carnage, his face a mask of shock and anger, but almost immediately his whole focus returned to the boy on the altar. He looked down at the dagger in his hand, and with a grimace turned back to his task. The sacrifice was going to happen at any moment. Macaven had the dagger raised in the air and in his other hand was the book. He shouted out more Latin words.

I can't let him kill the boy. I pushed and shoved my way to the bottom steps of the altar. Macaven, the madman that had killed my family, was moments away from slitting this boy's throat. I will not stand by and watch him kill again. I have to stop him. A red hot, blinding rage burst through me, and I rushed up the steps.

Macaven spotted me, and he dropped the book and raised his hand as if to work a spell, but I was moving too fast. I lowered my shoulder and plowed right into him. We both flew off the altar and hit the ground in a tangle of limbs. I grunted in pain as I hit the floor. The knife flew out of Macaven's hands and skidded across the room. I forced myself to move—I rolled toward the dagger and made a grab for it, cutting my flesh as my fingers wrapped around the blade. My blood slid down the steel surface, but I ignored the pain and pulled it toward me. I held the dagger tight in my hand and lifted it up as more of my blood dripped down its handle.

Out of the corner of my eye I saw one of Macaven's minions moving toward me. He was a giant of a man, towering over everyone in the room.

At the sight of him I froze, unsure what to do next. Nothing short of a tree trunk would bring this guy down.

Luke and Freddy appeared out of nowhere, plowing into the huge man's side and sending him stumbling across the altar.

Freddy began wailing on the massive man with his bolt cutters while Luke struggled to hold the giant down.

Luke looked over at me and yelled, "Kill him!" in a strained voice and pointed to where Macaven was beginning to climb to his feet.

I had the knife. I raised it and started forward. Macaven lifted his hands and screamed out. Banshees began to form in the air around him in an angry tornado. They swirled between us. How can I get to him? By the time I reached him, I would be flayed alive or worse. The spirits suddenly turned in my direction and rushed forward. I raised an arm up over my head but remembered I had no magic to protect myself against the assault. I closed my eyes and waited for them to swarm over me.

A shockwave punched through the air and knocked me back off my feet. I opened my eyes and turned to see Luke holding on to the enormous man's leg with one arm as his other free hand waved in the air. Latin words flew from his mouth. He had called forth his own banshees to protect me.

Luke's banshees rose up and washed forward like a tidal wave, crashing against Macaven's spirits. High pitched, wrenching screams filled the air as tortured souls clashed and smashed into each other. Each time the spirits collided, a wave of energy exploded out from them, shooting through the room. Macaven's spirits were overwhelming Luke's with superior numbers and darker intent, and I could see Luke struggling. A few of Macaven's banshees broke through and headed toward me. As they neared, I raised my hands in front of me, shouting out in rage at the swirling spirits.

The first banshee struck me, slashing with ghostly, painful claws and leaving long gouges across my shoulder blade. Blood began to flow freely, sticking my shirt to my back and trickling down my spine. They'll kill me if I don't do something. Did I have the magic to defend myself? I'd helped a spirit cross over to the light, but these creatures had little in common with the light; I could feel the waves of evil coming from them. Another painful slash across my back, and then a deep cut into my shoulder.

Whatever I was going to try, I had to do it now.

The slices on my back began to burn, and the pain seemed to wipe away my uncertainty. My anger flared back up. Macaven deserved to burn for what he had done. Fire. I'd used flames to sever the tie of the dying child from this world to the next. Could I bring the fire forward again?

I closed my eyes and tried to remember the words I had spoken from the book. This time there was no devil's berries ointment to induce the twilight sleep. I had to find my way back to that mental state all on my own. My life depended on it. Anger and pain sharpened my focus. I imagined the fire in my mind, then glanced down to see flames flicker to life at the fingertips of my empty hand. I'm doing it, I'm doing it! I pushed all the pain and rage pumping through my veins into those flames.

I opened my eyes wide, reached out, and with every ounce of strength I possessed, pushed the fire out toward the banshee closest to me. A blast of red orange heat radiated out and encircled it. The creature's screams filled my ears. Ash and embers floated through the air.

Drops of molten liquid rained to the floor from the empty space where the banshee had just been.

I paused for a second in complete disbelief. Even among the death and chaos, the enormity of what I had just done hit me. I have magic as powerful as Luke's, maybe even more powerful. I'd used it to protect myself.

I was no longer a victim in this game.

I closed my eyes and reached for the fire once more. I

pushed it out toward the spirits still encircling me. Screams of pain and horror filled the air as one after another was consumed by fire.

Another shockwave hit me, and I fell back again. I felt blood trickling along my arm. I looked down at the dagger still clutched between my fingers. The dagger. I'd forgotten about it. Without it, Macaven couldn't finish his spell. If I could release the souls trapped in the knife, then Macaven wouldn't be able to raise his demon.

And my father would be free.

I forced myself to my feet. The dagger felt warm in my hands. All I had to do was focus on the light. I could do the same thing I'd done for Thomas—I could free my father's spirit from this prison and help him cross to the other side. Without my father's power, Macaven wouldn't be able to release his spell.

I closed my eyes, ignoring everything around me. The dagger vibrated in my hands for a moment but then stopped. I concentrated harder. I could make out whispers on the wind. I could hear the tormented cries of the people Macaven had killed whirling around me. Vengeance, they want vengeance. I squeezed my eyes shut and tried harder. The dagger in my hands started to hum. The humming grew louder. I opened my eyes to see the dagger glowing orange. Is it working? Am I releasing my father's spirit?

The colored light slowly began to morph, first into gray, and then darker. I heard the sounds again. The ones I'd listened to when I stood before the great expansion of inky blackness during the rituals, the unearthly snarls and unworldly sounds of dragging and thumping. I opened my eyes.

I was back there now, on the edge of the abyss.

I could see it in front of me. Something within it seemed to call out to the dagger. Suddenly the blackness stretched toward me, swirling around the weapon.

I heard Luke yell my name right before the world around me exploded.

My body was thrown like a rag doll through the air and across the room. I slammed against something hard, and everything went dark.

~

WHEN MY EYES FLUTTERED OPENED, I cried out in pain. White hot fire shot across my temples. I forced myself to sit up, and stars blazed across my eyes. Something hot and wet dripped down my face. I reached up and touched my forehead. It was warm and sticky. I put my fingers down in front of my face and looked at them, confused. It was blood—I was bleeding.

I looked around and found myself back in the room. I'd been thrown into a wall. I was lucky I hadn't broken my neck.

That's when I saw it floating a few feet away.

I thought it was a cloud of black, but as I looked closer, I saw it wasn't a cloud at all. It had a shape—a human form—like a body, though not the body of a man or woman. It was something else. There was a head, arms, and warped limbs.

As I looked at it, I felt a pain radiate between my eyes. I blinked. The thing's head was turning toward where I lay. A set of four, dark red eyes focused on me, and I felt nauseous and sick to my stomach.

I heard a deep, rumbling voice echo within my head. YOU HAVE RELEASED ME, it growled.

The dark thing's face morphed, and I was looking into the face of my father, but this was not the kind and loving man I knew. These eyes were red and full of evil.

A wicked grin spread across its face.

"Who are you?" I whispered.

Its face morphed. My father's features disappeared, replaced with something warped, something that no longer resembled anything human. *THEY'VE NAMES FOR ME, BUT NAMES HOLD POWER. WHY WOULD I BE SO FOOLISH AS TO TELL YOU MINE?* Its voice vibrated in the recesses of my mind.

"You're a demon?" I didn't need to ask the question; I knew the answer. My worst nightmare was now standing before me.

I had somehow released the demon.

*THAT IS WHAT THEY CALL MY KIND. I PREFER SOUL EATER, OR PERHAPS LEGION.* It went on in a villainous voice, *WE ARE LEGION!* It laughed with a sound like cracking granite.

With a shock, I found that I recognized its presence. This was the dark presence I had felt during each ritual. This thing had come out of that black abyss. This was the thing out there that had made me feel like a deer being hunted. It was this creature, this being. It was this demon.

As if reading my thoughts, the demon bowed in my direction. *YOU ARE CORRECT. I'VE BEEN WATCHING YOU SINCE YOU BEGAN YOUR JOURNEY INTO THE DEATH ARTS.* The demon laughed. *WHEN YOU TRIED TO HEAL, IT WAS ENOUGH FOR ME TO FIND YOU.*

Pieces started clicking together in my head. "Macaven kept finding us. It was you—you led him to us."

*I DIDN'T THINK THE DEATH DEALER BRAT HAD IT IN HIM. I WORRIED HE'D KILL YOU WITH HIS INEXPERIENCE DURING THE RITUALS.* Its voice slid across my mind like dirty, oily water. *I WAS WRONG, THOUGH...HE DID SUCCEED. LOOK AT WHAT HE'S DONE, HE'S CREATED YOU IN YOUR NEW FORM, JUST AS YOU SHOULD BE. HE MADE YOU FOR ME.*

I was frozen, horrified. "Made me for you?"

*YOU THINK I'D ALLOW MYSELF TO COME FORTH ONLY TO BE BOUND TO SUCH A PUNY, WORTHLESS CREATURE?* It

309

gestured toward where Macaven lay on the floor, holding his head and looking dazed. *I NEEDED YOU TO SET ME FREE. AND HERE I AM, UNBOUND, NOW ABLE TO DO WHATEVER I PLEASE...AND THAT PLEASES ME AS WELL. YOU'RE MINE NOW, AND THAT PLEASES ME EVEN MORE.*

I reached up with a trembling hand and wiped away the blood dripping down my forehead and into my eyes. When I'd been thrown through the air, I'd hit my head against the wall. Maybe I have a concussion. Maybe this isn't real. It can't be real.

I took a deep breath and willed myself to wake up from this terrible nightmare. I felt dazed, confused. I looked around the room at the bodies strewn across the floor. The creature stared back at me. No, this wasn't a nightmare. I could feel my blood chill at the realization that this was really happening. I had done this. I'd created this creature. "What do you want from me?"

*I CHOSE YOU. I MADE YOU WHAT YOU ARE.* Suddenly, I was looking into my father's face again. *TRUE, TO BE RELEASED INTO THIS REALM I NEEDED TO ENCAPSULATE THE SPIRIT OF ONE WITH INCREDIBLE POWER INTO THE DAGGER, A POWERFUL BRIDGE TO HELP GUIDE ME INTO THIS WORLD. IT WAS BECAUSE OF YOU. I KNEW YOU WOULD NEVER TAKE THE JOURNEY YOU NEEDED TO TAKE IF YOUR FAMILY WAS ALIVE.*

I shook my head. "No, Macaven killed my family."

*OF COURSE, HE DID AT MY BIDDING.* It looked over at Macaven. *DO YOU THINK THIS FRAIL CREATURE IS CAPABLE OF CREATING SUCH AN ELEGANT PLAN ON HIS OWN?*

It couldn't be true, what the demon was saying. It's not true. I raised a trembling hand to my forehead. My words barely came out. "You killed my family because of me?"

*I SET YOU ON YOUR PATH. I HELPED GUIDE YOU ALONG. OF COURSE, WHAT I TRULY WANT, TRULY NEED, YOU AREN'T*

*YET READY TO GIVE. NOT YET...BUT SOON ENOUGH. FOR OUR FATES ARE TIGHTLY WOUND TOGETHER, COLINA.* I shuddered as it used my name.

*BUT FOR NOW, I GIVE YOU A GIFT, SOMETHING YOU DEEPLY DESIRE IN RETURN FOR GRANTING ME MY PHYSICAL BODY. FOR FREEING ME, I'LL GIVE YOU A PRETTY PRESENT ALL WRAPPED UP WITH A SHINY BOW...I'LL GIVE YOU YOUR INNERMOST DESIRE.*

I heard the remembered words whispered across a breeze, *Revenge will be yours, but it will come at a price.*

The dark thing started floating across the room. It was heading toward Macaven. The mage was slowly picking himself up off the floor. He looked uninjured. He seemed to sense something moving in his direction and turned. When he saw the demon, his face lit with pride.

Macaven yelled across the room, "Rise up, my brothers and sisters. Our day of glory has finally arrived! We've raised a piece of the greater darkness and bound it to our will. Our enemies will fall before us now! They'll be consumed by hell's own flames." As the surviving coven members began to rise from the floor and move toward Macaven, he faced the demon.

"Hellion, you've been raised by our will. Our enemies are yours. Your power is ours to command." With an evil grin, he pointed a hand red with sacrificial blood in my direction. "She came to the bait, just as you said she would, our pact is complete. Now her purpose is fulfilled, and she must pay for the damage she's done. The coven has been crippled, and she has to die."

The demon laughed again, a wicked sound. *NO, YOU HAVE IT WRONG. YOUR USEFULNESS IS DONE. YOU FOOL. AN UNBOUND ARCH DEMON, COMMANDER IN THE DEVIL'S ARMY, IS NOW BEFORE YOU. I AM FREE TO USE YOU AS I WILL.* A deep growl came from the demon's mouth. *BUT*

*YOU'RE NOT WORTHY TO SERVE IN MY ARMY...YOU WILL FEED MY HUNGER INSTEAD.*

Macaven stumbled back, his eyes showing white with horror. He screamed at me. "You released it before we could bind it! Do you know what you've done? You've unleashed a demon into the world with no one to control it!"

The demon, I released it, but not on purpose. I had only wanted to help my father, but I didn't save my father's spirit. My father was now part of that unholy creature. An unholy creature I was responsible for setting free.

Macaven raised his arms and shouted a spell. Orange light flew from his hands. Members of the coven still capable of action turned and ran from the demon, but three stood to fight, adding their power to Macaven's. Their spells reached the demon, enveloping it completely.

Whatever they were hoping to do didn't work.

As the orange cloud washed over the demon, it laughed and waved its clawed, long fingered hands, leaving a trail of fire in the air, and the cloud slowly disappeared. The demon clapped and a crack of thunder filled the air. A black storm that materialized from nowhere rolled toward the closest of the robed mages. The storm hit him, and he exploded, sending a splatter of blood and chunks of flesh into the wall behind him.

Macaven directed banshees at the demon, but it just drew in a deep breath, and right before my eyes, inhaled one banshee and then another into itself. It seemed to grow more solid with each soul it took in.

I realized that James's spirit was rushing toward the creature. My brother's spirit would be the next one consumed.

"James!" I screamed his name, but there was nothing I could do. I watched helplessly, tears streaming down my bloodied face, as the demon sucked James in.

Both my father and brother were trapped within the wicked being.

The demon finished off the banshees and then paused a moment before blowing a cloud of ashy black smoke into its hands. It moved its palms around as if molding clay. It worked and worked until it seemed pleased. It dropped the object to the floor. The impact of it caused the ground beneath us to shake. Ever so slowly, the thing grew and morphed until it took the shape of a monstrous dog. It looked like a massive pit bull on steroids. The dog's eyes glowed with flickering red fire as it moved to stand beside its master.

It can't be. There are no such things. But it is, I'd seen a picture in one of Luke's books, the animal standing before us was a hellhound, a creature straight out of myth and nightmare, pulled from the air by the demon. The demon lazily gestured, and its hound leaped at the next mage. It passed right through his falling body, ripping his soul away with a pair of red, gleaming teeth. What remained of the mage dissolved into flame.

The hellhound stood gnashing its teeth as it gobbled down the mage's glowing red soul. It then turned to the last of Macaven's supporters. A spout of flame jetted from the hellhound's mouth, lighting the man's robe on fire. The man screamed, and his hood fell back, revealing the graying hair of the death dealer who'd fought Luke at the magic shop. The hellhound leaped at the man, ripping off a smoking chunk of flesh from his face and swallowing it whole. His terrified screams echoed out from the growing column of flame. As the screams died down, the hound shook its head and out sprayed a cloud of ash and embers.

Amidst this chaos, the demon continued toward Macaven. It floated a few feet from him, completely unconcerned as Macaven flung spell after spell at it. Each spell broke harmlessly against its cracked, black skin. When it was finally close enough, it reached out and touched a finger to Macaven's forehead.

Macaven screamed. From the touch sprang welts across his face and body. He raised his hands and watched in horror as they erupted in bloody, oozing blisters. The blisters multiplied until they covered every inch of exposed flesh. They began to rupture, and the smell of infection and rotting flesh filled the room. Macaven touched a hand to his face, and a huge section of the skin slumped away, showing the gray, dying flesh beneath.

I looked away, no longer able to stomach the sight of my vengeance. I had given up so much to see the men who murdered my family die horribly, but even my darkest fantasies didn't prepare me for this reality. I had sacrificed my future, my innocence, I even died, and now that it was happening, I just felt sick.

I couldn't block out the sound. Wet, gurgling screams continued to tear through the room. The sounds he made were more terrifying than the banshees.

When the world was silent again, I looked back. Macaven was dead, I was sure of it. His limbs were twisted in unnatural angles.

The demon turned toward me again, its eyes glowing brighter. I stood frozen as it came closer. It reached a slow hand out and delicately wiped a claw across my face. My skin burned and blistered under its touch. Its claw came away smeared in my blood. I shrank back as it raised the finger, bright red with blood, to its mouth and sucked with evident pleasure. It gave me a wicked smile. Without warning, the dark creature twisted and spun, morphing before my very eyes.

Where it had been, a little girl now stood.

Dark pigtails hung from each side of her head and freckles

spread across her nose. It was the color of her eyes, a reddish orange not found in nature, that gave her true identity away. And when she grinned, my stomach turned. The smile was not that of an innocent child. It was an unclean, unholy grin...one that was somehow oddly familiar.

"I'll come for you when the time is right, Colina, and what fun we'll have." Her little girl voice was somehow even more chilling than the booming demon voice. Before I could think of what to say or do, the child turned and skipped across the room. She stopped by a broken display case that had once held an assortment of magical artifacts. With a childlike cry of delight, she pulled an antique doll from the wreckage. Its shredded dress fell away as the demon girl picked it up, but that didn't seem to diminish her pleasure. She clutched the smoking doll to her chest as she turned and headed toward the door. Flames erupted behind her as she went. The room slowly began to fill with smoke as she glided out.

The demon child whistled over her shoulder, and the hellhound followed, shrinking as it went until it was the size of an average pit bull. An air of menace radiated off them both as they exited through the flames.

The demon's words kept swirling around in my head. It killed my family because of me. It wanted me to become a death dealer so I could help release it. It was all a sick and wicked plan to get itself released, unbound. I couldn't believe it; everything I had been through, the horror, the nightmare, the rituals, had all of it really just been part of the creature's plan?

I looked across the room. Bodies lay everywhere like discarded rag dolls. The dead and injured littered the ground around me; moaning and screaming filled the air.

I caused all this destruction.

In a moment of insanity, I'd rushed in, hell bent only on revenge, and as a result, I set all of this in motion. How many people died because of me? And my family...I was the reason they were dead. Macaven might have killed them, but it was because of me that he went after them in the first place.

Luke. I suddenly, desperately wanted him by my side. He would know what to do. He would help me make everything alright again. It was my fault the creature was loose, but we could go after the demon. We would find some kind of spell in one of the old books that would force that thing back to hell. If someone had found a way to kill and force demons back into oblivion in the past, then there was a way. We just had to find it.

Maybe by doing so, I could find some kind of redemption for the things I'd done.

A fire was blazing on the other side of the room, the candelabras had been knocked over in the fight. Black smoke swirled into the air and up toward the ceiling. I had to find Luke and Freddy, we needed to get out of here before the whole hotel went up in flames.

I moved through the room looking for Luke among the carnage, my heart in my throat. Then I saw him by the altar.

A part of the gray stone had fallen and crushed him.

"Luke!" I cried out his name and rushed toward him.

Darla was with him. She cradled his head in her lap. I could see blood streaming out from beneath the stone that trapped him. I reached out and screamed his name again. "Luke!"

I was almost to his side when hands grabbed me.

It was Freddy—he wrapped his arms around my waist. "You can't touch him."

"I can heal him. Let me go." I struggled to get free.

Freddy's arms tightened around me. "You can't heal him, he's dead."

"No, no. He's okay, let me go, Freddy, I can heal him!"

Darla was gently stroking Luke's forehead, tears streaming down her face.

316

Freddy said in a harsh voice, "I won't let you turn him into a zombie."

I stopped struggling, stunned by his words.

"He told me what you can do. There's no saving him, Colina. He's been crushed to death. The stone weighs a ton. Luke's dead —" Freddy's words ended in a choked sob.

I shook my head back and forth. "He...he can't be dead. He's not dead."

Freddy pulled me closer. He leaned in and whispered in my ear, "Listen to me. You can't help him."

My head was spinning. *Luke's dead.* Those two words screamed inside my head. I couldn't believe it. I wouldn't believe it. I can heal him. I started struggling against his grip again. "I can save him! Let me go! Luke!"

Black smoke was now billowing in clouds on the other side of the room. People were rushing out in all directions.

Freddy started dragging me out of the room.

I screamed, kicked, scratched, and bit at Freddy, but he didn't let me go.

When we were finally outside, he threw me to the ground. I started to get up.

Darla appeared at Freddy's side. Her eyes were full of tears. "You did this. You killed my brother," she hissed.

I shook my head. "No, no..."

Darla wiped away her tears and yelled at me. "You wouldn't listen! You wouldn't wait. He tried to protect you. He went in there because of you, and now he's dead!"

Luke's not dead. I don't believe it. I can't believe it. I stood there in a daze as flames were glowing in the windows.

The hotel was engulfed in fire.

People in black robes rushed from the exits. But there were others, too, running across the grounds, others dressed in regular clothes.

"Those people in the basement. We need to get them out!" I yelled at Freddy.

Darla watched the people racing across the yard and said, "I set them loose. I went down to the room when Freddy and Luke came after you. All the hostages are free."

I had gone back into the hotel with the intention of saving the innocent people Macaven held hostage, but I hadn't given them a second thought once I set my sights on him. I had been so bent on my revenge, so focused on seeing Macaven die, that I hadn't cared at all what happened to anyone else. I had killed a man in cold blood, and then watched as the zombie I created killed a dozen more.

I was responsible for it all. For my family's death. For Luke's death.

It was all my fault.

I slumped toward the ground, my chest burning. This couldn't be real. This couldn't be happening, it had to be a horrible nightmare that I would wake from at any moment.

Freddy grabbed my arm and tugged me up, pulling me into the forest. I was pulled and shoved through the woods. I didn't resist. Instead, I moved as if in a trance. When we finally made it to the car, Freddy pushed me inside.

Luke can't be dead. This is not happening. I'm dreaming, and I'll wake up. Any moment now...

CHAPTER

# THIRTY-FOUR

I lay in Pagan's bed, staring blindly at the ceiling. The drive back had seemed unreal, like some horrible dream. The whole way back Darla had cried, sobbed, and moaned for her brother. Freddy had been silent, and I had stared out the window, unable and unwilling to process what happened.

I kept waiting to wake from this dream—I was desperate to wake and find Luke back at my side.

But Luke is dead.

The words rang through my head. They forced me off the bed onto my feet. I walked over to the window. Storm clouds gathered outside. I wondered when it would start raining. It was cold in the room, but I didn't care. I welcomed the chill—it matched the one surrounding my heart.

The traveler had warned me. She'd said the awakening was dangerous, and she'd been right. The awakening had triggered something inside me. The rituals had changed me. I'd become darker, reckless—I'd given in to my anger and rushed to seek my revenge, not caring about the consequences.

Because of my actions, Luke was dead.

The demon had granted me my innermost wish—to see

Macaven dead. But watching his body crumple to the floor hadn't given me any true pleasure.

Revenge hadn't brought my family back.

I'd tried to save my father and my brother but failed them both. Now their spirits were forever intertwined with a demon —an evil creature that was out in the world doing who knew what unspeakable things. It was my fault the demon was free. My reckless behavior had set that monster loose. And if the creature hadn't lied, if it told the truth, then my family was dead because of me.

I shook my head, trying to make sense of it all. Was I really just a puppet in the twisted creature's game? The demon had said our fates were intertwined and that it would see me again...that I wasn't yet ready to give it what it needed.

The memory of its words sent a chill down my spine. What does it all mean?

I threw myself down on the bed, closing my eyes and trying to clear my thoughts. Every time I tried; I saw the image of Luke's lifeless body crushed under the stone. I had fought against my feelings. I had been so scared to open my heart and let him in, but now I knew without a doubt, somewhere along the way, I'd fallen in love with Luke.

I hadn't truly realized it until I looked down at his broken body. In that moment, I knew how much I loved him. How much I needed him.

And now it was too late. He was gone. I'd lost him forever. No tears streamed down my face. I felt nothing now but a dark, deep void.

As I lay quietly, a cold breeze ran across my cheek, and I felt a pressure against my arm. I opened my eyes and sat up. Something was here in the room, something not of this world. A breeze rustled against my neck.

*I'm here, Colina.* The words slid across my mind.

"Luke?" It's him. His spirit was there with me in the room. I could feel it. I sobbed and reached out. His spirit was with me, but I couldn't touch him. I couldn't hold him. "Luke, I'm so sorry..." I hesitated and looked around the empty room.

I can do this. I can finally tell him how I feel. It's not too late to let him know how much I care.

"I love you." The words were finally out. My declaration was met with silence. The sadness, the heartache I'd forced back until now, came crashing down on me. I'd experienced every girl's fondest wish, I met the boy of my dreams, but my story was a little different.

I met the boy. I loved the boy. I killed the boy.

Then I heard it. A soft whisper floated toward me from across the room.

"I'm here. I'll never leave you."

THE CEMETERY DIDN'T LOOK any less spooky in the daytime. I was on a hill close by, watching the proceedings from behind a tree. Fifty people were gathered in a semicircle, all dressed in black. I'd watched six strong men carry Luke's casket through the cemetery from afar. It now rested near an open grave.

Storm clouds filled the sky. It hadn't started raining yet, but a cold wind whipped through the trees.

"Thank you," whispered across my ears, and a cold chill ran across my fingers.

I looked up into the face of Sarah's ghost. Her spirit stood before me. She seemed almost solid.

"Because of you, I'm finally free. I wanted to thank you before I go."

"Were you the one guiding me, helping me find Darla?"

Sarah nodded, and her image started to go translucent.

A light, bright like the sun, appeared only a few feet away. Like before, there were forms, shapes at the other end of the light. An incredible feeling of love and joy radiated out from within the light, and voices began calling out Sarah's name.

Sarah turned toward the light, but then looked back to me. "My family is calling. Because of you, I can finally go to them." She looked down at the funeral procession. "I've a message to pass on to you before I go."

"A message from who?" Is it my mother? Can spirits communicate with each other on the other side? I hadn't seen or heard from my mother since the night we worked the Ouija board spell.

"Don't forget who you are," Sarah whispered as the light reached out and engulfed her. She disappeared.

"Don't forget who you are." Those were the same words the traveler healer had told me when she gave me the protection pouch. But I had forgotten who I was. I was no longer the gentle healer. I was no longer on a path of light. I walked in darkness now death and destruction shadowed my every step.

I set the demon free. It was out there, running loose in the world disguised as a little girl.

And Luke... he was still here with me in spirit, but I desperately wanted to feel his arms wrapped around me. The image of his lifeless body flashed before my eyes.

I gave myself a mental shake. I wouldn't think about that now. I would lock those images into the deepest, darkest corner of my mind. Maybe one day I would deal with them...but not today.

It was then that I felt another presence, but it wasn't a spirit this time. It was a person. I said her name but didn't turn around. "Darla."

"I knew you'd be here." She waited for me to say something, but when I remained silent, she continued. "Macaven's coven is broken. My guild is hunting down those members responsible for the killings. There'll be a reckoning for what they did, for the lives they took. They hid their actions by blaming the deaths on the Redeemers, but everyone knows the truth now. Word has spread about what happened. Rumors have started about my kind. People are blaming us for those creatures at the hospital and for the massacre at the hotel.

"My family is in danger because of what you did. I know that you can raise the dead. Freddy told me what you did at the hospital, and I told my family. They had to clean up what you did at the hotel. That thing you left...all those people dead..."

I turned and looked at her. A black scarf covered her chopped hair; her dress was long and black.

I forced myself to ask the question. "How many?"

"Twenty dead, a dozen more in the hospital." Her eyes filled with hatred. "You saved me, and for that I'll give you this warning, my family wants you dead. They blame you for what happened to Luke. I blame you. He should never have gone back into that place. He's dead, and it's all your fault. Don't come back here. If I see you again, I'll kill you myself."

I started to walk away, but she grabbed my arm. "Luke is around, I can feel him. We tried a ceremony to move his spirit into the light, but he won't." She sobbed. "I know it's because of you. Freddy told me what you did for Thomas, you can make Luke go into the light. You can free him."

I shook my head. The thought of losing what little I had left of Luke scared me.

"Please, you can do it," she pleaded.

"No. No, I can't." I shook off her grip and walked away. I loved Luke. I would never let him go.

The sky overhead opened up and rain poured down. There was nowhere left for me to go. My clan would never let me come back once they found out what I'd become...once they

323

discovered the terrible acts I'd committed in the name of revenge. A sob escaped my lips. Nothing seemed real. I was going through the motions, but inside I felt numb.

No, I thought to myself. That isn't true. Inside I felt lost in a sea of hopelessness and despair. At times this sea of emotions washed over me so strongly that I felt as though I could no longer breathe. I felt like I would drown.

Luke was dead. It was my fault. I could never take back the things I had done to avenge my family.

I wiped the wet hair from my face. Luke's death had been violent and unexpected, which meant that, for a short time at least, his spirit should be unsettled, roaming the in between.

But Luke's spirit was here, with me. I could feel him around me at different times.

*Possession.* The word gave me hope. Luke had said a spirit could overpower someone weak, or someone on the edge of insanity. Wanda's spirit had possessed me. Her very essence had filled me, moved my body and limbs at her command. With Luke's help, I'd been able to force her out...but what if I hadn't? Wanda would have been able to roam the world using my body.

*Possession.* I was a death dealer now; I could bring him back. Luke could possess someone and come back to me. I could help force his spirit back into a living body.

I looked up at the dark sky and rain fell across my face. I didn't have a lot of power. I'd survived the rituals, but I hadn't finished the death dealer training. There had to be someone out there who could teach me. I could find books that would help me learn spells.

*Possession.* It was my one chance to bring Luke back. If there was a way to bring him back, I'd find it.

The thought of stealing a body and forcing another soul into it should have horrified me, but it didn't, all I could think of was bringing Luke back. I was prepared to do whatever necessary to see Luke at my side again. I was no longer that healer, that naïve girl who walked into the magic store. I had gone through the rituals, gone through the chaos, and all of that had changed me. I could feel a deep well of anger and violence in my core that hadn't been there before. I was becoming everything my parents had despised and hated.

I wrapped my arms around my body, pushing away my doubts and indecision for just a moment, and looked out toward the cemetery.

"Whatever it takes," I vowed.

And as I said the words, I felt a chill run across my neck and a ghostly touch slide down my cheek.

# Acknowledgments

Love and smooches to Nerd Boy and Mom for always being supportive of all the creative endeavors and especially for carrying the heavy load on all the daily chores so I can spend more time writing.

As always to my best friends Author Marie Harte, Teri Chapman, and Laura Rivas, thanks for being such great friends! You guys are always there for me!

Big thanks to my friends and Alpha Readers Author A.K. Mulford and Author Jamie Applegate Hunter for pushing me to revise the series as a New Adult. And I could not have done this without the help of my friend Alpha/Beta Reader Author Corri Emelia, who spent way too many hours combing over this book trying to help me find all the typos and mistakes.

Big thanks to TikTok Beta Readers: Author A.M. Deese, Mello Wilsted, Halley Newhouse, @yukonshawn, @brooke_and_books, Author Lily Snow, Author Emmy R Bennett, and Author BL Wilson.

When I started doing TikTok videos in 2020, I never imagined I would make so many friends. Thank you, AuthorTok and BookTok community, for making my world less lonely and filling my days with laughter. TikTok is such a chaotic, fun place!

# ALSO BY CATRINA BURGESS

**Awakening (The Dark Rituals Book 1)**

**Possession (The Dark Rituals Book 2)**

**Revenant (The Dark Rituals Book 3)**

**Legion (The Dark Rituals Book 4)**

# AUTHOR BIO

**Chaos - It's not just a lifestyle, it's a state of mind!**

I am writing New Adult Paranormal Romance as Catrina Burgess and New Adult Angsty Contemporary as Friday Burgess

**ABOUT ME:** I write because it helps keeps the darkness away and reminds me that there is magic in the world. I live in an old mining town in Arizona. At night this place is definitely spooky and I swear I've heard the wind giggle, and sometimes there's a very odd, very paranormal angry breeze that blows at night. Luckily, I love all things that are spooky. I'm addicted to coffee and chocolate. I've been living with chronic fatigue syndrome/ME for 12 years.

I've been known to eat pizza for breakfast, and I'm the queen of the board game Stratego. I've never been beaten. NEVER!

**You can follow me at:**

**TikTok:** https://vm.tiktok.com/ZMeLE8Hry/
**Website:** www.catrinaburgess.com
**Instagram:** https://www.instagram.com/catrinaburgess/
**Twitter:** @catrinaburgess.1
**Facebook:** https://www.facebook.com/catrina. burgess.5

Printed in Great Britain
by Amazon

23769160R00193